Edges First

By

Jay W. Murphy

Copyright © 2015 Five Stars Publishing, LLC

Library of Congress Cataloging-in-Publication Data is available.

ISBN: 978-0-9895076-4-6

Thank you to my parents for giving me the freedom to live, love and celebrate life. Your example of a loving marriage has always been an inspiration to me. For my wife, without your encouragement the pages that follow would surely be blank. To my children, hearing your laughter releases me from the grip of gravity and takes me to a dimension filled with pure joy. I am, without a doubt, the luckiest man in the world.

"Trust your instinct to the end, though you can render no reason."
- RALPH WALDO EMERSON -

Introduction

—§—

Tony James has just arrived back home in Portland, Oregon after a life altering encounter with the Central Intelligence Agency. At an early age and out of sheer necessity, Tony began developing an incredible and reliable ability to instantaneously sense dominant personality traits. While in D.C. he was cast into the Petri dish of government chaos. Tony was poked, prodded and mentally tested to exhaustion. Now, Tony James is testing the waters as a new secret weapon within a clandestine division of the CIA. However, in the dark recesses of the underworld, a surprising group emerges and targets Tony. He becomes the missing piece to the decades long puzzle of personal and government conspiracies. Does Tony have what it takes to navigate the two worlds and survive?

Chapter 1

The home phone rang out just a few seconds before she heard the doorbell. She hesitated, glanced at the kitchen phone and decisively chose to answer the door. Quietly gliding through the swinging door she took her apron and tossed it over the back of a chair. As was her usual practice she took a peek through the slightly frosted glass frame of the entryway. Her heart rate jumped. She opened the door to find two police officers in full uniform standing side-by side. One male and one female.

"Ma'am, may we come in?" asked the female officer after the door opened.

She appeared frozen in time as if only hearing the sound of the officer's words and not understanding them. Staring at the sight of her two uninvited visitors brought a lack of sensation to her entire being. Still holding the door open she stared unfocused.

"Ma'am, may we enter? We need to talk with you."

Finally regaining her senses she said in a burst, "Oh, of course. I'm terribly sorry."

The female officer, Lambert, entered first with her large partner, Rice, trailing right behind. Most law enforcement departments have pretty much the same protocol when it comes to this kind of visit…straight and to the point.

"Would you like to sit?" she asked as any proper host would do.

"No Ma'am," answered Lambert.

Officer Rice slowly sidestepped to place himself partially to her side and behind the woman they were

1

calling upon. Without a hint of emotion in her voice Officer Lambert said, "I'm very sorry to inform you...your husband is dead."

Rice was prepared to catch her if she fainted. However, she stood without movement, unflinchingly staring directly into the female officer's eyes. Not knowing if she were about to keel over, Rice moved his arms slightly outward just in case he needed to catch her.

"W—What did you just say?"

"I'm very sorry to be the bearer of such awful news," Lambert said in a softened tone. "May we sit down?" Using only her eyes Lambert notified Rice to guide her into the living room.

Slowly settling her into a comfortable four-legged chair, Lambert and Rice sat on the adjacent couch facing her. Both officers remained silent as protocol dictated. Once Lambert sensed it was time to speak she took a breath and began.

"Ma'am, do you understand what was told to you while standing in the foyer?"

No answer and a dazed look in the poor woman's eyes. Lambert gave a quick glance then nodded at Rice as if they had a silent language between them. Officer Rice pulled a grainy picture from his vest pocket and delicately placed it on the coffee table. He slowly slid it toward her hoping her eyes would come back into focus. Lambert found it odd that there wasn't one family picture in the entire room to help them verify the man from the photo in front of them on the table.

Her eyes, though still glazed over, began to look downward at what laid in front of her. She stared as if the god of granite had placed the rest of her body in a tomb of immovability. Lambert and Rice had seen it before. This woman is in sensory overload.

"Ma'am, can you hear me?" asked Lambert.

Still staring at the photo of her husband she slowly looked up at the two officers and asked, "What?"

"Ma'am do you recognize the man in the photo?"

"Yes. He's my husband."

Rice's body language relaxed as his thoughts of this new widow sitting in front of him seemingly had not gone into shock. He'd seen it a number of times before. Having a female partner break the news seemed to have the desired effect in delivering such dreadful information.

"Do you understand what I told you about him?"

"Yes, I do."

Lambert and Rice looked at each other and knew they were thinking the same thing; *how can she be so calm?*

Rice spoke in his deep baritone voice, "Ma'am, do you comprehend you have been informed that he is deceased?"

In a voice slightly above a whisper she answered, "I do."

Almost as if they had practiced it, both Lambert and Rice raised their eyebrows. They couldn't tell what emotion had taken hold of the new widow. Maybe she was void of emotion at the moment. It wouldn't be the first time they'd seen it.

"May we ask you a few questions Mrs. Shelton?"

"Please, call me Audrey."

Both officers took pause as they found this to be another strange response. Usually hysterical crying and questions came rushing at them. Audrey Shelton seemed to be a blank slate.

Lambert filled the awkward silence and asked, "When was the last time you saw your husband?"

"Last night before he left for his board meeting."

"Was that the meeting for a company called Computer Information Technologies?"

"Yes. He's President and CEO."

It wasn't lost on Lambert or Rice that she used present tense. A normal reaction to the news just received. However, Rice now had his small notebook and pencil out ready to take notes of the conversation. Experience from years on the force moved him to document what he deemed to be important information.

At the precise time Rice was ready with his notepad Audrey broke down dropping her head into her hands. She screamed, "NO! WHY!? THIS CAN'T BE TRUE!"

Rice set his notebook down on the coffee table. *I hate it, but this is more like it*, he thought.

"Are you sure it's him?" asked Audrey through heavy tears.

Lambert, giving a head nod to the photo, replied in a soft tone, "If that's your husband then he has been positively identified".

"But how–?"

"Apparent heart attack."

Audrey picked the picture up as more tears streamed down her face. She then held the photo to her heart and began rocking herself as she sat. Lambert and Rice gave her as much time as she required before asking any more questions. After a few minutes Audrey began to compose herself.

"Audrey was your husband under any undue stress as of late?" asked Lambert in a soft soothing tone.

"W—why do you ask that?"

"Just a typical question we have to ask in a case such as this."

"He has been under extreme pressure at work. CIT hasn't been doing so well as of late so he's been pushing as hard as possible."

"Has his health changed recently?"

"Andrew has always been extremely health conscious and very active."

"So this is not something you would have expected?"

"Obviously not," Audrey said a little more sharp-toned than anticipated. "He's been under pressure from the board of directors to improve the bottom line. It's been almost a year since a new market had been successfully tapped by the head of sales. Ryan O'Connor has been trying to draw in government contracts, but nothing has come to fruition yet."

Officer Rice handed Audrey the police report and said, "This is for you to look over at a later time."

Audrey took the papers and happened to see the time of death as she began to set them down on the table.

"Am I reading this right? The time of death was determined to be about midnight? He was found alone at his chair in the boardroom at CIT by Ryan O'Connor?"

"That's correct," said Rice.

"But the meeting was scheduled to begin at 11pm and possibly go into the early hours of the morning."

Lambert chimed in this time and said, "Everyone we interviewed said the meeting was to begin at midnight. Are they all mistaken or did your husband make an error?"

"Andrew would never have made a mistake about this meeting. His chairmanship was on the line. A discussion and vote was going to take place. He told me it was the first topic on the agenda. Andrew said if he was home late that it was good news. That's why I didn't worry as it got late and he still wasn't home."

"I'm sorry to have to ask right now, but what time did your husband leave home?" asked Lambert.

"It was around 10pm."

"How long does it take for him to get to the office from here?"

"No more than fifteen to twenty minutes at that time of night."

Rice popped in with a question. "Why was this meeting scheduled so late on a Monday and why would they work into the early hours of the morning? Why not hold this meeting during normal business hours?"

"I don't know. Ever since he started CIT both of us have put in long and odd hours. I guess it just seems normal to us."

"Old work habits from the start-up days I guess," affirmed Rice.

"I suppose so," said Audrey.

Audrey asked, "Where did they take him?"

"Mr. O'Connor insisted on following the ambulance directly to the hospital. He told us they were close friends and he would take care of things at the morgue."

"Is that where Andrew's body is right now?"

"Yes, would you like us to escort you?"

Dabbing her eyes with a tissue she said, "No, but thank you both for sitting with me. Unless you have any other questions I'd like to be alone now."

Officers Lambert and Rice each handed her their cards. "If you need anything please don't hesitate to call either one of us. Are you going to be OK? We prefer not to leave you alone."

"I'll be as OK as can be. I would prefer to be alone right now. Thank you for coming."

As Lambert and Rice shut the squad car doors they looked at each other. Rice said, "Now that's a new one for the books."

Lambert replied, "I feel for her, but she's one interesting lady."

Chapter 2

—§—

Present Day

Four days after returning from Washington D.C Tony James sat in his car and pondered the meaning of the words from the text message he received on his new Smartphone: REMEMBER, NOTHING IS REALLY AS IT SEEMS. The only person who ever said that to him was agent Elizabeth Wolf just as they were entering the government building at Langley. Somehow her words helped him get through a very difficult couple of days.

Tony lifted his eyes from the phone screen and quietly said, "It has to be her. But, how did she hack *this* phone. It came directly from SSD Director Don Williams. Wait a minute! This could be the beginning of some kind of training. That's got to be it. Is this my first test as part of the CIA's Savant Syndrome Division? Am I supposed to alert my handler here in Portland or do I contact the one in Washington, D.C.? That's an easy call…its Audrey. I don't want to deal with Senior Special Agent Dennis Forman so soon."

Hmm, I never asked what my actual title is. Am I an agent? A contractor? Employee? I'll ask Audrey when I talk to her next time, he thought.

He placed the phone into normal mode by following the instructions provided.

"I'm going to need to read this entire instruction book then shred and burn it. I hope I can remember everything. It's amazing how this looks to be an exact duplicate as the one issued by CIT."

Tony pulled out of the corporate headquarters parking lot of Computer Information Technologies and headed for home. He was looking forward to completing his week off. As he drove, the embryo of a thought began to form.

Am I now living in a glass house filled with listening devices and cameras?

Shaking off the dread of such a life Tony focused on getting home to Jacquelyn and the kids.

Pulling into the driveway he found a car blocking his entry into his garage. Tony didn't recognize the vehicle. He put his car in reverse and parked on the street. As he walked by he noticed the rental sticker on the back license plate frame of the unknown car.

Tony quietly opened the front door to hear a male voice he did not recognize. A feeling came over Tony that, for some reason, turned his blood to ice. The words *Changing Colors* penetrated his entire being. He picked up Nick's little wood baseball bat then stood quietly to hear what was being said. He didn't hear Sam or Nick.

They must be playing next door, he surmised.

Tony heard the man say, "This upgrade will provide the added security of optional cameras throughout the house. It enhances our ability to react to whatever threat may come your way."

"What's the charge for that option?" asked Jacquelyn.

Tony set the bat down and loudly closed the front door. He said, "Jacquelyn, I'm home."

He rounded the corner to find a middle aged man sitting at the dining room table with Jacquelyn. Glossy literature strewn about. Jacquelyn was holding a packet of papers.

"Tony, please say hello to Stan Davidson. He's with Rest Easy Security Systems."

Mr. Davidson stood and said hello with a firm handshake. "Your lovely wife and I were just going over the security options for your home."

Tony focused his attention on Stan Davidson while the man began to blather on about his company's state of the art security systems. The word *phony* penetrated him as warnings went off in his head.

"Nice to meet you Stan," said Tony. "Will you please excuse us for a moment?"

"Absolutely," said Davidson.

Jacquelyn and Tony walked far enough out of ear-shot to have a quiet private conversation.

"Are you out of your mind letting a perfect stranger into our home without me being here? And, when did you decide we need a security system?"

"What are you talking about? You sent me a text me earlier today telling me to expect him."

"I didn't send you a text, Jacquelyn," Tony said with distress in his voice.

Jacquelyn put her hand to her mouth as she gasped. "Are you saying—?"

Tony cut her off.

"How long has he been here?"

"About a half hour," she answered quietly.

"Was he within your sight at all times?"

"He did walk into the living room while I made coffee. I'm so sorry Tony."

"That's OK. Stay right here," Tony said calmly.

Tony went back into the dining room and asked, "Stan, when did you make this appointment?"

"I don't make the appointments. I was notified by my office just this morning," he said.

"Well Stan, we didn't make an appointment," said Tony.

"I don't understand," he said.

"Neither do we," said Tony.

"So this has been a huge waste of my time? That's just great." Then he mumbled softly, "She wasted my time."

That sent Tony over the edge.

"Get the hell out of here!" Tony said pointing to the front door.

The salesman, obviously irritated, looked at Tony and began collecting the literature laid out on the dining room table.

Tony took a step forward then said, "Leave it and get out now!"

In a classless sarcastic tone the salesman said, "If you change your mind…"

Tony escorted him out the front door. He then looked a little more closely at the brochure he held in his hand and noticed there was no address, phone number or web address. Tony quickly went back to the dining room and checked a few more pieces of literature finding the same result. He quickly rushed passed Jacquelyn on his way back to the front door to catch his license plate number, but he was too late. Jacquelyn stayed motionless not sure why Tony was looking so closely at the literature.

"I don't get it. Why are you so interested in those brochures?" she asked.

Dismissing her question Tony looked at Jacquelyn and said, "He's gone."

Jacquelyn, not a simple lilting flower, asked Tony once again about his interest in the brochures.

"Do you see a phone number, address or website on any of this stuff?" asked Tony.

After great scrutiny Jacquelyn said, "I can't believe I missed that! What should we do...call the police? That guy's a conman," she said.

"Good idea. I'll do that while you call next door to make sure the kids are alright. And pass the word on to the rest of the neighborhood about this guy," he said.

Tony had no intention of calling the police. His objective was to call on a higher power...Audrey Shelton.

Just then his Smartphone vibrated in his pocket. Tony was going to disregard it, but his normal setting for an incoming text was one vibration. This came in as a double. He quickly figured it was on the *other* part of his phone. After punching in the code he found he was right.

The text read; MONDAY 9AM MEETING...MY OFFICE

"What the —?"

While Jacquelyn was on the landline with the neighbors next door, checking on Sam and Nick, Tony called Audrey from his Smartphone.

"Hello Tony," Audrey said in an upbeat tone. She added, "You got my text?"

"I did, but how did you know I was going to call you at this particular moment?"

"I didn't. I just wanted to tell you we have a conference call meeting in my office on Monday at 9am with Mr. Mercury."

"So you weren't —?" Tony didn't finish. He wasn't sure if this was part of his training or something completely coincidental.

"I wasn't what, Tony?"

"Nothing, I'll see you Monday."

"Have a good rest of the week," Audrey said.

"Thanks, you do the same," he said. *Something's not right here, but I have no idea what it is. Until I figure it out I'm keeping my mouth shut*, he thought.

Tony finished out the week spending most of his time with Jacquelyn & the kids. They all had extra fun at the Oregon Zoo near Washington Park. Sam loved seeing the elephants again and Nick enjoyed the train ride as if it was his first time. Tony also completed a few projects around the house. On the top of his list was installing new deadbolt locks to the front and back doors.

Sunday night brought an unusual feeling for Tony. He normally dreaded Monday mornings. But, tonight he was actually looking forward to what his new responsibilities will bring him. Before he got into bed he realized his urge to tic from Tourettes, even with the added stress of Wednesday's unwanted visitor, had settled into what he considered to be extremely mild. His medication was doing its job. No major tic release from holding back seemed to be required anymore.

Chapter 3

—§—

1995

Audrey Shelton screamed at the top of her lungs at Ryan O'Connor and the only man on duty. Audrey was in a panic standing in the hallway of the hospital basement.

"How could you let this happen!?" shouted Audrey at the two men in front of her. The power of her voice seemed to have the muscle to travel and wake the patients in the Intensive Care Unit.

The man in the white lab jacket held up his clipboard in a defensive manner. "I can't tell you how this happened. All I can say is the paperwork is right here. I just follow orders."

"Well you screwed up! You didn't do the right thing!" shouted Audrey.

Ryan moved to place his hands on Audrey's shoulders. They were quickly swatted away. "Please try to calm down Audrey," he said.

"Why should I calm down? They cremated my husband's body without me seeing him one last time!"

The lab assistant said, "He's been here two days. We figured no one was going to claim the body. It's procedure."

Audrey glared at Ryan and said, "I was told you were taking care of things here!"

"Audrey, I tried calling you, but you wouldn't answer. Not that I thought this mess would ever take place." Ryan glared at the lab technician.

"I needed time alone. But, how could this happen!?" asked Audrey as her emotions took a turn.

"Mr. O'Connor, do you want to take the ashes with you?" asked the man in the lab jacket.

Audrey grabbed the container from him and said, "I'm not leaving him here just so you can use him for an ashtray!" She turned on her heals and stormed out.

Ryan O'Connor grimaced at the man with the clipboard then quickly followed Audrey to the elevator door. As they waited he could see her begin to fortify her emotions.

"I'm so sorry Audrey."

Staring straight ahead it appeared Audrey was looking through the steel door into another world. No response. The elevator door opened and Audrey stepped in with Ryan right on her heels. Ryan pressed the button to the parking garage. Not a word was spoken. The elevator stopped and Ryan held the door for Audrey. She calmly stood her ground without so much as looking at him.

"Get out," she said in a menacing tone.

Ryan stepped out and watched Audrey holding Andrew Shelton's ashes as the elevator door squeezed shut. He stood for a moment and felt the weight of the world on his shoulders.

"I'm the one Andrew trusted. I'm the one he asked to show up early for the meeting. I'm the one he looked to have his back. Why couldn't I have been there just a few minutes earlier? "I never expected it to be like this," he mumbled wiping a tear from his right eye.

Chapter 4

Present Day

"Right on time as usual, Tony. How was the rest of your time off?" Audrey asked as she sat behind her big desk on the thirty-third floor.

"Hi Audrey, I hope you had a nice weekend. Visit any nice coffee shops?"

"I had a very pleasant weekend. Thank you," she replied dismissing his question.

"So is Dennis calling here or are you calling him?" he asked.

"Something I've been asked to tell you is that we are not to use real names with regard to anything associated with our government work with SSD."

As quick as ever, Tony followed up by asking, "So is Nubmnuts calling here or are you calling him?"

"Tony, be nice. He's someone you want on your side" she chided.

"Are you sure about that? Remember I'm just sticking my toe in the water to see if this is something I really want to do. So, what should we call each other within the context of SSD business?"

"I was sent a list."

"You mean we can't pick our own code names?" asked Tony pretending to be dejected.

"I don't think code name 'Nubmnuts' would be appreciated," Audrey grinned.

"Let me see the list," said Tony.

"That's another thing you will want to remember. Don't print out certain documents unless you absolutely have to," she said in a tutorial tone.

Tony listened to her reasoning and understood the purpose. Audrey and Tony sat down at the round conference table. Audrey set her Smartphone down after entering her special code to access the non-CIT part of her phone.

"I've got a question about these phones. What if I accidently lost it?"

"We'll get you another one. But, don't lose it," she said wagging her finger.

"Can it be compromised if someone tried?"

"Funny you would bring that up. I thought the same thing awhile back when I was issued mine. So, I had one of our techs check it out under the auspices of him thinking CIT was looking at purchasing a cell phone software manufacturing plant. If he ran across anything unusual he was to report it to me, and only me, immediately. He found nothing out of the ordinary. Apparently they've done a pretty good job of making these things incredibly secure. I was also notified by my handler that my phone was undergoing a diagnostics test that was not authorized. Kind of spooky they knew about it so quickly if you ask me."

I never thought about Audrey having a handler, Tony thought.

Tony gave a silent facial response telling her he was somewhat impressed about the phone technology.

However, his main focus was thinking about how Jacquelyn got a text from his phone. Especially from *that* particular part of his phone.

"Is it possible our friends out East can send a text to you and make it look like it came from either part of my phone?"

"You mean even if you didn't send it?"

"Right."

"You know, after all these years in the information technology business I think just about anything can be done. Given that, however, I have never experienced something like that nor even heard about it," said Audrey.

Interesting, he thought.

"Why would you think of something like that, Tony?"

He preferred not to tip his hand and replied, "I guess just being a techie myself and new at this cloak and dagger stuff that I question the capabilities and morality of my new employer. For all I know they can clone each of our phones and take them over at any time."

"Actually that makes perfect sense in an extreme case I suppose...but, I don't think we need to concern ourselves about things like that."

I think we should and I do, he thought.

Audrey looked at her watch and said, "Time to make our call."

After pressing the numbers on the keypad she placed it on speaker then on the table between them. The digital tones were audible and quick. Audrey turned the volume down just a little.

"On time as always," boomed the voice Tony recognized immediately. "Are you both there and free to talk?" asked Senior Special Agent Dennis Forman.

"We're both secure and contained," responded Audrey.

Tony gave her a look. *I forgot she's been at this kind of thing for a while*, he thought.

"Let's get down to business then. Audrey, I'll be emailing you an itinerary of items that Tony will need to complete so he can be up to speed on some important protocols and procedures. Tony, we've equipped Audrey's computer with a program that re-invents any attachments we send. It looks like a regular business email, but once opened with the CPT program it transitions to what was really written."

"What's CPT stand for?" asked Tony.

"Good question. Code Protected Transmission," replied Dennis.

Tony was impressed. His expertise is computer technology and yet he felt a little intimidated.

Dennis seems different. He said that I had a good question. Maybe Audrey is right about him. But, then again maybe I'm right that at his core he's like mercury, he thought.

"Speaking of technology have you read and destroyed the instructions of your new com device Tony?"

"You mean my new phone?"

"Yeah, sorry...too many years in the field," replied Dennis.

"Yup, all set. If I need help I'll turn to Audrey."

Audrey gave a nod to Tony.

"OK. Tony, we have a line on a potential SSD asset that we need your help with. All pertinent information will be in the second attachment of the email. Audrey will brief you."

"What do you want me to do?" asked Tony.

"Exactly what you were hired you for. Give us your assessment of the POI."

I remember being designated as a 'POI'. I already feel sorry for whoever this Person of Interest is, thought Tony.

"I don't have time to spell everything out for you, Tony. That's what Audrey's for," barked Dennis.

Ah, that's the Dennis Forman I'm used to. Agent Nubmnuts, thought Tony.

Dennis continued. "From here on out the only time we are to use our real names is when all parties are safely secured and contained. If you aren't then use code names only. You got that Radar?"

Tony hesitated then realized Dennis was talking to him. "Better than rabbit ears I guess", quipped Tony.

"Rabbit ears...I should have thought of that," Dennis said playfully.

"Audrey will fill you in on the other names, but from here on out my name is 'Repairman' in a non-contained environment. Got that?"

I still think 'Nubmnuts' is better, thought Tony. "Repairman...got it," said Tony.

"All right then let's get to work. Audrey, have you discussed the shadow's edge with Tony?"

"It's on the agenda after this call," she said.

"Good. It's important. Also, I'd have agent Wolf send you the email, but she just left on vacation. I'm sending you the documents now. Talk with you two later."

Audrey pressed the 'End Call' button on her Smartphone. "I have to check my email inbox. Dennis is incredibly prompt when he says he's going to send something."

Don't I know it, thought Tony.

He remembers still holding the phone after talking with Dennis for the first time when he immediately received an email Dennis said he'd be sending.

Audrey took her computer off mute and said, "It's here."

"A couple of questions Audrey. Am I a government employee, agent, contractor?"

"Your official title is 'Information Specialist' and you are considered an at-large consultant for Homeland Security, Savant Syndrome Division. Hardly anybody knows that division even exists. It's really part of the Central Intelligence Agency. It's funded in a way you don't want to know about. Remember, under the threat of government prosecution, you can't divulge that to anyone." she answered.

Tony James, Information Specialist for the Central Intelligence Agency, Savant Syndrome Division. I like the sound of that, he thought.

"Your other question?"

"What's the shadow's edge?"

"Oh, it's really not a big deal especially in your case. But, it happens. At some time you could find yourself acting on your own needs and wants instead of the interests of The United States. We call it the shadow's edge because one split-second decision and you find yourself either on the right side or the wrong side of the law...in the light or in the shadows for the rest of your life."

"I'm glad it's no big deal," Tony said sarcastically.

Chapter 5

—§—

1995

Audrey went directly from the hospital to Greenhill Funeral Home by the river to hire them to take care of the details for Andrew's memorial service. Before entering she took hold of her emotions. Checking her make-up and hair in the rear-view mirror she couldn't believe how tired she looked.

Audrey entered the main entrance hearing a single subdued tone that signaled the arrival of a guest. A man with graying hair at his temples in a classic black suit entered the room. He moved in a very deliberate manner.

"Hello, my name is Steven Miller," he said slowly and calmly as he extended his hand.

Audrey turned and said, "Hello Mr. Miller. I'm Audrey Shelton."

"Please, call me Steven. I'm so very sorry for the loss of your husband."

Audrey just stared at him in silence shifting Andrew's ashes from her left to right arm.

"I read about it in the paper", he said trying to put Audrey at ease. "Let me help you with that."

He gently placed the container on the mantel above the fireplace. It looked very much out of place since the ashes had yet to be placed in a suitable urn.

"I would like to make sure Andrew has a proper private memorial service," said Audrey.

"Please, let's have a seat over here to discuss your needs," said Steven gesturing with a sweeping arm and a much practiced comforting expression.

Audrey and Steven went over the details and settled on having just a few people who would be allowed to attend. She also requested that nothing be placed in the newspaper announcing any details of the service.

"It is most appropriate two marines attend the service to present you with the flag," said Steven.

"Oh, I hadn't thought of that. Alright," she said.

Steven thought about trying to offer more, but he knew he was dealing with a woman who knew exactly what she wants. Audrey thought she saw the wheels turning in Steven's mind so she cut him off before he opened his mouth again.

"OK. We're done here. Andrew wanted it this way," she said.

Two days later a very simple and quiet memorial service was held for Andrew Shelton. No fan-fare and no long line of people to listen to with their obligations of saying how sorry they are about Andrew. Besides the two marines it was just Audrey, Ryan O'Connor and Andrew's younger brother, Mark. Mark flew in from St. Louis the night before. He and Audrey aren't very close so he stayed at the downtown Marriott. Mark was Andrew's only sibling and their parents had previously passed away. After the service both Ryan and Mark were surprised no burial ceremony was to take place.

"Audrey, are you sure you don't want to have a place to go and talk with Andrew?" Mark asked.

Audrey, wearing black, simply said, "No, Mark. Andrew asked to have his ashes spread in a very special place and I intend on keeping my promise."

24

"But, you can still have a headstone," replied Mark as if it were more for him than Audrey.

"Mark, Andrew will always be with us. He touched our lives in so many ways. I don't think staring at a chunk of rock will do anyone much good."

Seeing that Audrey was perfectly comfortable with the arrangement he said, "You can always change your mind later if the mood strikes you."

"Thank you, Mark." *Now butt out*, she thought.

The three of them walked out together with Mark giving Audrey a hug then peeled off from her and Ryan as he was parked on the other side of the building. From the looks of the sparse parking lot the funeral home appeared to be closed. Ryan walked Audrey to her car.

"Audrey, I know this is really bad timing, but a board meeting has been called for Monday at 8am. Since CIT no longer has a President and CEO we are, by law, required to name Andrew's successor."

"Why are you telling me this? What does that have to do with me?" she asked in a sullen tone.

"Nothing really. I just wanted to you to hear it from me. Also, as the current Director of Sales I expect I will be named Andrew's successor."

"What gives you that idea?"

"I've spoken with Bob Robinson and Brian Harris and they're in favor of having me take the reins."

"What about Mike Turner?"

"I don't see why it would go to anyone else. Are you going to be OK?"

"At the moment I really don't care what happens to anyone or anything. Why would you even consider bringing this up now?" she said curtly.

It was as if a fog had lifted from Ryan O'Connor's mind. He'd been thinking of this day for some time. Ryan almost asked for her blessing then decided against it.

What if she said no.? That would be a problem. One I could overcome, but why open a can of worms with the mood she's in, he thought.

Audrey made a call to Janine Sheppard. The purpose of her call was simple; notify her if anyone from Langley shows any interest in involving themselves in Audrey's business. Janine Sheppard and Audrey had their initial training together. They became close friends, but as time passed they drifted. Audrey was convinced Janine would be of greater benefit to work at Langley and try to climb the ladder. With three sons to look after, Janine really didn't have the heart to be in the field and was a much better fit within the confines of the home office. Janine agreed especially after her one year hiatus after working with her handler.

Monday morning arrived and with it came a cold driving rain. Ryan O'Connor felt like this day was never going to get here. Three of the four board members, appearing somewhat somber, were in the conference room discussing a multitude of personal topics when the door opened. Ryan stepped in and glad-handed each man he'd known for many years. He acted as if he were running for public office. He went so far as to use the old 'two-handed grab and hold' handshake with each of them. Ryan extended his right hand then, once hands were engaged, he lightly grabbed the forearm to covey the observance of the intense closeness of their

26

relationship. He learned this little trick while watching how business is conducted in the nation's capital. Ryan felt exuberant, but tried not to show it.

The four men settled down and took their regular seats across from each other at the highly polished oval conference room table. Interestingly not one of the "type A" personalities took the vacant seat at the head of the table vacated by Andrew Shelton.

Just seconds before the meeting was called to order the door opened and Audrey Shelton entered the inner sanctum of the CIT boardroom. It wasn't the first time she was in here, but it was the first time during a board meeting.

Each man quickly got up and made sure Audrey felt welcome and poured out their condolences since they were not given the opportunity since Andrew's death. Audrey didn't play the 'poor me' part. She was put together and knew her role.

After the round of hellos and condolences the men took their seats. Audrey closed the door, but did not leave. She confidently walked over and sat in Andrew's chairman's seat. To a man, save one, each of them had an identical thought and for good reason.

"Are you planning to stay Audrey," asked Brian Harris.

"Well, if no one objects. After all, I did help start this enterprise and have been part of the many integral decisions all along the way. Though my physical presence in these board meetings has been absent my ideas have not. Andrew sought my advice on almost every aspect of this business venture."

Half standing, Harris asked, "Do any of you object to Audrey sitting in on this meeting?"

Not a single man disagreed and even seemed eager to welcome her. Ryan, on the other hand thought, *you don't belong here*. He was the only one thinking this way.

Since it appeared unanimous Audrey was more than welcome to stay for the meeting. Harris set the wheels of the meeting in motion though not really in charge. Ryan thought lying low early on would be a good strategic move. He knew the pieces of the puzzle would fall into place.

"OK, let's get down to the nomination process for CIT's new President and CEO," said Harris in a straight forward business tone.

Bob Robinson piped up and said, "I would like to be the first to nominate Ryan O'Connor. His experience speaks for itself."

Harris looked around the room and was looking for a second. He didn't want to be the second nominating vote. He was now flirting with a completely different idea. No face was looking at him except Audrey's.

Time slowly went by and Ryan began to feel like he had to make his move, but he was waiting for Harris to second his nomination.

What's he waiting for? he thought.

Ryan then pushed. "Brian?" he asked.

"My thoughts are to allow a free and open nomination process and then we'll vote Ryan."

Ryan shot him a look that could kill.

"Does anyone —?" Harris began.

Mike Turner cut him off and spoke in a soft voice. "I would like to bring a discussion to the floor."

"Go ahead Mike, this isn't Congress," said Harris.

He turned to Audrey and said, "I'd like to know if this board would consider Audrey Shelton to succeed Andrew as President and CEO."

Audrey looked at Mike in such a way as to give the impression of surprise and confidence at the same time. She said nothing, but nodded affirmatively.

Ryan just about fell out of his chair and said, "That's ridiculous!" He quickly back peddled saying, "She's just lost her husband for God's sake."

The rest of the men in the room finally lifted their heads as if awakened by a magic spell.

"I nominate Audrey Shelton", said Mike Turner.

Coming off as to be polite Harris said, "I'll second her nomination. We now have a second. Does anyone want to nominate anyone else before we vote?" asked Harris.

Ryan looked at each board member, but they averted making eye contact. He wasn't getting any support from them. Staring directly at Brian Harris, Ryan gave him a pleading gesture. He needed someone to second his nomination.

Harris didn't want to go back on his word to Ryan, but he also knew what would be in the best interests of one Mr. Ryan O'Connor. The tension in the air seemed so thick it could be cut with a knife. Finally, Harris buckled to the pressure of his word.

"I second the motion for Ryan O'Connor."

Ryan let out his breath. He didn't even realize he was holding it in.

"We have two candidates. Does anyone else want to place a name into nomination?" asked Harris.

No one spoke. The nomination process was brought to a close.

"Then we have Audrey Shelton and Ryan O'Connor on the ballot to succeed Andrew as President and CEO of this fine corporation. Each of you has a ballot in front of you. Please write the nominee for whom you'd like to be Andrew's successor. Please be sure to sign and date the bottom of the ballot," Harris instructed.

Each board member picked up their black Mont Blanc pen and discretely wrote down their vote. Audrey remained a spectator since she is not part of the board of directors. Harris instructed them to conceal their vote by turning the ballot over until such time as they are called upon to voice their choice.

Ryan O'Connor did the math in his head. *With my own vote, Bob's and Brian's it's a done deal. I'm in*, he thought.

"OK, looks like we are all set to reveal our votes. As directed by charter each vote must be verbalized and presented in writing so each board member can hear and see it clearly. Ryan, we'll start with you."

Ryan O'Connor proudly lifted his ballot and pronounced, "I cast my vote for myself, Ryan O'Connor."

"OK Mike. You're up," said Harris.

"I cast my vote for Audrey Shelton," he said softly as he held up his ballot.

"We have one vote for Ryan and one for Audrey. Bob you're next," said Harris.

"I have cast my vote for Audrey Shelton," he said without looking at anyone.

That means the best I can do is tie. There will be a re-vote. These guys are just making Audrey feel good. I can count on them in the second round vote, Ryan thought.

"I have the last ballot and cast my vote for Audrey Shelton," Harris said decisively. "Each of you please show your ballots so everyone can see and verify them. Does everyone see three votes for Audrey Shelton and one vote for Ryan O'Connor?"

The board members gave Harris the confirmation that it is a three to one victory for Audrey Shelton. Harris inspected each ballot.

"Congratulations Audrey, you are the new President and CEO of CIT," declared Harris.

Chapter 6

—§—

Present Day

Tony sat across from Audrey while she opened Dennis' email using her personal laptop computer. She connected it to a docking station so she could utilize her regular keyboard and larger monitor. As he watched he became quite impressed with her typing speed.

Wow! It's like she's pretending to just hit any key, he thought.

"Do you want to see how the CPT program works," she asked.

Tony hesitated. *I'm not sure I want to know everything about this stuff. But, maybe it'll come in handy someday*, he thought. "Sure," he said as he rounded her desk for a good view of her computer monitor.

"As you can see this is the first attachment…PDF1."

"Yeah, he's gifted when it comes to naming files," said Tony.

She double-clicked it. The PDF file opened and looked exactly like a typical business letter. Audrey then opened a little program called 'Hard Drive Re-Set' under the 'Accessories' program files.

"That's a clever name for the CPT program. No one would ever attempt to re-set their hard drive on their own," said Tony.

Audrey clicked on it and the blue screen of doom appeared. "That's a false front. It provokes an unwanted user to shut the computer down for fear of wiping out the hard drive. It's really harmless."

"Brilliant," said Tony.

Audrey sat back and waited before the blue screen disappeared and the CPT program started.

"I need to enter my security code. Will you kindly look away Tony?"

Tony couldn't help himself from looking when he found her keyboard directly in his line of sight from the reflection of the window. He watched as he heard her keyboard click along at a furious pace. *Hmm, only nine characters. I can see she's entered that password more times than she can count. Why didn't I look away?* he wondered.

The CPT program opened showing nothing more than the letters CPT in a one inch square dead center in the middle of her monitor. She dragged the box down to the lower panel and released the mouse button when it was held over the file she chose...PDF1.

Tony thought he was possibly having another hallucination. He couldn't believe his eyes. The business letter opened up to full screen then began to dissolve as if grains of sand began swirling clockwise then falling through an invisible funnel. Once that was complete the process reversed itself. This time it slowly brought up and pieced together the intended document.

"That has to be one of the coolest things I've ever seen," said an elated Tony. "I'm amazed at how these guys come up with this stuff," he added.

"What do you mean these guys?"

Tony looked at Audrey and saw a little grin. "You mean—?"

"I'm not *just* a pretty face," she mused.

The 'Double-edged sword' meaning for Audrey took on another dimension for Tony.

"OK, apparently there is a young man that has shown an ability to smell C4," said Audrey after reading the first few lines of the document.

"You mean the explosive?" asked Tony in a surprised tone. "Dogs can do that," he added derisively.

Audrey had kept reading ahead silently. "Yes, but this guy dreams about it first. Turns out he's been accurate every time. Called 911 the last two times and law enforcement found him to be correct."

Tony moved past Audrey and asked her not to read any more information to him. He sat back down at the round conference table. Audrey cocked her head to the side of her monitor staring at him.

"What's wrong," she asked.

"It sounds too weird," he said in a deflated tone.

"Why would this be any stranger than your talent Tony? And I mean that in a good way," she added.

"No, I don't mean this person's ability, talent...or whatever. It's just something I haven't told you and I feel uncomfortable talking about it."

"I'm only here to help Tony. Whether you want to talk or not is completely up to you. I won't be offended," she said.

Tony hesitated then blurted, "If I know too much about a person before meeting them it can block my senses at the initial meeting."

"I get it. It's like you need a blank slate," said Audrey.

"Exactly," he said. "However, that's not always the case. It's just the best scenario if I don't have any preconceived ideas about them."

"Well then I won't read any more to you. Is that what you want?"

"I think it's for the best," he said.

"OK, then I'll just provide you with the bare necessities of your objective. How does that sound?"

"Perfect," Tony said. *Perfect. What have I gotten myself into?* he questioned.

Tony stayed seated at the conference table while Audrey gave the basics of the objective.

"You are to meet this person —." She stopped herself. "You need to know if we're talking male or female don't you?" she asked.

"No. Not really, but you've already tipped me off it's a guy."

Audrey let her eyes linger just a fraction too long for Tony's taste. "Does it really matter to you," he asked her.

"Oh...no of course not," she answered back as if caught with her hand in the cookie jar.

"Just tell me when and where. Give me as brief description of the POI and I'll take it from there. I presume they want to know if this person is for real or not."

"That's exactly right and anytime this week by Friday afternoon in San Diego. There's a restaurant *this person* eats alone at outside every single work day. He or she always wears tennis shoes with his suit. Oh, shoot! I just did it again."

"OK, that's enough info." I'll work out the details of which day to go based on my workload and the weather report for San Diego," he said.

"Have you ever been to San Diego, Tony?"

"Nope."

"I can tell you not to worry about the weather. It will be sunny and seventy-two degrees," she said with a grin.

"How do you know?"

"Because it's always sunny and seventy-two in San Diego. Why do you think everyone wants to live there? But, I love the fact you were thinking ahead like that. You never cease to surprise me and I'm not sure why."

"How are you going to work this out with Jacquelyn," prodded Audrey.

"Nice try."

"What?"

"You have no idea if I told her about this whole thing and your fishing. Shame on you Audrey Shelton," Tony finished with a tone dripping with sarcasm. He followed up with, "What's my cover?"

"You either read too many spy novels or watch too many movies. You have no cover. Just show up, eat lunch and report back to me what you find out," said Audrey almost rolling her eyes.

"I just remembered, you never told me the other code names," he said excitedly.

"Alright, but I'm only going to say this one time and no jokes if you find any one of them even slightly humorous. I can't remember the last time we used them by the way."

"Scout's honor," Tony said as he placed his right hand on his heart.

"You were never a scout were you?" she said.

"I was a cub scout for almost two whole weeks. When I found out we only glued Popsicle sticks together instead of going camping I went AWOL."

They both had a good laugh.

"You already know yours is Radar. Dennis is Repairman. Director of Savant Syndrome Division is Missile. Agent Bobby Stark is Rockford and agent Elizabeth Wolf is Hollywood. The rest you don't need to know right now."

"Aren't you missing someone?"

Sheepishly she said, "I am Dagger."

I can't believe how close that is to double-edged sword, thought Tony. "I'd say you have the coolest name out of all of us. Why Dagger?"

"Each name has either a little story behind it or something that just sounds right at the time. It's an easy and safe way to communicate just in case. Like I said I can't remember the last time any of them needed to be used," she said.

I wonder what the story is behind the name Dagger, he pondered.

Audrey could see Tony was thinking about something and likely the origin of her code name. "Before you try and figure out how my name came about don't waste your time. It was given to me a long time ago and back then they just pulled the next one in line and handed it out."

Nice try Dagger. There's a story behind it, thought Tony.

Chapter 7

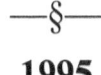

1995

On Saturday, two days prior to the CIT board meeting, the mail arrived at each home of the men who will be attending on Monday. Mike Turner, an avid reader, looked up from his book and heard the mail truck stopping and starting at each house. He's always friendly with the mail carriers and enjoys a quick hello when home on weekends. As was often the case the mail carrier handed Mike his stack. They exchanged pleasantries then he turned back toward his house. As he walked back up the driveway he flipped through each piece of mail. One parcel made him scratch his head.

That's odd. This one's from the Internal Revenue Service. It's marked 'URGENT'. Probably some policy notice that everyone, including me, will throw away, he thought.

He entered the house and grabbed the letter opener from his study. Expecting a form letter he unfolded it and began to attempt to quickly read and dispose. Mike instantly realized it was more than a form letter so he got his reading glasses. He found them lying on top of his book in the other room. Mike then went back to his study to clearly read the letter. Standing, at first, he found himself getting weak-kneed as he began read further.

"This is definitely no form letter! Oh my God!" he exclaimed.

The last sentence made it very clear that he was in no way to communicate any piece of information contained within it to anyone else especially a fellow CIT board member.

"I can't believe it," he said staring in quiet alarm.

About an hour later, on the same side of town, Bob Robinson also heard the mail truck. Bob has a different personality than Mike Turner in that he views his weekends to see as few people as possible. Bob speaks to so many bank executives during the week he just needs to lay low. He let the mail truck deliver to his house and then two more before briskly walking out to retrieve it.

Bob set the mail down on the kitchen counter then opened the refrigerator. He grabbed his bottle of Coors and opened it. After taking his first swig he shuffled through the mail. He too was surprised to see a letter from the IRS. Not so alarmed by the word 'URGENT', Bob took a long pull from the bottle of his favorite weekend beverage. Then, holding the envelope in his left hand he reached for his letter slitter with his right. Upon opening it he stopped frozen stiff.

"I'll be a Son-of-a —."

He couldn't believe his eyes. Moving his beer bottle on the counter he re-read the entire letter. Then he read the same sentence about no communication especially to a fellow board member once again.

"What the hell kind of crap has he been pulling!?"

"Did you say something Dear?" his wife asked from the other room.

"No, just…talking to myself."

"That's how it starts you know," his wife said jokingly.

This is no joke, he thought.

Brian Harris didn't get home until 6:15pm. He helped his daughter haggle with car sales people all day. He was bushed. Harris' wife, Deb, had retrieved the mail already. As always she placed it in the basket on the counter by the phone. Brian paid no attention to it. They had a nice dinner together and discussed how the car shopping went. After a blow by blow they cleaned up the dishes and were ready for a relaxing evening.

The next morning Harris was up well before his wife. He wished his body clock could change for weekends. Sauntering to the kitchen to make coffee he gave a fleeting look at the pile of mail in the basket.

Coffee first, he thought.

Harris opened the front door and picked up the Sunday newspaper that was delivered in the wee hours of the morning. With a chill in the air he quickly stepped back into the warm confines of his suburban home. He returned to the kitchen and set the paper on the counter next to the mail basket. The elixir of life began to fill the house with the aroma Harris started with each Sunday morning. He stopped at the mail basket and began to flip through the envelopes.

"Junk, junk, junk, bill…what's this?" he finished in a quizzical tone.

He separated the envelope from the rest setting it down on top of the newspaper then poured himself a cup of fresh hot coffee. Harris blew on the steaming brew, took just a small sip then set his mug down to open the curious envelope.

"This has to be a joke!" he said staring at the letter. There's no way Andrew would have ever done anything to put himself or CIT in a compromising position with the IRS."

Harris picked the envelope up for inspection and said, "Postmarked out of Washington, D.C. Must be the real deal."

He sat down, letter in hand, at the small round table next to the bay window.

"But, I just don't see how Andrew could have possibly abused company funds for personal gain."

Harris stared out the bay window and said, "He's— he *was* the most honest person I've ever known in the business world. It's the reason I agreed to become a board member. A private off-shore bank account? I just can't believe it," he said.

As a corporate attorney Harris realized that litigation is imminent. In particular the next President and CEO will be in the hot seat on this one.

"I'm not going to be on the wrong end of the enormously deep pockets of the US Justice Department, in particular when it comes to the IRS. They'll destroy Ryan O'Connor and enjoy themselves while doing it. I can't talk to him or I risk my own neck according to this letter. What am I going to do? I just can't saddle him with this burden. But, I can't inform him either."

Looking out, the bay window became a glossy haze as Harris thought about how he had been misled by his friend Andrew Shelton. He became angry and melancholy at the same time.

"I have no idea what I can do. I'm not going to be drawn into something as tawdry as embezzlement charges by the Internal Revenue Service. Even if the government is wrong, which is unlikely, the negative publicity is going to hit the next Chairman extremely hard. His business life is over. Andrew may have dodged one by having his heart attack. I have to think of a way to save

Ryan and make damn sure I'm not implicated by association. I had no knowledge of this and have done nothing wrong. I'm saving my own skin. What a way to start a Sunday," he said.

Chapter 8

—§—

Present Day

Tony finished his meeting with Audrey and thought about the origin of Audrey's code name, Dagger, as he drove from downtown Portland to his home office in the suburbs.

What a coincidence her government code name is Dagger and the very first feeling I got from her was double-edged sword. That can't be a fluke. It's who she is. Mine is Radar, which makes sense. I'm not so sure about her explanation concerning how she got her code name. The way she let her guard down this morning was strange too. It's as if she felt she finally had someone to mentor and share this stuff with, he thought.

Tony took the turn down his street, pushed the remote garage door button and pulled the car onto his side of the garage. Jacquelyn was still teaching at school. He needed to get caught up on some work since he'd been off the past week.

He began with his usual routine. Tony turned on the television for background noise. It was already tuned to ESPN. He set the remote control down on his desk to have ready access to the mute button if a call came in.

It took about an hour for Tony to sift through his email inbox eliminating the ones that required no action on his part. Once through that he realized he was a little hungry and grabbed a protein bar. Tony ate it as he slightly rocked in his desk chair watching SportsCenter. As soon as he was done eating he went right back to work, this time on the emails that required action.

"Wow, they sent me OSRs knowing I'd be gone? What were they thinking?"

Tony contacted the first Off Site Repair client. The client said she is very satisfied with the service she received.

Apparently you think I'm calling to follow up to verify that your computer problem had been completed to your satisfaction, he thought.

It was and Tony went with the flow of the conversation. He then wondered if all the rest were taken care of as well.

Contacting customer service he said, "Hi Molly its Tony."

"Welcome back Tony. Did you go anywhere fun on your vacation?"

Fun? Vacation? Audrey must have put a memo out covering me, he thought.

Tony thought about making up a lavish story just for grins, but knew he couldn't do that to Molly. The two of them have a very good working relationship so he didn't want to mess that up.

"No, no place fun this time," he said. *Unless you call going to Washington, D.C., or more specific Langley's Prison Hotel a fun-filled vacation*, he thought.

After the small talk Molly verified that each OSR sent to him was a duplicate and they all were handled by his associates throughout the country.

"We had trouble with just one potential customer though. Never heard of the place before. They're not a customer yet and based on the fact we couldn't help them I doubt we're going to ever get them."

"Did you check them out?" asked Tony.

"Didn't have time, sorry. But he did specifically ask for you by name," she said.

"For me? Why, is the company in the area?"

"I'm not sure. Like I said it was one of those real quick calls, you know? I've got my notes right here and my handwriting looks like I was in a big hurry. Must've been a heavy call day. All I can make out is something about a big white bird. Wow, that's really bad. I need a vacation!" said Molly.

"OK, anything else I should know? Otherwise ignorance is bliss", he added.

"You should know lots of things, but nothing I can figure out," Molly said with her odd sense of humor.

"Well I guess we're up to speed. Thanks. I'll talk to you later," said Tony.

With all of the Off Site Repairs taken care of Tony's rest of the day just opened up. He rearranged his priorities.

"I'm heading to the club and getting a little time on the racquetball court then get in a good weight lifting session. After that I'm going to figure out when I'm going to get to San Diego. Wait, I better set up San Diego first," he said changing his mind on a dime.

Tony accessed the SSD part of his phone and called Audrey. The number of rings seemed to go on and on.

"What, no voicemail?" he mumbled.

In a very hushed voice Audrey said, "I'll call you right back."

Tony looked at his phone. She didn't give him a chance to say a word.

After just about one minute Tony's phone rang in a slightly different tone than normal. It was close to his normal ringtone but just a little higher in tenor. He looked and the screen read 'Private Caller'.

Ah, I bet all calls come in like this. I had hoped it would say Dagger, he thought kiddingly as he answered.

"Hi Aud—", Tony said before he completed her name.

"I'm secure and contained. Are you?" she asked not giving Tony a chance to use her name.

"Yes. I just have a question," he said.

"Good, is everything alright Tony?" an agitated Audrey asked.

"Yes, like I said, I just have a question," he said.

"Didn't you read the protocol for urgent versus non-urgent calls?" she shot back.

"No, I'm sorry I didn't see anything about it. There is such a thing?"

"Yes," Audrey replied curtly.

Tony still wasn't used to hearing Audrey talk like this.

"Just before you press the send button press pound then wait for two beeps. Once you hear the two beeps you can press number one for urgent or number two for non-urgent then press send. I stepped out of a CIT meeting because if you place a call without waiting for the beeps the default is set to urgent," she said.

"I'm so sorry, but I didn't know."

"That's OK. It's my job to make sure you understand these things," Audrey said calming down to her normal tone. "What's your question?"

"How do I make flight plans? Do I go through CIT's booking agency or what?"

"No, don't ever do that. It creates a document trail. Normally Don's office takes care of this. You have the number in your contacts listed under the 'Music' app."

"Music?" Tony repeated contorting his face in confusion.

"Music, then open the 'Plane White T's' file. And that's P-L-A-N-E not P-L-A-I-N like the group," she said.

If this weren't so serious I'd let her know she's pretty up to date with her music knowledge, thought Tony.

"OK got it," said Tony.

"Did you just write that down?" she asked.

"Yes I did."

"In an all business tone she said, "Never, ever write anything like this down. You will have to memorize things like this. If you forget you can always contact me. I have to get back to my meeting. Do you need anything else?"

"No, I'm really sorry Audrey."

"Don't worry about it. We'll get the bugs worked out. I'm glad you're quickly jumping on your visit to San Diego. Talk to you later."

"Bye," he said.

Tony looked at the notes he scribbled and immediately ran the paper through the shredder. He then found the correct contact and waited for the two beeps and pressed send. A woman's voice answered on the other end.

"Trinity Corporation, how may I help you?"

"Eighteen - One – Four – One - Eighteen," replied Tony straining to remember the initial part of the code.

"I'm sorry, but you must have called an incorrect number," she said.

At first Tony thought he made a mistake, almost ended the call, and then realized this was part of the procedure.

"Um...Romeo - Alpha - Delta - Alpha - Romeo," Tony quickly replied in a concise monotone manner.

After a brief silence and clicking within the connection the woman said, "Radar, please confirm status."

"I am secure and contained," he said timidly almost rolling his eyes. *If this wasn't so serious I'd laugh*, he thought.

"Line is secure...go ahead."

"Am I calling the right number to make flight arrangements?" he asked.

"I see this is your first time calling. What can I do for you sir?" she asked in a suddenly sweet tone.

"I need to make travel plans from Portland to San Diego and back with an open ticket for Friday."

The woman never gave her name and Tony didn't ask. He could hear her typing on a keyboard just as fast as Audrey.

"Message received and confirmed," said the woman. "You are all set under your civilian name and can board any flight to and from San Diego tomorrow."

"That's it?" asked Tony.

"Unless you require something else," she said.

"No, that's all I need."

"Terminating communication sir," said the woman.

The line went dead as part of protocol. Tony looked at the phone then verified the transmission had been severed on his end as well. He of course made this call through the SSD portion of his Smartphone.

A moment later he received his open ticket with a complete flight listing via email. He knew there was no way to trace its origin, nor did he want to. He had learned that each email deletes itself in twenty-four hours unless he preferred to eliminate it immediately. Tony figured he'd take the 9:10am flight there and return on the 2:35pm. He memorized the flight numbers then pressed delete.

When Tony returned home from the meeting with Audrey and Dennis his mind was preoccupied. He didn't notice the blue and white utility van parked down the street.

"Do you have any concerns about your man who placed the bug?" asked the scrambled mechanical voice via cell phone.

"No, I insulated myself with five degrees of separation just like you taught me. He doesn't have a clue who actually hired him. Besides, he's been paid very well to keep his mouth shut."

"Well done," said the voice in a satisfactory tone.

"Sounds like he's made plans for his first assignment," said a woman in the counterfeit electric company uniform.

The voice asked, "When and where?"

"Friday…San Diego."

"Who's the target."

"Unclear at this point," she said.

"Tail him and please don't get caught."

"Understood.   Do you want me to continue my surveillance any longer today," she asked.

"No, give him some space.   You better get going before he heads out to pick up his kids from school."

"OK.   I'll call you Friday from San Diego," she said ending her transmission then setting the silver cell phone down.

She picked up the small black handheld digital device and verified it had cloned the James' wireless garage door opener code.

Chapter 9

—§—

1995

After all the polite hand shaking and congratulations Audrey officially accepted the office of President and Chief Executive Officer for CIT. She signed the papers that Brian Harris had drawn up. It was as easy as changing the first name from Andrew to Audrey. Any grade school student could do it, but Harris is an attorney and therefore it fell into his realm of responsibilities.

Ryan O'Connor tried to put on a good face however his true emotions seeped through the cracks. He thought there was still a way to win if he could only get Brian and Bob alone. He gave Audrey a quick hug while eyeing the two men he needed to talk with.

"Congratulations Audrey," Ryan said.

"Thank you Ryan. I know you wanted this. I need you by my side. Will you consider temporarily moving to the thirty-third floor until I get my feet planted firmly on the ground?" she asked.

"I'd be happy to," Ryan said vacantly.

"I'm going to need your expertise, especially with the government market channel," she said.

Ryan O'Connor would say yes to just about anything at the moment. All he really cared about is getting Brian and Bob alone so they could plan their next step.

"Well boss, I guess I'll see you in the morning," Ryan said with half a smile.

"Wonderful Ryan and thank you."

Not more than fifteen minutes later Ryan O'Connor, Bob Robinson and Brian Harris met at the corner pub. It was almost empty since it was still well before the lunch crowd. Ryan was the last to arrive. Robinson and Harris sat across from each other in the booth at the far back left corner of the bar named 'The Office'.

Even before sitting down next to Robinson, Ryan said, "What in the hell just happened? I pray you two have something up your sleeve!"

The two of them gave a knowing look at each other. Ryan felt like an alien from another planet.

"What's that look about?" he asked in an alarming tone.

Harris said, "Keep your voice down. We need to tell you something."

"I'm all ears," said Ryan showing control.

Harris, being an attorney, automatically became the mouthpiece and said in a hushed tone, "You read the letter. We're not supposed to be talking about this."

"About what? What letter are you talking about?" asked Ryan.

"Did you read your mail over the weekend?" asked Harris.

"What does that have to do with anything?" he asked in frustration.

"Everything," Robinson injected.

Ryan looked from Robinson to Harris with a look of complete and utter frustration. He took a breath and started over.

"I have no idea what you two are talking about. Let's get back to the subject of how we're going to remove Audrey as President and CEO and vote me in."

Robinson and Harris once again looked at each other and realized Ryan really hadn't read the letter from the IRS.

"Will you two stop that!?" blurted Ryan.

Harris leaned in and quietly asked, "Did you or did you not read the letter from the Internal Revenue Service which arrived on Saturday?"

"I didn't get a letter from the IRS. What are you talking about!?"

Harris promised himself he wouldn't get entangled in this mess. He chose his words carefully so he asked Robinson, "Would you please discretely like to explain it to him?"

Robinson took the lead and said, "I thought you just didn't care about the IRS letter and wanted the chairmanship regardless. Now I know you didn't have a clue when we were nominating and voting."

"A clue about what!?" asked Ryan in a hushed yet demonstrative flourish.

"So you didn't read the IRS letter," Robinson asked just to verify.

Ryan leaned back and said, "I'm going to make this perfectly clear to both of you. This is the first I'm hearing anything about a letter from the IRS...PERIOD!"

Harris remained quiet and became very uncomfortable. He stared at the salt shaker and allowed Robinson to proceed so he could honestly testify to saying nothing of the details regarding the letter if it ever came to that.

"All of us received a letter from the Internal Revenue Service from Washington very clearly spelling out felonious activity by Andrew before he died."

"Come on. Andrew was the straightest arrow I've ever met. There's no way he'd do anything illegal," scoffed Ryan.

"Then explain why each of us received a letter stating CIT's taxes are off and he was embezzling money placing it in an off shore account," replied Robinson.

"Come on...No way, Bob. I'm not buying into that," Ryan said as he sat back.

"The letter stated that any board member who communicated to anyone about this issue will face the judicial system. We're placing ourselves in jeopardy as we speak," Robinson said flatly.

You mean as YOU speak, thought Harris.

Ryan sat quietly for a moment then said, "But, I still don't get why you both went rogue and voted Audrey instead of me."

"Part of the letter very specifically stated that the new CEO will have to deal with this issue. Not the entire board. You see Ryan, we saved your ass today," Robinson said bluntly.

Ryan's eyes were as big as saucers. He couldn't believe his ears.

"So was Mike in on this as well," asked Ryan.

"Don't know. I didn't talk to anyone because of that letter," said Robinson.

Ryan turned to Harris. "I did not speak one word of this to anyone," he said clearly.

"Then how the hell did Mike Turner decide to nominate Audrey?" asked Ryan.

"Do you want to take this Brian?" asked Robinson.

Harris gestured with his left hand for Bob to continue.

"The way I see it Mike got the same letter and decided, just like the rest of us, to obey the directive of silence between us. So, when the opportunity came with Audrey sitting in on the meeting he jumped at the chance to throw her under the bus hoping the rest of us would follow. The rest is history."

Ryan became red in the face with fury. He stared straight through Bob Robinson as if into another dimension rarely seen by the other two. When he settled down he spoke in a very cautious tone.

"So you're telling me all of you got this letter this weekend and didn't bother telling me about it?"

"Why would we? I figured each of us got one," answered Robinson looking to Harris.

"Did any of you knuckleheads contact the person that sent the letter before we had our meeting?" asked Ryan in a condescending tone.

"I didn't," said Robinson.

There was no way for Harris to stay silent any longer so he very precisely said, "I took no action."

"You guys are lucky you didn't vote me in. I'd fire you right here on the spot!"

Ryan got up and said, "Stay right here. I'm going to get my cellular phone out of my car. I'll only be a few minutes."

Upon Ryan's return he asked to see the letter. Harris didn't move. Robinson reached into his briefcase and handed it to Ryan O'Connor. He first read it then looked for the phone number and a contact to call.

He punched in the numbers and a man answered, "Wagner."

"Mr. Wagner this is Ryan O'Connor of Computer Information Technologies Corporation."

"What can I do for you Mr. O'Connor?"

"I'm calling to verify you sent each board member a letter regarding an alleged felony by our recently deceased CEO, Andrew Shelton."

"There's a case number just under the date. Can you give it to me?"

"Yes, it's BD23725126416."

"Let me plug that into the computer. Yes, I have it right here. Why are you calling?"

"I just want to verify this came from the IRS. You know how many scams are out there," said Ryan.

"Well, I can assure you this is no scam and at this point I cannot speak about this case until the indictment order has been issued. However, while I have you on the line, are you the new CEO?"

Without hesitation Ryan O'Connor said, "No, that would be Audrey Shelton. Thank you Mr. Wagner."

Ryan couldn't get off the phone quick enough. He sat quietly thinking about what just happened. Then he raised his head and looked at his two fellow board members.

"I owe you guys an apology. You saved my hide today. I can't thank you enough. Audrey Shelton thinks she's hurting now. Just wait."

Chapter 10

—§—

Present Day

After practicing his racquetball backhand and getting in a solid workout, Tony went home for a late lunch and to make a few phone calls for CIT. His watch alarm went off at 2:00 P.M. reminding him to take his medication. He thought about how fantastic it's become that his life is no longer totally held captive because of Tourettes.

I'm not completely free yet, but getting closer, he thought.

He reset his alarm to remind him to pick Sam and Nick up from school at 3pm. Jacquelyn has her fill of school all day long as a teacher. The last thing she wants to do is go to another one though she loves to hear the excitement in the kid's voices as they pile into the car.

Time flew by and Tony's watch alarm rang out. Time to get the kids. Sam and Nick are on the same campus, but not in the same school. Samantha always waits for Nick outside his school on the little swing-set so Nick will find her and she can have some fun while waiting.

Tony drove up honked his horn and the two of them came running as if competing in the Olympics. Sam touched the car first and yelled "Shotgun." It's a game that Nick will have to grow a little more before he has a shot at beating his big sister. Both got in and buckled up. Tony reached back and made sure Nick's seatbelt was secure.

"You're getting close Nick. Sam looks like she's worried you're going to beat her one of these days," Tony said to encourage a little competition.

"I'm not worried," Sam said nonchalantly.

"You should be," said Nick.

"Dad, can we play next door before dinner?" asked Sam.

"Not today guys," said Tony knowing he and Jacquelyn needed to address the security breach. He then added, "But, I'm in charge of dinner tonight and I feel like Chinese."

What came out of Sam's mouth next made Nick laugh so hard snot blew out of his nose.

"That's funny, my friend Li Chang is Chinese and you don't look at all like anyone from her family."

Now that is funny! But, I can't laugh because it's also bordering on racism, thought Tony.

"Sam, Nick, listen up. That's not a good joke. It's not polite to separate people by something called ethnicity. It's a fancy word to say where people from other countries are born. Do you guys understand?" he asked.

Tony handed Nick a tissue. He wasn't sure they got the message, but he let it go for now. He made a mental note that a little more parental diligence in this area is required. Tony wasn't overly concerned. However, he didn't want Sam and Nick thinking that it's OK to go around saying things remotely close to this.

Once home Tony offered both either an orange or an apple before they ran away and played upstairs. Both said they wanted an apple. Unfortunately, there was only one left. Tony explained the dilemma and decided to leave it up to them to come to an agreement. He placed the apple between them on the kitchen counter as they sat on stools.

Good practice for the real world, he thought.

Sam said, "Since I'm the oldest I get to choose."

"No way," Nick retorted.

"I have a question," announced Tony. "Are either of you going to eat the whole apple?"

"Probably not," said Sam.

"Me neither," said Nick.

"Think about a way that the two of you can enjoy the same amount of the apple," Tony prompted.

Sam's face lit up turning to Nick. "I know. I'll eat this one while Dad goes to the store and gets another one."

Nick didn't like that joke too much. He grabbed the apple, turned and took a big bite out of it.

"Hey! I was just kidding," she said. "Dad!" she said using two syllables.

"Well Sam you better think the next time you joke about food with your little brother. Nick, put the apple back down."

"What I was really thinking was that we could cut it in half and share it," Sam said with a disgusted look on her face as she stared at her brother.

"Now that's a great idea. I'll cut it so the part Nick already took a chunk out of becomes part of his half," said Tony.

He took the apple, turned away then smiled as he got a knife out of the drawer. *She's coming up with some doozies today*, he thought.

"When both of you are done with your snack have fun. I've got some work to finish so please keep it down. When Mom gets home its homework time, OK? After that I'll order the food."

Tony made sure the dead bolts were secure before returning to his office. After about an hour Tony heard the garage door.

Jacquelyn's home, he thought.

After what seemed to be a lengthy few minutes Jacquelyn hadn't come into the house yet. Tony began to wonder what was taking her so long. He opened the house door to the garage and to his surprise her car wasn't there. However, the garage door was open.

That's really weird, he thought.

Tony called Jacquelyn's cell and she picked up on the third ring.

"Where are you?" Tony asked in an almost demanding tone.

"Hello to you too," said Jacquelyn.

"I'm sorry. Did you just open the garage door then go somewhere and not close it," he asked.

"No, but I'm just turning down our street right now so I'll see you in a few seconds." Jacquelyn ended the call without saying goodbye.

She walked through the door and asked, "Are you still a little freaked out about that security alarm guy?"

"No, I think I just made the mistake of not closing the garage door when we came home," said Tony not really believing his own words. "How was your day?"

"Nothing out of the ordinary, thank God."

"How was yours?"

"Don't ask," he said deflecting the question.

"That bad, huh?"

"No…just don't ask," he said kiddingly. "Everything was just fine."

After dinner Tony and Jacquelyn discussed their options regarding the conman that wormed his way into the house. Jacquelyn asked Tony if he looked into how someone could send a text and make it look like it came from his phone number.

"When it comes to technology the crooks are almost always one step ahead of the good guys. I asked the question, but the only answer I got was it's possible, but unlikely."

He didn't mention the context with which he asked or that it was Audrey that gave the answer.

"So, what should we do?" asked Jacquelyn.

"I think it'd be a good idea to look into installing a security system. It would be nice to be able to know we have an extra layer of security around here. Not that a burglar would get much, but I'd feel better if I'm out of town or something. I know how to hook everything up to our computers so we'd save a few bucks there," said Tony.

"OK. Would you mind doing the legwork up-front on this since you have the technical background?"

"Not at all...makes sense," said Tony. *I want to try and find out about the company that hacked my phone anyway*, he thought.

"Sam and Nick came running down the stairs to give their mom a big hug hello.

They both spoke so quickly and simultaneously about a bad joke and an apple. Jacquelyn looked to Tony for help. She loves her children, but she's around other parent's kids all day in school. She wasn't sure what they were talking about.

"I promised I'd cook Chinese. You up for it?" he asked.

"Dad, why would you cook a Chin—?"

"Don't say it. It's wrong" he said stopping her quickly.

She closed her mouth, but a twinkle in her eyes told Tony he needed to have that discussion about ethnic jokes sooner than later.

"They get that from you, you know," Jacquelyn said accusingly.

Nick and Sam then both pleaded with her to say yes. "Of course," she said giving Tony a knowing look. "But, both of you have to finish your homework first, OK?"

The kids rushed off to get their books and begin their work.

"You're cooking? So what take-out joint are you calling," she needled.

After dinner had been delivered and devoured, the kids went back upstairs to play. Tony and Jacquelyn quickly cleaned up and sat down to relax in the living room.

"Audrey's sending me to San Diego Friday. Just a fast day trip," Tony said to follow up quickly.

"You mean a long day and no overnight?"

"No overnight stay. It's just a quick trip with normal business hours or maybe even shorter. But, you'll have to pick the kids up because I'm not sure I'll make it back in time."

"That quick of a trip? What's so important that can't be done via an internet meeting?" asked Jacquelyn.

"Audrey says she needs me face to face in order to properly coordinate with this guy about plastics," he said.

"Plastics? I thought CIT's more into the software business than hardware," said Jacquelyn.

"Well, as a computer company we need to maintain our edge when it comes to our servers. I won't get into the details about materials and best practices on how to keep servers cool and energy efficient."

"Yes, please don't. So is this one of those extra CIT ambassador trips?"

"Exactly," he said nodding his head.

"This came up kind of quickly didn't it?"

"It did. But, we agreed for me to take the promotion because of the extra money remember?"

"I know. I just don't like it when you're gone like this."

"It's probably going to be a shorter day than usual," Tony said confidently. He followed up with "How did your day go today?"

"It was pretty normal except a substitute teacher was sitting at my desk when I got in this morning. She already had my computer booted up. All of us are required to keep our lessons on the school's intranet now. There was some kind of mix up and she thought she was taking all my classes today. I should've let her. But, that's about as exciting as it got," she said with a healthy sigh.

"Was this one of your regular subs," asked Tony.

"No, she's new and very pleasant. She wrote down her number and told me to give her a call if I ever needed her to sub for me. I put it on the fridge. I'm not sure why I did though."

"Why's that?"

"First, the school takes care of setting up our substitutes. They have a list of pre-qualified teachers for each class. Second, she gave me her number but, didn't put her name on it and now I forgot who she said she was."

Later that evening, with Jacquelyn already in bed, Tony searched for anything he could find on the internet with regard to Rest Easy Security Systems. He found absolutely nothing. As he sat back thinking about moving ahead and researching a real security system his mind began to drift. Tony's senses kicked into hyper drive and he thought he saw a pattern beginning to emerge.

First there was the Rest Easy Security Systems guy. Then a phantom text to Jacquelyn. Then there was the garage door. I know I closed it. Next Jacquelyn had another intruder, nice person or not, in her classroom today, he thought.

Tony closed his eyes and tried to picture the license plate of the rental car that was parked on his driveway. A picture finally squeezed out between the cracks.

"Hertz Airport," he declared with wide eyes. "The frame around the back plate read 'Hertz Airport'. Why would a local security system sales guy be driving a rental from the airport? I guess if he lives by the airport and needed a car I suppose that's where he could get a rental while his car was being repaired."

Tony mulled that over for a few minutes poking holes in his theory on purpose. However, he felt like he was possibly onto something, but it was getting late and he needed to get some sleep. He logged off the computer and began to head for bed. He stopped and realized the kitchen light was still on. Just as he flipped the switch off, he noticed something and turned the light right back on.

He walked across the tile floor and looked at the pink sticky note Jacquelyn had placed on the refrigerator. Tony examined the note. It definitely was not Jacquelyn's handwriting, but also definitely female with large swirls and loops.

Hmm...this handwriting seems oddly familiar. I think I've seen it before, he thought.

Tony couldn't place where or when he'd seen this handwriting previously. The answer seemed to be just out of reach. He stared at it for a few more moments, yawned, but couldn't place it.

Ah, well, maybe with a good night's sleep it'll come to me tomorrow, he thought.

Chapter 11

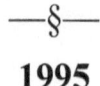

1995

Audrey arrived home after the board meeting and collapsed onto her couch. The very same couch officers Lambert and Rice had occupied recently. Across from her sat the empty chair officer Rice had guided her to just in case she fainted at the news of her husband's fatal heart attack. She slipped off her shoes, curled her legs up and rubbed her aching feet. Once feeling more comfortable she picked up a flip style cell phone and placed a call. She entered the ten digits from memory. Audrey listened intently as her call finally went to a mechanical sounding voicemail. Audrey tapped the cell phone's microphone three times, paused, then once more before she ended the call. She turned the phone off and flipped it closed. She sat back with just a hint of a grin then let out a small sigh.

"I'm the President and CEO of CIT," she said as if needing to hear it out loud.

Audrey closed her eyes. After a few minutes of silence the noise of the landline phone rang out. She remained quiet, and still, with her eyes remaining shut. Two rings then the phone went silent. Audrey smiled as she placed a pillow behind her head and stretched out on the comfy couch. Her calmness in the middle of chaos has always been one of her strengths.

After ten minutes she opened her eyes and said, "I have to get to work. Women in the workforce need to be twice as good as men just to create a level playing field."

After getting her briefcase from the closet she walked to the den where Andrew used it as his office away from the thirty-third floor of CIT. She gingerly sat down in his old chair on wheels and gently felt the solid wood desk. Audrey looked at the barren wood grain desktop and adjusted the chair to fit her just right.

"Nostalgia later. Time to get to work," she said aloud.

Once the computer booted up she browsed the files and took inventory of the system Andrew used to keep everything organized. Audrey knew she was going to have to work very hard and also need some inside guidance from Ryan O'Connor.

Calling from her new home office she asked the young man at CIT to create a new email address for her.

"This will be ready for you before the end of the day," the young man said proudly.

"No, that won't do. I need it in the next five minutes," said Audrey in a very patient tone.

"But, with all the new—"

"I don't think you understand," she said cutting him off. "I require my new email address in the next five minutes so I can communicate to our family of employees that I am the new President and CEO of CIT."

The young man swallowed hard, now understanding exactly who he was talking to. He said, "Yes Ma'am. You'll have it within five minutes after I get off the phone with you," he said nervously.

"Thank you. I appreciate your help. Will you kindly send me a test email so I know it's active?"

"I certainly will."

Within minutes Audrey was indeed up and running with her new email account. She wrote a glowing report of the work Andrew had done giving birth to a company with unmatched integrity and reputation within the industry and community. She sent it to every person within the corporation.

Ryan O'Connor had gone back to his office at CIT and was casually reading an industry report when the arrival of Audrey's email chimed.

"What the—? She not wasting any time is she?" he said.

He read the lengthy email and then sat back with his feet up on his desk and chuckled. Ryan noticed Harris and Turner were not on the email list so he forwarded the message to them.

"She has no idea what a short ride she's on," he said thinking of the IRS problem. *I haven't talked to Mike, Brian or Bob. We need an organized plan to tell her*, he thought.

Ryan waited a few minutes then placed a call to Brian Harris at his law office. Harris, Robinson and Turner are on the board, but O'Connor is the only board member and CIT employee.

Harris' assistant announced that Mr. O'Connor is on the line. He picked up the phone, "You miss me that much already?" he joked.

"We need to figure out a plan to inform Audrey of this IRS thing," said Ryan.

"Why?" asked Harris.

"What do you mean, why? Did you read the email she sent out that I forwarded to you? Based on her glowing report of Andrew's integrity she's delusional and as board members it's our responsibility. Come on, it'll be fun," he laughed.

Harris said, "I don't think we need to say a thing to her."

"Why not?"

"Well, the IRS letter states we are not to discuss the matter with anyone. I presume they mean it," said Harris.

"But, that's lunacy. We're the board of directors. It's our duty and obligation to notify her. Remember, she didn't get a letter because she wasn't a board member yet," said O'Connor.

"I know what you're saying is right, but if we don't follow the law we could wind up joined at the hip with our new President and CEO. I don't look good in prison orange. I'm staying clear of this mess at all cost," Harris said pointedly.

"That's pretty harsh Brian."

"It's reality Ryan."

They both hung up the phone not feeling very good about their quick conversation. Usually they're both on the same side of almost every issue.

Well, I can at least count on Bob Robinson and Mike Turner, he thought.

"Hi Bob its Ryan. You got a few minutes?"

"Ryan, I told you earlier, you should be thanking us not giving us grief," he said jumping to conclusions about this call.

"You're right about that, but that's not why I'm calling. I want to have an organized plan to notify Audrey of the IRS problem she's about to walk into."

"I'm not going near that subject unless I have to. You read the letter. We are not supposed to discuss anything related to it. Besides, why should you care? Once this is over Audrey will be out and you will then be voted in as President and CEO. It's only a matter of time."

That makes sense, thought Ryan.

At the end of the conversation he placed the phone back in its cradle and paused with his hand tentatively resting on his phone. O'Connor needed to run things over in his mind before he calls Mike Turner.

If we say nothing we don't get dragged into a mess with the government and I wind up with the gold medal. If we say nothing Audrey will be blind-sided by the IRS and she has the power to fire me, but Brian, Bob and Mike are safe because it takes a full vote to release anyone from the board of directors. They're only saving themselves. Maybe Mike will have a different take, he thought.

"Mike Turner speaking," he said answering his phone.

"Mike. Ryan."

"Ryan, I haven't spoken to you in hours. How've you been," he said joking around.

"Mike, where do you stand on notifying Audrey about this IRS problem?"

"I've thought about it and decided it's in my best interest to stay clear of the whole thing. After all, I had no hand in creating it," he bristled.

"But, don't we have an obligation as board members to notify her that she's walking into a buzz saw? Based on that email she just sent out she had no idea what Andrew was up to."

"The time to notify her was before we sealed her fate and voted her in," said Turner.

Ryan thought about that for a moment and said, "Well…maybe your right."

"I know I'm right."

"OK, thanks for your thoughts Mike."

Once again Ryan found himself alone and out of the loop from his associates. He just sensed something wasn't feeling right and it was gnawing at him.

All three of them are looking out for themselves. Maybe I should take their lead, he thought.

The chime from his computer interrupted his thought process. A new email came in. This one also came from Audrey. He opened it up and found her to be reaching out to him.

"She's asking me to be her right-hand man. Vice President of Sales and Marketing with a pay raise to boot," he said to the screen.

He re-read two sentences out loud that changed his entire view: "If you will be kind enough to guide me early on I will make sure you are taken care of when the time comes. Andrew would have wanted it this way."

"How do I say no to that?" he said as he exhaled.

Ryan wrote her back and told her he appreciates the promotion and will gladly help in any way he can. His finger tips hovered over his keyboard thinking if he should tell her about the Internal Revenue Service problem. He wrote:

"Can we meet in your office yet today?

Her reply came back quickly.

"Sorry, but I'm at home and won't be in until morning. How about 9am?"

Ryan confirmed back to her then wondered if he was doing the smart thing.

I know I'm doing the right thing, but I'm not so sure it's the smart thing, he thought.

Chapter 12

—§—

Present Day

Friday morning seemed to come quickly as Tony's internal body clock was once again right on schedule…5:35am. The first thing that greeted him was a short eye blinking tic episode.

Well, that hasn't changed much. Maybe someday, he thought.

Tony looked out the bedroom window and saw a very rainy day in store for the Portland area. He thought about what Audrey had said about the weather in San Diego and the idea seemed to warm him up a little.

Jacquelyn was up early and already had her first cup of coffee. She turned in early last evening and awoke refreshed after getting well over eight hours of sleep. She saw Tony gazing out at the rain.

"You poor thing, just thinking of San Diego must make you sad," she kidded with a little jealousy in her voice.

"Why do we live here?" asked Tony still staring out the window.

"Oh, I don't know, family, friends and jobs. You know those pesky unimportant things."

"If San Diego weather is so great then why don't we move there?" he asked sincerely still staring at the rain.

"Because our life is here and your happy…got that," she said teasingly.

"Oh, yeah, I forgot," said Tony playing along.

"While you daydream I've got to get ready for work," she said.

Abruptly Tony asked, "What did that substitute teacher look like that was in your classroom yesterday?"

"Why, are you in the market for a sub?"

"No, I have my reasons for asking. Isn't it strange how just in the past few days we've had unwanted visitors at home and now at your school?"

"Don't let your imagination get the better of you Tony. It was just a simple mix-up at school."

"Will you do me a favor?" he asked.

"We don't have time for that right now," Jacquelyn said mischievously.

"Who put a quarter in you this morning?"

"Sorry, I just don't think there's a connection between that con man and a substitute teacher," she answered.

Tony paused then said, "Your right, maybe I am letting my imagination get the better of me. But, just in case, will you check into how she happened to be there just to ease my mind?" Tony asked with pleading eyes.

"Vulnerability is not one of your best qualities. But, I know you won't stop asking until I check it out. So, I'll look into it…OK?"

"Thank you Jacquelyn," Tony said with a wry grin.

Jacquelyn said, "Well I have to get ready. Since you can't take the kids to school that doesn't give me much time. Will you help get the kids going?"

"Of course."

The James gang began their day with Jacquelyn teaching, Sam and Nick learning and Tony off to sunny San Diego for a brief encounter with a possible asset for a covert division of the United States government.

Just another typical day, he jokingly thought.

Before checking in at the ticket kiosk Tony went to the Hertz car rental located on the third floor of the parking structure. He went inside.

"How may I help you?" asked the young woman behind the counter.

"My car's in the shop. How much is it to rent one for the day?" Tony asked.

"If you're having car trouble I have to refer you to one of our other Hertz rental locations. We only have enough cars for airport customers at this location. Here's a map with all our locations throughout the Portland area. Is there one that suits you?"

"Thanks for the map. So I have to be an air traveler to get a car here?"

"I'm terribly sorry, but we only have so many vehicles."

"OK, thank you," said Tony. He turned to walk away then turned back and asked, "How would you know if I told you I were an airport traveler or not?"

"We require all rental customers to provide proof of their flight information."

"Are you sure that's legal?"

"I just follow the rules. Would you like to speak to my manager?"

"No...just wondering. Thanks."

Tony deplaned at the San Diego International Airport on time. He was thrilled to see palm trees as he hailed a cab. Tony put on his sun glasses and politely told the driver to drop him off at the NBC building at 225 Broadway. He carried his briefcase and purchased the San Diego Union Tribune newspaper to blend in with the local downtown crowd. He also asked to be dropped off at this particular location so there wasn't a record of him being dropped off at the Thai restaurant.

The ride only took about fifteen minutes. Tony paid the cab driver with cash then walked into the NBC building. He got his bearings and headed straight out the other side onto Broadway Circle. Looking to his left he saw the restaurant. Tony looked at his watch and knew he had about forty-five minutes to kill. He walked to sit on a rustic bolted down bench for a front row view of the outdoor seating area across the street.

Eleven in the morning and it's about seventy degrees with no humidity. I could get used to this, he thought.

Opening the newspaper he practiced how he would conceal himself. This time not because of Tourettes. Tony decided to practice turning his head in one direction while keeping his eyes behind his sun glasses on an empty restaurant chair across the street.

This is going to be just perfect. Although I didn't expect as many trucks traveling on this stretch of road, he thought as one traveled past blocking his view briefly.

He looked at his watch once again and began to people watch. Tony noticed the foot traffic had picked up. The restaurant employees began to raise the shade umbrellas on the tables of the outdoor seating area. It looked to seat four people per table with eight tables outside.

Why would anyone want to eat inside on a day like this? Tony questioned.

Fifteen more minutes flew by as Tony scanned the newspaper slightly less than his target area. His stomach grumbled.

I knew I should have eaten something before settling in for the job, he thought.

A few people began to be escorted to the empty round tables outside.

"OK...Showtime. Let's focus," Tony mumbled.

A faint echo of a familiar feeling began bothering Tony, but he chalked it up to nerves. He looked around in a casual manner. Tony decided to push the feeling away and focus on the task at hand.

Less than one hundred feet away from Tony stood what appeared to be an older woman wearing a fashionable straw hat and rather large sunglasses at the right corner of the NBC building. She lifted her left hand to her face pretending to read a text on her phone. Using her ultra-slim digital camera, which looks like a Smartphone, she zoomed in on Tony and snapped a few pictures of him as if he were posing for a newspaper advertisement. She acted casual, but remained focused on Tony then panning to the restaurant across the street. On her hat she wore a small pin that avid golfer's often wear. Tony only noticed the pin because he's seen it a million times from watching the Masters golf event on TV. What he didn't know was the pin is a very high-tech ultra-sensitive wireless directional microphone. The woman made sure she pointed it right at Tony as often as possible.

Meanwhile, across the street, each time the hostess emerged from the shadows of the restaurant Tony gave a laser-like focus on the lunch-time patrons following behind. At this point he paid no attention to any female. He knew his target to be male.

The crowd began to grow and still Tony did not see, or feel, his target. However, he continued to get a nagging feeling, but he just couldn't pinpoint what it could be. Tony made sure he wasn't going to get distracted from his assignment. He doubled his efforts. Tony heard a rumble coming down the street from his right. An old green McNight's Fish delivery truck drove past between him and the restaurant.

Maybe I didn't pick the best spot, he thought.

He looked around, did a double take when noticing something from the corner of his eye, but decided this spot has the best line of sight other than being in the NBC building with binoculars. Tony shook off the idea of what he thought he may have seen just a few seconds ago.

I don't think I'd get a good read if I was in the building. Besides, it's a beautiful day, he thought

He looked back to the restaurant and said quietly, "Only one table left. Maybe he's not coming today."

It seemed like it took an eternity, but finally the hostess emerged with one menu in hand. The first thing Tony saw come into sight a few steps behind her from the shadow of the restaurant and into the sunlight was exactly what he had hoped for.

"Bright red tennis shoes," said Tony not realizing he verbalized his thought.

The slim twenty-something with floppy black hair, carrying his sport coat over his shoulder, followed the hostess. As he sat they chatted for a few moments like they were old friends. Tony noticed she didn't even give him the menu.

This is where he eats lunch every workday. He already knows the menu. So this guy has a dream about plastic explosives then calls it in? I wonder how Director Don Williams would plan to use him. He looks like he drives a VW Beetle and makes house calls for Best Buy, Tony thought.

Still strategically peering from behind his newspaper Tony placed his entire focus on the floppy-haired young man. The feeling that came flooding at Tony hit him like a fifteen foot wave. The words that accompanied this feeling were *Broken Savior.*

Hmm, I wonder if that helps confirm what SSD suspects of him. Does he really dream about C4 then call it in and rescue people? Pretty cool if he does...but I don't think so. I should ask how they came to find out about this guy. Dreams aren't something the government would know about. Maybe he told the police or firefighters. I think he's a fake anyway. Broken savior. Guaranteed he sets it up ahead then calls it in. I wonder where they got their intel? Intel...maybe I do watch too many movies, thought Tony.

Tony heard someone yell his first name. It came from behind him and inside the NBC building behind him.

Must be some other Tony, he thought.

He folded his newspaper, got up off the bench then walked into the building. He was no more than twenty feet inside when he heard the explosion and then felt the ground shake. Suddenly, he was showered with tiny balls of glass from the skyscraper entrance in which he stood, eyes closed, covering his head with his briefcase. The glass is designed just like a car window. It won't break into shards. It rained down little beads of glass.

Everyone in the atrium of the building ran away from the explosion except for Tony. He looked at the gaping hole from which he had just walked through where there used to be multiple doors. When he got outside he tried to see where the explosion originated. The thought never occurred to him there could be more explosions.

Turning toward the bench he left just minutes ago confused him. He looked further left then shifted his eyes back. There was a good reason he missed locating the bench. It's been blown away. With the smoke and debris it became difficult to see, but Tony instinctively needed to find the genesis of the explosion. He began to move straight ahead. People were running in the opposite direction.

A green delivery truck that was apparently passing by at the time of the explosion was up on the sidewalk with flames billowing out. The driver side door was open. Tony ran toward it.

"Empty. Thank God," he said looking in from about ten feet away.

Knowing not to stand around a truck on fire he moved to see across the street to the restaurant. Thick smoke blocked his view. He covered his mouth and nose with his hands and saw the chasm that lay waste where the outdoor seating used to be.

"Oh my God, none of those people could have survived that blast!" he said.

His ears were muffled from the strength of the explosion. He heard the sirens, but thought they were blocks away. Tony looked and saw the red lights of a fire truck through the smoke had already parked. Firefighters frantically pushed their way toward the flames of the building that used to be the Thai restaurant.

As Tony ran out of the smoke and down the street he caught a glimpse of an unbelievable sight. A bright red tennis shoe disappearing around the corner of the NBC building. Tony went into a full athletic sprint trying to catch up with the POI.

"Hey! Stop!" shouted Tony.

He rounded the corner and did a three-sixty. Tony lost him.

That's not possible, he thought.

He held his nose and blew air into his nostrils to try and pop his ears to hear clearly. One of them cleared while the other still remained muffled.

I don't think Audrey or Dennis would want me to go on the record and be a witness to this. I have to get out of here, he thought.

Tony swiftly walked to the front of the NBC building where he had been dropped off by the cab when he arrived. He took an inventory of himself.

No injuries. My clothes are full of soot. I can't go anywhere without people asking questions. I should've stayed away from the aftermath. However, if I hadn't I wouldn't know our POI is still very much alive. He left before the blast, he thought.

Tony re-entered the NBC building. He found the men's bathroom, entered and shook the soot from his hair then washed his face, arms and hands. Tony took off his shirt and pants and shook them out. After a brief inspection he quickly put them back on. Tony cleaned his briefcase and looked at himself in the mirror from head to toe.

OK, I'm presentable enough, he thought.

Tony re-exited the building, crossed the busy street and walked east on the opposite side of Broadway until he found a clothing store. He quickly purchased one new shirt and a pair of pants. The kid at the register had a bored to death look about him. Tony quickly entered another downtown skyscraper and changed his clothes in the bathroom stall reserved for handicapped people.

This seems familiar, but for a completely different reason. I'm not so sure I wouldn't trade back right about now, he thought referring to his previous need for tic release.

Once dressed, he inspected the clothes and realized his shoes were still a little too dirty. He cleaned them off, went back outside and began walking at a leisurely pace. As he did so he took his Smartphone from his briefcase, entered his code and made a call.

Audrey picked up and cheerfully asked, "How's the weather down there?"

Not feeling the least silly as he had envisioned he shakily said, "Not secure or contained."

Audrey's voice changed to have almost a robotic tonality to it, "Confirmed. Leave out names and anything you don't want others to hear. What's your situation?"

Tony explained as he walked trying to look like just another business person not letting any use of his time go to waste. He spoke softly. Tony then listened as Audrey gave him very specific instructions of which he would follow. It wasn't anything he wasn't doing already. Tony walked about ten blocks then hailed a cab to take him back to the airport. He got on a plane and headed for home.

As soon as Audrey ended her call with Tony she called it in and asked, "Was this who we think it is?"

"Who else would it be?"

"Should we tell Tony?"

"He's on a need to know basis. And, he doesn't need to know this."

Chapter 13

—§—

1995

After changing elevators on the thirty-second floor Ryan O'Connor rode the private elevator one more floor up to the thirty-third. He was a few minutes late for his 9am meeting, but felt he held most of the cards so he didn't feel too badly about making Audrey wait.

"Good morning Ryan," Audrey said politely as the elevator doors opened directly into her office.

"Good morning to you Audrey."

"Please, have a seat right here," she said placing him in front of what is now her desk. "Can I get you a cup of coffee," she asked.

Ryan felt the anger begin to build seeing her behind that desk. He put on his famous infectious smile and said, "Yes...black. So how does it feel being the top dog around here," he asked.

"Bitter sweet," she replied not meeting his eyes.

"Oh, right...sorry," said Ryan feeling like a complete jackass due to her loss.

"I'm sorry Ryan I need to filter that out," she said.

"Hey, you have every right to feel any way you need," he said sincerely.

Handing him his coffee Audrey asked bluntly, "So, when can you begin to move your office up here? I need to be brought up to speed as quickly as possible."

This took Ryan by surprise. Even with his new title he thought he'd have the choice to keep his office right where it is while Audrey had to handle the Internal Revenue Service. Ryan only wants to warn her and not play a major role in this mess.

"Do you really think that's necessary?" he asked.

"Yes. You and I are going to work very closely together. I need your help."

Ryan began to wonder if Audrey knew about the Internal Revenue Service problem. *Why else would she be so insistent on me sharing an office with her.*

"Audrey, don't you think you should have the big office to yourself? After all you're the President and CEO. We don't want any confusion with that." said Ryan trying to sell her on possible misperceptions.

"I'm not concerned with anyone's perception of me Ryan. I just need to get up to speed with the important issues facing CIT and taking them on. I can accelerate the process with your knowledge of the day to day business activities," Audrey said plainly. She added, "This will be temporary."

Looks like I'm on the wrong track. She doesn't know, he thought.

"Audrey, would you mind if we sit at the table instead of having a desk between us?" asked Ryan.

"Oh, I'm so sorry Ryan I never—." She stopped then started again. "What was I thinking making you sit across from me? See, this is why I need you so close. It's not just the big issues, but something as little as this," she said motioning her right hand across the desk.

Ryan felt better now that the playing field became a little more level with both he and Audrey sitting at the round conference table. Audrey had her notebook and pen at the ready. She made notes on occasion as they conversed. Ryan began to feel like a professor with a high level student with an insatiable appetite for knowledge.

After conversing for about an hour Ryan began to see Audrey in a different light. He became more convinced than ever Audrey knew nothing of her husband's corporate deceit.

She just wants to continue the good work Andrew had done before he went off the reservation. I better tell her before this goes too far. I have to do it in such a way she doesn't think she was set up, he thought.

"Audrey, I know how much influence and the numerous ideas you must have had while Andrew was running CIT," Ryan said.

"Being together when he started CIT brought us closer together," she said in a melancholy tone.

"Did he ever share the financials with you?"

"That's an area that became an issue in our marriage early on. He would tell me how he often times made payroll by the skin of his teeth. At the time I didn't have the stomach for it so he no longer shared that kind of information with me. Thankfully the business took off and the subject never again needed to be discussed.

"I'm not Andrew, but I need to have one of those hard discussions with you right now," said Ryan sitting casually with his hands clasped resting on the table.

"Is CIT in financial trouble?" Audrey asked with panic in her voice.

"Not exactly," said Ryan.

Audrey's eyes became as big as saucers.

She said, "Just tell me in plain English. If there's a problem we'll fix it."

"There is a problem and you are the only one who can fix it," he said as he got up to get his briefcase from next to the chair in front of the desk.

Audrey stared at the briefcase before Ryan had picked it up then she cautiously asked, "What is it?"

Ryan set his briefcase on the table and pulled out a copy of the IRS letter he got from Brian Harris. He took it from the large manila envelope. Stapled to it was a photo copy of the envelope that was mailed to Brian Harris. He quickly re-scanned the letter then handed it to her.

"This is the problem, Audrey."

She looked at the first page and turned it landscape style. Audrey looked up at Ryan with confusion in her eyes. Next she flipped it to the IRS letter turning it back to portrait view with the staple in the upper left corner. She creased the two pages at the staple. Reading quickly she sat up straighter as if feeling a stab in the back with each paragraph moving down the document. By the time she had finished she was at the edge of her seat almost ready to stand.

With pain in her eyes and her mouth already partially open she stared at Ryan O'Connor then asked, "Is this for real?"

"Unfortunately it is. I verified it for myself."

"But—?"

"Audrey, I spoke to Mr. Wagner from the Internal Revenue Service myself," Ryan said pointing to the contact name on the document. "This is real," he said leaving the obvious unsaid. *I'm not going to trample on Andrew's grave,* he thought.

Audrey re-read the letter. Ryan remained silent as she did so. When she finished she flipped back to the copy of the envelope. She raised her eyes to Ryan then again back the page.

Leaning over to Ryan she held the pages and pointed to the postmark, then said, "Do you notice anything unique about this date?"

Ryan didn't respond choosing to accept her question to be more of a statement. He just looked at her.

"Ryan, this postmark is just prior to the board meeting. The very same board meeting in which I was voted in as President and CEO. How could you not tell me before you voted me in?"

Thinking quickly Ryan said, "Audrey I voted for myself if you recall. I never got one of these letters." He pointed to Harris' name and address. "If anything its Harris, Robinson and Turner you need to be asking not me," he said calmly.

In a puzzled tone she asked, "You didn't receive a letter?"

"No."

"But, Brian, Bob and Mike did?"

"Apparently," said Ryan walking the fence on that answer.

Audrey got up and began pacing as she read the letter one more time. She absent-mindedly sat down on her chair at her desk with her back toward Ryan and stared out the window. Ryan knew he needed to remain silent.

Finally Audrey swiveled her chair back toward Ryan. "When did you find out?"

"Not until well after the board meeting took place."

"Why didn't you call me right away?" she asked with a sting in her voice.

I'm not going to get grilled over this. It's her problem. Her husband created this mess. She was so willing to ace me out as President and CEO and now she's going to try and push me on this? I don't think so, he thought.

"I didn't call because this is the sort of thing we need to discuss in person like we're doing right now. Someone in your position should know this. And I don't appreciate your tone. Do you really think I would have voted for myself if I had this information? If you do then I now know what you really think of me," he said emphatically.

Audrey paused then said, "You're right. I didn't mean to attack you Ryan. It's just that now I find myself in a very difficult position because of the other three board members. They knew by voting me in that they were sending me into the lion's den."

She's smarter than I've given her credit. She cut right to the heart of the matter, he thought.

"I guess it's understandable. Here you are ready to work hard to expand Andrew's legacy and find out...well you know," said Ryan.

"No, I don't know and neither do you. I'm going to fight this with everything I can give. Andrew is the most honest and caring person I have ever known."

You mean was, Ryan thought.

"Are you sure fighting the government, especially the IRS, is a good idea?" Ryan asked hopefully leading her to come to her senses.

"I'm not letting anyone, and I mean anyone, soil Andrew's legacy," she said clinching her jaw when she finished.

"But—?"

"Look Ryan, I'll handle the IRS. You and I are the only ones that were out of the loop during the board meeting. I need your help getting rid of Harris, Robinson and Turner off the board. The reasons are obvious."

Hmm, I really would only answer to Audrey with new inexperienced board members. And her inexperience would put me in a position of power that could be greater than if I had been elected CEO with the IRS problem. All the benefits without the burden, Ryan quickly calculated.

"Woe, wait a minute Audrey. You're talking about firing three board members who are my friends and have served this company well. Besides, with the IRS problem hanging over our heads, I don't think we'd find anyone of substance to replace them," he said.

"Who said anything about replacing them?" she said pointedly.

"You have to replace them," Ryan replied.

"Says who?"

"The commerce department of the state of Oregon, that's who."

"Show me where it states we must have five board members. If my memory serves me right you became a board member because of your value to incoming revenue via sales. Brian Harris was tapped because of his relationship with Andrew as an attorney. Bob Robinson was the banker at the time of legal organization of CIT. And Mike Turner stood up at our wedding. There is no reason we can't shake up the existing board. Besides, do you really think any of them want to be a part of this IRS thing?"

Audrey saw Ryan sitting with his left arm across his stomach. His right elbow resting on his left arm. His right hand lightly grasping his chin with his thumb and index finger, signaling his deep thought process.

"And besides, do we really need five? If we must have board members why not just have three? We will have to vote on many different business items, but this way you and I can control the outcome of each. I'm going to add a poison pill to the framework just in case either one of us loses our mind and decides to try and pull a power play."

Wow, there really is more to her than meets the eye, Ryan thought.

"Those are really good ideas. I think you're right about Brian, Bob and Mike. I think they'd like to be as far away from this IRS thing as possible. You've got a real handle on this I don't think you need me up here at all."

"No, I want you here for short period of time. You work on some names for the reorganization of the board of directors while I work on the Internal Revenue Service. At the same time you can work on cultivating more relationships to gain government contracts. How does that sound?"

"Sounds like a plan Audrey." Lifting his coffee mug he said, "Here's to the future of the new CIT."

Chapter 14

—§—

Present Day

Tony placed his secure call to Audrey once his car exited the traffic at Portland's International Airport. He needs to let her know he's back safely and provide a verbal report.

I have no intention of putting anything in writing when it comes to my new shadow employer. More importantly, I want to know why the hell I was put in a situation where I could've been killed, he thought as he waited for the connection.

After normal phone protocol had taken place Audrey asked, "Are you OK?"

"OK!? I just escaped a bomb blast that could have killed me! No I'm not OK!"

"We are so sorry Tony. All the information we acquired did not show any sign of danger or you would not have been activated." She paused then asked, "You believe me don't you?"

Tony cut right to the heart of it. "No, I don't believe you."

Audrey, taken by surprise, emphatically said, "How can you think I would put you in harm's way?"

"Two plus two makes four, Audrey. It happened."

"Yes, it happened. That doesn't mean I would purposely allow you to be hurt or worse. My God, you have Jacquelyn, Samantha and Nick!"

Tony heard complete sincerity in her voice and took a deep breath and finally said, "OK, then you have to be more diligent when agent Numbnuts provides you information on the next POI. I no longer trust him."

"I will. Now, I'm going to ask you again. Are you OK?"

"I'm fine. A little shaken up, but I'm fine. Not so sure I'm cut out for this stuff. I'm not sure exactly what just took place. I had plenty of time to think on the plane and something's bothering me."

"What's that," she asked.

"I noticed a lot of cameras that certainly have me recorded sitting across from the scene. How do I handle the questions that are sure to come my way once the police review the scene?"

Audrey said, "Right after you called me from San Diego I made a call to make sure the appropriate authorities take control of all surveillance properties. Just so you know the police will be legally handcuffed by the government. They will never see the video recordings."

"You did that with one phone call?"

"Yes," she said as if this were an everyday thing.

"Let me guess...agent Numbnuts, right?" He continued, "So, you're saying I won't be exposed because of the cameras?"

"That's correct."

"What about the ones that are privately owned. Like where I bought my shirt and pants?"

"Tony, it includes them all. Besides, where you made your purchases are not in line of sight where the explosion took place. Do you really want to know how that gets done?" she asked knowing the answer.

"No," he said succinctly. *Good to have Big Brother on my side for a change*, he thought.

"I have a question for you Tony. Who taught you not only to think about cameras, but to actually look for them? They're not always easy to spot."

"It's just the way I'm wired I guess," he answered not really knowing the answer.

"Nobody taught you?"

"No."

"You are one smart cookie, you know that?" she said as a statement more than a question. "I'll be working at CIT late tonight. Can you come by and fill me in with the details?" she asked.

"No, I'm sorry Audrey. I'm going home to my family. How about we get together in the morning?"

"That won't do. Something like this requires immediate attention," she said.

"Then let's talk right now while I'm driving."

"That will be fine," said Audrey.

Tony gave her as much information as he could remember then he got to the meat of the reason why he went in the first place.

"I have an assumption of what it could mean, but I'm sure that probably doesn't really mean anything to SSD," said Tony.

"You are selling yourself way too short Tony. Your interpretations of the feelings you get are taken very seriously. They break the code for us. As a matter of fact without them you would likely be the only person to know the true character of this young man," explained Audrey. "So, tell me," she added.

"Broken Savior," said Tony.

Audrey repeated it as if just to hear the words from her own mouth then asked, "What does it mean?"

"I can tell you he's not what SSD is looking for. He was likely the only survivor who was seated outside at the restaurant if that tells you anything."

"And you don't think that's a coincidence?"

"Not at all. He obviously had to leave before the explosion. I also think he had help."

Audrey paused then asked, "Why do you think that?"

"I tried chasing him down. There's no way that scrawny kid could have gotten away from me without someone's help. I'm guessing you already likely know from his file he's not an athlete. So the question is, how'd he disappear into thin air?"

That is amazing, thought Audrey. "Do you have any proof," she then asked.

"Only a guess."

"And that is…?"

"There was an older lady wearing a straw hat with large sunglasses that somehow seemed out of place. I didn't pay much attention to her, but I just wonder about her."

Incredible! thought Audrey. "Why her?" she asked calmly.

"I really don't know. Most of my attention was on the restaurant across the street at the time. Maybe it was just the pin on her hat."

"What do you mean?"

"Nothing really. I recognized the golf pin and maybe that's why I noticed her."

Of all the people milling around you still somehow find the needle in the haystack, she thought.

Just minutes before Tony phoned, Audrey had just ended a call with agent Forman. He had contacted Audrey and told him they found a straw hat, sunglasses, a professional grade latex mask along with a sophisticated directional microphone two blocks away from the explosion. The memory chip had been removed. Audrey thought about Forman's exact words. 'This kid had an accomplice. He's not what we're looking for. Our asset's presence must be completely erased and move on'.

Audrey said to Tony, "Well it's not unusual to get a little paranoid when on active duty. Especially when it's your first time."

"I'm not going to lie. I was nervous and now we both know it was for a good reason."

You have no idea, Tony, she thought. "I had the financial channel on in my office. It was breaking news about twenty minutes after the explosion. I'm basing the timeline on when you had called me from there. NBC showed the hole in the ground from the twentieth floor of their building. Frankly I'm amazed anyone walked away."

Twenty minutes, I definitely was gone by then, thought Tony. "As I said, It's too amazing. This kid blew the place up and killed innocent people. He needs to pay for what he did," said Tony.

"If you're right, I agree. Another agency will see to that. But, exactly why do you think he is the one responsible? There isn't enough evidence yet to support your conclusion," she said.

"I don't think it was a coincidence he sat in that exact spot."

"So you're saying that makes him the one who planted the explosive?"

Something bothered Tony. It may just be Audrey's tone or more likely that she was now questioning him about his observations.

I better tread lightly, he thought.

"Thinking it, but not saying it," Tony replied.

"Fill in the blanks for me Tony. How do you know he survived? There hasn't been a confirmed body count or any victim's names released yet," asked Audrey.

"Our POI was wearing bright red tennis shoes."

"So?"

"Just as I was about to leave the explosion area I happened to catch a view of one of those shoes rounding the west side of the NBC building. I took off after him, but like I said, it was as if he vanished into thin air."

"Are you sure it was him? It could have been someone else wearing the same shoes," said Audrey.

"Not those shoes. We're talking Las Vegas neon lights red shoes. I've never in my life seen shoes like that until I saw them on him at the restaurant. I know I was closing in on him, but when I rounded the corner he was gone. Nobody moves that quickly."

"What are you saying, Tony?"

He paused for a second then said, "Nothing. I just find it strange everyone else dining outside the Thai restaurant is hurt or worse and this guy just happens to be leaving the scene with clean shoes? It only adds up to—." He stopped short of completing his thought.

"It only adds up to what? Come on Tony I've known you long enough to know you have a definite take on this," said Audrey prodding.

"Before I answer you did anyone call in a possible explosion at that particular restaurant today?" he asked.

I know where he's going with this. If I answer yes then Tony would likely end his association not only with SSD, but CIT as well. He'd want to know why he wasn't warned of the danger he was placing himself in, she surmised. *But, I can't lie to him. I'll take my chances.*

"Somebody did call it in. Until now there has always been a successful conclusion to each one."

"Meaning what, exactly?" Tony asked sharply.

"No explosions of course. We have yet to confirm if it was our guy on this one," she said closing her eyes waiting for a full eruption from Tony.

Tony remained silent for a few moments then said, "I don't like the sound of that Audrey. But, God only knows why, I trust you. I'm going to choose to believe you knew I wasn't' in danger based on a clean track record of no previous explosions," he said.

Audrey breathed again and said, "Thank you Tony. Please remember there is risk just crossing the street. I would never purposely put you in harms-way. I'm so glad you are OK. As always this is confidential information. No one can know about this. I'll provide your report and if Dennis needs to follow up with you he will be in contact," she said in a relieved tone.

After they ended their conversation Audrey swiveled her chair to look out the thirty-third story window. She envisioned everything Tony told her.

Don was right. Tony is truly exceptional and is a natural. He is the key to the success of SSD...and more, she thought.

Tony got home and was met by Jacquelyn with a smooch on the lips. Nick and Sam came running downstairs a little too fast and Nick took a spill. Sam stopped with a look of concern on her face.

Just like the tough little boy that is Nick, he quickly got up said, "Hi Dad," then continued on through as fast as he could.

Samantha, standing still, was now relieved that she wasn't in trouble for her little brother's fall and said, "You're not getting away from me!"

Jacquelyn and Tony watched the two of them bolt through the house. Tony asked, "So, a pretty normal day, huh?"

"Just another—" she stopped and sniffed Tony. "What's that smell?"

I forgot how good her sense of smell is, thought Tony.

"You didn't hear the news? There was an explosion in downtown San Diego today."

"Oh my God I never even thought you would be near something like that! I saw it on TV."

"It actually happened across the street from where I was. I heard it then pebbles of glass rained down from the windows of the building I was in."

"Are you OK? You're not cut are you?" asked Jacquelyn looking him over.

"I'm fine, but I had to buy these clothes or I don't think anyone would sit next to me on the plane," he slightly kidded in a calm tone. He added, "It's really quite amazing how they can make glass break so it won't hurt anyone."

Relieved, Jacquelyn gave him a wry look and said, "Go take a shower. You smell."

Tony gave her a salute as if to say yes ma'am.

And throw those clothes down the clothes shoot right away," she shouted. In a much quieter voice she said, "Then I'll burn them...not just because they smell, but because their ugly. What were you thinking?"

Tony came back downstairs wearing his jeans and his favorite hooded sweatshirt. The aroma of something cooking pulled him toward the kitchen. He found Jacquelyn with her index finger on a cookbook page.

"What's this?" he asked.

"It's called cooking from scratch," she said light-heartedly.

"I've heard rumors of such a thing before," he kidded back.

"What's on the menu?"

"Salad, chicken stir-fry and cornbread."

"Want some help?" he asked.

"How about since I'm doing the cooking you take clean up duty?"

"That seems fair," he said.

The James family had a nice dinner at the dining table. Each went through the highlights of their day. Both Tony and Jacquelyn love spending time as a family as often as they can. It's their belief that a meal with conversation brings everyone that much closer to each other.

After dinner the kids asked to be excused then went to watch a TV show together while the table was cleared. Jacquelyn began to pick up a couple of glasses from the table.

"Hey, what are you doing?" asked Tony.

"Taking these into the kitchen," she said.

"No, no, no...you go sit down and relax. The deal was you cooked and I clean up, remember?"

"Oh, I don't mind," she replied.

"OK then I'll go sit with the kids and watch TV with them," he said setting the plates back down on the table.

"Hold it right there. You agreed to clean-up duty. Now bring those plates in here. I'll go sit with the kids," she said with a grin.

"OK, that's more like it and thank you for making dinner. It was delicious," Tony said sincerely. "Nick, Sam, don't forget to thank Mom for making dinner."

"Thanks for making dinner Mom," said Sam.

"Yeah, thanks Mom," added Nick craning his neck without taking his eyes off the TV.

Tony saw exactly what he was looking for...a smile coming to Jacquelyn's face. Jacquelyn sat for only a few minutes as Tony cleared the table. She got up and headed for the kitchen to help Tony with the dishes.

"What are you doing in here?" he asked.

She gave him a kiss and said, "Just helping you out. Besides, that show gives me a headache if I watch it longer than five minutes."

While both were working in the kitchen Jacquelyn said, "I set the DVR to record the evening news. I would think the San Diego explosion should be a top story."

"Sounds good, but let's make sure the kids aren't around. The news is always so depressing," said Tony.

The cable company van had parked a few houses down the street just prior to Tony arriving home. The woman inside wore the appropriate uniform with the name 'Danielle' embroidered on her shirt. Her ID tag, with color photo, hung around her neck. If anyone questioned her, the name and face would check out. She made sure of it.

'Danielle' sat in back with a pair of headphones in her right hand held up to her right ear and a disposable cell phone held in her left and in the middle of a conversation.

"Yes. They did talk about his trip to San Diego and the explosion that took place," she said.

"Anything specific as to why he was so close to the blast?" asked the scrambled voice on the other end of the cell connection.

"No. It's really interesting how he can get so close to being specific yet really say nothing at all. He's really frustrating or he has a gift. His wife recorded the evening news and they're going to watch it later specifically to hear what's said about the San Diego explosion. Maybe I'll get a little more detail from him then," she said.

"If that doesn't pan out we may need to put ears in his car as well. Give me a call back if you learn anything important," said the voice.

'Danielle' turned off the phone, removed the back cover and took the battery from its compartment. She placed it in a backpack knowing she'd dispose of each piece in separate locations later. Sitting back she positioned the set of head phones on top of her head to patiently listen in on her target's conversation. The sudden blaring in her ears forced her to turn the volume down.

The home phone rang. The ringer had been left on the highest volume level for some reason. It was likely the kids had been a little too loud to hear it on low.

Looking at caller ID Jacquelyn answered ending the ear piercing ring blast saying, "Hi Mom."

Tony knew this was his queue to finish rinsing and placing the dishes into the dishwasher. Jacquelyn and Betty could talk for quite a long time. He finished up then sat with the kids for as long as he could stand the show. Tony lasted about four minutes.

"Do you guys want to play a board game?" he asked falling on deaf ears. "How about playing Apples to Apples?"

Tony picked up the remote and muted the program and began to repeat the question. He was met with an onslaught of surprise and groans for the disruption of Sam and Nick's program.

"OK, OK. Here, enjoy your show," he said quickly un-muting the sound.

I'm bored, he thought as he looked at the kids lost in their show and Jacquelyn on the phone.

He went to his office down the hall and sat in his comfy chair with his personal laptop. *I might as well investigate what security systems would best fit our needs*, he thought.

After some extensive research on the internet he paused and realized he has the best security in the world at his disposal...The US Government. After seeing the CPT program on Audrey's laptop he figured she would be the perfect place to seek advice. He picked up his Smartphone and placed a call to her.

"Hi Tony," she answered politely.

"Hi Audrey, is this a bad time?" he asked.

"Based on the ringtone this must be CIT business. You didn't make a mistake using the wrong part of your phone did you?"

"No. Actually, this is a personal call," he said.

"Oh, to what do I owe the pleasure?"

"I'm doing some investigating about home security systems and realized you're probably the perfect person to call and get a recommendation," he said.

"Are you thinking of beefing up security because of today, Tony?"

"In part, but mostly since we had that conman stop by."

"What conman?" Audrey asked sitting up a little straighter.

Tony, almost brushing it off, quickly explained what had happened.

"Why didn't you tell me about this right away?" asked Audrey in a tone fit for a mother.

"Well, it's really none of your business, but I told you now. Do you have a recommendation?" he asked with just a hint of an edge to stop her from making this into a prolonged part of the conversation.

"Tony, something like this must be reported immediately given your new responsibilities, even if it's just to me. I'll take care of this and we'll put it on your CIT expense account. You really need to be a little more open about these things. However, I understand you are new to this new world of adventures," she said softening her tone towards the end.

I suppose an explosion that could've killed me could be categorized as an adventure, he thought.

"Are you saying this won't cost me a dime?" he asked in a surprised tone.

"That's correct. You and your family need to feel safe in your own home," she replied.

As soon as 'Danielle' heard Tony say hello to Audrey she sat up straight to listen intently to his side of the conversation. She adjusted two knobs on a digital receiver to zero in on the clearest audio. The background noise from the television and Jacquelyn's conversation seems to be distorting some of his words. She knows everything said is being recorded via a wireless recorder, but she took notes in bullet form anyway.

She scribbled her notes on the yellow note pad only to preserve them just in case technology failed. 'Danielle' preferred not to have anything in her hand-writing, but knew she'd destroy the evidence once verifying there hasn't been a glitch in the recording.

Used to hearing both sides of a conversation, it struck her how much Tony James listens based on the long pauses between each time he speaks.

This is not going the way I want. He either needs to talk more or I need to hear the other side of the conversation. Maybe I'll learn more when he and Jacquelyn watch the news. This could be trouble if he's allowing CIT to install a security system, she thought.

She took out another disposable phone and placed her call.

"Sorry to call you so soon, but we're going to need to move much more quickly than expected," said 'Danielle'.

"Why?"

"Because as soon as a new security system is put in place at his home they will find our listening device," she said calmly.

The reasoning was sound so the voice said, "We'll be OK. Piggy-back off whatever system they install. Make sure you update me if anything important is said when they watch the news tonight."

"As promised," she answered.

_____

"Jacquelyn and I really appreciate that Audrey. When and who can I expect to call me?" Tony asked Audrey.

"Are you in your office tomorrow?"

"No. But, I will be on Thursday," he said.

"I'll have it installed Thursday then," she promptly answered.

"I appreciate it Audrey, but who will be doing the installation and what are they installing?"

"I don't think we need to get into the details right now so I'll get you that information when we are together. OK?" Audrey said in a leading tone.

"I understand. Will you at least send me some basic information so I can go over it with Jacquelyn?" he asked.

"Sure, but I can't send it like you saw on my computer today. I'll have to doctor it up a little and send it via CIT email. That will help Jacquelyn won't it?"

"Now, now...you're fishing again," said Tony wagging a verbal finger at Audrey.

Audrey let it slide. "Do you understand?" she asked.

"Yup...got it," he said.

"Can I do anything else for you Tony?"

"That should do it for now. Thanks," he said.

They said their goodbyes. After ending the call Tony sat silently looking at his Smartphone.

This phone is enough of an intrusion. Well, at least part of it. I don't know if I want the government intruding any further. After all, I told them my personal life is off limits. Maybe I'm over-reacting. But, I want Jacquelyn and the kids safe when I'm not here, he thought.

With the kids tucked in their beds Jacquelyn and Tony sat down to watch the evening news that she had recorded. They relaxed on the couch with Tony sitting on the right and Jacquelyn resting up against him. Tony put his left arm around Jacquelyn after picking up the remote with his right.

She looked up at him and said, "I've been meaning to ask you about how it's going with your Tourettes."

Those big brown eyes melt him every time. "MY Tourettes?" he asked.

"You know what I mean."

"Just so you know I have never claimed it as MY Tourettes. MY tormentor, yes but, never MY Tourettes. But, with the medication, diet and exercise it's improved so much I can't even come close to explaining it," he said.

"That's wonderful! I'm so happy for you Tony," she said as she lifted herself up to give him a smooch.

"You know, I found myself in a situation today where I would normally need to release a stockpile of tics and was surprised to find it wasn't needed. That is, at least not today."

"Wow! That's new. What do you attribute the big change to?"

"I think the biggest thing is the new medication from Dr. Dillon, but without watching my diet and keeping up with focused exercise I don't know if it would be working as well as it is."

"Well, from my perspective you seem very focused lately and I don't think anyone would guess you even have Tourettes," Jacquelyn said emphatically.

"Was it that noticeable before?" asked Tony bracing for her answer.

"You hid it so well before, I think only those closest to you who even knows what Tourettes is, might have figured it out. That's not too many people because you've done an incredible job. Do you ever regret going through all the trouble to hide it from everyone?"

"Yes, every time I see someone who I think has the disorder. I feel for them in a big way."

"Have you ever considered joining a local group to help those who are afflicted by Tourettes?" she asked.

"I'm just getting used to my new self right now. But, I think that's a great idea later on down the road. I could maybe help someone even if I didn't choose the best path."

"What do you mean…best path?" asked Jacquelyn.

"Just that I think if someone's comfortable in their own skin, with the tics, then my path would be totally wrong for them," he said.

"Tony, it would take a very rare person to be OK with severe or moderate tics in front of others. What you've discovered works for you. I think you could reach out and be surprised to find people grateful for the information you possess. It's up to them what path they take."

"Maybe you're right. I'll give it some thought," he said then kissed her.

"Now let's get to the news," said Jacquelyn in a tone that punctuated the end of that topic of discussion.

Tony worked the remote with his right hand and located the program then pressed play. As expected the San Diego blast was the top news event of the day. Both Jacquelyn and Tony watched and listened carefully. However, Tony didn't focus on the exact center of the screen. Like watching an upcoming opponent in racquetball he searched the edges for anything out of the ordinary.

"Why would anybody purposely do something like this to those poor people? And why on earth do they take credit for such violence?" questioned Jacquelyn.

As Tony pressed the rewind button to watch it again he said, "There are some sick and some evil people in this world. Some are just plain sick and some are just evil. Then again there's both."

"That's a scary thought," she said.

They both watched it one more time. Tony found it odd that the blast hole was just a few feet above where the young man with the bright red tennis shoes had been sitting. He rewound it and played it again.

"Tony, how many times are you going to watch this?" asked Jacquelyn in a manner to which she really meant to say enough already!

Tony thought, *I'm certainly no expert, but that doesn't look like the building blew from the inside out. It looks like it got hit by a projectile.* He drifted back to the scene and then remembered the truck. *Hmm...I wonder?*

Jacquelyn got up and said, "That's all I need to see. This world is getting crazier by the day."

She went to the kitchen to turn the ringer on the phone down to its normal setting. Tony muted then rewound the recording and paused at a specific point. He pressed slow motion as he focused his eyes on one particular female ATF agent on the scene.

I'm either joining the crazy people or there's something very familiar about that particular agent from the Federal Bureau of Alcohol, Tobacco, and Firearms. She isn't carrying anything and doesn't look like she belongs. No one's talking with her. But, she's got the ATF jacket. Can't buy those at Wal-Mart. Come on. Lift your head up so I can see you. OK now my imagination's getting the best of me, he thought.

Jacquelyn came back into the living room and said, "I understand why you have such an interest in that, but let's watch something to lighten the mood before we go to bed. I won't sleep otherwise."

Tony saved the newscast on the DVR to take a closer look when Jacquelyn wasn't around. They found a sitcom to ease Jacquelyn's mood. Each found fast relief and felt the events of the day melt away the further they got into the comedy.

'Danielle' gained nothing from Tony watching the news report. She had zilch to go on so she decided not to call back. She quickly stored her gear. As she started the van she put the shift into drive then immediately placed it back into park.

"How stupid…I almost forgot the orange pylons I placed in front and behind the van."

She got out of the driver's side door and walked to the front of the van to retrieve that one first. She carried it to the back then slid it over the other one as a voice blared out in the distance. She opened the back of the van and deposited the pylons and quickly closed the door. Walking toward the driver's side door she became startled by the presence of a man about six inches taller than her.

"Hi," said the thin middle-aged man wearing faded jeans and a graying pony tail.

Danielle instinctively reached her right hand behind her to grab her snub-nosed twenty-two pistol hidden at the waistline just under her shirt.

With relief she thought, *Oh God, another one of those tree hugging hippies that never grew up.*

"Working on the Denton's phone line?" he asked in an odd tone.

She pretended to scratch her back and removed her hand from the gun. Trying to give him the brush-off she said, "I'm afraid I can't discuss that with you sir."

"OK, but I got a question for you. How can I get you guys to get those damn wires away from my trees in the backyard? I've been calling for over six months now and this is the first I've seen your truck on my street. So, I figured if you're too damn busy I might as well come right out and talk to you about my problem face to face."

You have a problem alright. Back off before I put my knuckles to your Adams Apple, she thought.

Thinking quickly she replied, "Sir, I work strictly on DSL internet service. I can't do anything about the tree line issue."

"You work for the same company, don't you?"

"Our lines run underground."

Knowing she didn't need this type of interaction she quickly added, "Let me get into my vehicle and put a natural resource impediment notation into the NRDC via my computer." *That sounded official enough*, she thought as she just made it up.

"That a girl. I knew I'd eventually find the right person to get the job done."

Danielle pretended to enter everything into her computer. She asked simple questions such as his address and correct spelling of his name.

"Your call tag confirmation number is G210-001," she said confidently.

"Thanks. Danielle is it?" he said focusing on her employee ID tag.

Noting he wasn't wearing a wedding ring and knowing the type she abruptly said, "Well I have to get home to my husband. You have a good evening."

As she drove up the street she said, "Good luck with those trees. Don't wait too long for the job to get done."

_____

Jacquelyn said, "That hit the spot, nothing like a good comedy to put my mind at ease."

"I need to shut my work computer down. I'll be up in a minute," said Tony.

"Promise you won't get caught up in work. You'll be up late and still wake up at the same time then be tired all day."

"I promise. I'll be right up," he said.

Chapter 15

—§—

1995

After Audrey met with Ryan O'Connor about the roles each would take on, she decided to work from home the rest of the day. Before she left, Audrey called human resources to aid Ryan in moving him to his new interim thirty-third floor office.

"Leave his current office furniture right where it is. This is just temporary. Find a desk that will fulfill his needs that we already have available. As a matter of fact, take one of the boardroom chairs so he's comfortable. Just not my chair. If you can't find a desk that fits the chair please notify me," said Audrey.

"We have plenty of desks. Nothing fancy, but plenty of them," said Kelly in a pleasant tone on the other end of the phone.

"That's good. Please call him and ask if he requires anything special. Remember, this is only a temporary situation. After I make one more phone call I'll be out the rest of the day."

"I'll call him right away and coordinate everything," said Kelly.

O'Connor heard his phone ringing as he unlocked the door to his office. "Ryan O'Connor," he said answering.

"Mr. O'Connor this is Kelly in human resources. I just got off the phone with Mrs. Shelton regarding the coordination of moving you to the thirty-third floor."

"She called you already?"

"Yes. We coordinate all moves within CIT," Kelly said proudly.

"Is Bonnie there?" asked Ryan.

"Yes, would you like to speak with her?"

"Yes," he said a little too quickly.

After a brief stint on hold Bonnie, Kelly's boss, answered saying, "Hello Ryan. I hear you're moving up in the world…literally"

"How do you know that?"

"Mrs. Shelton said you would be calling. Trust me; Kelly is the best person to coordinate your move. She'll have you settled in by morning."

"Audrey called you?"

"I just got off the phone with her minutes ago. I like her. She is very adamant to leave your current office alone and set you up temporarily in her office. You won't miss a beat, trust me."

"Did she call you or—?"

"Of course she called me and I can tell you I'm very happy to have Kelly take the ball and run with this."

"OK, thanks Bonnie." *So much for trying to avoid the inevitable*, he thought.

On her way home Audrey stopped at the small law firm of Swan and White. Their specialty is corporate law.

The young receptionist with a tiny-sized Cindy Crawford style mole on her cheek curtly greeted Audrey in a distant tone.

"Welcome to Swan and White. I'm Jean. You're Mrs. Shelton I presume?"

"Yes, Simon must have told you I would be stopping by."

"He did. Mr. Swan is on a call at the moment. If you want coffee I'll get you some," she said as if it would put her out.

"No, that's quite alright."

"Please, have a seat. I'm sure he'll be with you in just a few minutes," said the receptionist.

"Thank you," said Audrey turning and rolling her eyes.

Audrey found a chair with a view of the street. As she gazed out the window the past came flooding back to her.

Simon Swan grew up in the suburbs of Portland going to the same high school as Audrey only one year ahead. In those days Audrey had a little crush on him. Simon attended George Mason University and ultimately graduated in the top ten percent of his class.

He stayed in the Washington D.C. area for a couple of years, but never really liked the intense pressure of high stakes political law. Simon met Dawn White in law school as they both interned at the Justice Department at the same time. She grew up in Eugene, Oregon. So, he and his law school friend, Dawn White, moved back home to Oregon, married and opened what is now their very own law firm.

Since it is such a small place Audrey heard the door down the hall open and then the slow step and slide of Simon Swan coming toward her down the hall. The echo made her stomach do a flip for multiple reasons. Audrey felt the slow piercing of guilt thinking back to how Simon suffered his injury.

Years earlier, while Simon was still in undergraduate school, Audrey was visiting Washington, D.C. and looked Simon up. They got together for dinner and had far too many drinks at the famous Constitution Eatery just next to the National Convention Center and Hotel. They moved their reunion to the convention bar and talked until closing. Neither was in any shape to drive so they decided to get one room since neither had much money at the time. They agreed it was strictly a one night platonic stay for safety and monetary reasons. Simon hadn't met Dawn yet and Audrey and Andrew weren't one-hundred percent committed to each other.

Audrey awoke first the next morning finding Simon in bed right next to her. She slowly looked about the room and saw clothes strewn all over the room. Her stirring then woke Simon. He greeted her with a groan without opening his eyes at first. A few minutes later they cautiously looked at each other. Their clothes were strewn about the room. Both came to the realization of what must have happened then smiled at each other. They agreed that this was just a one-time thing and nobody else needs to know.

By 11am Audrey and Simon were walking side-by-side through the parking lot when a man wearing all black clothing, including a black knit mask, appeared out of nowhere. Audrey was talking to Simon then stopped abruptly with her eyes open wide. Her expression pulled Simon's attention to what she saw. He watched the man raise his arm upward from his side as if in slow motion. The man had a gun. Simon's automatic reaction wasn't anything Audrey expected. He moved quickly and covered her like a bear protecting a cub. The shot rang out and Simon drove Audrey to the ground. Then came another shot. This time, however, Audrey recognized it as a much larger caliber round. She heard a sound as if a large sack of potatoes hit the ground. Though she couldn't see because of Simon covering her, she knew the second shot didn't come from the same gun or direction.

Simon was unconscious and Audrey didn't know just yet why he wasn't responding, but she screamed hoping it wasn't what she figured it to be. She struggled to free herself from his weight thinking one, or both, gunmen likely had her in their sights. Audrey then saw Simon's back and she froze. The brackish purple liquid was spreading through the back of his rumpled dinner jacket. Off in the distance she heard sirens. Audrey figured someone heard the shots and called 911 immediately. She looked for the second shooter as she lay at an awkward angle pinned under Simon's weight. Her decision not to run and hide came only when she realized it shouldn't have taken so long for a second shot to come her way. Audrey finally freed herself and applied pressure with her hands on the exact center where the pooling blood appeared to be oozing from Simon's back. The police and EMTs arrived just seconds later and took over.

Simon was rushed to the hospital and emergency surgery performed. During the operation a nerve had been accidently nicked by the surgeon. Because Simon was unconscious and sped into surgery he did not fill out or sign any release forms. He was informed about the surgical mishap. The hospital administrator tried to get Simon's signature on a release waiver, but he wanted to see how his rehab would go first. After months of pain and frustration, Dawn convinced him to sue for damages.

Dawn White had successfully represented him as his legal-council. He used some of the settlement funds from the law suit as seed money to start their new firm. When they married Dawn legally hyphenated her last name to White-Swan. She thought it to be cute. Most people found it to be amusing...Dawn White-Swan. Both thought the law firm name of Swan and Swan didn't sound quite right so they settled on Swan & White.

As if in an echo chamber the sound finally registered with Audrey.

"I'm so glad to see you Audrey. Dawn and I are so sorry about Andrew," said Simon as he gave her a hug.

Audrey finally turned her head and thought; *I still love that mop of red hair.* "Thank you Simon, is Dawn in?"

"No, she's gone for the day courting a new corporate client. I'm sure she would love to see you. She'll be so disappointed you missed each other. I'll tell her you stopped by. Come on into my office so we can talk."

After pleasantries and catching up on each other's lives, Audrey then came right to the point bluntly asking, "Will you consider becoming at-large council on retainer for CIT?"

"But, you have your own attorneys and damn good ones at that. Why would you need us?" he asked.

"Because there are times when people only agree with the boss," she said directly.

"Is there something specific going on that's bothering you," he asked more as a friend.

"Maybe, maybe not...it depends if Swan and White are my new law firm," she said with a slight grin.

"I'm so sorry Audrey. I should never have asked you a question like that. You're my friend and—."

Audrey jumped in leaning toward him and said, "Here, read this. I've taken the liberty of drawing up the papers so we can talk in confidence right now."

Simon read the short document and said, "There are a few things I would revise, but this is sufficient enough for us to be able to talk in confidence today. Dawn and I can formalize a document that you can look over and sign later. So what can we do for you today," he asked in a more upbeat business-like tone as he signed.

"I have two issues that need your attention at this time. The first has to do with the Internal Revenue Service and the second is regarding the formation of a new board of directors," she said succinctly.

"That's right in our wheelhouse, but I have to tell you Dawn is the resident corporate tax expert."

"I know what needs to be done. It's just that I don't want CIT's attorneys to be the ones to talk to anyone from the IRS. I've put a muzzle on them. To me it's just not good business practice to have them engaging them in this particular situation. So, this is where you and Dawn come in. I want CIT's law department to stay in the background keeping as much distance from those IRS leaches."

"OK...and what is it you would like us to do for you in the matter of your board of directors?"

"That's an area where I have no clue how to go about eliminating them," she said pointedly.

"Eliminate your board of directors?" Simon asked almost stunned.

"Long story...I won't bore you. I need you to advise me on how to go about it and remain in good standing with the bi-laws of CIT and the State of Oregon. Not to mention our Federal Government."

"OK, either bring or email the current documents so I can dissect them. I've done this before. How many board members do you want?"

"One," she said flatly.

Simon raised his eyebrows and said, "You fancy yourself a dictatorship then?"

"I knew you would grasp my needs quickly." Audrey stood. "It's great to see you Simon and please tell Dawn I'm sorry I missed her. I have to get going. I will send you the documents you need later today. How fast can you be prepared?" she asked.

"That depends. How much is our retainer fee?" he asked with a smile as he stood leaning a little to one side.

"Your right, I guess I'm getting the cart before the horse. Send me the retainer agreement you feel is in the best interests of you, Dawn and CIT. I'll read it tonight and we can be in business first thing in the morning. Here's my card. I would prefer you didn't send it to my CIT email account."

"Something this sensitive…I completely understand. All this can be done discretely, but on the up and up," he said.

"Of course. My personal email address on the back of my card. You can send it there. However, all communication regarding the IRS issue should go to my CIT email address."

"Got it Audrey," Simon said like a friend she can count upon.

Stick with me and play your cards right. You and Dawn will have more business than you ever imagined, thought Audrey.

Audrey returned home and flipped off her shoes looking like a bad field goal kicker. She went directly to the answering machine in the kitchen to see if any messages were waiting. Untucking articles of clothing on the way she arrived and saw the digital read-out indicating four messages. She pressed play.

"Hi Audrey, this is Mark. I'm just checking in to see if you need anything. If you do, don't hesitate to give me a call."

I'm not sure if that was sincere or pathetic. That's an odd message to leave on a new widow's answering machine. Can't you wait to at least talk in-person? she thought.

"Hello Audrey, this is Steven Miller from Greenhill Funeral Home. My thoughts are with you and if you require anything I want you to know I'm here to be of service to you. Have a blessed day."

I give the guy credit. He knows how to follow up and make sure he gets good word-of-mouth advertising, she thought.

"Mrs. Shelton, this is Larry Sullivan with information about Andrew's life insurance policy. Please call me at your leisure at 207-555-2321."

Nice try. I know that's a Portland, MAINE area code. People have called here by mistake in the past. Dismal con attempt, she thought.

At first listen, the fourth message seemed to be a hang-up. However, Audrey waited then heard exactly what she hoped to hear. It was what she had been waiting for. Five soft taps to the microphone then a pause and an additional four more.

"Yes! No more short-hand Morse code," she said excited yet quietly.

Audrey erased each message then picked up her cell phone and pressed each digit by heart. After listening to the electronic outgoing voice message came the beep. She tapped her phone's microphone five times then ended the call.

She immediately contacted her cell phone provider and said, "Please cancel our existing account. My husband no longer is in need of his phone. I'll be in tomorrow to sign the paperwork for my new account. I enjoy the level of service you provide and do not want to switch, but I do want to obtain a new cell number for myself."

The customer service person at the store not more than five miles from Audrey's house said, "There's no need to make you come in and do that. We change phone numbers for people all the time. I recognize your voice Mrs. Shelton. May I put you on hold while I prepare your new number?"

Pleased with the expediency of the young man she said, "Yes, and thank you." *Easier than I thought it would be.*

He came back on the line and said, "Once we end our call just power your phone down, wait five minutes then power it back up. Your new number will show on the screen. Make sure you write it down because this will only show this one time. Of course when you get your bill it will be on there as well."

"Thank you so much. I greatly appreciate you being able to take care of this over the phone. If I have any trouble I will call you back from my landline."

After five minutes she indeed had a new cell number then thought, *I wonder if CIT were to provide cell phones and service if we could save money. I'll put that on my things to-do list.*

Sitting at her desk in the den she booted up her personal computer and logged on to a free email account that has never sent nor received a single message since its creation. It remained active just by logging in occasionally. This email account, however, is about to blossom with messages. Her handler taught her this method of communication. The only downside is that only one person could be logged into the account at a time. So, after writing each draft she had to log off and wait a few minutes, or more, to check back to continue to communicate. She was also taught using an internet café, or library, is by far the safest way to use this method.

Audrey wrote her first email, but did not press send. Instead she saved it as a draft. Her instructions were to never place an email address or subject in their respective places. Audrey followed those instructions perfectly. She logged off and waited exactly ten minutes. While waiting she started the coffee maker. With her hot brew now resting on the coaster next to her she logged back into the email account. Excitement rushed through her as she saw her draft email had been deleted and a new one ready to read.

Success! No more phone calls and tapping the microphone. This really is a much better way to communicate without anyone else knowing. As long as we don't send the messages and make sure we delete the drafts there is no trail to follow. We're the only ones that know about the email account and the password. Now this is the way to communicate! she thought excitedly.

After reading the new email draft that appeared Audrey immediately deleted the message. She then wrote about her move to hire a local law firm. She wrote in generalities and kept to the plan of not using names. Audrey made sure it was understood that the IRS will be taken care of by legitimate means for perception purposes only. The new law firm will think they are in the driver's seat, but that's just not the case. She saved the draft and logged off.

Ten minutes later, logging back on to the secret email account, Audrey once again saw her draft had been deleted with a new one in its place. She opened it and read exactly what she was hoping for as a response. She logged off after deleting it.

Audrey used an external hard drive often to back-up and store large amounts of CIT information for Andrew since he worked from home until wee hours many mornings. She attached the hardware and quickly located the CIT bi-laws documents and sent them as attachments to Simon Swan from the email address she wrote on the back of her card. This is her personal email address that many others have.

"I'm not waiting until the retainer document is in place," she said boldly after pressing send.

She disconnected the external hard drive then sat back taking a small sip of her coffee as she stared at the email inbox. Her thoughts turned to the future without any board members to interfere with her decisions at CIT.

My word will be law, she thought.

A new message came in from Simon as a reply to Audrey's email.

You're right on time Simon. I knew you wouldn't disappoint me, she thought.

Audrey read his email and then opened the attachment which she knew would work just fine even before she was out the door at his firm. She spent the next fifteen minutes scouring the retainer document making sure she wasn't committing to something unwanted.

"I trust Simon, but he is a lawyer," she said with a grin.

After her review process she sent an email back countering the retainer fee.

I don't want to look like I'm an easy client, she thought.

After a few more emails back and forth they arrived at a fee with which they both agreed upon. She wrote she would stop by his office to sign the paperwork in the morning.

"OK, now on to the IRS issue," she said to herself.

Chapter 16

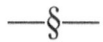

Present Day

Tony entered through one of the front doors of the seven story building at exactly 7:55am. It's his first and only scheduled client visit of the day. He had been informed, right after his vacation to Punta Cana with Jacquelyn, that a prospective customer had specifically tried to reach him. No other person would satisfy the caller. Molly, Tony's trusted customer service representative, and Tony didn't know he was visiting this very same prospective client.

He found the entryway to be lavish with sculptures, paintings and very expensive furniture. Tony walked directly to the receptionist. On his way the feeling emanating from her to him was *Caring*.

Tony chatted with her, mostly about nothing, for a few moments then handing his card to her he said, "Tony James with CIT. I'm here to see the operations manager."

He had a flash-back after she asked, "Do you have an appointment?"

Tony almost by reflex wanted to say that he was here to schedule one, but caught himself. "Yes I do," he said nicely.

"I'll let Ms. Freund know you are here Mr. James. Please have a seat," she said with the echo reverberating off the cavernous walls.

Tony felt an odd sensation about the ambiance of his surroundings. They seem so familiar to him. He then heard the receptionist's voice.

"Mr. James, she will see you now. The elevators are to your left. She's on the sixth floor. She will meet you as you exit the elevator."

Tony rode up to the sixth floor. Even before the doors opened he got a piercing feeling...*Fraud.*

"We're running out of time. This has to move along or I'm going to have to take other measures," said the scrambled voice on the other end of 'Danielle's' latest prepaid cell phone.

"There's plenty of time. You worry too much. Trust me we can get it done almost according to plan," she said.

"Almost?" said the voice in a parental tone.

"Sometimes the variables on the ground change and we have to adapt and change with them," she said.

"I've taught you almost everything I know. I trust you will get the job done."

"I know I'll get it done," she said confidently.

"Where are you right now?"

"I'm sitting in a car with binoculars waiting for him to exit a building. He's at what I presume is a client of CIT's.

"Is it a big client?"

"In terms of dollars, I have no idea, but I assume very big. It's a law firm and it appears they occupy all seven floors of the stylish building. From the outside they look to be very successful. But, you and I know looks can be deceiving," she said.

"You're right, however that's very good news. Let me know when he leaves and make sure you have a directional microphone on him. We need to record everything that comes out of his mouth. We might get lucky. Do you understand? We need to take advantage of every opportunity. Did you plant the listening device in his car?"

"Already operational," she said ending the call then dismantling yet another disposable phone.

Tony James left his client and walked to his car in silence.

After getting in and shutting the driver side door he said, "Wow, what a crook! There's no mistake that lady really should be called Ms. 'Fraud' not Freund. I've never had a client this size demand such an intricate proposal to be sent via email the same day. She's playing games. And that ugly mole on the side of her face! Doesn't she own a mirror? I guess that's what can happen when people age poorly. This is a big contract so I need to get back to my office to complete an all-encompassing proposal based on what I found to be unbelievably extensive needs here. I wonder what she's up to. It feels like we have too many clients like this. There seems to be so many shady people in the corporate world these days."

After starting the car Tony then turned on ESPN radio while he pulled out of the parking lot. He traveled home listening without saying another word. It wouldn't have mattered if anyone was listening in as the radio was drowning out all possibility of understanding anything he would have said.

He arrived home to work on the proposal for the new client. The law firm of Swan, White, Jenkins and Webster required a comprehensive update of their antiquated computer systems. Tony put aside his feelings about Ms. 'Fraud' to complete a full assessment of where they are currently and where they want to go with regard to information technology.

"Maybe it's just me. Maybe I'm the one who's hiding things and only seeing the bad side of corporate America these days. The receptionist passed my test. So did a few of the others I met there. I wish I had met the person who hired Ms. 'Fraud'! I'd like to warn them. Maybe I'll get the chance," he said.

After making a few coded notes Tony's stalker made a call saying, "I think we just hit the jackpot."

The voice on the other end asked, "Oh, in what way?"

"You know that law firm he was at earlier today? He must have gotten one of his feelings about the operations manager and called her a crook."

"So?"

"So, his big heart wishes he could meet the person responsible for hiring such a person," she said in a leading tone.

"Remember a perceived crook isn't always a crook or bad thing. Why, what are you thinking?" asked the voice.

"We both know an operations manager doesn't have any real power. They always need approval from higher up. We need him to get to the top dog. Even I was able to hack into their archaic computer system and found the name of the person who hired her many years ago. He's THE top dog. He started the law firm with his wife. If we can somehow get them face to face there's a good chance he won't be able to stop from spilling the beans on the operations manager. Once Mr. Big Shot looks into it and finds Mr. James was right…he's in. He'll have his complete confidence," she said proudly.

"How can you be so sure he would tell the head of the firm about a long time trusted employee?"

"I didn't say anything about her length of employment," she said bitingly.

"Obviously someone doesn't reach that level unless they've been around for a while," said the scrambled voice brushing her comment away.

"You'll have to trust me that I just know," said 'Danielle'.

"All right, once he's in I can try to pull some strings. Just a reminder, we're still a few assets short of the team we are trying to build. However this sounds like it could be a gold mine," said the voice.

"I'm staying on top of that," she said confidently.

Tony completed what he thought is the perfect integrated solution to replace the computer chaos at Swan, White, Jenkins and Webster. He re-read every word and made sure everything is in its proper place.

Sitting back and letting out a lengthy exhale he said, "OK, time to send this off to Ms. 'Fraud'."

Once that was complete he got up from being strapped to his desk for hours and had the urge to release a few quick tics. They were very mild in comparison to what he had experienced in the past. However, being shackled to his desk all afternoon made him realize he needed to get some exercise. Before he left Tony decided to call Ms. 'Fraud' and confirm she did in fact receive his proposal.

Better to over-communicate than leave it to their out-dated technology, he thought.

While in her office earlier in the day he took note of the extension number on the digital read-out on the phone on her desk. He called guessing correctly it would bypass everyone and she'd pick up as this is her direct number.

"Jean Freund speaking," she answered.

"Hi Jean this is Tony James with CIT. I'm calling to verify you received my computer system proposal."

She looked at the time first, then without pause checked her email inbox. "I have it. Thank you, Mr. James. Is there anything else?" she asked.

"No, I just wanted to confirm you had it on time," said Tony.

"That's very nice of you. I'll read it and get back to you," she said then ended the call abruptly.

"Goodbye to you too," said Tony looking at his phone in disbelief. *She's got a personality like a fish*, he thought.

He decided to workout at home this evening instead of going to the club. Looking at his prioritized task list he realized he hadn't put much time into investigating a home security system.

This can't be that tough, he thought.

He proceeded to use the internet to find exactly what is available for a tech-savvy person who wants a do-it-yourself system. Tony found so many similar systems that really only differed in the varying degrees of oversight and response authority if he decided to chose to use one.

"Wow, I can run just about any one of these components from a Smartphone! There's even an app that lets me know if a non-authorized device is in the home or business. Not sure I need it, but it's cool so I want it. Who needs a big security company when I can buy, install and monitor everything myself? I better call Audrey and let her know I'm going a different way. I don't need the government having access to my home," he said looking at his computer screen.

"Hello Tony."

"Hi Audrey."

"I'm very sorry, but I'm in a bit of a hurry, she said apologetically.

Knowing she wouldn't have answered if she didn't have a minute Tony said, "You can cancel the security installation. I'm going another way."

"Oh, and what way is that?" she asked in a surprised tone.

"None at all or I'm doing it on my own. Likely none at all." he said.

"Why would you do that when you can have the best security system in the world for free?"

"Remember when I told you and Williams that when I'm at home my private life will remain private? Well, I got to thinking about your gracious offer and it crosses the line for me. Thank you so much for your generosity, but I'll take care of this myself," he said hoping it wouldn't cause a rift between them.

"Are you saying you don't trust me?"

"No, I'm saying I don't completely trust the government," he said in an almost sarcastic tone.

"Well, I don't have time to argue the merits of a government security blanket with you at the moment so let's put this conversation on hold for another time, OK?" she said hurriedly.

"No need. I've made up my mind. I'll take care of it so please don't waste any of your valuable time or government resources on this," said Tony.

"OK, it's your life and I respect that. I have to get going so we'll have to talk later," she said matter-of-factly.

"Thanks Audrey. You're a good friend," said Tony knowing what button to push.

Audrey paused then said, "You're most welcome Tony. Just for the record, I do remember you telling us ahead of time you would keep your work and home lives separate."

The call ended quickly and Tony went about piecing together his needs to install the type of wireless security system he requires. He had already decided on false cameras. Tony also saw too much trouble with a website based system. Tony knew how to hack better than most, but didn't act upon the knowledge except to help clients know their vulnerabilities in a legal manner.

I don't need to worry that someone's watching us in our own home. I just want unwelcome visitors to think someone is watching, he thought as he opened another new tab while working on the internet.

After an hour of finding the right pieces to put the system together he checked out Radio Shack's website. To his surprise he found every piece of technology all in one place. Tony decided to skip going to his local store. They know him too well. He drove to the bank then the Radio Shack store across the river and purchased everything on his list. Not taking any chances he paid cash and told the clerk it was for his in-laws.

When the clerk asked for his phone number he calmly waved his hand and said, as if he were a Jedi Knight, "You don't need my phone number."

The clerk shrugged his shoulders and nodded in agreement.

Tony just about busted out laughing thinking, *Hey, it worked!*

I'm not telling a soul other than Jacquelyn about this. The last thing I need is for Big Brother to enter my home and monitor us every second of the day, he then thought.

Jacquelyn came home and proclaimed, "I'm tired."

"Long day?" asked Tony.

"It seemed that way. Oh, remember that substitute teacher that made the mistake of coming to my classroom? Well, I saw her today."

"Not again?" asked Tony.

"This time I saw her walking out of Nick's school as we drove by," she said.

"Well, she must be a pretty good teacher if she's subbing in this school district," said Tony.

"I know all the subs. This one's new. Do you remember Drew Brenner? He's the principle at Nick's school," she said guiding Tony.

"Sure, I remember. He's a nice guy. He's very involved with Special Olympics activities if I recall."

"That's him. So, I decided to call him from the minivan and ask who the new substitute teacher is. You know what he said?"

Tony shrugged.

"What new substitute teacher?"

So we talked about how Nick is doing and then I turned the conversation back to the new sub. He told me none of his teachers called in and required a sub today. So I asked him if he was interviewing for new subs today. He said no then inquired as to why I was asking."

"What'd you tell him?"

"I told him about the woman that showed up in my classroom and that I saw her at his school after I picked up Sam and Nick."

"What was his reaction?" asked Tony.

"He figures it's probably one of the moms and I must have been mistaken. He has a point in that I was driving by when I saw her. But, I could swear it was the same person," she said voice trailing off at the end.

"Well, you did the right thing regardless," said Tony giving her a big hug.

"By the way the kids are next door playing until dinner," she said quietly.

"Then why don't you go upstairs and relax. I purchased the equipment to install the perfect security system today. I'll take care of that while you take a hot bath and let your busy work day melt away."

After installing the security system Tony realized a flaw in his plan. He is going to run and monitor everything from his Smartphone. The only one he has looks like it's from CIT, but its government issued.

"No way am I coming this far to protect my privacy and then let them take control because it's their phone. I'm buying a separate phone just for the security system."

Tony called up to Jacquelyn, but she couldn't hear him over the running bath water. He phoned the Weavers next door and let them know he was running out for a few minutes and Jacquelyn was resting.

"I'll be back in thirty minutes," Tony said to Connie Weaver.

"Take your time. The kids are having fun and Joe won't be home for awhile," she said.

Tony arrived back home and walked across the lawn to pick up Sam and Nick.

"Thanks again for letting the kids stay a little longer today Connie," said Tony.

"Oh, it's no problem. I like having them over. Sue and Justin love it when they're here," she said.

"Next time our house, OK?" Tony asked, but was more of statement.

"That would be great," said Connie.

Later that evening Tony showed Jacquelyn the new security system...cameras and all. Her reaction was pretty much what he had expected. His determination to keep his family safe came through every pore in his body. The new phone, the exact same model issued by his employers, had a partial charge and it was time for a test and demonstration to help Jacquelyn see the benefits of what he put together.

"Here's the command center," said Tony holding it in his palm.

"It's a cell phone," she said with apprehension in her voice.

"Smartphone," he corrected.

"Excuse me...Smartphone," she said sarcastically.

"We can run everything from this," Tony said proudly.

"From that?" she said skeptically.

"Yup, right from the phone."

Tony had it turned off so he and Jacquelyn could go through the process together while sitting on the couch together. He held it so both of them could see. He turned it on. Once the home screen appeared ready he swiped the numerals on the touch-screen with his right index finger in the shape of a seven. This allowed access.

"This icon holds all the controls —."

"Stop right there. I know you get into this technology stuff, but it bores me to death. Just show me what it does then get rid of those cameras," said Jacquelyn cutting Tony off from his little seminar presentation.

"You really should know how to use this Jacquelyn," said Tony.

"All in good time," she replied.

Tony turned the entire system on and began explaining the different benefits to Jacquelyn when all of a sudden a red flashing dot appeared on the screen. It showed the layout of the living room. An indicator read: NON-AUTHORIZED EQUIPMENT FOUND

Jacquelyn asked, "What does that mean?"

"I must have installed something wrong," said Tony as if only talking to himself.

Getting up from the couch he turned then walked toward where the red dot showed the problem. Stopping at the table next to the front window he was alerted he was basically standing right next to what was causing the alarm notification.

"I didn't install anything over here," he said turning his head toward Jacquelyn.

She got up and sidled up to his left side leaning on his shoulder with both her hands. Then, together they searched around the underside of the table.

Jacquelyn, studying the screen, said, "Maybe just move the phone around this area. It might be like the game we play with Nick. You know, you're getting hotter, colder…," she said still staring at the red dot on the screen.

Tony realized there was a sound icon on the screen so he touched it. A rather quick beeping sound began and either sped up or slowed down as he moved.

"Apparently we're being told we're right on top of whatever we're looking for," he said.

"Whatever it is we should get one for Nick so we can find him really easy," Jacquelyn joked.

"I wonder what I screwed up?" he asked.

Tony moved the phone from the base of the lamp to the top. The beeping turned into one solid high-pitched tone. He handed Jacquelyn the phone then took the lampshade off and was so surprised to find one of the smallest microphones he's ever seen. He pointed it out to Jacquelyn. She reached out and snatched the piece of hardware handing the phone back to Tony.

"Is this one of the things you installed? Maybe it's malfunctioning?" she said.

Tony looked at the tiny device in Jacquelyn's hand then into her eyes and said, "I didn't put that there."

"Then who did?" she asked.

"I don't know, but it isn't like the ones I installed," he said.

"You installed eve's dropping microphones?" she asked alarmingly.

"Yes, they're for when we aren't home. They'll record everything just in case we need it."

"So how did this one get here and why is it here," she asked.

Tony silenced the Smartphone from the annoying tone then put his right index finger to his lips signaling to Jacquelyn not to speak another word. He held out his hand and motioned her to give it to him. Tony walked directly toward the back door with Jacquelyn right behind. Tony touched one icon to disable the alarm system before opening the door. He placed the device on the concrete and stepped on it crushing it into pieces.

As soon as he did this he thought, *I should have kept it and handed it to Audrey then tell her I'm out if games like this are going to be played.* Then another thought hit him. *I don't have proof she's responsible for this. She might not be involved.*

Tony and Jacquelyn swept the entire house to make sure there weren't any more of these devices. They found none.

"Jacquelyn, I think it's safe to say that bug was put there recently."

"How could you know that?"

"Because I saw a little dust on the frame holding the lampshade and that thing had no dust on it," he said as if noticing this is normal.

Jacquelyn looked at Tony and realization set in at the same time for both of them, "The security system conman," they said almost in unison.

I'm not so sure he's just a conman, thought Tony.

Chapter 17

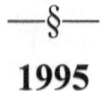

1995

Audrey reached into her briefcase and retrieved the copy of the IRS letter Ryan O'Connor gave to her. After re-reading it a few times she was prepared to move to the second stage of her strategy. Audrey composed two letters. The first, being to Simon Swan regarding her vision for the situation of the CIT board of directors. After tweaking it a few times she was satisfied and printed it out on plain white paper. She did not sign it. Next she wrote a letter contesting all implications the Internal Revenue Service leveled at Andrew. This she printed on CIT letterhead paper and boldly signed. Audrey laid the two letters side by side on Andrew's old desk satisfied with her work. She shut her computer down and called it a night.

The next morning, on her way to work, Audrey stopped by Simon Swan's office and signed the paperwork hiring his firm on retainer for CIT. She expressed to Simon that she knows the Internal Revenue Service has the most influential reputation, and resources, as the biggest bully on the face of the earth. What she didn't share is that she must create the appearance of a delicate balance between cooperation and pushing back. If she pushes too hard, one way or the other, she will not achieve the desired outcome.

First they both signed the document placing the law firm of Swan and White on retainer for CIT. Next, she handed him both letters she had written last night. Simon sat back and read them.

Knowing Simon would comment on the difference between the CIT letterhead document and the plain sheet of paper she stated, "As I said I want to keep the strategy very private. Hence the reason the board of director strategy document is not on CIT letterhead, nor signed. I want deniability for the time being. I don't want a leak to be traced back to me before I'm ready."

"That's fine. You're covered under attorney client privilege either way," he said not looking up. Even if the government wanted to they couldn't touch this."

I know. That's why we're doing it this way, she thought.

"Just so you understand the IRS issue is another matter. There is the possibility, no strike that, a probability they will require all records pertaining to your case. I can of course slow the process down, but eventually they almost always get their way. Dawn can speak to that better than I can."

I know that too, she thought.

"Audrey, I will get right on the elimination process of your board of directors, but I think it would be best if Dawn sits in on this meeting regarding the IRS issue," he said reaching for his phone.

"Actually Simon, I have a meeting I need to attend at CIT, but I think you're right. Will you and Dawn look this over then we can get together later today? It will give me a chance to see Dawn and catch up with her as well," said Audrey.

"After lunch?" he asked.

"That sounds fine. I will call you to confirm," she said.

"Great. Dawn is looking forward to seeing you."

Immediately after her CIT meeting, Audrey left her office and made a phone call from her car to Dr. Richard Wilkins, PhD of the University of Portland. Her old finance professor was very happy to hear from one of his favorite former students.

"Audrey, how are you?" he asked in his old growly German accent leaning back in his chair.

"You remember?" she said with delight.

"Yes, yes...how could I forget my top student. To what do I owe this pleasure?" he asked in his raspy old German inflection.

"Are you still up on current global financial banking issues and the extent of the reach of the Internal Revenue Service? I'm looking to settle a bet."

"That is a very broad question Audrey. I thought I taught you to do your homework, invest wisely and never wager your hard earned money," he said.

"You're right, but this is just a friendly dinner wager. I'm sorry to have asked such a wide open question. Let me narrow it down. If the United States Government, specifically the IRS, has opened a case against an individual do they have the authority to freeze a Swiss bank account?"

"What side of the wager are you on?" he asked. "Did you forget the Swiss banking act of 1934?" he asked sounding just like her professor again.

"No, I remember it started with the French then it saved the Jewish people millions because of the protection of the individual against the power of the German State," said Audrey proudly.

"I couldn't have said it better myself. I believe no bank whose business is to shield money and keep

146

everything so private would ever entertain the idea of providing information to anyone much less the IRS," he said emphatically.

"So the act still stands strong today?" she asked.

"You would be correct. I have never heard of any cooperation to any government agency especially the IRS. If banks begin this practice then their depositors would move their money so quickly their heads would spin," he answered.

"I guess I just won a free dinner. Thank you so much Dr. Wilkins," said Audrey.

"Please, you're a grown woman now. Call me Stephen," he said with a smile.

"Remember what I taught you. Anyone who has only one secure private bank account with the Swiss should move approximately sixty percent of their money to the Cayman Islands and back every so often. It not only keeps the banks honest, but the money stays ahead of anyone who is sniffing around. Besides, if you visit Jamaica it is only about three hundred miles to the Cayman Islands," he said as if he were lecturing.

"Well, someday I hope I have enough money to make that trip for just that purpose," she said.

"What do you mean someday?"

"Your right I should be more optimistic and plan my trip now," she said in light-hearted tone.

Audrey ended the call and made one more before heading over to Swan and White law firm. She was looking forward to seeing Dawn. It had been too long since the two of them had spent any meaningful time together. They are the same age and have many of the same interests. She and Andrew were so happy when they announced their wedding. Andrew and Simon seemed to have had fun going out as couples, but neither man considered their friendship close. It wasn't often the men joined them.

Audrey entered the front entrance and Dawn happened to be walking past the receptionist's desk on her way to Simon's office.

With a double-take, Dawn's eyes opened wide as the two greeted each other with a great big hug.

"Audrey!" said Dawn just about to burst at the seams.

"Dawn. Look at you. Beautiful as ever," said Audrey sincerely.

"How long has it been?" asked Dawn.

"Too long," said Audrey.

"I was just on my way to Simon's office with your file. Do you want to go to my office and catch up before we talk business?" asked Dawn.

"That would be lovely." Audrey answered.

The two of them spent about one-half hour going over old times. Audrey avoided the subject of Andrew's passing for another time and Dawn respected her wishes. With the door shut they couldn't hear Simon's shuffle and step. He knocked at the door.

"Come in," said Dawn.

"Am I interrupting you girls?" he asked smiling as he entered.

"Yes, now go away," Dawn said kiddingly. "Actually we were just about to head down to the conference room," she added.

The fifteen foot by twelve foot conference room comprised of a single bland rectangular table with six utilitarian chairs available to choose.

Very sparse. This will change, thought Audrey.

Simon and Audrey sat across from each other with Dawn at what could be considered the head of the table. This allowed Dawn and Audrey to review the copy of the IRS letter that was sent to Brian Harris and Audrey supplied to Simon.

After the review and a question and answer session Audrey said, "I like your plan. Especially you calling this Mr. Wagner personally first before beginning any written correspondence," said Audrey.

Prior to meeting with Dawn and Simon, Audrey's second phone call was placed from a pay phone before arriving at Swan and White. It was to a colleague. She made it clear it was imperative everything had been set up properly.

During that call she said, "Please contact Mr. Wagner of the Internal Revenue Service and tell him we need his full cooperation with the law firm of Swan and White. Everything will be in place within the hour."

The man on the other end of the line simply said, "Affirmative."

Listening to Dawn it was clear she had every detail nailed down and Audrey couldn't have been happier.

"Thank you for being so comprehensive with your plan and don't let these guys get you down. I'm not letting them trash Andrew's good name. Lord knows these twits I have as board members have already spread the news around town," Audrey said forcefully.

"Don't be so sure about that Audrey. They are under strict guidelines not to speak to anyone about this matter. As I think of it, maybe I should send each of them a letter reminding them of their responsibilities. They're still board members and bound by law." said Dawn.

"Writing them is a great idea. However, I'd like to move quicker than that. I have their email addresses. You can email them right now while I discuss other business with Simon," said Audrey.

"I like the way you think Audrey Shelton."

"I'm so glad we've reconnected Dawn."

As Dawn got up she gave Audrey another big hug.

This one has to be because of Andrew, Audrey thought.

Simon moved one chair over so Audrey could see what he had put together regarding the removal of the board of directors at CIT.

"Did you remember to bring a few pieces of blank CIT letterhead?" asked Simon.

"Yes, right here," said Audrey pulling a few sheets from a folder within her briefcase.

"OK, I've done my homework regarding the bi-laws document you sent me and I'm really quite surprised," he said.

"Oh, in what way?" asked Audrey.

"Andrew's attention to detail. He not only specified how many board members there would be but, he specifically named each person who would fill those positions."

"That can't be good," said Audrey in a deflated tone.

"Quite the contrary. Because he names the board members, including himself, it now opens the document up for legal revision."

Audrey lifted her head and raised her eyebrows then said, "Go on."

"This is a mistake many entrepreneurs make. When they place names into board positions and a person no longer has the ability to fulfill his or her duties it activates a revocation of said document under the law. In a nutshell, this document is currently worthless," he said holding up the pages in one hand.

"Are you saying because Andrew can no longer perform his duties that he can't just be replaced?"

"Not quite. He can be replaced and he has...by you. However, the document covering the legal mechanics is null and void."

"Does that mean I don't need to do anything but tell the other board members their services are no longer required?"

"Unfortunately it's not that easy. Under the statutes a board meeting must be held and the issue of the current state of your bi-laws must be rectified."

"What do you mean...rectified?" she asked emphasizing the last word.

"Simply modified or eliminated by majority vote," Simon said flatly.

"Let me make sure I understand what you are telling me. I need to call a board meeting with the men I no longer want on CIT's board and just ask them to modify the document to bring us into alignment with the law?"

"That's one way," he said tilting his head a little.

"OK, then tell me another," Audrey said with authority.

"I'm happy to. I've laid out a plan that will allow you to not only have that board meeting and also get what you want without trouble. I can't imagine them voting themselves out of a position on the board of directors," he said.

"You're right about that," said Audrey.

"I think its best they resign of their own free will," said Simon without emotion.

Audrey stared into Simon's eyes to see if he was kidding. She found his familiar deep hazel green colored eyes staring right back at her. "You're kidding right?" she asked meekly.

"I wouldn't kid about something like this Audrey. Here's how it works.

Chapter 18

—§—

Present Day

Tony went out to the garage to make a sweep of the minivan. Nothing showed up on his new security Smartphone app. He then checked out his car just in case. As he entered his car, the red dot suddenly appeared once again notifying him a listening device is nearby. The audible warning beep was so quick he felt as if he were on top of it already. Moving the phone all around the inside of the car he waited to hear the solid tone when the target was found. He reached the phone up with his right hand moving toward the rear-view mirror.

"Bingo," he declared.

Tony tapped the icon to turn the alarm off then inspected the rear-view mirror. To his surprise he found nothing. He sat back and wondered if his new toy was not functioning properly. Tony raised it back up without sound and the dot was glowing as red as ever. He set the phone back down and felt along the edges and then behind the mirror. Feeling a small bump his heart rate jumped as he turned the mirror to see the exact same type of listening device that he had just crushed on the back step.

What in the world? Tony wondered.

He decided to leave the bug right where it was...on the back-side of the mirror. He got out of the car and checked the rest of the garage and was relieved not to discover anything else. Tony didn't want to scare Jacquelyn so he said nothing about what he found.

The next morning Tony drove in silence to the same Radio Shack store. Using duct tape he covered the tiny round button shaped listening device to hopefully muffle the sound if someone was indeed listening. The kid who was on duty at the store last night wasn't there.

"How can I help you?" asked a voice rounding the corner from behind boxes of electronic supplies.

Tony turned and deliberately looked at his gold name tag.

Good, he's the manager.

"Doug, I have a small listening device and I wonder if you sell these here," said Tony holding the black button stuck to a small piece of duct tape.

The manager examined the small piece of hardware then looked back up to Tony. "Where'd you get this?" he asked.

Evading his question Tony responded, "Smaller than what I'm used to seeing."

Doug walked behind the counter and turned on a light to view the device under a magnifying glass.

"We don't sell anything close to this type of product," he said emphatically.

"Who does?" asked Tony.

"The military," Doug deadpanned.

"Huh?"

"See, right here, these letter and number combinations indicate military grade. But, I've never seen one like this before. Where'd you get it?" he asked again.

I think I know, but I'm not sure what the guy's real name is, Tony thought.

"It's on and I would like to turn it off without destroying it. Do you know how to do that?" asked Tony.

"Oh, that's what the duct tape is for. If it's like the others I just need to twist the top portion to the left. It's almost seamless until it's under the magnifying glass." With a slight turn Doug handed it back to Tony and said, "Smart move putting duct tape on it."

"So, if I want to activate it I just twist it back to the right?"

"Exactly. See these two lines? They just need to line up" said Doug.

"I never even noticed the lines before. But, how do I know it's on," asked Tony.

"You won't unless you have a detection device." Doug began to turn and say, "We carry two types if you're interested, but—."

Tony cut him off said his thanks and was on his way. In the car he verified the little bug was indeed off by looking at the uneven line separating the top and bottom.

"Damn him! I just knew following a techie around would be harder than I thought," she said sitting in her car near the electronics store. *I hate to have to provide this update, but better sooner than later*, she thought.

She made the call and got exactly what she expected...an earful.

"It's time for me to make contact with him," said the scrambled voice.

"But, you'll blow your—"

"Don't be so naive," the voice said cutting her off. "I have no intention of revealing my true identity. Manipulate a chance meeting with him. I'll play the role of an associate from the law firm he just sent that computer proposal to."

"I don't understand," she said.

"Better to have this plan in place and not use it than be caught trying a last minute effort. Just take care of it."

"Oh, so now I'm your secretary," said 'Danielle'.

"A very smart person once told me sometimes the variables on the ground change and we have to adapt and change with them. Well, this is one of those times," said the voice.

"What if we did this a different way. A way so you don't have to jeopardize your identity."

"When you think of it let me know. In the meantime let's at least have something in place."

"OK. I'll do it. But, I really don't think it's the best idea," said 'Danielle'.

Tony received a text on the secret side of his phone. It was from Audrey asking if he could meet with her right away. He texted back confirming he'd be at her office in about thirty minutes.

As Tony entered Audrey's office he sensed she seemed to be carrying extra emotional weight on her shoulders. He also broke focus to observe any feeling he might have with the infamous two-way mirror on the wall.

Nothing...good, he thought in relief.

"What's wrong Audrey?" he asked as he pulled up a chair in front of her desk.

"Why do you think something is wrong?" she asked in a quiet tone.

"Sorry, it's quite apparent to me," he replied.

"I thought I held my emotions in check pretty well. No fooling you is there," she said turning her eyes back to her computer monitor.

"Is there something I can do to help?" asked Tony.

"Let's sit at the table so we can both see what I need to show you," she said.

She took her personal white laptop out of the docking station, replacing it with a CIT issued black one. Audrey then placed the white one in between them as they sat down. Tony remained silent. Audrey filled him in that Dennis Forman had sent her some information regarding the San Diego incident.

"Audrey, before we start I have something on my mind that I think we need to address," said Tony.

"And that would be?"

"I have no training," he said leaving it put to wide open interpretation.

"Tony, for what you do there is no training."

"What I'm talking about is self-preservation in the face of danger," he said sincerely.

Audrey thought a few moments and said, "You are right. With your proclivity to take action we need you to at least be prepared to protect yourself from harm. I'll set it up."

"Thanks."

"Now, back to what this meeting is about. Tony, what I'm about to show you is sensitive and confidential."

She turned the screen just a nudge so Tony had a clear view. The screen was gray. Audrey placed one finger on the touchpad revealing the play icon for the video he was about to see.

Tony sat up and pulled his chair a little closer to the computer. The video showed a view of the inside of what appeared to be the restaurant before the explosion. Nothing seemed out of the ordinary with waitresses and waiters moving in and out apparently from a ceiling mounted camera. Patrons seated chatting and eating.

"Do you recognize the restaurant?" asked Audrey.

"I know it's the Thai Restaurant, but I've never been inside before," said Tony.

"Pay close attention to the next thirty seconds, it covers a span of five business days," said Audrey.

The video had been cut to show a young man with tennis shoes following the hostess through the inside dining area then turning right to the outdoor seating area.

"That's him!" Tony said moving even closer to the screen.

Audrey said, "Keep watching."

After showing this portion of the five business days Audrey paused the video. "Do you notice anything Tony?"

"Pretty broad question, but yes I do. He's being shown to the same area of the outside patio. They always turn right once outside," he said looking at Audrey.

"Very good Tony, now let's move on."

The next portion of the video was again from a different fixed camera inside the restaurant. It somehow zoomed all the way to the other side of the street. Tony was about to ask why a restaurant would need a camera to zoom that far, but figured big brother had to be involved. He recognized himself on the bench he had sat upon just recently. The video continued, showing cars and an occasional small delivery truck impeding line of sight. Then it hit Tony like a ton of bricks.

"Pause it!" he said. Can you go back and play the last ten seconds in slow motion?"

Audrey pressed pause then asked, "Why? What are you looking for?"

"I'm not positive so I need to see it one more time."

She played it back in slow motion just as Tony asked then paused it again.

"May I?" asked Tony.

"Be my guest."

Tony took control of the touchpad. He replayed the same footage three more times. He then froze the video just after a truck had cleared the view to the NBC building across the street. He stared at the upper right corner then sat back closing his eyes thinking back to when he was there himself.

"What is it Tony...the truck?" asked Audrey sitting straight up.

He opened his eyes and refocused on the woman in the hat and sun glasses. Tony replayed it one more time to make sure.

Staring at the screen Tony said, "Audrey let's come back to this part. Can we go ahead further?"

Audrey acquiesced and allowed Tony to take full control of the touchpad. As the video moved along Tony's hunch paid off. He remembered his feeling of being watched that day. The woman had taken the same interest in the young man in the neon red tennis shoes as much as Tony. Just before the explosion he saw himself walk into the NBC building. The woman lingered only a few seconds longer, looked up the street, then backed away out of view on the side of the building.

Tony let the video play out with the sudden disconnection he knew to be from the explosion.

"Is that it or do you have more footage from other cameras," he asked.

"What caught your attention, Tony?"

She didn't answer my question, he thought.

He wasn't sure why she did this so he deflected her question asking, "Why did you want me to see this?"

"Well, because you were there. We thought you might have a unique perspective. Do you?" she asked pointedly.

"I'm not sure. Would you mind if I spent a little time going over it some more," he asked.

"That's why you're here."

"Is there more footage," Tony asked testing her again.

Audrey's desk phone rang. She got up and took the call. "Alright, thank you for expediting the matter. I'll be right down," she said into the phone.

Saved by the bell, thought Tony.

"Emergency?" he asked.

"Not really, but when someone goes the extra mile for you it's disrespectful to make them wait. I have to go down to the twenty-second floor, but I shouldn't be long. Will you wait for me?"

"I have a High Speed High Density back-up drive in my briefcase. I could just make a copy—"

"That's not allowed Tony. I've been cleared to show you, but that is it," she said bitingly.

Tony was surprised at her reaction and didn't like being talked to in this manner. Especially since he had been put in danger without notice.

With a poker face he said, "I understand. I brought my briefcase in with me so I suppose I can get something done until you get back," he said giving a nod to the briefcase sitting across from her desk.

"Do you have your laptop with you?" she asked.

"No."

Audrey walked back to the table and logged off her white laptop shutting it down. She then went back to her pristine desk, set it down, then logged Tony into CIT's intranet through the black laptop already in the docking station.

"There, you can access your email then we will continue when I get back," she said.

Tony sat down at Audrey's desk as she politely said, "Adjust the chair or your knees will be black and blue from knocking into the desk. I'll be back shortly," she said as she walked to the elevator.

You're concerned about my knees bumping the desk, but not me getting blown to pieces? he thought.

Tony, sitting in his boss's chair, watched Audrey enter the elevator and waited until the door closed. He swiveled one hundred-eighty degrees to look at the view of downtown Portland.

"Nice to be the big shot," he mumbled.

As he swiveled back his eyes caught the flash of white before looking at the twenty-two inch computer monitor in front of him. He pushed the image from his mind. Tony logged into CIT's intranet and clicked on the 'NEWS TODAY' link highlighted in blue. It took only a few seconds before he could begin to read the information. However, in those precious few seconds, Tony turned his head to the right and quickly glanced at Audrey's white laptop then back to the monitor.

Something's up, but don't even think about it, he thought.

Tony began reading the CIT news update. His mind wandered back to the image of the white laptop once again. He knew he could easily hack in without anyone ever knowing.

I'm not that kind of person, but then again I'm not stupid either, he reminded himself.

Staring at the monitor he just couldn't shake the idea that the video was just sitting a couple of feet from him.

I risked my hide and now I can't even see it without permission, he thought staring through the monitor. *Who the hell do they think they are? I'm not going to let them walk all over me again*, he decided.

162

Though Tony didn't catch any feeling from the white framed mirror like before, he did take the precaution to walk over and cover it up with a tablecloth.

Just a precaution, he thought.

Tony quickly turned to the white laptop and found the Wi-Fi button on the right side and turned it off. Then, opening the clamshell, he powered it up. At the home screen he entered the password he remembered seeing through the reflection of the window:

'iamdagger'

At first Tony's only interest was to make a copy of the video. Then he remembered the CPT program as well. He thought he might have to open the video using it.

Screw it. They didn't play fair with me. Now it's my turn. It'll be faster just to copy the hard drive. He pictured being held against his will in the D.C area and began a slow burn. *Pay-back's a bitch*, he thought.

Very quickly Tony took the HSHD back-up drive from his briefcase. It's the size of Smartphone. He quickly attached it to Audrey's personal computer via a USB Port. With a few keystrokes a small orange bar appeared in a light blue box indicating the duplication progress being made. Within four minutes a full copy of the hard drive had been captured. Tony disconnected the hardware and placed it back into his briefcase still sitting in front of Audrey's desk. After moving back to the home screen Tony quickly opened the diagnostics and deleted the last action taken from her computer's memory. Tony flipped the Wi-Fi switch back on, shut the computer down and closed it. Tony quickly returned the back-up drive to his briefcase. Then, just because he's seen it in movies, he wiped the computer keys so his finger prints wouldn't be found. He was never there.

Tony removed the tablecloth from the mirror and placed it back where it belonged.

Chapter 19

—§—

1995

"If you just eliminate each of the current board members they will rebel. Then you've got a real public relations problem on your hands. You could also be looking at a law suit, especially from Brian Harris. Trust me I know Brian and his pride. He's a good guy, but as an attorney he wouldn't think twice about going after you for a few bucks over this," said Simon.

"So what do you suggest I do?" asked Audrey.

"Look this document over. It's your new bi-laws naming only one Chairman of the Board and two other members. No names," he said.

"But, I just told you I don't want any other board members," Audrey said emphatically.

"Please look at page six. It does not specify, by name, who the board members are."

"You already told me there are no names. What benefit does that provide me? I still have to deal with two other board members. It's not what I want."

"Well, you still have to make sure you remain legally sound. Here's the beauty of my plan."

Simon slid a one page document in front of her.

"This is an affidavit placing me and one other person on the board with you. It prescribes all authority of my votes by proxy to you," he said proudly.

"Are you saying I place you on the board? Is that legal since you wrote the document? No conflict of interest?" she asked.

"Believe it or not, it is very legal. It's a loophole in the law that has yet to be reconciled. I know enough State Senators who have their own corporations and use this to keep full control along with complete deniability. Politically speaking I don't see it changing any time soon."

"Are you sure?"

"I better be. I'm their attorney."

After reading the document she asked, "Why would I place you on the board?"

He paused then said, "Let's just say we want to leave CIT as healthy as possible for the next generation."

Audrey melted just a little, but didn't go anywhere near talking about the elephant in the room. Looking into his brilliant green eyes she flashed back to the passionate night they spent together. They were young dumb and it was a mistake. However, she has no regrets.

"I get your point. Who do you suggest I place into the other seat," she asked.

"Who would benefit you and CIT by having as a figure-head board member? More importantly who do you have influence over that will mostly agree with you?"

Audrey didn't need to search for a list of names as she said, "Ryan O'Connor. Not so much for loyalty, but more for appearances."

"Isn't he already a board member? Also, isn't he the one who wanted to be Chairman?"

"Yes."

"Then why would you want to tip your hand and ask him to sign a document shutting him out of the very process in which he would rather control himself?" he asked.

"He wouldn't have seen this document. You and I would be the only ones to know about this arrangement. Even if Ryan votes against me from time to time it will still be two to one in my favor. He's a valuable asset to CIT and it would pump his ego and also keep him from jumping to a competitor," said Audrey.

Simon sat back with his thumbs on his chin and the tips of his fingers over his mouth in steeple shape as if he were praying. His wheels were turning to play devil's advocate. He could find only one hole in Audrey's logic.

"I like it," he said leaning forward. "But, he's eventually going to want to know who the other board member is and why he or she doesn't show up for meetings?"

"How many board meetings are required by law?" asked Audrey.

"By law, only one review per fiscal year. But, it sounds like Andrew held at least one per quarter. Won't you raise questions by doing it differently?"

"I'm not Andrew," she said succinctly.

"Good point. Do you want me to sign? If you haven't noticed I wrote a declaration of termination clause into the document. If the Chairman of the Board, you at this time, has a change of mind then the termination clause can be executed without delay. It's fool proof. So, do you want me to sign right now?" he asked again.

Audrey turned the document back to Simon for his signature.

"I'll be right back. I have to load the printer with the CIT letterhead you gave me. Then I'll sign it. Once signed, you will need to get it notarized. I'd do it, but my signature is the topic of the document which is a conflict of interest. You can go to your bank or someone trustworthy to get this done," he said.

"I don't want this going beyond just the two of us." she said.

"I have a friend who's a Notary that I trust. On occasion, she allows me to cover the documents so she will have no knowledge of their contents. I've done the same for her," said Simon as he signed and dated the document.

"Are you talking about Dawn?" she asked.

"No, I'm not. It wouldn't be legal. We're in a gray area already. If contested there could be a problem since she's not only my wife, but my partner as well."

"Looks like I chose the right lawyer," Audrey said with a smile.

Simon gave a pleasant smile back to Audrey then pointed and said, "You just need to sign and date it right here."

Audrey went home to write an email draft explaining exactly what she had just set up with Simon Swan. She waited ten minutes then checked to see if her latest secret email draft had been deleted. It hadn't. Audrey gave it fifteen more minutes and then found a new draft with an empty subject line. After reading it she smiled at the response and logged off.

She hopped into her car and drove over Willamette River to make a call from a pay phone on Martin Luther King Jr. Drive. She never spent much time here and that was the point.

The woman on the other end of the call answered politely, "Trinity Corporation, how may I help you?"

"Four - One - Seven - Seven - Five - Eighteen," said Audrey.

"I'm sorry, but you must have called an incorrect number," replied the woman.

"Delta – Alpha – Golf – Golf – Echo - Romeo," said Audrey.

After a brief silence and crackling noises within the connection the woman said, "Dagger, please confirm status."

"I am secure and contained."

After a brief pause the woman said, "Confirming line is secure...go ahead."

"My message is to Repairman. Contact Mr. Wagner of the IRS and have him email CIT's board members in two hours. That includes the Chair Person. The message is to contain the threat of legal action with regard to case number BD23725126416. Provide an escape hatch for each in the form of their resignation. Once again they are not to discuss this matter with anyone."

Audrey then remained silent.

"Message received and confirmed," said the woman.

The line went dead. No goodbyes or parting words. Just a sterile dead line as protocol required. Audrey paused then hung up as well.

Audrey sped back home to her office. She sent off an urgent invitation for an emergency board meeting for tomorrow morning at 8am. Audrey stayed by her computer waiting for Brian Harris, Bob Robinson, Mike Turner and Ryan O'Connor all to reply.

No responses came back immediately. Audrey kicked her shoes off and lay on the couch to catch a power nap. She heard an elevator chime off in the distance. Audrey then heard it once again. Slowly she opened her eyes realizing she wasn't at CIT. Another chime then another, but this time understanding it is her computer calling to her with new email messages. She got up very refreshed and walked over to her desk.

Excellent, everyone can make it. Apparently they all got Mr. Wagner's notice and scared the crap out of them. This will make the meeting so much easier, she thought.

The next morning Audrey was in her office by 6am. She stared out at the thirty-three story panoramic view and ran meeting scenarios through her mind. By 7am she had her template. By 7:30am she quietly rehearsed her role to perfection. Now feeling very comfortable Audrey began to head to the board room at precisely 7:55am. She intended to be the last to arrive.

Opening the door Audrey said, in an all business-like tone, "Good morning gentlemen."

The men were already in their seats. Mike Turner glanced at his watch. Audrey noticed the intense expressions on their faces.

I wonder if the pre-meeting chatter topic was about Mr. Wagner's email to each of them, she thought.

"Good morning Audrey," they said back not quite in unison.

Audrey took her chair at the head of the table as the men half stood as she did so.

"What's this about Audrey?" asked Brian Harris holding what she presumed to be the email from Mr. Wagner.

"First, let me say thank you for agreeing to meet on such short notice. I know each of you have very busy schedules and I appreciate your reaction time to my request for a meeting this morning.

"How could we not meet after receiving this from the IRS," said Bob Robinson holding the very same email.

Well, Bob, I'm surprised you have the balls to bring it up first, she thought.

"I presume you all received the same email I did?" Audrey asked holding her own copy up for everyone to see.

This time Ryan O'Connor did receive notice as well. He seemed to be acting as if he was now part of an exclusive club and feeling comfortable and in tune with the group.

"Audrey, originally the letter that was sent to these men stated only the Chairman of the Board would bear the brunt of a possible penalty from what Andrew did," O'Connor said acting like the ring leader.

As if her eyes could burn a hole into O'Connor she replied, "Andrew has done nothing wrong! You obviously feel otherwise! I don't want you on this board if that's how you see it!" she scolded.

"I misspoke. I'm sorry Audrey," O'Connor said remembering the screw up at the hospital morgue. "I meant to say allegedly."

"I understand, sorry," replied Audrey. *Now that I jumped down Ryan's throat and set the tone I need to watch it and take it easier on him than the others the rest of the meeting*, she thought.

Mike Turner gave a look to Brian Harris as if he were a kid in grade school who just found the answers to an upcoming test. Harris remained cool and didn't tip his hand, but he figured he knew what Turner was thinking.

"Does this amuse you Mike?" Audrey poked.

"Quite the contrary Audrey, I think it's sad," he said.

"Sad? Are you saying you're sad for having served on this board with one of your best friends? Some friend you are. His body is barely cold and you want to stomp on his grave," she said with a flourish.

"That's not what I meant," Turner said raising his voice.

"Good. Because if you have your doubts then I suggest you resign right now," Audrey said forcefully knowing his quick temper.

"Relax Audrey. Why are you taking this out on me?" he asked sitting as if he is above it all.

"We have a crisis here of monumental proportions and you're advice is to tell me to relax?" she asked with her voice becoming louder.

"Yeah! That's exactly what I'm telling you to do...relax!" he shouted not to be outdone by Audrey's shrill tone.

"This is serious business Mr. Turner!" she said slowly holding up the email.

"Yeah, serious enough to get each of us heavily fined or worse! I'm not going to jail!" he said meeting her challenge.

I knew Mike would be the first to pop. His angry streak is just what I was hoping for, she thought.

"Come on. Both of you settle down," said O'Connor trying to defuse the situation.

Bob Robinson and Brian Harris stayed silent and out of the fray as Mike Turner now turned his anger toward Ryan O'Connor. Robinson slipped Harris a quick knowing look while the fireworks were going off around them.

Once there was a break in the action Brian Harris very calmly said, "May I ask a few questions?"

Everyone turned their eyes to Harris. Audrey was counting on the only attorney in the group. Everybody except Audrey recognized him as a natural leader. She thought of him as a snob and a bully.

"Why all the acrimony?" he asked. "Shouldn't we be focusing on how to solve the problem rather than fighting with each other?"

Turner, still hot said, "Sure you'll be just fine. You're an attorney and can keep yourself out of this mess!"

That's it boys turn on each other, thought Audrey.

"What the hell does that mean?" asked Harris.

"Just that you and your lackey, Robinson over there, will find some kind of legal protection while the rest of us blow in the wind!" retorted Turner.

"That's—"

Bob Robinson cut Harris off.

"What do you mean by that!" said Robinson physically standing to his own defense.

"You know very well what I mean. I'll say it plain as day. When the going gets tough you go running to Harris!" scolded Turner.

Robinson made a move to reach over the table as he said, "You piece of shit! I'm—."

Ryan O'Connor grabbed Robinson and pulled him back to his chair.

"Now sit there! You stay where you are Mike! Everyone calm down and listen to me! We've gotten past rough bumps in the road before. There's no reason to think we can't do it again," he said.

O'Connor found he was the only one standing and finally sat down.

"Now, I suggest we control our tempers and allow Audrey to conduct this meeting," O'Connor said in a much calmer tone.

That a boy Ryan. Now it's you and me against Turner, Harris and Robinson. This is going much better than I anticipated, she thought.

Audrey said, "Ryan is right. We have overcome adversity before—"

Turner shut her down and said, "Correction…Andrew, Ryan, Brian, Bob and I have overcome adversity before. You, on the other hand, have never faced anything like the adversity the Internal Revenue Service is mounting against us."

Ooh, that almost hurt Mike. Sticks and stones…, she thought.

"Mike!" said O'Connor with a disappointing yet pleading look.

Still you and me against them Ryan. Way to go, thought Audrey.

Turner paused then took a turn looking each man directly in the eyes.

"Ask yourselves one question. Do I want to go to war with the United States Government with Audrey Shelton at the helm?"

Audrey stood for effect. "Are you suggesting I step down!?" she asked incredulously.

"No. I'm flat out saying it. Step down Audrey. You can't fill Andrew's shoes," he said steely-eyed.

"The only way I'm going anywhere is if I decide to make that decision!" she said sitting back down.

"Then I believe we are at an impasse. I make a motion to remove Audrey as Chairman of the Board. Who will second?" Turner said trying to force his will upon the others.

Silence filled the room.

"Ryan?" he asked.

Ryan O'Connor blankly stared at his friend then defiantly slowly shook his head no.

Turner knew he pissed Bob Robinson off so he went to Brian Harris next.

Harris looked at Ryan O'Connor instead of Turner and also shook his head no.

Mike Turner didn't even bother asking Robinson. Not because of their earlier altercation, but he knew the numbers. Audrey will remain as Chairman of the Board. He knew his fate.

Come on Mike don't disappoint me, thought Audrey.

After what seemed like an eternity of silence Mike Turner stood and said, "I resign."

Atta boy Mike. Fall on your sword. One down and two to go, thought Audrey.

"Come on Mike think about what you're doing. Don't make an emotional decision like this," said O'Connor.

Audrey looked at Robinson and Harris. They were just staring at Turner, but said nothing. This told Audrey volumes.

"Mike Turner has placed a motion on the table to resign as a board member of CIT. It is in our bi-laws that we do not need to vote. It is up to the Chairman of the Board to either accept or reject a resignation. However, I do want everyone's input regardless," said Audrey in an all business tone.

"He's just pissed off. Let him cool down. He'll be fine," said O'Connor.

Turner shook his head at O'Connor then turned, briefcase in hand, and walked out the door.

Audrey looked to Robinson and Harris. Neither one of them said a word. Ryan stared at the door in disbelief.

Audrey then said, "I'll take it by your silence that I should accept Mike's resignation." She paused, more for effect than anything else then said, "I guess he's off the hook with the IRS. Resignation accepted."

The look in Robinson's and Harris' eyes indicated to Audrey that the light bulbs just went on.

Took you boys long enough, she thought.

Harris looked at Robinson then said, "I believe there is a time for each of us to know when we have given of ourselves and can give no more. I'm proud of the work we've done here. I've been especially proud of the relationships we have built over the years. However, there comes a time when we all must realize when we've surpassed our usefulness and allow others to guide this great company. So, I too resign as a board member."

Spoken just like the hack attorney you are. Dominos anyone? thought Audrey.

"Brian, just because Mike—" Audrey began.

"This has nothing to do with Mike. It's my duty to step aside if I feel I have nothing else to give. Please accept my resignation," he said.

What a load of crap, thought Audrey. "If that's what you want Brian, and there are no objections, then I reluctantly accept your resignation."

With his notepad and pen already packed back into his briefcase he got up shook hands and said, "I'll see you around."

Another one bites the dust, thought Audrey.

Ryan piped up turning to Bob Robinson saying, "You're staying, right?"

Bob began packing his briefcase and said, "I can't say it any clearer than Brian. Please accept my resignation Audrey."

"Are you sure Bob?"

"Yes."

"I wish you would reconsider."

"It's for the best," he said calmly.

And there's the dagger, she thought.

"OK, resignation reluctantly accepted," she said followed by a heavy sigh. "Thanks for everything you have contributed Bob," she said after shaking his hand.

The door shut and Audrey turned to Ryan and asked, "Are you going to leave me too Ryan?"

"You know I'm not going anywhere, but what are we going to do?" asked Ryan shell-shocked.

"We'll be just fine," she said.

"Fine! How can we be fine? This Mr. Wagner from the IRS is at our front porch ready to eat us alive!" he said.

"I'll make you a deal. You keep forging ahead with our venture into government contracts and I will make sure you are kept from having anything to do with this IRS situation," she said.

"How can you guarantee that?" he asked.

"If you don't receive written notification clearing your name from this thing, from this Mr. Wagner, then I will personally go to Washington, D.C. and throw myself to the lions," she said boldly.

"You would do that for me? Even after what happened at the morgue?" he asked sincerely.

"I swear on Andrew's soul," she said placing her right hand over her heart.

Ryan paused, leaning toward Audrey and quietly asked, "Is this because—"

"We agreed never to discuss that...ever. And for the record...no." she said

Chapter 20

—§—

Present Day

Tony heard the elevator return to the thirty-third floor. The doors opened and Audrey energetically stepped out. Tony lifted his head after a few more keystrokes completing a work related email.

"You're back and you seem to be in a hurry," said Tony lifting his eyes from the computer monitor.

"I didn't want to keep you waiting any longer than you should. Let's get back to what we were doing," she said.

Tony logged off his account and, purposely using a double meaning said, "Thanks for letting me use your computer."

"I'm glad you could be productive. Let's go back over to the table," Audrey said as she picked up her white laptop.

"Is there more footage or are we just going to cover the same stuff we already saw?" he asked.

"You saw something and it could be very important," Audrey insisted as she booted up her personal computer.

This time Tony watched Audrey to see if she used the CPT program to open the video. She did. He watched the sands of time swirl then the play icon appeared. *That really is very cool,* Tony thought still amazed at the hidden program. Then he wondered; *Why doesn't she have to use another secure password to use the program? Big mistake.*

They started at the beginning once again and Tony let it run as he tried to think of a way to satisfy Audrey's curiosity while trying to get out of her office. He knew she had to provide a report. If he gave her nothing then he might be looked upon as uncooperative or nonessential. Tony already had the feeling he wasn't being told everything. He didn't want to tip his hand and add fuel to the fire.

Tony asked Audrey to place the video into slow motion. He had an idea that just might satisfy her and for those for whom they both work.

"Freeze it right...there," he said.

Audrey let it run a little too long and said, "You know where to pause it. Here, take control of the computer."

Oh, I plan too. Especially later and not here, he thought.

He turned her laptop slightly toward himself and paused it exactly where he wanted. It once again showed Tony sitting on the bench across the street looking to his left. His face is very discernible as he had lowered the newspaper for only a few seconds.

"Do you see anyone you recognize?" he asked.

"Of course. That's you on the bench," she answered.

"Anyone else?"

Audrey scoured the screen person by person and finally said, "I have no idea."

Tony first pointed then zoomed in on the woman in the straw hat and sunglasses.

"Now do you recognize someone you know?" he asked.

"That looks like—", she stopped short. She examined the blurry image then said, "That almost looks like me!"

"Is it?" Tony asked completely straight-faced.

Audrey looked at Tony and said, "You know that's not me. I was here in Portland on Friday."

"Sounds to me like we're going to need to verify that Audrey," Tony said without so much of a hint of sounding like sarcasm.

Finally catching on she playfully slapped him on the arm and said, "You called me from there you turd."

"But, I called your cell phone not your office number", he said finally smiling.

Audrey turned back to the image staring back at her. "Uncanny how she does look similar to me. How did I miss that before? Pretty grainy footage though."

"Let's face facts Audrey, you're losing your touch," Tony kidded.

"But, what are the odds..." she said with her words evaporation into thought.

Tony took advantage of the opportunity by saying, "Looks like you have something new you need to add to your report."

Still lost in the visual, Audrey said, "Uncanny isn't it?"

Tony leaned in just a little and asked, "Wouldn't this be better if we discovered it first and not agent Numbnuts?"

Audrey seemed to break out of her spell and said, "What?...yes, of course, you're right. I better get this in right away. Thank you Tony. Would you mind going over this one more time after I submit my report?"

"Why don't you just make me a copy and—" Audrey cut him off.

"I would love to Tony, but you know I can't. Besides you wouldn't be able to open it anyway."

That's what you think. "OK, I understand. Maybe someday," he said.

"Thank you for understanding. I'm sure in due time you will have everything at your disposal," she said comforting him.

Maybe sooner than you think, he mused.

"Well, I hope I helped," said Tony as he got up from his chair.

"Tony, although this POI didn't turn out to be a potential asset, you sped the process along by at least three months."

"Glad to help. Next time let's make sure we aren't in the middle of a war zone, OK?"

Audrey smiled and said, "I will do everything in my power to protect you."

"Thanks. I have to get going. Let me know when you have some self-defense training set up for me."

"I have it on my list. We will get to that in short order," said Audrey.

Not fast enough, he thought.

Once the elevator door closed completely Tony couldn't help but release a few minor facial tics. Tony was really on edge. He went over his justification of copying Audrey's computer hard drive.

If you guys are going to put me in harm's way and not tell me then I'm taking matters into my own hands. It's either that or I'm getting out, he thought.

Tony looked at the elevator numerals descend as he unintentionally tapped his hand on his briefcase knowing the valuable contents inside.

As Tony drove toward home his Smartphone rang. Looking at the screen it showed it to be Jacquelyn. Using his hands-free call system he answered by pressing a button on the steering wheel.

"Hi Jacquelyn. I just got into the car and should be home in about a half hour. How's your day going?"

Complete silence on the other end of the phone. Not even static.

"Jacquelyn?"

Tony's digital dashboard notified him the call ended. He pressed another button on his steering wheel then used a voice command to call Jacquelyn right back. Tony, listening to the fourth ring, was finally placed into voicemail. He ended the call without leaving a message.

She must be trying to call me back, he thought.

After waiting what seemed to be an eternity he realized she wasn't calling back. Using voice command he called her once again. Yet again it went to voicemail. He ended the call without leaving a message.

Maybe she pocket dialed me by mistake. Wouldn't be the first time, he thought.

Tony brushed it off and continued to drive turning on the radio to catch up on the latest sports news. He got home and found the garage door to be open.

Jacquelyn's car isn't here. I wonder if she forgot to close it. Can't be, that's not like her, he thought.

Tony exited his car in the garage and did a quick visual inspection of the garage door opener which is fastened to the finished drywall garage ceiling. His eyes followed the green wire to the press pad next to the door to the house. Tony walked over and pressed the button. He stood watching the ceiling unit rotate as the door began to close. He turned his head to watch if the door was tracking properly. The door closed perfectly.

Hmm, everything seems to be working just fine. Maybe she thought she pressed her remote and was in a hurry. This thing seems to be acting up lately, he thought.

Just before unlocking the door to the house Tony paused and stood frozen looking at the key he was about to insert. Staring, without moving, he thought he heard something in the garage. It sounded like slight movement against a cardboard box.

Tony held his breath as he continued to try and hold his body still. *Is someone in here?* he wondered.

He remembered when he installed the garage door opener unit that he set the light bulb timer to five minutes. Tony had four more minutes of light then the garage would go completely dark. Of course he could flip the light switch, but he wasn't sure if that short amount of time could be the difference between an injury and a fatal injury if someone was indeed in there with him.

Tony's heart began beating rapidly now. He tried to control his breath by very quietly breathing through his mouth. He heard another noise. Tony stopped breathing. His heart pounded inside his chest as if it were trying to punch its way out. This time the sound seemed more like a short quiet hum. He slowly turned to gather in the view of the garage.

Then in a burst of quick movement he saw the flash of color. Tony caught a glimpse of the red blur shoot out from under his car coming straight toward him. He attacked as instinct took control of his body.

Just as he went into a full body leap forward he shifted sideways landing awkwardly against his car. Tony watched as the small remote controlled car was about to slam into the base of the doorway to the house where he had just been standing. Tony instinctively covered his head hoping there wasn't another explosion aiming to take him out.

No explosion. Just impact. Some kind of instinct took over as he quickly stood turning to look everywhere for additional movement within the garage. Looking back at the red RC Racer, wheels still spinning, he recognized the toy car.

It's Nick's! he thought to his surprise.

As he went over to pick the toy up and stop the spinning wheels his phone rang and made him just about jump out of his skin.

Wow! Am I on edge. I'm going to push Audrey for some self-defense training sooner than later, he thought.

Tony fumbled and dropped the car. He pulled the Smartphone from his pocket and quickly answered.

"Jacquelyn," he said breathing hard.

"I'm sorry, am I interrupting your workout?" she asked.

"I wish. Did you try calling me within the last thirty minutes?" he asked.

185

"What's wrong?" she inquired without answering his question.

"It's nothing. I'll explain later," he said.

"OK...I just wanted to tell you Nick was playing with his—"

"Don't tell me. Are you going to say he was playing in the garage with his RC Racer?"

"Yeah, how'd you know? You didn't run it over did you?" Jacquelyn asked in a concerned tone.

"I found it. Or, I should say, it found me. It almost gave me a heart attack."

Jacquelyn laughed. "He wanted to take it to school, but I wouldn't let him. The little stinker tried to sneak it into the car. I was running late so there was no time to put it back in the house. I set the car and the remote next to the large box on the garage floor. I didn't want you to run it over when you got home," she said.

"Well, I found it and I think we owe him a new one," said Tony.

"So you did run it over?"

"I'll tell you about it later," said Tony.

Tony entered the house and locked the door behind him while finishing his call with Jacquelyn. He quickly put that phone away and took out his new personal one. The security system recognized Tony's phone via the Bluetooth signature signal. No alarms would go off unless, of course, he didn't disarm it within two minutes. He did.

Accessing the home security app he quickly roamed the house looking for anything out of the ordinary. In particular he hoped not to see a red dot and hear the beep of someone intruding on their privacy.

All clear, he sighed.

Tony could feel the tension leave his body finally realizing how stressed he had felt. He wasn't sure if it was making a copy of Audrey's hard drive, the garage fiasco or both, but he needed to release just a few quick tics.

What a difference this medication is making for me, he thought.

He realized he had some time to dig into the contents on Audrey's hard drive so he set up shop at his desk. Tony completely unplugged his home Wi-Fi system then flipped the switch on the side of his computer to turn the RS off completely. By turning the Radio Signal switch off his computer now could not be located by any digital means. He further fortified it by plugging into an auxiliary pulse power source. This is the way some hackers practice their craft. If someone was trying to intrude, the power source would jump around like a squirrel jacked up on caffeine.

Once connected to his computer he first scanned the High Speed High Density external hard drive for any type of virus or malicious software. Tony needed to also make sure there wasn't any imaging software or keyboard tracking programs. He ran into this frequently as some companies like to keep track of every keystroke each employee makes. None detected. He re-ran the scans to be sure. It was clean.

Time to log into Audrey's files, he thought while giving his interlocked fingers two quick stretches in front of him.

Chapter 21

—§—

1995

Audrey left the mayhem of the board meeting walking with Ryan O'Connor down the hallway. She knew the meeting could not have gone any better. She smiled on the inside, but showed a face of concern. O'Connor on the other hand was truly beside himself.

"Audrey, I'll catch up and talk to the guys. They were just angry and got caught up in the moment. I can fix this," he said.

She stopped and reached out to touch O'Connor's arm and said, "Tell me something. Did they ever behave like this with Andrew?"

O'Connor's protective side came flooding out and said, "This isn't because of you Audrey. We've had our battles between each other over the years. I can reason with them."

I hope you can't. I'll just have to find another way to eliminate them, she thought. "You would do that for me?" she asked in a concerned tone.

"Of course. We're a good team. A good team doesn't break up in the middle of a crisis," he said gaining a sense of power.

You are such a puppet. But, you're my puppet, she thought.

"Thank you Ryan. I appreciate the effort. Let me know if you make any progress. I'm taking the rest of the day and working from home. I need to prepare just in case you aren't successful," she said.

O'Connor then asked, "Audrey, is it true?"

"Is what true."

"What you said in there. You know, that by resigning eliminates the personal threat of the IRS?"

"Yes."

"Oh. Maybe this could be tougher than I thought," said O'Connor dejectedly.

You're finally catching on, Audrey thought.

"Ryan, you have my word the IRS will not touch you."

"How can you do that for me and not for the rest of the board members?"

"Because you are an employee of CIT and I protect all my employees like family. Especially you," she answered.

"OK. I'll give it a shot, but just so you know I'm not going to mention that you're protecting me."

"Makes perfect sense. As I stand here, and I were one of them, I don't know if I would take my chances against the IRS either. Maybe they made the right decision. Even if Andrew had done something wrong, which I am convinced he did not, they may be dodging a possible reputation attack," she added.

"Yeah, maybe you're right," he said softly.

Of course I'm right. Now get going so I can move on to the next phase of the plan, she thought.

Audrey left the building and walked two blocks to The Cyber Roast Café. A small coffee shop with computer terminals in every booth. She sat in the back left corner facing the street entrance. After ordering her coffee she made sure not a single person could see the monitor as she typed.

The email address used this time is for the Trinity Corporation. Trinity is a legal corporation in the import export market for just about any product imaginable. It is the parent company of a network of growing corporations in a multitude of business sectors. Audrey's goal is to report that phase one is complete. CIT will soon become the next to be welcomed into the fold.

After writing her message, of which she only saved as a draft, she perused the Wall Street Journal as her coffee arrived. Sipping and reading. Really sipping and giving enough time for her contact at Trinity to respond to her latest update regarding her total takeover of CIT.

She set the newspaper down and went back to the draft email folder. Audrey was pleased her draft was replaced with a response. 'Phase two: Begin immediately'.

Audrey wrote one more sentence in another draft. It read: 'I require CIT's Ryan O'Connor to have success and produce a sizable order with the government'. She saved it as a draft once again.

Logging back into the email account a few minutes later, she read the response: 'We will set up a meeting for Mr. O'Connor to see Charles Blackstone in Washington D.C. ASAP. Your Mr. O'Connor will be on his way to becoming very successful. He will be contacted at 10:10am tomorrow to schedule an appointment. Make sure he's available'.

Perfect. But, there has to be a better way to secure our communications. I'll work on that when I get the time, she thought.

The next day Audrey sat in front of O'Connor's desk discussing his marketing plan when his phone rang. He excused himself and answered. Audrey remained seated looking calm, but feeling exited.

"Ryan O'Connor speaking," he said politely.

"Hello Mr. O'Connor, my name is Marcie Decker with the United States Government. I'm calling on behalf of Mr. Charles Blackstone about an inquiry you made a few months back regarding your company's analysis assessment services," she said courteously.

"Oh...yes...hello," O'Connor said sitting up straighter.

"Mr. Blackstone would like to meet with you next week at our Information and Technology Center building here in the D.C. area."

Gathering the information, Ryan quickly scribbled his notes on a piece of paper and said, "Thank you, Marcie. I look forward to meeting you and Mr. Blackstone."

"Mr. O'Connor we are not friends nor even acquaintances yet so if you don't mind please limit the use of my first name at least until we actually meet face to face," she said putting Ryan on the defensive.

"I'm so sorry Ms. Decker. Here in Portland we're—."

"Well this is Washington Mr. O'Connor and you will find simple nuances such as these are very important to the success or failure of your business here. I will place you on Mr. Blackstone's calendar. Be here no later than thirty minutes early. Thank you and I will see you next week. Check in with me first," she said.

"Thank you Ms. Decker. I look forward to meeting you in person and on behalf of CIT I appreciate the opportunity to meet with Mr. Blackstone."

Ryan laid the phone into its cradle on his desk like it was a newborn baby. He paused, looked at Audrey, then stood up and clapped his hands and said, "I did it!"

"Did what? Who was that?" asked Audrey.

"You're not going to believe it!" he said.

I'm so happy to pull your strings Ryan, she thought smiling at him.

"This calls for a celebration," he declared.

"For what?" asked Audrey.

"I'm in. I finally got in to see Mr. Moneybags," he said almost shouting.

"Get an order then we'll celebrate," Audrey said.

It's already arranged, she mused.

"Ryan, it appears you are going to be pretty busy with this potential I think it would be best if you moved back to your regular office. If I need anything I know where to find you," she said.

O'Connor was riding high on cloud nine and barely heard what Audrey said.

"I have a lot of planning to do. You mind if we cut our meeting short, Audrey?"

"Not at all. Let's meet on Friday so you can show me what you are going to pitch to Mr. Blacksmith," said Audrey.

"Blackstone. Not Blacksmith, Ryan said in a somewhat condescending tone."

I know. I've known him for a few years, she thought. "Whatever. Let's stay close and make sure we're on the same page. Alright?"

"You got it boss," O'Connor said effusively.

Right on track, thought Audrey.

O'Connor sat back in his chair and pondered the monumental effect his success could have on the entire company. Audrey got up from her chair in front of O'Connor's desk and walked directly across the room to hers. She picked up the phone and pressed three digits.

"Hi Bonnie, will you or Kelly please remove Mr. O'Connor's desk and re-establish him back into his old office? He's going to work from there from now on." She paused and listened then said, "Today. Thank you Bonnie."

"Audrey, you don't want me working in here anymore? I just got settled in," he said.

"You have plenty on your plate with our new prospect. Your total focus needs to be landing a government contract. I can manage and you're just a phone call away," she said.

"You sure are settling into your new role with ease," said O'Connor.

"Oh? You expected something else?" she asked.

"That came out wrong. I—"

"For someone who has the sales call of his life coming up you have a lot of polishing up to do," Audrey said knowing how to end a conversation.

Within thirty minutes two large men and an IT guy showed up to move O'Connor's things back to his old office. He was happy to return.

Audrey, satisfied she had showed Ryan that she was willing to lean on him, could now count on him to carry out the needed duties he was being paid for…acquire new business among other matters for which it's not necessary that he be aware. She needed her privacy back but, was satisfied that Ryan O'Connor is totally committed to her and CIT. Audrey now needed to focus on a resurrection of sorts.

Chapter 22

—§—

Present Day

Tony took note that Audrey didn't have a single icon on her desktop. He also noticed that she didn't even have a home page picture. His eyes were sharp enough to observe the tiniest little smudge on the upper right corner of the screen he was working from. He took a microfiber cloth and wiped the screen.

Hmm. The smudge is still there, he thought.

Tony grabbed the glass cleaner and gave the monitor a quick spray and wiped it down.

Still there. I wonder if—?

Tony manipulated the mouse and scrolled over the smudged area. The arrow turned from white to semi-transparent. Almost invisible then it reappeared.

What could this be? he wondered.

He moved the arrow over it time after time then let it sit directly on the small area and sat back to try and figure what could be causing this abnormality. After about fifteen seconds of letting it sit he left clicked and got a surprise. A small white pop-up box appeared.

"Ah-ha! An encryption password is required. That is so clever! Because this is a copy it inserted this extra layer of protection. I wonder if this is another one of Audrey's innovations."

Tony entered the password he remembered seeing Audrey enter: 'iamdagger'

Immediately the vacant blue home screen changed to an outdoor picture of a smiling man dressed in a tuxedo standing with a younger looking version of Audrey in a white wedding dress showing on the real home screen. They were holding each other with what appeared to be great affection and joy.

"Well, hello Mr. Andrew Shelton," said Tony.

Not content to think this was the only backdoor Audrey used to access and protect her computer Tony slowly moved the cursor around the screen to try and find another portal into the secret life of Mrs. Audrey Shelton.

"Looks clean," Tony concluded.

Something from his recent past pierced him.

Nothing is really as it seems. When it comes to stuff like this, not a bad creed to live by, he thought.

He started to move on then hesitated. Something in the background of the picture seemed out of place. He leaned in. The focal point of the photo was obvious. However, Tony never took in only the obvious. His instinct to look peripherally almost always paid dividends.

Tony attached a digital automatic magnification scope to look at the background closely. He turned on a second monitor so each area inspected only showed what the scope offered him. It helped him so as not to be distracted to where the human eye is naturally supposed to focus…on the two newlyweds.

Starting at the top left corner of the screen and automatically moving from left to right the scope clearly magnified each quadrant tenfold. As it moved across the foliage in the background Tony saw it. He paused the scope then backed it up just a little. He increased the magnification of the frame just a little more. Tony adjusted the clarity and could not be sure he should believe what he was seeing.

With great scrutiny Tony looked directly into the eyes of a very serious man in the dimly lit background. The man's left wrist was out in front of him just below his chin apparently talking. Tony squinted as he couldn't believe his eyes. He scrolled up and froze the scope on the man's face.

"That's—. He's younger. Is he Secret Service!?" Tony said with his jaw just about to hit the floor.

"Why does Audrey Shelton need to have the secret service protecting her at her wedding?" he said sitting back.

Tony let the scope run the rest of the digital photo and found no other abnormalities. He shook off the surprise he discovered. He already found more than he bargained for. Now was the time to dig into the files.

He found Audrey's folders and files to be very well organized. Each was labeled and almost all of them had subfolders with logical titles and uniformity to them.

That seems like Audrey, but almost too organized. Not a single file mislabeled or out of place. Just too well done from my experience, he thought.

Tony knew about programs that aided in formatting user folders and files, but this didn't match the criteria of those. This was something different all together. It was just too perfect.

Something's up, he decided.

Tony chose a simple folder named 'Finances' then a spreadsheet file labeled 'Funds Transfer' and decided to run it through the Code Protected Transmission program. He located the CPT program opened it then dragged the

197

file to into it. The sands began to swirl and right before his eyes the innocuous spreadsheet changed into what was really written.

He read it silently and without blinking. No small feat for him. Tony could not believe the spreadsheet turned into a document complete with letterhead. When it finished transforming he sat back staring at the monitor. Fear engulfed him as if it could jump off the screen and kill him.

What am I getting myself into? he wondered.

The letter, undated, was from the United States Government. The CIA to be specific, according the bold letterhead seal.

No real names used. Just code names. Addressed to Dagger from Ruido Blanco, he determined.

Ruido Blanco. What kind of name is that? Maybe a foreign operative? Tony wondered.

The letter went on to describe in detail a plan to launder millions of dollars through CIT using an asset named Lehrer. The money was to be split between two offshore banks in very specific yet odd amounts. The account numbers were in code.

I wonder why everything else is clear using the CPT program, but not the account numbers, Tony thought after his initial shock wore off.

Tony chose another folder and file at random and ran it through the CPT program. This time the sands swirled and brought back the exact file with no changes.

Obviously not a coded message, concluded Tony.

"How do I get through all these files without having to take one at a time? There has to be a way to figure out which files are in need of the CPT program and which aren't," he wondered out loud.

Then it dawned on him to look at the two files he had just opened. The extensions of the files were of course different since one was a spreadsheet and one a simple word processing document. After staring at the spreadsheet file name and extension for almost five minutes he became frustrated. Tony tilted his head back clasping his hands behind his head blowing out an exasperated breathe. Then he took a fresh look at the file name again.

"There you are!" he said excitedly.

He looked even closer and realized he was right.

A small dot appears prior to the first letter of the name of the file. A tip of the hat to you Audrey. It's barely even noticeable, he thought.

Tony now had a template to search all files that begin with a dot and cross his fingers they come up coded. His fingers typed quickly then hitting enter he seemed to go into a trancelike state watching both monitors scroll so fast only another computer could keep up. The scrolling finally stopped and the read-out in the bottom left corner of the screen showed one-hundred forty-two files found. Next it was time to put Tony's pre-dot theory to the test.

Opening the first folder entitled 'ALL EMPS' he found a Word document which should list all of the employees who work for CIT. He dragged the file down to the CPT program at the bottom of the page and the sand swirl began.

"I don't believe it. This can't be real," said Tony.

At that precise moment Tony's work phone rang and he just about spilled out of his chair. He looked at caller ID and saw it to be from Nick's school.

"Hello," he answered.

"Hello Mr. James, this is Sandy Johnson at Riverdale Elementary. I'm sorry to bother you."

"Is Nick alright?" he asked deeply concerned.

"He's fine…for the moment."

"I don't understand. What do you mean for the moment?"

"To my knowledge you are working from your home office. Is that right?"

"What does that have to do with Nick," asked Tony quickly losing his patience.

"If you are in fact at home it will help little Nick tremendously," she said in a calm tone.

"Does he need medication or something?"

"There is a piece of paper on your refrigerator with a phone number on it. Wait exactly ten minutes and call the number."

"How would you know what's on my refrigerator?"

"I wrote the note and gave it to your wife."

Tony paused then said, "That doesn't answer my question. Who the hell are you!?"

No answer back. The line went dead. Tony quickly pressed *69.

"Sandy Johnson," she answered in an upbeat tone.

Tony pulled his cell phone away from his ear and glanced at it. Quickly he placed it back so he could speak.

"You're Sandy Johnson?" he asked.

"Yes, how may I help you?" she responded.

Tony paused, held his breath then finally asked, "Did you just try calling me?"

"Well, that depends. Who am I speaking to?"

Oh my God! This is not the same voice of the person who just called me, he thought.

He struggled at first then asked, "Are you Sandy Johnson at Riverdale Elementary?"

"Yes. Who are you?" she asked sternly changing her tone.

Realizing he had a different person on the line he said, "This is Tony James. Nick's dad."

"Oh, Hi Mr. James. We just love your son. He brightens up every room he enters," she said cheerfully.

"I need to speak to Nick right away. It's an emergency."

"We'll round him up. Do you want to hold or take a return call?"

"I'll hold...and don't alarm him," Tony said with authority.

The minutes seemed like hours.

What is going on? he thought.

The sweet little voice came on the line and said, "Dad?"

"Nick. You're OK."

"Yeah. Why are you calling me at school?"

"Nick, have you talked to any strangers today?"

"Nope. But, I met a new teacher. Mrs. Conway said she might not be here tomorrow so she brought in a lady who's gonna be here instead."

Tony, trying to sound calm asked, "Did she give her name?"

"Yeah, but I forgot."

Tony knew better than to grill Nick at the moment then said, "OK buddy. I'll be picking you up from school today so please make sure you wait inside for Sam."

"Aw Dad. I wanna wait for you with Sam outside so we can play," Nick said disappointedly.

"She's going to be waiting for you inside at the front of the building. OK?"

"OK," Nick said in defeat.

"Good. I'll be extra early. You have fun the rest of the day. Will you please put Mrs. Johnson back on the phone?"

After what Tony heard to be a quick hand-off of the phone Sandy Johnson asked, "Are you all set Mr. James?"

"Yes, but I have a quick question. Who's scheduled to be Mrs. Conway's sub tomorrow?"

Sandy quickly accessed the school computer and came back to the phone and said, "Mrs. Conway is not scheduled to be gone tomorrow so there is no substitute scheduled."

"Nick just told me Mrs. Conway introduced her sub to the class for tomorrow."

"Oh, she's not a teacher. She's from the National Teacher of the Year program. We've nominated Mrs. Conway and she's made the first cut so their sending someone from Washington, D.C. here to observe. Nick may not have been listening completely."

"Have you met...wait what did you say her name is?" Tony asked.

"Yes. She was here last week setting things up. Her name is Danielle...Danielle Green."

Tony's mind raced, but his mouth couldn't catch up. He tried to place the name, but just couldn't think straight.

"Are you still there Mr. James?"

"Yes, I'm sorry. Did you say Danielle Green?" he asked awkwardly.

"Are you OK Mr. James? Do you have a concern that we should be aware of?"

If I could only tell you, he thought.

Without directly answering her he asked, "Would it be OK if I also monitored Nick's class for the first half hour tomorrow?"

"I'm sorry, but we don't want to put anymore undue stress on Mrs. Conway. We are so proud of her. Can you come by in the afternoon? Ms. Green said she will only be monitoring in the morning."

"I'll see what I can arrange," said Tony ending the call.

Why does the classroom observer have to be from Washington, D.C. of all places? Tony wondered.

Tony made a bee-line to the refrigerator. He removed the magnet, took a close look at the paper and quickly recognized the style of this handwriting.

"Agent Elizabeth Wolf!" he said with alarm. "But, that wasn't her voice on the phone pretending to be Sandy Johnson. Or was it?"

He looked at his watch and realized he was sixty seconds past his ten minute mark. Tony quickly entered the digits. The phone numerals made their normal sounds then he heard a voice at the other end.

"Trinity Corporation, how may I help you?"

Chapter 23

—§—

1995

Once again sitting in the back corner booth of the Cyber Roast Café Audrey feverishly communicated via the draft email system. This time using a completely different email address. Plotting the next move was more than just crucial. It was monumental in her eyes. She waited for the next new draft email to arrive.

What's taking so long? she wondered.

Something or someone stopped the flow of communication. Audrey reined in her imagination by leaning on her strength which is remaining calm in the face of hysteria. However, given the fast paced give and take that had been interrupted she could only think that something had definitely gone wrong.

Did someone walk in on him? Did he get a phone call? Stop it. Could be anything, she thought.

Finally it arrived with an apology, but no description of the interruption. Audrey read the communication twice to try and figure the meaning. She quite simply didn't understand what was meant to expect a visitor. Audrey eliminated the draft and wrote back asking for clarification.

It came back quickly this time. She didn't realize it, but she held her breath as she read. Sitting back staring out into the street Audrey tried to understand the words her eyes just consumed. The waiter came by and topped off her coffee without even the slightest interest in what she may be doing on the computer. Cyber cafes are built on knowing their customers want privacy.

Her blank stare broke and reflexively she said, "Thank you."

The young waiter simply said, "Uh-huh."

What in the world is going on here! This wasn't part of the plan. We never discussed it, she thought.

She wrote back asking for the reason for the visitor and a change in plan. Once again it was replied to with extreme speed.

"Just do as I'm told?" she whispered as she read the last sentence.

I get it. You're technically my boss, but you're changing the rules in a big way. This isn't how you've conducted operations in the past, she thought with concern.

She wrote back asking who to look for and the reason for the change.

'NOT MY DECISION', were the only words on the screen.

If not yours then who's? You're the head of this entire thing, she contemplated.

She decided to ask and did just that. No rapid response this time.

Maybe just another interruption on his end. I'll wait, she thought.

After checking for the new email draft she found hers still to be unread. Picking up her coffee and sipping while checking her surroundings she noticed a somewhat handsome man she had never seen in the café before.

I would remember him, she thought with an almost expressionless grin.

She always carried The Wall Street Journal in with her and now lifted it up to garner a better look at him. The man was dressed in an ill fitting gray suit, slightly crooked maroon tie and old black shoes that had been shined to someone's best ability. He appeared to be around thirty years of age, but she couldn't count on her estimate. His black mop hair had a touch of gray at the temples which would indicate only two things.

Either he's graying early or he's older than he appears. Who's he trying to fool anyway? she thought.

Audrey set her newspaper down and checked her latest communication. It was gone, but nothing yet in its place.

Thank God. He read it. Hang in here and I'll have my answer in a minute, she thought.

As she waited she became more and more interested in the man in the gray suit.

He seems a little out of place. Terrible spot to sit if he's looking for the best privacy. I wonder why he's here, she thought.

Audrey checked back with her communication and was completely taken by surprise. An instant chat pop-up window had appeared. Nothing written, but instant messaging was not part of their protocol. She quickly ended her internet session.

She deleted all browsing history as well as cookies that could trace her movements while she was utilizing their computer. Audrey returned to the home screen.

Suddenly another instant chat pop-up window appeared. This time it caused her to flush with fear. She knew all instant chat sessions can only be held while online and can be recovered and printed. This came while offline.

'HELLO AUDREY SHELTON'

A box appeared just below it for her to respond. Her instinct was to unplug the computer, but because her name had been used she froze.

'IT'S IMPOLITE NOT TO RESPOND', came another message.

Audrey stared at the words. They pulled her in.

'I KNOW WHO THE VISITOR IS AND WHY THE PLAN HAS CHANGED'

Oh my God! she shouted inside her head. *There should have only been one person besides me who knew I was online. How is this possible? A very competent hacker, that's how*, she deduced.

Audrey calmly picked up her large stylish handbag from the seat next to her. She rummaged both her hands around inside the bag.   She then casually, but very carefully, placed her bag right next to the tower drive computer residing next to her right leg on the floor.

As she moved her bag in place she watched the screen flicker then come back to clarity. She moved the bag once again and the screen looked as it were crying for help before it went completely to a blue screen. It finally read; 'FATAL SYSTEM ERROR'

Always a good idea to have a high powered magnet handy to destroy a computer hard drive, she thought.

She left a tip and exited the café door then turned right.

The man in the gray suit quickly logged off, gathered his things, and was in full pursuit. He had looked up in time and saw which way Audrey went and knew he could catch up with her. He stepped outside, looked down the street, but couldn't find her anywhere. The man began to briskly walk in the direction Audrey went scanning everything in his sight.

Audrey, right after clearing the front windows of the café, hurriedly ducked into the travel agency right next door and took shelter behind a large cutout of the Eiffel Tower. It provided perfect cover and a great view of the street. She watched the man walk by, but couldn't see his eyes as he was now wearing sunglasses.

"Interested in a trip to Paris?" one of the travel agents asked from across the room.

"Just dreaming," replied Audrey pretending to be looking at the cardboard cutout, but taking in the view of the street. Once feeling somewhat safe she said, "I need to powder my nose." She paused then asked, "Will you point me in the right direction?" she asked sweetly.

"All the way back. Last door on your left", said the travel agent quietly.

"Thank you."

Audrey walked through the establishment and exited through the rear door.

Thank God no alarms went off, she thought.

Audrey made her way back to her car at CIT and quickly drove to the airport and entered the newly opened Hertz rental on the third floor of the new parking structure. She had seen the grand opening billboards for this particular Hertz rental location around the city.

"I'm not taking any chances driving my own car knowing someone's on my tail." Then she thought, *I wonder if this guy who hacked the café computer is working alone. Good luck extracting any information from that hard drive*, she thought giving a small grin.

Audrey exited the airport driving a navy blue sedan. The type of car almost nobody is excited to drive because it screams boredom. She drove the car past her house noticing every spec of information she could take in. It had become second nature. Audrey then made another trip after rounding the block so she could see everything from the opposite perspective.

She turned her sun visor sideways to help shield her face. *OK, there he is. I'd recognize him anywhere. I wonder what he wants. He's not a pro that's for sure. Idiot...you stick out like a sore thumb,* she thought.

Audrey went around the block one more time then parked on the same side of the street as the man in the gray suit. Reaching into her bag she brought out small binoculars first to see if anything was unusual at her house. Satisfied to some degree she then focused on the man.

"He's just sitting there alone in plain sight. I don't get it," she said.

Well, in this business a little paranoia isn't a bad thing, Audrey thought.

She felt for her snub-nosed nine millimeter Glock in an inside pocket within her bag then got out of the rented car. Stepping around the back of her rental she placed the straps of her handbag over her right shoulder. Audrey positioned her hand inside with the firearm at the ready. She always has it locked and loaded.

At about fifteen feet away the man in the gray suit shifted and turned his head to the right to look at the passenger side mirror.

Finally, you see me. You can't be that dangerous if you let me walk up to you this close without making a move. And why would you move your head to tip me off while you're wearing sunglasses? Definitely not a pro, she thought.

He rolled down the passenger side window as Audrey walked up and leaned down on the car's open window frame resting her handbag with her right hand inside it.

"Who are you?" she asked sternly.

"Hi, Mrs. Shelton," he said in an upbeat tone.

"I asked you a question," she said sternly.

"I'm sorry. My name is Don Williams," he replied.

"Why are you stalking me?"

"I'm not—."

"I'll ask you again. Why are you sitting across from my house and stalking me," she asked slowly aiming her firearm at him within her handbag.

One false move and you're stalking days are over, she thought.

"I'm not stalking you. I'm the—."

"Answer my question," she said with a discomforting calmness.

"You didn't let me finish. I'm your visitor."

"You're my what?"

"From the email...you're visitor," he said pleadingly gesturing with his hands.

"Take those sunglasses off and put your hands on the steering wheel," ordered Audrey.

He did as he was told. Audrey smoothly opened the passenger door and got in without taking her aim off of him.

"What email?" she asked bluntly.

"I'm not supposed to talk details to you about all this unless we are in a secure location," he said clumsily.

"Very slowly, show me your ID."

He did as he was told and passed her his wallet. Audrey didn't lift a finger.

"Take your driver's license out and slowly hand it to me then place your hands back on the wheel."

"You're talking to me like you're going to do something to me if I don't obey your every command. I don't need this."

He took his right hand off the steering wheel and Audrey moved quickly. She lifted her right hand out from her handbag revealing the Glock.

"I think you do," she said pointing the pistol at his abdomen.

Audrey was trained not to raise a weapon for all to see while appearing to be having a conversation in a car. She certainly was prepared to pull the trigger at any moment, however.

"Wait! You have this all wrong! I was sent here to—.""

"You're right. We shouldn't be having this conversation out in public. Start the car and pull into my driveway. We'll have our conversation in my home," she calmly said still pointing her pistol at his abdomen.

Chapter 24

—§—

Present Day

"Trinity Corporation?" asked Tony with complete surprise.

"How may I help you," asked the female voice on the other end of the line.

Tony took a shot. "Agent Elizabeth Wolf gave me this number regarding a Danielle Green. Can you help me?"

"I'm terribly sorry, but neither of those names comes up in our employee directory. Sir, You must have misdialed."

She ended the call. Tony looked at his phone and verified he certainly had been disconnected.

"That was rude. I'm calling her back and—."

He paused looking at his Smartphone. Something was awfully familiar about that voice. Tony entered the secret side of his phone to find the phone number he called to make his flight arrangements to San Diego.

Who remembers phone numbers anymore? Everything is just one touch and go these days. I never looked at the actual number I've got stored in my phone to call for anything I need from my government job, he thought.

Tony looked the secret number up in the music category. He then looked up the 'Plane White T's'.

Hmm...no phone number is associated with it. I wonder..., he thought.

He pressed send and listened for the numerals to make their digital tones. Then a voice answered.

"Trinity Corporation. How may I help you?"

Same voice! he thought.

"Eighteen - One – Four – One - Eighteen," said Tony. He paused then said, "Romeo - Alpha - Delta - Alpha - Romeo."

Once again there was a brief silence and clicking within the connection then the woman said, "Radar, please confirm status."

"I am secure and contained."

"Line is secure…go ahead."

"I need to confirm we have an agent named Danielle Green."

After a brief pause the woman said, "I cannot provide you with any information to your inquiry," she said flat-toned.

"Can't or won't?"

"I cannot provide you with any information to your inquiry," she said once again.

"OK, I get it. I need to reach agent Elizabeth Wolf," said Tony.

Again she said, "I cannot provide you with any information to your inquiry."

"Who do I need to contact to reach her?" asked Tony. "And please don't say you can't provide that information."

"Radar, please contact your handler to resolve your inquiry. Do you require anything else?" she asked.

"No, thank you."

"Terminating communication sir," said the woman.

The line went dead.

Well, at least I verified the phone number the substitute teacher gave to Jacquelyn is the very same as the one I have stored in my phone. Does that mean she works for SSD or some other alphabet agency? he wondered.

Tony called Sam's school and verified she was in class.

Sam is very in tune with the nuances of unspoken emotion. I better not talk with her. She'll think something's wrong and grill me and I don't want her to worry. I'll leave a message to meet Nick inside the main entrance of his school. I'll get there extra early, he decided.

"Please don't tell me you can't pick the kids up," Jacquelyn said answering her phone.

"Well, hello to you too," said Tony.

"I'm sorry. It's been a rough day. I don't have much time right now," she said.

"Then very quickly, do you remember what that substitute teacher looked like that was in your room? You know, she's the one you also saw at Nick's school."

"Yes. Why?"

"I thought you didn't have much time and this could take some time to explain," he said.

"About five-seven and slender."

"Anything a little more specific?" he asked.

"Roughly our age. Maybe a few years younger. Long red hair. Dressed professionally. Why?"

"I know you're busy. I'll explain at home tonight."

"OK. Put that away."

"Huh?"

"Not you...one of my students. I really have to go. I'm so sorry Tony."

"Don't apologize. You have a job to do. I'll see you later. I love you."

"You too," she answered not letting on who she was speaking with.

It's got to be her. Well Danielle Green or agent Wolf you will not be happy to see me in the morning.

The next day Tony got ready with a determined mind-set. Tony had spared Jacquelyn the details of his conversation with the fake Sandy Johnson. He felt guilty about it, but didn't want her to worry.

He watched Sam run into school with her best friend Stephanie. Tony then drove over to Nick's school parking lot.

"Why are we parking here Dad?"

"I get to join you in class this morning."

"Really!? Are you the parent helper today?"

Tony thought about that and said, "Yes I am."

Last night Tony entered the school computer system and placed his name on the 'Parent Assistant' list and rescheduled Mrs. Brandt. He walked Nick into school, signed in, then right into the classroom. Tony kept an eye on Nick while also searching for Danielle Green.

"Good morning Mr. James. Is there something I can do for you?" Nick's teacher asked.

"Yes. I'm your classroom helper this morning. Do you have anything specific in mind for me?"

"I'm sorry, but I don't think you're on the schedule for today. Let me check the list," she said uncomfortably. As she brought up the list of parent helpers on her classroom computer she said, "I guess I should apologize. I must have misread the schedule for today. I thought Mrs. Brandt was coming in today. You are on the schedule. I think I'm losing my mind."

"That's OK. Simple mistake. Happens to us all," said Tony.

"We have a special guest coming this morning so all I really need you to do is sit in the back and make sure the children are behaving themselves."

"I guess I picked a good day to volunteer. Who's the guest?"

"Her name is Danielle Green. She's from Washington D.C. The Department of Education," she said excitedly.

"Wow!" Tony said pretending to also be exited.

"Apparently she's looking for ways to improve classrooms all over the country and she wants to visit us."

"Congratulations. That's quite an honor. How did this come about?" Tony asked trying to fill the gaping hole of information.

"I attended a meeting with Principle Blake and he told me he received a request about it," she said.

"By phone or email?" asked Tony.

"He showed me the email and obviously then phone conversations took place after that."

Email...good to know. I can track that if I need to, thought Tony.

"So he verified that this person is really from The Department of Education?" asked Tony.

"Of course. She has been on campus a couple of times already," she said looking at Tony with a slight awkwardness.

Tony sat in the back as instructed. More and more children entered the room until it was at full measure. Mrs. Conway announced to the children to take their seats.

She announced, "Nick's dad is our parent helper today and is sitting in the back of the room."

Tony gave a small wave to the kids.

"I need you each to behave extra well today. A special guest from our nation's capital will be joining us this morning," she said with a great amount of pride in her voice.

The bell rang. Mrs. Conway looked at the classroom clock, then the door and without hesitation turned on the Smart Board projecting a map of the United States.

Teachers are so prepared. Mrs. Conway obviously pre-planned for the possible tardiness of her guest, thought Tony.

Just as she asked her students who knows where the District of Columbia is located came a quiet one knuckled knock at the door. As soon as Tony saw the arm swinging the door open Tony got a powerful feeling. With only the hand on the doorknob and the arm revealed he was pierced by the word... *Understudy*. It opened slowly and today's special guest entered. Tony sat up as if ready to pounce.

Agent Elizabeth Wolf! How can that be? I don't get different words for the same person, he thought. *She's dressing the part at least, wearing an upscale pant suit perfect for the occasion. But, why would she be here. Does she know I needed to talk with her?*

Mrs. Conway welcomed her warmly and then introduced her to the students. "Class, this is Ms. Green. She's with the Department of Education all the way from Washington D.C. The purpose of her visit is—."

"Mrs. Conway, would you mind if I jumped in at this point?" she asked politely.

"Oh...of course not," replied Mrs. Conway stepping back.

Agent Wolf turned looked out into the bright wonder filled eyes of the children and said, "Good morning boys and girls. My name is Ms. Green. You may call me Danielle if it's all right with Mrs. Conway."

Mrs. Conway gave a gentle smile and a single nod.

She hasn't even noticed me yet. Wait until she does, thought Tony with anticipation.

"I'm here today to celebrate with you!"

Mrs. Conway gave a confused look.

"Of all the teachers in your city. Of all the teachers in the great state of Oregon. Of all the teachers in this wonderful country of the United States of America, Mrs. Conway has been chosen as...Teacher of The Year!"

The children erupted with cheers. The door to the classroom opened once again with Principle Blake leading a group of distinguished visitors wheeling in a cake on a table about ten feet long. Candles already lit and shimmering as they traveled. Among the guests are Mayor Grant and even Governor Dawson. A photographer followed in behind.

Sorry, but I didn't vote for either of you, Tony thought regarding the politicians.

After the official award had been presented the festivities of divvying up the cake brought the excitement to a new level of chaos to the classroom. Other teachers showed up while their own parent helpers stayed with their students.

Danielle Green finally took notice of Tony standing in the back of the room. Their eyes locked long enough for her to give him a vacant nod while she continued to smile.

Finally! She got around to noticing that I'm here. But, something's not right. Those are not the same eyes of the agent Wolf I know. Well same color and all, but something is very different, he decided. *'Understudy' instead of 'actress'. I wonder why? She looks the same, but there certainly is something different about her. Maybe 'understudy' and 'actress' really mean the same thing and I'm just imagining things,* he thought.

Out in the hallways the chatter and footsteps of children could be heard. Another women with a slightly bewildered look on her face entered the classroom and whispered into Mrs. Conway's ear. Mrs. Conway's smile barely lessened as she listened.

Mrs. Brandt I presume?

Principle Blake announced, "Everyone form a single line. We are all go to the gym to and celebrate with the rest of the school."

Tony kept his eyes on Danielle Green. He wasn't sure who it was standing in the front of the room. As the classroom finally cleared he found himself following just behind today's guest. They were the last two to begin exiting the classroom. She stopped suddenly. Shut and locked the door. It was only she and Tony left in the room.

Chapter 25

—§—

1995

Audrey didn't let the man in the gray suit say another word until they were both inside her house. She used her gun to point where her visitor should sit.

"Now...tell me your real name," she said sternly.

"I already did. I'm Don Williams. That's my real driver's license. I was sent here to help you with ongoing operations from a technical aspect. Will you please point that thing in another direction?" he pleaded staring at the gun.

"Why did you hack the computer at the café'?"

"That was stupid. I was trying to impress you. I thought if I impressed you it would be a good thing," he said.

"Are you that stupid?" asked Audrey.

"Look, I'm just an IT guy in a new job trying to make a good impression. I'm really sorry. OK?"

Audrey looked at him unflinchingly for a few more seconds then lowered her firearm.

"I think you're telling the truth, but I don't trust you. I'm going to verify what you've said."

The man in the gray suit relaxed just a little now that he wasn't looking down the barrel of a gun. Audrey then raised her pistol once again.

"In that drawer." She pointed with her left hand at the top left drawer of the desk. "You'll find a roll of duct tape. I see you wear your watch on your left wrist. Are you right handed?"

"Yes," he said timidly.

"Then place your right arm on the arm rest and tape it to the chair."

He did as she asked. Once this was accomplished Audrey quickly secured his left arm. She taped his feet together at his ankles.

"Now, just sit there while I check to see if you are who you say you are."

She rolled the man to the center of the room then stood at her computer terminal to logon to her secret email account. She went into another room to quietly call and verify his story. Audrey never took her eyes off him while on the call.

"Alright. It appears you're telling me the truth. Just one thing though. Why on earth would you compromise both of us with your little hacking stunt in the café?"

"I was trying to impress you and I didn't compromise anything or anyone," he said sincerely.

"How can you sit there and tell me that, you imbecile!"

"I used a third party IP digital scrambler."

"Exactly my point! Who's the third party?" Audrey asked stingingly.

"You are," Williams said succinctly.

"How in the world can I be the third party when I was your target?" she asked as if this guy has so much to learn.

"Before you entered the Cyber Café I installed the software on the computer you used."

"See, that's my point. How could you possible know what computer I would use?"

"Because I had been put in charge of monitoring your digital footprint and that is the terminal you always use when at the café," he said without even the slightest hint of smugness.

Audrey paused and looked at this man in a new light then asked, "Why are you here exactly?"

"Would you mind"? he asked looking at the duct taped on his arms and ankles.

"I'll cut the tape after you answer my question," she said.

"I'm here to finish your cyber training," he said as if waiting for an eruption.

"You? You are going to train me?" she asked with slight laughter.

"Yes," Williams said flatly.

Audrey looked at him for a long pause. *Either he must be very good or they wouldn't send him here or he's as bad as his first impression. If the latter is true I will boot him back to Langley in no time*, she thought.

As Audrey cut the duct tape she said, "I'm sorry I had to treat you this way."

Relieved he said, "You didn't have to treat me like this, but I get it. I was told to report back how you handled this situation."

"Are you serious!?"

"Dead serious."

"Well skip the part about the duct tape will you?"

"Actually, I think they would like to hear you took a precaution like that."

She looked at him with a new set of eyes. *He's been given more information and control than I thought.*

Audrey put her hand out as if waiting for a reciprocating handshake. "Fresh start. I'm Audrey Shelton. Nice to meet you Mr. Williams."

Williams looked at her with skepticism, but was courteous and replied, "Nice to meet you Mrs. Shelton."

"OK then. From here on out you help me complete my cyber training and I will let you stay here until we're done. OK?"

"I don't want to put you out—."

"I'm not letting you show your face to anyone around here. So, here is where you will stay and here is where my training takes place. We'll start first thing tomorrow morning," she said as the final word on the subject.

Don Williams just nodded and thought; *This is working out better than I had expected.*

The next day came quickly and Audrey placed an egg timer on the desk where her cyber training would take place.

I can't afford to have this greenhorn waste my time, she thought.

To her surprise Williams was already up and had his first cup of coffee.

"I hope you don't mind, but I made coffee," he said vaguely making a point.

"Let's get down to work," she replied.

They both sat at her desk in the den. Audrey was pleasantly surprised to know Williams had done his homework. She was no newbie to the workings of computer technology. Not just the legal methods anyway. Williams broke the ice by not treating her as his student or trying to take a superior role. He played it right. They were equals moving toward a target together.

The egg timer went off.

"What's that for?" Williams asked.

"Time's up for now," she said.

"What am I supposed to do the rest of the day?" he asked.

"Wait until I get back. I've got a computer company to run. Remember?" she said testing his resolve.

"So, one hour in the morning and that's it?" he asked.

"You catch on pretty quick."

"But, we should be working all day and into the evening—"

Audrey put her hand up and said, "I've got more on my plate than you can imagine. So, when I get back we will resume. OK?"

I know exactly what's on your plate, but I'll play along, he thought.

"All right. When can I expect you back?"

"When I walk through the door," said Audrey as she left the room.

"What am I supposed to do all day?" he yelled.

"You'll figure it out," she said as the back door shut on her way out.

"OK. Well I'm not under any communication restrictions like you," he said to himself.

Don Williams got up and watched Audrey back out of her driveway and zip down the street. He poured himself another cup of coffee and went to work on a project that he thought just might draw some positive attention. And not just from Audrey.

Williams casually snooped around Audrey's computer files for awhile and found nothing but a boatload of CIT work related material.

Everyone has secrets. I wonder where she keeps hers? It might be better if I don't find anything about the secret life of Audrey Shelton at the moment. Finding myself nose to nose with a Glock isn't my idea of fun, he thought.

"I need an extra hard drive," he said to himself. There's got to be a local computer store around here."

Williams found the yellow pages and drove to the local Radio Shack and picked up a new Western Digital hard drive and a few other necessities. He paid in cash which he was given before he left the East Coast. Upon returning to Audrey's house he got right down to work.

Within an hour it looked as if Audrey's computer was hooked up on life support. Wires and clips hanging from everywhere. After writing code for three hours Williams finally took a quick break for lunch.

He buckled down once again at the computer and then beta tested his newest invention. Williams wrote two separate short paragraphs using Audrey's word processor program and saved each as a separate document on his new hard drive. He then dragged the first one into his new program he had minimized located at the bottom of the screen. At first he was disappointed as nothing happened. Then suddenly the document began to disappear as the screen began to look like it was dissolving. Once the document was completely devoured it re-appeared by reversing the pixels until it reveled what was really written. He sat back and smiled.

Excited he said, "This is like writing with invisible ink! Now all communication can be run through my new program without anyone having to know what's really written. A perfectly innocent email attachment or letter can be sent without having to worry about the true content being discovered. This is so cool! This should give me an edge with not just Audrey Shelton, but everyone back east. This is just the thing I need to position myself to move in any direction I want if I play my cards right. What am I talking about? I always play my cards right."

What should I call it? Their so big on everything using the alphabet. How about 'The WPP'? 'The Williams Protocol Program'. I love it! That'll get me noticed!

Williams installed the WPP on Audrey's computer so she can be the first to use it in the field. He knew it would have to be approved first, but it just might change her first impression of him.

I have to copy this program and code it so it can self install on the recipient's computer so the real communications can read exactly as it had been written. Makes no sense to only have one computer with the program, he thought.

It only took him an additional hour to accomplish this and get Audrey's computer back to not looking like its guts were hanging out. He was about to send the WPP when he heard Audrey pull into the driveway.

228

Entering through the back door Audrey shouted, "Williams! I'm home! How was your day of watching the soap operas!?"

She entered the den and found Don Williams exactly where she thought he'd be. On the couch watching TV.

"I can't believe they hired you. Couldn't you think of anything else besides watching TV to keep your mush brain alive?"

Williams took it all in. He knew how he was going to angle his way into Audrey Shelton's heart.

"How was your day?" he asked.

"Fine. I'm going to quickly eat then let's get back to my cyber training and you can get the hell out of here," she said dismissively.

"Mind if I join you?" he asked.

Audrey didn't answer. Williams turned the TV off and followed her into the kitchen and they both ate sandwiches while standing. He tried small talk, but Audrey just wouldn't engage.

"OK. Let's get back to it," ordered Audrey.

Williams quickly finished and once again found himself following in Audrey's wake.

"Before we get back to your training, would you mind if I show you something I created today?"

"Did you carve a letter opener or something?" Audrey asked in a patronizing tone.

"I think you'll like this," Williams said pulling the chair out for Audrey to sit down at the computer.

"Thank you," she said sort of mumbling.

"I got to thinking about the way you were communicating at the café today and how easy it was to piggy back and see what you were doing," he started.

"Well, isn't that why you're here? To teach me the skills to do just those types of things?"

"It is, but I think you might like this a little more," he said calmly.

Williams had Audrey create a short paragraph using her word processing program. Then he asked her to locate a simple CIT document anywhere within her computer files and open it.

"Where is this leading?" Audrey asked impatiently. "Now what," she asked still impatient.

"Just let the program open then I'll instruct you," he said.

The WPP opened and Williams said, "Now minimize it."

Audrey did as instructed.

Williams knew this was when he was going to make a name for himself. He kept his tone soft and his instructions clear.

"Drag this document down to the minimized WPP and that will do it."

Audrey sighed, but did as instructed.

As the screen began to dissolve the document into tiny pixels Audrey said, "What did you do to my computer!"

The document disappeared.

Audrey began to stand thinking he destroyed her computer and said, "If you infected—"

She stopped as the pixels began to reverse themselves.

"What the—"

The document that she wrote appeared. She stared at the computer screen. Slowly she looked up at Williams then back to the document on the screen.

"What just happened!?"

"You just experienced the newest evolution in agency communication technology," Williams said proudly.

It wasn't lost on Audrey exactly what she just saw. "So you brought and installed a program that lets me write what I really want to write then use this program to conceal it? That's genius!"

"Well, you're right about it being genius, but wrong on your premise," he said.

"What do you mean?"

"While you were gone today I made myself useful and created the Williams Protocol Program," he said proudly.

"You did this just today?"

"Yes."

Audrey pinpointed the exact need of this new program and asked, "If I'm sending this to someone else won't they need to have the program to open the real document?"

"Yes."

"Then this is the dumbest program I've run across in a long time," she chastised.

"That's why I also wrote code to automatically send a copy to the recipient so they can use it immediately."

Audrey stared at Don Williams for what seemed to be an overly long uncomfortable period. She realized what an incredible asset this computer geek truly is. She began to grin. It grew into a full blown smile.

"You are going places Mr. Don Williams! I intend to be at your side along the way," she said excitedly.

"Thank you Mrs. Shelton."

"No. Thank you and please call me Audrey."

Chapter 26

—§—

Present Day

She stood no more than a foot from Tony after she locked the classroom door. Her action took Tony by surprise. He stepped back. The only two in the classroom.

"What are you doing here Elizabeth?" asked Tony.

The attractive redhead stood perfectly still and looked deep into Tony's eyes as if she were searching for some sign of pre-cognition.

"Are you just going to stand there and stare? What the hell are you doing here?" he asked sternly.

She continued her stare.

Suddenly it hit him. "You're not agent Wolf are you!?"

"No, I'm not," she said with a slightly sharper tone than Elizabeth.

"But, you look just like her," he said half stunned.

"You're quick. Identical twins do have that reputation. Personally, I don't see it. She has a small birthmark the shape of Florida on her neck and I don't," she said slightly tilting her head while wearing a wry grin.

Tony froze and peered deeply to see if this really was agent Wolf the actress.

"Are you just going to stare at me or can we have a conversation," she asked.

Tony snapped out of his gaze and said, "OK, but who are you?"

"My real name is not important, but you can refer to me as Danielle Green for our purposes."

"You visited my bride's classroom and gave her a phone number to call if she needed a substitute teacher. I don't understand. Is this some kind of training for me or something," said Tony.

"Bride. What an interesting way of saying ball and chain. The two of you have been married for some time now. I think it's time you appropriately call her your wife. By the way she's gorgeous. You're a lucky guy. Ever get tired of her?" she asked tilting her head to the other side.

"What do you want?" he demanded.

"Well, I'm staying in town for a while and I wouldn't mind your company from time to time," she said inching toward him.

Tony stepped back and said, "Hold on! What do you think you're doing?"

"Afraid of a little attention Tony?"

As if a light switch had been flipped Tony realized this woman seemed to know exactly what she was doing.

This is a tactic. Nothing more and nothing less. Let's see how she responds to a counter attack, he thought.

Stepping so close and looking down into her eyes he softened his voice and calmly asked, "Where are you staying?"

She slipped to her left and replied, "I'm around."

"You are so transparent thinking you can come at me thinking I'll bite on this sexy come-on from you. What do you really want?" he asked directly.

"Oh. So you do think I'm sexy," she said in a mischievous tone.

"Nice try. Now answer my question," Tony said turning his frame toward her.

"Well, your file doesn't do you justice," she said in a more business-like tone.

"My file? Are you—?"

"No. I'm not directly with the Agency if that's what you were going to ask. I don't have much time right now. I have to be in the gymnasium to present the award in just a few minutes. Will you meet me afterwards to talk?"

Tony paused and said nothing.

"I think you'll be very interested in what I have to tell you," she said beginning to move back toward the door.

An identical twin sister. Agent Wolf said nothing about having a twin sister. What's this all about? This doesn't pass the smell test. I certainly don't trust her, he decided.

"No. I won't meet with you."

She reached for the door and just before opening it she said, "Your bride really is very pretty. I'd hate to see anything happen to that lovely face of hers," she said in an ominous tone.

Danielle Green quickly slipped out the door and began briskly walking down the school hallway knowing she just picked a fight with a very dangerous man. Didn't matter if he knew it yet or not.

Tony stepped into the doorway and watched her move quickly down the hall. He decided not to go after her and grab her by the neck and drag her outside for threatening Jacquelyn. He was stunned. Tony let her slip away for the moment.

I better catch up with her and not let her out of my sight. I'll meet with her in the gym right after the award ceremony. Nobody threatens my family and gets away with it! he decided.

As Tony walked toward the gymnasium he entered his code into the secret portion of his Smartphone. Tony knew he couldn't let anyone hear his conversation so he stepped back into the hall for a moment.

"Well hi there," said Audrey answering her Smartphone without using Tony's name.

"I am NOT secure or contained," he said seriously.

Audrey sat straight up in her CIT office chair and said, "Urgent matter?"

"Yes. At my son's school. I need help."

"On my way. Communicate via text from here," said Audrey.

"Confirmed," said Tony ending the call.

He stepped back inside the gymnasium to keep his eye on Danielle Green. As Tony opened the door and saw the entire place decorated like a pep rally. His eyes scanned the dais and found Danielle Green.

With Smartphone in hand he wrote a text to Audrey looking up every few seconds to make sure as not to lose sight of Ms. Green. His instructions to Audrey were to sign in at the school entrance, showing a digital camera to get her past security, then go directly to the gym. He pressed send.

A light bulb went on and Tony thought *a camera.* *What was I thinking? I almost forgot...I have one in my hand*, he thought.

Tony lifted his Smartphone, zoomed in on Danielle Green and took two pictures of her. He sent one off in a text to Audrey typing; 'TARGET'

While driving, Audrey opened the text and glanced at the photo. She pulled her car over and used her index finger and thumb to expand the photo Tony just sent.

What's agent Wolf doing there! I thought she's on vacation. How can she be a threat to Tony? she wondered.

Audrey texted Tony back; 'AGENT WOLF IS THE TARGET?'

Beginning to drive again Audrey waited for Tony's response. It finally came.

'NOT AGENT WOLF - NAME IS DANIELLE GREEN'

This time Audrey not only stopped her car, but nearly felt her heart stop.

Dannie? This can't be! she thought.

She looked at the photo again. Made a decision. She texted Tony; 'BIG PROBLEM - CAUGHT IN TRAFFIC'

Tony felt his phone vibrate in his hand. A new text from Audrey. He read it and didn't understand.

How can you be caught in traffic this time of day? Maybe there's an accident. Of all days when I need her here most. Well, I'll just have to handle this on my own, he decided.

Immediately after deleting Audrey's text Tony looked up and saw Danielle Green looking at her phone. She looked up then slunk over to Principle Brenner and whispered into his ear showing him her phone. He nodded his head and Danielle Green walked directly out the door on the opposite side of the gym as Tony. She nodded to the photographer and he went the other way.

She's leaving! I have to get to her! She won't get away with threatening Jacquelyn! he thought.

Tony exited the doorway where he was standing. Walked into the hallway then around the corner where Danielle Green had left, but found absolutely no sign of her anywhere.

The exit door! he shouted in his head.

He opened the door outward and took one step outside before he fell flat on his face as if he had been struck by lightning. Danielle Green, hiding behind the now open door Tasered Tony. She didn't wait around for him to stop quivering like a fish out of water. He never knew what hit him.

It took Tony more than a few minutes to begin to return to normalcy. He pushed himself up from the grass feeling totally disoriented and a sharp pain in his back.

"Damn it! How could I be so stupid!?"

He pulled on the electrical wires like ripping off a bandage. His back arched as the claws drew blood as they pulled from his flesh.

"Jacquelyn! I have to get to Jacquelyn," he said almost incoherently.

He looked around as he got up brushing himself off and then said, "Oh no...Nick!"

The door he exited from had been shut and didn't offer a doorknob from the outside. An obvious precaution for the school. Tony had to hoof it to the front of the school and re-enter at that point.

Once inside he saw the award ceremony was now over as children and adults alike were scattering in all directions. He darted for Nick's classroom dodging everyone in his path.

Peering through the corner of the classroom window he saw Nick calmly seated at his desk.

Thank God he's alright, he thought.

Next Tony looked for Audrey. Grabbing his phone he saw it had no power.

"The Taser," he said.

"What Taser?" asked a familiar voice.

"Audrey! Thank God you made it. I have to warn Jacquelyn—"

"Hold on Tony," Audrey said trying to pull him back to normal speed. "First tell me what's going on."

Tony and Audrey found an empty classroom to talk. He quickly filled her in completely. That is up until he got his brains scrambled.

"Are you sure it wasn't agent Wolf just playing another role? She's one of the best."

"At the moment I can't be 100% sure of anything. But, I remember that even before she entered Nick's classroom I felt her presence. Do you remember what word is attached to agent Wolf?"

"Yes, you said actress. Like I said maybe she was just playing another role or something we weren't told about," Audrey said.

"You're right about the word actress when it comes to agent Wolf. But, the word that came to me today was *understudy*."

Audrey nodded her head slightly from side to side as she said, "Actress...Understudy. One in the same to me."

"Feels completely different to me," said Tony.

"Are you sure you're thinking straight? Your back is still bleeding a little."

"I think I'm fine. No telling for sure. I have to be certain Jacquelyn is protected."

"I'm already on it."

"But, then she'll know," he said absentmindedly.

Audrey raised one eyebrow and said, "So you haven't told her about your new job after all."

"Scrambled brain or not I have to protect Jacquelyn!"

"Aren't you forgetting someone else? asked Audrey.

"Huh?"

"Samantha. Your daughter?" she said calmly.

"Oh my God! My brain is still off!"

"Sit down and don't worry. I have sent people over to take care of both of them," said Audrey.

"But, that will just freak Jacquelyn out!"

"Not the way we handle it," Audrey said confidently.

"What do you mean?"

"Audrey put her hand on Tony's shoulder and said, "Trust me."

Tony searched Audrey's eyes to find a reason not to then said, "You mean trust you like the explosive trip to San Diego?"

"Not now Tony. We can discuss that at another time. Right now security for your family is the primary concern."

Tony thought about it then quietly said, "OK."

Just then Audrey took her hand off Tony's shoulder and touched her ear. She looked off in the distance for a few moments then spoke into a transmitter on her left wrist.

"Affirmative."

Audrey looked back at Tony and said, "Your family is accounted for. Everyone is keeping their distance so Jacquelyn, Samantha and Nick have no idea they are being watched."

Tony let out a quick burst of breathe he didn't realize he had been holding in. He seemed to be coming around a little bit more.

"Hey! What about me?"

"What about you?" asked Audrey.

"Who's watching over me?"

"The best person for the job...me," she said with a warm smile.

"Tony, we need to put you through a crash course."

"On self-defense?"

"Most people would call it that. However, I want to take it a step further. Cancel everything you have going for the next few days. I'll get you the details, but you need to start tomorrow morning."

"After today…the sooner the better," said Tony.

"You seem to be thinking better now. Tell me about what happened here today."

Tony filled Audrey in regarding everything from the time he set foot in Nick's school to the present. He provided very specific details about his encounter with Danielle Green. Tony also had a few questions about her, but kept them to himself for now.

"I made a call about the picture you texted while I was on my way over here. Our database came up empty as far as any covert activities are concerned. She really is with The Department of Education," she said.

"I've learned that means nothing. You're the CEO of a successful corporation. I doubt you would let anyone share information about you. Would you?"

"No, I suppose your right. You think she has a connection other than just The Department of Education?"

"I have no doubt she does. I think I need to take her up on meeting with her while surrounded by agency people for my protection," he said.

"You're not ready for something like that Tony."

"Well, starting tomorrow morning I'll be more ready than I was today," he said reaching over his shoulder feeling the insert points from the Taser hooks.

Chapter 27

—§—

1995

Audrey treated Don Williams so well over the next couple of days after he had designed his new communication program. He accomplished his goal of impressing Audrey and she was so thankful that she became a tireless student for him.

"Well, Audrey, I can't think of another thing that I could possibly teach you. How did you become such a quick student of cyber tactics?"

"Simple. You just had to gain my trust and, as you can see, I have a little natural ability," she answered.

"You have that and then some! No wonder why you were tapped to run a computer technology company. Well, at least that's your cover, anyway. But a good one."

He doesn't know the whole story, she thought.

"Are you heading back to Langley from here?" she asked.

"No, my brother lives in Los Angeles and I'm going to try and visit him."

"Oh? You never mentioned you have a brother. Is he as good as you?"

"Audrey, you're one of the good guys so keep this between you and me. I learned everything I know from him. He's a genius with anything related to computers."

"What's his name?"

"Sefter," said Williams.

Audrey made a funny face and said, "Sefter?"

"He changed his given name years ago," Williams said a little embarrassed.

"Is Sefter now his first or last name?"

"It's just Sefter. It's his first and last name. Just…Sefter."

"What was it before he changed it?"

"Theodore"

"Are you kidding me!? Your parents actually named him Ted Williams? Did your father have a baseball dream he couldn't live up to?" she said with a laugh.

"Now you know one of the reasons why he changed it."

"Why Sefter? And did you say you are going to *try* and see him?"

"Long story, Audrey. You know how family can be."

"What's he do for a living?"

"His real job or how he makes his money?" Williams asked back.

"Either one," said Audrey hoping for the latter.

"In his legitimate job he's a program analyst for an investment firm.

She paused then asked, "And that's how he makes a living?"

"How he makes his real money, and he's loaded by the way, he writes certain types of financial programs that people like you and me frown upon. He was busted as a thirteen year old for hacking into the Chicago Mercantile Exchange. Man, were my parents pissed!"

"I can imagine!" said Audrey soaking in the information.

"He was an early adopter of the whole child emancipation thing," said Williams.

"So he left home at a young age?" she asked.

"No. He failed to win his case because he hacked into the Justice Department and erased his record. Had he just left well enough alone he probably would have succeeded."

"So if someone looks him up in the phone book—"

"Yup. He's the only Sefter in the world. But, you won't find him in any phonebook," Williams said smiling and shaking his head. "He doesn't play well with others," he grinned.

Sefter. Good to know, thought Audrey.

"You want another cup of coffee, Don?"

"Sure"

As Audrey poured she asked, "So, how did you come to work for the government?"

"My dad pretty much pointed me in that direction. After my brother had his troubles he was dead set on one of us becoming respectable in his eyes."

"I get that, but did you know someone in a position to give you a job within your chosen field?"

"My dad set up an interview, but from there it was all me," he said with a slight edge.

"Sorry, I didn't mean anything by—"

Williams cut her off saying, "Sorry, I guess I'm just a little sensitive when it comes to my dad."

"Why is that?"

"My father wasn't the best role model in the world. He'd be gone for up to a month at a time leaving me, my mom and brother to fend for ourselves."

"What's his line of work?"

"More like what *was* his line of work."

"What do you mean?"

Williams had a distant look as if he were off in another time and place. He heard Audrey's question, but just slipped into the past. Williams then heard Audrey's voice bringing him back to the present.

"Was he fired or something?" she asked.

Slowly, Williams gathered his thoughts and replied, "Let's not dig up old bones right now. What about you? How did you come to work for the Company?"

Audrey shut him down quickly by saying, "You know that's classified." She read an emotional change in Williams and said, "Let's just say I was recruited."

Williams nodded as if he knew what that entailed and said, "Enough said. I know we shouldn't be talking about this right now. However, I now completely get why you're so good with cyber tactics. Who trained you initially?"

"You wouldn't know the person if I told you," she said hoping to dodge the question.

"I know a lot of people. Try me."

"Let's leave this subject for another time as well. Agreed?"

"Agreed. I'm sorry, but I don't get to talk about work with anyone."

"I understand. It can get lonely. When you get back to Langley I want you to look up a man named Jeff Statz. He'll be a good person for you to know as you progress in your career. I'll call him for you while you're visiting your brother, or rather, attempting to visit your brother."

Williams tried not to, but his back went straight as he sat and his eyes opened very wide. He caught himself, but not before Audrey took notice.

"Do you know Jeff Statz?" she asked.

"I've only heard his name," he lied. *She knows my dad. How high up are her connections?* he wondered.

Audrey knew all too well she had hit a nerve, but elected to let it go for now. She needed to get back to work and Williams had completed his training with her. She would dig into the connection between Don Williams and Mr. Jeff Statz at another time.

Williams set his coffee down and said, "Well, it's time I better get going. Hopefully my brother will be waiting for me. It sure has been a pleasure getting to know you Audrey."

"Likewise and I'm really sorry to have mistaken your intentions at first."

"Are you kidding me? I was told you were good. I just didn't know how good. It's been a real eye opening experience getting out into the field and seeing how a pro functions."

"Come on; let's get you to the airport. I have to return that rental and get my car." said Audrey as she stood.

"You mean that's not your car?" asked Williams.

"Just another little tactic for us field operatives," she said.

Suddenly Audrey's printer began churning then printing. Audrey excused herself and reappeared holding a single sheet of paper.

She looked up from the page with a confused look and said, "It's for you."

Taking the page from Audrey, Williams read the nine words that froze him like an ice cube. It read: I'M WATCHING YOU LITTLE BROTHER. WHO'S YOUR NEW GIRLFRIEND?

Audrey began, "How the hell did he—?"

"Don't ask. He's just simply the best at what he does."

Chapter 28

Present Day

Tony, Jacquelyn and the kids sat at the dining room table enjoying a wonderful meal together. Getting home first, Tony had changed his clothes so he didn't have to explain the dirt and blood stains on his shirt.

"Nick had an exciting day today. Didn't you?" Tony asked him.

"I did?"

"Yes. Mrs. Conway got an award...remember?"

"Oh, that."

"What do you mean, 'Oh that'? It's a big deal."

"Really?

"Yes, really."

"Well, I guess it's a big deal to her, but all we cared about was eating cake and getting out of class," said Nick.

"You got out of class? For how long?" asked Sam.

"Two periods," said Nick.

"You're lucky. I was stuck in class all day," Sam said enviously.

"Wait a minute. Are the two of you saying all you care about is getting out of class and really don't care Mrs. Conway was named Teacher of the year?" asked Jacquelyn.

"Yeah," they said in unison.

"Those are your kids," Jacquelyn said to Tony.

After dinner was over and the night drew to a close Tony knew he had some explaining to do. In their bedroom Tony walked over and quietly closed the door.

"Tony. Not now. The kids could still be awake," she said in a loud whisper.

Without a word Tony opened his closet, picked up the shirt and pants he was wearing earlier in the day and showed Jacquelyn.

"I need to tell you something," he began.

Tony let the pair of pants roll down showing the dirt stains from his encounter with Danielle Green.

"What happened to those?" asked Jacquelyn expecting a simple answer.

Tony paused, didn't answer, and then showed her the front of the shirt with dirt and grass stains. He dreaded the idea of having to turn the shirt around, but he did.

"Oh my God, Tony! Is that blood?"

Tony still didn't answer and removed the shirt he was wearing and turned around so Jacquelyn could see the small spike marks from the Taser points. She moved closer to him as his head hung down and turning his back to her.

"Tony, tell me how this happened," she asked with despair in her voice.

As he turned to face her Tony lifted his head and said, "You might want to sit down for this."

Looking at the wounds on Tony's back almost sickened Jacquelyn. Her love for him is overwhelming. But, she knows this isn't easy for Tony either.

"Remember what I told you about agent Wolf?"

"She did this to you!?"

"Please, keep your voice down. And not just for the kids," he said looking around. Then Tony followed up with, "No, it was Danielle Green."

"Who's Danielle Green?"

Tony craned his neck to try and look at her making a face as if she had two heads then said, "The person from the Department of Education who presented Mrs. Conway the Teacher of the Year award."

"Oh, right." she said.

Jacquelyn calmly asked questions as she examined then applied antibacterial cream to each small wound on Tony's back. Tony answered her questions very directly. As she made her way to each area with the light touch of her fingers she asked one very distinct question.

"Did she use a T6 or T8 on you? It looks like it must have been a T8 given the size of the marks."

Tony once again turned his head and tried to look at Jacquelyn and asked, "How did you know this is from a Taser? More importantly, how would you know the difference between a T6 and a T8? I don't know anything about Tasers."

"I...um...must have read it somewhere at some point?" she said slowly.

"So you don't remember the supposed dignitary in your profession who gave out the award at Nick's school, but you know the models of Tasers based on just looking at the puncture wounds on my back," Tony said unexpectedly.

Jacquelyn stopped her nurse-like touch, stepped back then asked, "What are you insinuating, Tony?"

"It's just an odd thing that you know about Tasers based on an observation of my back," he said turning and staring.

Jacquelyn didn't budge, let out a sigh then said, "All right. Right after you and I agreed you would take the government job I felt it would be prudent to be able to defend myself if necessary. Pepper spray didn't seem like it would be enough." Then she proudly added, "It is my right."

Tony stood tall and strong without his shirt on facing her and remained silent.

"You know how I feel about guns. So, the next best thing for me is a Taser. I had it with me when that security alarm guy was here. I wasn't about to take any chances. In order for me to have one I had to take a class and obtain a permit. That's where I got my information. I'm sorry I didn't tell you Tony, but I thought if you knew you would step down and you can do so much good for our country."

Tony continued to just stare.

"Say something Tony," Jacquelyn implored.

He took one step forward, wrapped his arms around her and gave her one of the biggest hugs he has ever given. Surprised, but relieved, Jacquelyn reciprocated throwing her arms around Tony.

"Whoa! That hurts!" said Tony.

"I'm so sorry Tony. I forgot! Are you OK?"

After the sting subsided he said, "Never better."

Jacquelyn wrapped her arms around his waist then rested her head onto Tony's bare chest. Their embrace seemed to last forever as they both felt that much safer in each other's arms. The meaning of time escaped as they held tightly.

"I'm so proud of you Jacquelyn."

She lifted her eyes to him and just stared.

"What?" he asked.

"I'm just wondering?"

"Wondering what?"

"How you're protecting yourself if something, God forbid, goes wrong."

Tony wrapped her up once again then picked her off her feet as if she were light as a feather and looked her into her big brown eyes.

"I've asked for training. Audrey's setting it up. Just so you know I intend to carry some kind of weapon with me at all times and I don't mean pepper spray or a Taser."

Jacquelyn looked deep into his eyes and said, "I expect you to become the best marksman you can possibly become. I don't like the idea of guns lying around the house though."

"Why would anyone do something so stupid as that?"

"You see the same news report as I do. Just putting you on notice that I want you to protect yourself, Sam and me, but I want any and all firearms in a safe where no one else can get at them...including me and especially the kids."

"Scout's honor," said Tony.

"Were you ever a scout?"

"Absolutely! When I was in grade school I was a Cub Scout," he said with a grin.

"A Cub Scout doesn't count," said Jacquelyn.

"You're right. I was only in it to go camping and do cool stuff. I quit after just a few weeks of making crap out of Popsicle sticks."

Tony left his shirt off so the antibacterial cream could soak in. He then put a shirt on and went downstairs to his office. It wasn't too late for him to call Audrey.

"Hi there," she answered.

"Secure and contained," said Tony.

"Likewise," said Audrey.

"Sorry to bother you Audrey, but I need to find out how to go about protecting myself."

How does he stay one step ahead so frequently? she wondered.

"I was going to tell you in the morning. We have your program set up and it begins this Friday at 9am."

"That's great! When you say program, what do you mean?"

"Well, I discussed it with Dennis and Don and we all agree you don't need boot camp or any type of hell week."

"What's the difference," Tony asked.

"The purpose of boot camp is to bring an individual who is used to doing things his or her way and break them down to think of the group as a whole. You know, to put the individual agendas away."

"And hell week?"

"It's what it sounds like. Just to be open about it, Dennis did want you to go through hell week."

"What a jerk!"

"Not really Tony. He is so intrigued by you that he felt it would be a good idea to see how well you would do under extreme circumstances. Believe it or not, Tony, Dennis thinks very highly of you."

"He sure has a funny way of showing it."

"True, but remember he's been through the battles and wars. Anyway, we decided to focus on an AIT. That means Advanced Individual Training. Specifically, it's firearms training and a small amount of self-defense for you."

"That sounds perfect, Audrey."

"Firearms training is first on your agenda. Tony, this man is not from the Portland area. He is flying in with a convict flight out of Dallas. He's a tough man on the outside—"

"Yeah, yeah…he's a real softy on the inside. I'll be the judge of that," retorted Tony.

"I guess you would be the best one to really know. Anyway, he will provide you with exactly what you need. I will give you his bio in the morning so you know why we have chosen him. I think you will be very pleased. He's the best in the business."

"If you don't mind Audrey, I would prefer not to know anything about him. I like to experience my own first impressions. As you know, the more information I have about someone the harder it is for me to make the most accurate assessment possible."

"OK, then let's make this a little more interesting. He will make contact with you and the two of you take it from there," said Audrey.

"I look forward to meeting him," Tony said.

Friday morning came quickly and Tony found himself at his desk looking at the clock for what seemed to be the millionth time.

When is this guy going to call? Audrey originally set us up for 9am. He should have contacted me by now. Maybe he's not coming. Should I call Audrey? No, not after telling her I didn't want to know anything about him, he thought.

Just then Tony's Smartphone rang. He looked at caller ID.

"Oh good. It's Molly," he said to himself.

"Hi Molly, how's my favorite Customer Service Rep today?"

"Tony, I'm always doing well. Especially since CIT announced they were starting to allow my boss to listen in on my conversations with incoming calls," she said sarcastically.

"Well, why don't you just get the person's name and number then call them right back. If they only listen to incoming calls you'd be all set," Tony said kiddingly.

"Not a bad idea," said Molly as if she was really considering the idea.

"How can I help you Molly?"

"I just got off the phone with a guy in Portland that screwed up his entire network. It's above my head and he's willing to pay the extra expedite fees to get him back up and running if we can get to him before noon. This would really help my paycheck," she said not so subtly.

Tony glanced at the clock once again and thought; *If this so-called firearms expert is this late then he can wait for me while I help Molly out.*

"You know what? I'll change my schedule and take care of it for you right away. You deserve an extra bonus," said Tony.

"Thanks Tony. I knew I could count on you. The guy's name is Charles Fullerton. His business is located near downtown Portland at 1225 N. Hillmar St. His phone number is 503-555-6262. I'll call him and tell him to expect you."

"OK. I should get there within thirty minutes. Did he say what system he's running? "He did. Let me go over my notes with you—"

"You know what Molly? Let me call you from the car. It'll save time and your boss can listen in at how good you are at your job."

"Thanks Tony. Talk to you in a few minutes."

Tony approached the one story brick building and entered through the front door. It's a nice enough neighborhood, but has seen better days. He expected a receptionist to greet him then realized it seemed almost too quiet. Tony wasn't sure how many of the cars parked on the street were for Fullerton & Associates.

By the looks of things I don't think anyone's here, he thought.

"Hello?" he said.

No answer.

"Anybody here?" he said raising his voice a little louder.

Still nothing. Tony walked back outside and verified the address on the front of the building. He pulled out his Smartphone and called the number Molly had given him.

"Fullerton & Associates," said a man with a heavy New York accent.

"My name is Tony James and I'm just outside your lobby. I'm looking for Mr. Charles Fullerton."

"Who?"

Tony looked at his phone wondering if he dialed the wrong number.

"I'm with CIT looking for Mr. Fullerton to help—"

"Oh, yeah, right…the computer geek. I'll be right there," the man said without the slightest realization he just insulted Tony.

This should be a load of fun, Tony sarcastically thought.

Tony went back inside, set his briefcase down and looked at his surroundings. Just as he was about to inspect a Portland Chamber of Commerce award hanging on the wall he felt the piercing of the word *Mercenary*.

As Tony turned around he found himself in the presence of a fifty-something year old man pointing a rifle at him. Without hesitation the man squeezed the trigger and hit Tony directly in the chest.

Tony's body flung backward hard into the wall with the Chamber of Commerce award knocking loose as he slipped down to the floor. His eyes were closed. He couldn't breathe. Tony, slowly and barely opening his eyes, looked at the man with the rifle and saw him remain steady as a statue still pointing the barrel at him.

As the pain began to sink in Tony looked down at his shirt and was shocked at the amount of red ooze. The plaque on the wall finally slipped off its nail and gravity helped it find the top of Tony's head. Everything went black.

Chapter 29

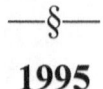

1995

Audrey returned from the airport eager to take her clandestine communication platform to a whole new level, thanks to Don Williams. But, before she could do that she had to make sure the Williams Protocol Program was completely safe. She also needed to write a few new lines of code for added security before sending it off.

She sat at her desk at home scrolling through page upon page of code that made her eyes weary. Finally she found the block of safety line codes.

"You learned something from Sefter, didn't you Don," she said scanning the screen.

What's this? I knew it! You little snake in the grass. You planted an 'admin echo retriever' in this thing! There's no way I'm entrusting my life to your snooping eyes. OK, if you did that then you had to install a backdoor, thought Audrey.

After several hours removing, modifying and adding lines of computer code Audrey rubbed her eyes and was almost ready to take the new version of the Williams Protocol Program for a test run.

I changed quite a lot of his program, she realized. *He may be very good at writing code, but the Williams Protocol Program? Really? This needs a more generic name. One that sounds boring so as not to attract attention. How about...Code Protected Transmission?* she thought.

"CPT program. It has a nice non-descript ring to it. Could mean anything," she said to herself as the program completed running its diagnostics.

Audrey went back in and changed the name of the program then did a test run using a new open domain free email address. It would only be used this one time. She sent a formal looking business letter to herself. The attachment, which had the name 'DAGGER' in big bold letters imbedded in it, went along for the ride.

She didn't have to wait long for her email to arrive into her inbox. There was no information in the subject line. Audrey opened the attachment.

"Perfect. It looks exactly like the business letter", she said excitedly.

She opened up the CPT program, minimized it then dragged the business letter attachment down hovering over the new CPT program. Within moments the screen dissolved and staring her in the face was the word 'DAGGER'.

A smile came over her as she sat back with pride and a healthy dose of relief. Then she realized something.

How am I going to communicate if I'm the only one with this program? she wondered.

Audrey quickly had her answer.

Send the entire program as an attachment from my CIT email address. It will take some time for it to upload, but it will work if I compress the file. I'm going to have to let him know ahead of time to look for it.

She quickly wrote a draft email explaining how everything will work. Then she waited for a response. It took close to an hour then she heard the new email arrive.

She opened the new draft. It read: 'EXCELLENT!'

Once her email was sent she knew it could take up to two hours for the attachment to download for him. She was tired and her eyes were blurry.

"I need a little shut-eye," she said to herself as she stretched and yawned.

Her eyes seemed to not want to cooperate with what her brain was telling them to do. But, she did, in fact, fall asleep. Finally she opened one eye and saw the room sideways. As if there was a fire she jumped up off the couch and made a mad dash to her desk. She quickly checked to see if she had a new draft in her inbox.

She stood silently staring at a new draft that had been sent forty minutes ago. It had the word, 'Hello' in the subject line. Audrey sat down almost afraid to open it. She thought about how Don Williams' brother, Sefter, had surprised them by taking over her printer.

I know I protected myself from anyone trying to keep an eye on me electronically. Sefter or anyone else isn't going to get through to me now, she thought.

Audrey opened the new draft email. She already had the CPT program minimized at the bottom of her screen. She opened the attachment. A lengthy business letter from an accounting firm she never heard of before. The moment of truth. She dragged the attachment into the CPT program. It seemed to hesitate forever before dissolving and allowing the true message to appear.

It read; 'HELLO DARLING. I MISS YOU SO MUCH. YOU ARE AN INCREDIBLE WOMAN! I DON'T KNOW WHAT YOU SAW IN ME, BUT I'M GLAD YOU SAID YES WHEN I ASKED YOU TO MARRY ME. INTERESTING HOW WE'VE KEPT THAT ONE PARTICULAR VOW. YOU KNOW, THE ONE ABOUT TIL DEATH DO US PART. I FEEL

MORE ALIVE TODAY THAN ALL THOSE DAYS SINCE MY, SO CALLED, 'HEART ATTACK'. I LOVE YOU AUDREY SHELTON. YOU ARE MY LOVE. YOU ARE MY LIFE. I'VE NEVER FELT SO ALIVE!

WITH ALL MY HEART,

ANDREW'

Chapter 30

—§—

Present Day

Lying on the floor with his eyes still closed, Tony heard a muffled voice off in the distance telling him to pull it together.

"Hey! Yo! Wake up!" said a man's voice in a New York Italian accent.

The man lightly slapped Tony's face with his left hand while holding his head with his right. He switched hands then said to himself, "Damn it. I got blood on my hand."

"Hey James…you're bleeding. Wake the hell up!"

The piercing voice brought Tony back to consciousness. As he began to move, Tony slowly started to open his eyes. To his surprise a man's face was inches away from his. Realization finally set in and he struggled to move away from him. Pain seared his chest.

"You…shot me!" Tony said fearfully.

Tony successfully pushed the man away from him, but he was slumped against a wall. Tony then looked down and almost passed out once again.

"Oh my God!" he said looking down at his red soaked chest.

Then he felt the pain in his head and believed it was part of the dying process. He slowly placed his hand on top of his head and felt the moistness of his own blood. Tony pulled his hand down to look at the crimson covering his fingers. As he looked at the man he saw the same red on his hand and didn't know what to think. Tony felt woozy.

With a grimace and a soft raspy voice Tony asked, "Who are you?"

"Don't be so dramatic. It's just a little cut on your noggin," said the man.

Tony's eyes widened as if he were in the presence of the devil himself and quietly said, "You see all this blood from my chest and you only comment on a cut on my head!?"

The man began to laugh.

"You're one disturbed individual," said Tony.

"Do you feel like you're die'n?" he asked.

Tony stared in disbelief.

The man laughed even harder then said, "You think you'd be sit'n there talk'n to me if I really wanted you dead?"

Confused, Tony looked at the man then realized he was right.

I'm breathing fine now. My chest hurts, but my head hurts more. How does that make sense? he wondered.

"While I gotcha sit'n all quiet I wanna ask you a question. How did you hear me before I shot you?"

Tony continued to stare in disbelief.

"I mean, I was as quiet as a mouse. You got super hearing or somethin'?"

I've got something all right, but it's not super hearing, thought Tony.

"You might need a stitch or two on your head. L'me take a closer look."

"Get away from me!" Tony said gaining strength back in his voice.

"Look, I'll pay for the shirt if that's what you're worried about."

Tony, a little foggy from the bump on the head said, "You shot me! Why would you do something like that? I have a wife and two kids. What are they going to do without me?"

"Huh? I think that bump on the head has got you wacked out."

Tony remained motionless and fixated on the man's eyes.

"It's a homemade recipe," the man said bending down as if talking to a child.

He reached over to one side, picked up the rifle and said, "It's a paintball rifle idiot. I didn't mean to hurt you."

Tony took a whiff of his red soaked shirt then ripped it open to discover only a red welt the size of a quarter, but growing. Realization finally set in.

"You shot me with a paintball?"

"Now your noodle's cook'n kid."

Tony began to stand up, but felt woozy from the head injury.

"Hey, hey, hey…sit down," the man said in a concerned tone as he gently dropped the rifle and tried to help Tony ease onto the couch.

"You ambush then shoot me and now you're concerned about my well being?"

"Hey, I didn't take into account you would hear me and turn around so quick. I meant to shoot you in the back."

"Oh, that makes much more sense now," Tony said in a tone dripping with sarcasm.

"It was to make a point hotshot," he said.

After Tony got situated the man asked, "How did you know I was there anyway?"

"First, I'm not the least concerned about answering any questions from you. Second, why would you—?"

Tony stopped short of asking his question and gave a quick left jab to the man's prominent nose. The man flew backwards as blood quickly appeared from his nostrils.

"What the hell are you doing!?" shouted the man.

Tony got up with a grunt of pain and stood over him ready to get some answers of his own. In a blur, Tony suddenly felt a delayed electric pain from his groin. The man had kicked him in the crotch.

"Never, and I mean never, allow yourself to become a target like that," said the man as he spoke in a nasally tone as blood continued running from his nose.

Barely able to speak Tony asked, "Mr. Fullerton I presume?"

"Call me Charlie," he said losing the New York Italian accent. "Charlie Tankerton. My friends call me Tank. It's a pleasure to meet you."

Tony was trying to get through the pain.

"You'll be alright. Your balls will hurt, but you'll be alright," said Tankerton.

Once the pain began to subside Tony asked, "Then who's Fullerton?"

"Just a name I used to get you to come here. It had to be a legit name or you wouldn't have come. Am I right?"

"That's true," said Tony quietly.

"I'm real sorry about your head. Even I didn't see that one coming. You weren't supposed to know I was there."

"OK, so you're the guy from Texas who's supposed to teach me self-defense and how to handle a pistol," said Tony.

"That's almost right."

"Almost?" asked Tony.

"I'm not from Texas."

"I was told you were," said Tony.

"You're memory is a little off, maybe from that bump on your head. I was visiting in Dallas then caught a flight from there to here. I'm from no place you've ever heard of before so don't ask."

Both men stood up and flipped the red covered cushions over and sat down to lick their wounds and talk.

"Why the extravagant set-up?" asked Tony.

"I do everything to bring the best out in each of my trainees. I'm the best. Didn't they tell you?" answered Charlie Tankerton.

"I was told you're the best, but I don't think this was necessary," said Tony.

"You'd be surprised. This gives me a baseline of your instincts. Let me tell you, you're instincts are exceptional. Raw, but exceptional."

"Is this where I'm supposed to say thanks?"

268

"Nope. I'm just glad you're not like the last person I trained. What an imbecile."

"Did you succeed?" asked Tony.

"I always succeed."

"So why is he an imbecile?"

"This person was afraid of his own shadow. You on the other hand, somehow not only heard me, but fought for your life. You even drew blood from me. I can count on one hand how many men can say that. I like that. Congratulations on your entrance exam. You got an 'A'."

"Why not an 'A+'?" asked Tony.

"Because I'm still alive. No one has ever gotten an 'A+'."

Tony thought about the technique used and decided to embrace the fact he needs Charlie Tankerton. He also realized Audrey would never put him in the hands of a hack.

"Well, thanks Tank," said Tony knowing full well a rebuke of using his nickname was likely forthcoming.

"You're welcome, Tony. I think we're going to become fast friends," said Tankerton.

Chapter 31

—§—

1995

Audrey stared at her computer screen almost afraid to move. She and Andrew hadn't communicated this intimately, even though just in email form, since the day of his 'death'. A flood of emotional memories came rushing out. The police officers. The phony funeral. The letters she wrote to the CIT board members to scare them with the IRS threat. All the planning and not being able to tell a soul. Most of all she felt cut in half being away from her love, her husband. Tears began to flow. She touched the computer monitor where Andrew's words emitted a lifeline from him to her.

"I miss you so much Andrew," she said wiping a tear.

Then, after a long pause, she realized, *I don't have to sit here and long for him. Both of us can now at least read our very own words.*

Audrey wrote a very long love letter using the CPT program. She wasn't sure where Andrew is living at the moment so she asked. His reply came quickly.

"The Cayman Islands. Grand Cayman to be exact. I'm moving to Little Cayman Island tomorrow. I've been working on setting up a computer terminal over there so I can connect to the internet from my villa."

"Perfect! Staying close to the money." she said as if talking directly to him.

"You didn't purchase a villa did you?" she typed then pressed send.

"Of course not! I am renting a home on both islands under the names we decided upon. Remember, we agreed this was the strategy." he wrote.

"Sorry, I didn't mean to say you would deviate from the plan or do anything to compromise us. I've been immersed in so much here at home. I can't wait to tell you all the details when I see you. Remember, I have my passport ready. I miss you so much."

"I miss you too. I want you by my side. But, we can't be seen together. More importantly, I don't want you followed. You know how Big Brother can be. You never know who might be looking if you leave the country right now. By the way, you might not recognize me. I've lost 22 pounds!"

"Oh how I wish I could see you."

"Does this program work with pictures?"

"It wasn't built for them, so let's not take the chance."

"Then patience my love. All in good time Audrey."

"Have you checked on the money? Is it all there?" Audrey wrote.

"I have and it's all here. We will move some of it at the appropriate time and I will move with it. Although, I'm getting pretty used to this weather down here."

"Hey, don't get too comfortable. I want to enjoy it with you," Audrey kiddingly scolded.

Suddenly something odd happened. Both Andrew and Audrey's screens flickered for a few seconds. Then large red capital letters began scrolling across. It read: 'THE OTHER BIG BROTHER IS WATCHING'

Their screens flickered once again and the scrolling message disappeared. Andrew quickly logged off and wiped his hard drive clean. Audrey remained logged on believing she was safe.

"What the hell was that!" she said finally talking at the screen.

She quickly went to work on finding the source of the intrusion, but came up empty. Frustrated, Audrey unplugged her computer and sat back staring at the dead screen in silence. The whirring of her computer fan no longer running made her aware of how alone she truly had become. It was as if the sound had instantly developed into an audible link to Andrew.

Her logical mind raced to find answers. She scribbled down the words that had scrolled across her screen.

The OTHER Big Brother? Who could that be? she wondered.

She pounded her fist on the desk then said, "Think, Audrey think!"

I don't know who to turn to that I trust. I certainly can't call it in, she thought.

After staring at the words 'The Other Big Brother Is Watching' she realized this could be a set up by the Agency.

No, that can't be right. The Other Big Brother. Big Brother is Langley. So, who's the OTHER one? Is there another agency at play here? It could be an oversight agency. I have to pull the hard drive and destroy it. Wiping it clean might not do the trick. I can work on it off-line with my back up hard drive. Thank God I back everything up daily, she thought.

She heard a car door shut outside close to the house. Then another. Audrey got up from her desk and peaked out the front window to see a police car in her driveway.

She tilted her head just a little and wondered; *What are they doing here? There's no way this can be connected.*

She glanced back at her computer and then the bottom right drawer. Her firearm. Just in case. The doorbell rang and Audrey calmly walked to open the door.

"Hello officers," she said in a neutral tone.

"Hi Mrs. Shelton. Do you remember us?"

"I'm sorry, I—. Oh, wait...Officer Lambert, right?" she said to the female in uniform.

"That's right," said the officer with a proud polite smile.

"And...I'm sorry I don't remember," she lied to the male officer.

"Rice. Officer Rice," he said in his deep voice.

"That's right. You gave me your card. Would you like to come in?"

Audrey extended her arm as if she were inviting them in to stay for dinner.

"Please, make yourself at home."

"Thank you Mrs. Shelton," said Lambert.

"Please, call me Audrey."

Officer Lambert didn't want to sit in the exact same place during her previous and only unpleasant visit. She chose a practical chair. As she sat she quickly took note that there still were no pictures of her late husband anywhere in the living room.

"Officer Rice, make yourself comfortable."

Rice decided to take the chair Audrey occupied during their previous visit.

"So, to what do I owe the pleasure?" asked Audrey as she settled onto the middle cushion of the couch.

"It's part of the department's community outreach program to follow up with you to see if we can be of any assistance since our last visit," Lambert said delicately.

Oh, thank God! This has nothing to do with what just happened on the computer, she thought.

"You didn't have to stop by to do that. You could have just called. I'm fine," said Audrey.

"Do you have someone helping you?" asked Officer Lambert.

"Helping in what way?" asked Audrey a little confused.

Officer Rice jumped in and said, "You know, just everyday things."

That really clarifies it, Audrey thought sarcastically.

"Oh, this place? I can handle most things myself. When I can't, I hire out," said Audrey.

"Well, that's good to hear," Lambert nodded.

"Mrs. Sh—Audrey, unfortunately we need to talk to you about the night your husband passed away," said Rice.

Audrey's demeanor didn't change.

Rice and Lambert gave a brief glance at each other knowing they both remember thinking how odd Audrey had reacted during their first visit delivering the news of her husband's death.

"Audrey, this is a task we are given during a follow up, such as this, if one of our detectives digs up a minor anomaly. They really don't expect to get much clarification so they leave it to us to report back," said Lambert.

"In this case it's more about the hospital's management than anything else," said Rice.

Audrey remained silent and let them do the talking until they got to the point.

"I'm sorry to bring this up, but do you recall when you went to the morgue to recover your husband's remains," asked Lambert.

"It's not something I will likely forget. Why?" asked Audrey.

"Who was with you when you recovered your husband's ashes?"

As if you don't know, Audrey thought.

"Ryan O'Connor," answered Audrey.

"Was there anyone else with you?"

"No, it was just me and Ryan," she said.

"Was there a hospital employee that you met with," Lambert continued.

"Yes, of course."

"Do you remember his name?"

Audrey paused for effect then said, "No. I'm sorry; I think I was too upset."

"I'm sorry to ask you this, but were you upset about something more specific than your husband's passing?"

"Isn't that enough?" answered Audrey.

"Our detective uncovered a last minute personnel change that apparently has no explanation."

"I don't understand," lied Audrey.

"The hospital had a Ms. Claudia Graham scheduled to be on duty in the morgue the day you were there. Do you remember meeting with her?"

You know very well she wasn't there, but I'll play along, thought Audrey.

"No, if I recall correctly a man was on duty," Audrey said a little more animated.

"Can you describe this man, Audrey?"

Audrey shifted her eyes as if trying to remember then said, "He was just a guy in a white lab coat that screwed up."

"Screwed up how?"

"I couldn't bring myself to identify Andrew's body right away so it took me awhile to finally get the courage to go to the hospital. When I got there I found they had already cremated him and put his ashes in a brown box. I was so upset. The poor guy got an earful from me. I know it wasn't his fault. Ryan O'Connor was supposed to have been taking care of everything. I think I was completely out of my mind when I yelled at both of them."

"That's understandable given the circumstances. Can you describe the man in the lab coat?"

Oh no! Something went wrong, thought Audrey.

"Everything's a blur at this point," said Audrey hoping they would cut her some slack.

"Give it a try. You might surprise yourself. You already remembered it was a brown box and the man was wearing a white lab coat. Do you remember if he was wearing a name tag?"

"I'm sorry, I don't."

Officer Rice pulled out his small spiral bound notebook and flipped it open ready to take notes.

"You seem to remember colors. What color hair did he have?"

No sense lying and getting myself in trouble, thought Audrey.

"Brown, I think."

"How tall? Just a rough estimate."

"Six feet or a little over."

"Any distinguishable marks on his face, neck or hands. Was he wearing any jewelry?"

"Not that I remember. What's this all about?" Audrey asked trying to head off a million questions.

Officer Rice said, "There was a tire slashing that morning."

Audrey looked at him very confused.

He followed up and said, "The tires were that of Ms. Claudia Graham."

Oh Dennis, how could you be so stupid! thought Audrey.

Chapter 32

—§—

Present Day

Tony, now back in his car from his appointment with Charlie Tankerton, called Audrey from his secret side of his Smartphone.

"Hi, how are you?" answered Audrey.

"Actually, I've been better," he said rubbing his chest.

"What's wrong?"

"The self-defense trainer you sent to ambush me. That's what's wrong."

"Tank? What do you mean…ambush you?"

"I made a call on a new prospective client for CIT and it turned out to be Chuckles. He shot me in the chest," said Tony purposely to get Audrey's attention.

"Good ole' Tank. Hasn't changed a bit. What did he do this time?"

Not the response I was looking for, thought Tony.

"He shot me with a paintball rifle with red paint. I thought I was dying. Those things really hurt," said Tony in an alarming tone.

"You're lucky," said Audrey.

"Huh?" *Again, not the answer I expected*, he then thought.

"Usually he catches everyone so off guard he nails them in the back," she said in a matter-of-fact tone.

"I'm on my way to get a couple of stitches," said Tony.

"Stitches, why do you need stitches?"

"The blow to my chest knocked me backward into a wall and then some award landed on my head."

"Oh, I'm so very sorry," Audrey implored.

"Who the hell is this guy?" asked Tony.

"He's only the best of the best at preparing you for any unplanned conditions that may arise."

"Unplanned conditions? What a nice way of saying when I need to protect myself with lethal force," said Tony.

"Correct. He has trained over two thirds of the Secret Service. He's now out on his own. I was lucky to get him for you."

"What's his story…just the short version."

"He came to the attention of the Agency during his tour in Vietnam. His hand to hand combat experience is second to none. The stories are fascinating, but somewhat gruesome. Once State-side, he graded out so high in weapons school they fast-tracked him to become an instructor. Tank didn't like the cookie cutter training curriculum so he offered to change it. Well, actually he decided to change it without asking. That's a problem when it comes to an established program that had been in place for so many years. So, he couldn't get his way and left. He's a freelance instructor and doesn't need to advertise. I've had training sessions with him. I trust him with my life and you should too, if you know what's good for you," said Audrey.

"So, what you're saying is he didn't like the rules and told management it was his way or the highway?"

"You got it."

"Hmm.   No wonder we got along so well after I realized I wasn't bleeding from my chest."

"Well, he did that to the very person who is in charge of the protection detail for POTUS," Audrey said as if she were a proud big sister.

"What's POTUS," asked Tony.

"I'm sorry.   President Of The United States," she answered realizing her inside Washington slang.

"So, I'm in good hands and not with some nut job who's going to accidentally kill me?"

"Correct on the first part," said Audrey playfully.

"Very funny, Audrey."

"His techniques can be somewhat unique, but they are very effective. I assure you. Are you on board?" she asked.

Tony paused, taking note of the throbbing pain in his head then said, "We'll see. I'll be with my new best friend for the next couple of days. You'll cover for me?"

"Of course. No need to check in until you and Tank are done. That is unless he really does kill you. Then no need to call."

"Very funny Audrey."

Tony required exactly two stitches just as Tank had predicted.   He was thankful the doctor didn't have to shave any of his hair. Once home he and Jacquelyn took Sam and Nick out for dinner to one of their favorite burger joints.   It was Nick's turn to choose and there wasn't any doubt where they would be dining tonight...McDonald's.

"Just what I need. A bunch of kids yelling and playing as loudly as possible," he said to Jacquelyn.

"Did they give you anything for pain?" she asked.

"They offered, but I turned them down."

"I bet you wish you hadn't," she said tilting her head slightly towards the children.

"You're enjoying this aren't you?"

"Just a little. Here you are, Mr. Coordinated, getting a lump on his head from a file cabinet. I meant to ask. How's the file cabinet?"

Tony didn't tell her about Charlie Tankerton.

"Very funny. Everyone's a comedian today," he said.

"You know I'm just kidding around. Here, I have some Tylenol in my purse. You want a couple?" she asked sincerely.

"Yes! Thank you."

Tony leaned in and asked, "You got your Taser in there?"

"Shh...someone might here you," she scolded.

"What's the big deal? I think you should take it one step further—"

"We'll talk about this another time. You know how I feel about...you know."

"You can say the word Jacquelyn. It won't hurt anyone."

"Fine. You know how I feel about guns," she said in a whisper.

"Mom, Dad! Come play with us," shouted Nick from the ball pit.

The next day came around quickly and the James family moved in a pattern a Swiss watch maker could appreciate. Once Jacquelyn was out the door Tony dropped the kids off at school then headed to an address Tank had given him for his first lesson. Tony didn't know what to expect.

He pulled his car into Fields Indoor Target Shooting Range and felt a sigh of relief.

At least he won't ambush me here...I think, thought Tony.

Tony entered the firing range and scanned the entire area for his instructor, Tank. He walked around and found nobody minding the counter. Then he heard a single shot somewhere on one of the firing lanes. He stood still and waited for another shot. It didn't come.

"Hello? Anybody here?" asked Tony craning his neck behind the counter.

Finally a squat gray haired grandpa looking man rounded the corner and asked, "You been helped?"

"No. I'm meeting an instructor for a private lesson."

"You must be looking for Tank. He's on lane nine. Sign here and I need your driver's license. You got muffs?"

"Muffs?" Tony said more surprised that this man knows Charlie Tankerton.

The man held up a pair of earmuffs and said, "You gotta wear muffs if you're going out there."

Tony grabbed the volume controlled earmuffs, put yellow tinted safety glasses on then entered the firing range. He could not believe his eyes.

"The whole trick is to control your breath. Squeeze as you exhale like this."

Tony saw the entire staff and every single patron of the firing range watching Tank shooting his pistol with one arm duct taped behind his back. In disbelief, Tony saw Tank unload nine more rounds into the paper target with the silhouette of a man's head down to his chest at the farthest point of the range.

"Well, let's see who owes who," said Tank.

A man flipped a switch and the target began its long journey back to them.

Upon inspection of the target Tank said, "Looks like you owe me another full day's range time tomorrow and complimentary ammo son."

The man was slack-jawed looking at the precise grouping right between the eyes of the paper silhouette.

"Now, you want me to use my dominant hand or have you had enough?" asked Tank.

Tank then noticed Tony and said, "All right everyone. Show's over. My star pupil is here. Thanks for the ammo and the range time. Next time I'll shoot blindfold and we can put some real money on the line."

The crowd dispersed as Tony walked towards Tank.

"Good morning Tony. How's your head?"

"I'm fine, but—"

"Walk with me Tony," said Tank.

"You sure are the popular kid on the block," said Tony.

Without breaking stride Tank said, "I know these types of people. I needed to let them know whose boss around here. Besides, we now have all the free ammo and range time we want."

"So, you don't think by drawing attention to yourself doesn't expose you just a little too much?"

"You have to remember, Tony, I'm not the spook...you are. Besides, how else am I supposed to advertise?"

Tony ignored the prodding then asked, "But, I thought you only took clients brought to you from government sources? Tony asked.

"Oh, I've branched out from just government clientele. Do you know there's a whole world of anti-government people just waiting to be taught the things I know? More than fifty percent of my clients are non-government."

"The way Audrey spoke about you I just assumed—"

"You know what happens when we assume."

"Yeah, I know—"

"No you don't. People get killed. That's what happens when we assume in this business. I'm not here to teach you to kill anyone, unless you have to. I'm here to teach you how to protect yourself from being killed," said Tank.

Tank and Tony removed their ear protection once they exited the range and re-entered the main lobby area of the building.

"Well, Tank you show those guys who's the boss?" asked the man behind the counter.

"Sorry 'bout that Franklin. I didn't expect—"

Franklin held up his hand in a stop signal manner and said, "As soon as I saw you I had a roll of duct tape ready. I knew what you were up to. Seen it before."

"A man can only take so much grief. So, I took matters into my own hands," said Tank.

"Hand...you mean hand. Anyway, don't worry about it. I laid a nice bet with Ackerman and Lufkin that within ten minutes of range time you'd be shooting left handed with your right arm duct taped behind your back. I made out pretty well, but in the end my guess is I'll break even on your range fees and ammo," said Franklin.

"If not, I'll make up the difference. You know I'm good for it," said Tank.

"Me Casa Sue Cassia," said Franklin giving a wide gesture.

"My client and I are going to use one of your classrooms for a couple of hours. That OK with you?"

Franklin just nodded.

Tony and Charlie "Tank" Tankerton entered the classroom closing the door behind them. Tank had already placed a locked suitcase on wheels in the corner of the room. He told Tony to sit and get comfortable while he set up.

"So, how do you know Franklin? Do you come here often?" asked Tony.

"No, I've spoken and demonstrated at the annual NRA conference numerous times. It's amazing how many friends I've made over the years. Besides, I taught his son how to shoot properly. Man, was he a mess when I first got hold of him. But, I straightened him out. The guy is not what I call a natural," said Tank.

"What's his son do that he needed your help? Tony asked.

"He'd tell you he's a private detective."

"And you think otherwise?"

"I think he's a two-faced lying punk, but it doesn't really matter what I think. Years ago I showed him how to become better and in a safe way. That's all I can do."

"You think he's lying about his profession?"

"Let's not waste time talking about a failure in the character department. Let's focus on making you into a guy that can not only protect himself, but others as well."

I wonder what this guy did to tick him off. Charlie Tankerton is one guy I'd hate to be on the bad side of, thought Tony.

"Your right, what's first," asked Tony.

"First, you're going to tell me why I was hired to train a computer geek that could sniff out an ambush," Tank said boldly as he sat on the edge of a table in front of Tony. "Albeit late of course," he added.

"Because I want to be trained."

"Cut the bull and tell me what agency of the government you work in, or are you on the other side. It makes no difference to me. I'll train you either way, but I need to know so I can tailor our time together to meet your exact needs."

Tony stared into the dead icy cold eyes of the professional marksman and almost felt the need to tell him everything.

He doesn't NEED to know. He WANTS to know. Big difference, thought Tony.

"If I told you I'd have to kill you," smiled Tony.

Tank didn't blink.

"It's a joke. Why do you take jobs blindly? Tony asked.

"It's how it works. I get a text from a phone I can't trace. I create a first meeting with the pupil to get my initial assessment then create a plan of action. Simple as that," Tank said.

"Isn't that a little naive," Tony asked to get a rise out of him.

"You haven't answered my question. Who do you work for?"

Impressive. He stayed on topic, thought Tony.

"If my employer wanted you to have that information then you wouldn't have accepted an anonymous text taking the job. So, let's you and I agree to work together so you can get paid," said Tony in a calm tone.

Tank didn't bat an eye. He just stared back at Tony. Tony calmly did the same. Almost a full minute went by without either one giving an inch.

Without shifting his eyes Tank said, "Looks like we're at a crossroads."

"Is it mandatory you know who my employer is? Tony asked.

"Yes," answered Tank.

"Then I'll have to say thanks, but no thanks." Tony began to stand.

"Hold it right there. You're going to forgo your training just because I'm pressuring you to divulge your employer?"

"No. Not at all. You're not the only trainer in the world," Tony said as he continued to remove himself from the confines of the desk.

"I'm not, but I'm the best," said Tank.

"That may be true, but you're crossing a line that I'm not willing to cross with you," said Tony as he began to walk toward the door.

"Congratulations Tony. You just passed your second exam," said Tank.

"Second?"

"Sure. The first was our initial meeting. Whoever trained you to sniff out an ambush did a pretty good job. Now, under the pressure of losing your firearms training shows me you have character. You wouldn't believe how many people give me an answer to that question. Now get back here and let's move along and get you properly trained."

Tank set up his computer and projector, dimmed the front lights and began by showing Tony numerous videos about gun history, safety and law enforcement. After the videos he began to take one firearm after another from the suitcase. He discussed, dismantled and reassembled each and every one of them.

"As I cover the topic of 'Stand Your Ground', I need you to complete these forms."

"What are they," asked Tony.

"Concealed Carry Weapon Registration forms. This is for the Utah permit."

"What's a Utah permit," asked Tony.

"Come on. Are you serious?"

"Yes. I don't know what a Utah permit does for me. I live in Oregon."

"You got skills, kid. I almost believe you really don't know." Tank paused then said, "I'll play along. It allows you to carry your firearm in almost every state of the union."

"Almost?"

"Yes. For instance, Illinois has passed a concealed carry law, but it's, in my opinion, a real bad one. It's so restrictive I don't even consider it to be real," said Tank.

Tony completed the forms as he listened to Tank describe home invasion tactics to be used if such a situation ever arises.

"Sounds like if someone breaks into my home in the middle of the night I have to leave my house if I have a safe exit? That's crazy!" said Tony.

Tank looked around as if looking for someone then appeared satisfied and said, "Most target ranges have intercom systems and can hear what's being said. That's what I like about this place. They haven't updated a thing in years. To answer your question, it's what the law dictates. I agree it doesn't seem to be right. Right is not the subject at hand. At the moment I'm teaching you what the law of the land is. I presume you're all about playing by the rules."

Tony disregarded Tank's last fishing expedition comment then asked, "So, have you ever had anyone break into your home while you were there?"

"Yes."

"Did you follow these insane procedures?"

"No. I shot the guy in the heart then shouted 'I have a gun'," Tank said with a growing smile.

"So, you're telling me to do one thing, but the law doesn't apply to you?"

"I'm telling you to use your best judgment. I'm giving you the law of the land. What I do is up to me. What you do is up to you. Right now I'm here to inform you of the law. We'll get to the other stuff later."

"OK, so you shouted 'I have a gun' so you could honestly tell the police you really said that, right?"

"You catch on pretty quick for a computer geek. Too quick if you ask me. If you aren't a disaster on the range we just might be able to move into some of the more interesting aspects of your training."

With the paperwork completed, Tank provided Tony with the basics, beginning with all the safety rules before allowing him to even touch one of the many hand guns.

"OK Tony, what's the first rule when it comes to setting your firearm down in front of you before you do anything else?"

"Make sure it's pointing down range," answered Tony.

"Good. Apparently you really were listening in the classroom," said Tank in a satisfactory tone.

Once Tank completed quizzing Tony it was time to get down to actually firing each and every hand gun he had brought with him.

"Why so many different guns?" asked Tony.

"You and I need to find the right weapons that are going to meet each of your needs," said Tank.

"Each of my needs?"

"Sure. One for home. One to carry and one you're going to leave in a safe deposit box at the credit union."

"Banks don't allow weapons in safe deposit boxes," Tony said sternly.

"That's why I said credit union. Credit unions are member based organizations and have different rules than banks," said Tank with a sly grin.

"I have no intention of carrying a gun on me at all times," said Tony.

"Then how are you going to protect yourself?"

"Quite fishing. I'm not telling you why you're training me."

"I read your jacket, so I already know," said Tank flat-toned.

"First, I have no idea what a jacket is and second you're a really bad liar."

Tank took a good long look at Tony then said, "You know very well 'Jacket' means file. And you're wrong. I'm a damn good liar," he said with a smile. "Come on. Let's head out to the range."

The partitions between firing lanes consisted of welded metal which allowed a clear view of every station on the range for safety purposes. Tank, with the permission from Franklin, hung numerous large sized targets on the partitions to give them some privacy. Tank wants paying customers not rubberneckers looking for a free lesson. Tony noticed a camera pointing at each lane from above and behind each and every one of them.

"Are we being recorded?" asked Tony with a nod to the camera.

"Of course."

"Why? I thought this place was outdated."

"It's the law. Do you know how many suicides are performed at firing ranges each year?"

"Suicides? At firing ranges? I never hear about that on the news," said Tony with a confused look on his face.

"There's a reason for that. Damn near every person who walks through the doors of any firing range is a very contentious law abiding individual. Do you remember handing over your driver's license when you signed in?"

"Yes."

"Then you can draw the conclusion why criminals don't frequent firing ranges. They prefer to shoot at empty beer cans or other stuff without the hassles of a paper trail. Plus, where they practice, it's free. Usually not legal, but free. No range fees. Not to mention those pesky cameras you pointed out."

"But, I still don't understand the reason for someone to take their life at a firing range of all places," said Tony.

"Every suicide that has taken place at a firing range has had one thing in common. Care to take a guess at what that might be," asked Tank.

Tony looked directly into Tanks eyes as if trying to extract the answer then said, "I haven't the slightest idea."

Tank said unblinkingly, "In every case their firearm was always pointed down range when discharged to prevent others from being hurt."

Tony's eyes opened wide with the full understanding of what he just heard.

"That's right Tony. Even in a suicidal state these people are so conscientious to go to great lengths to make sure they don't hurt anyone with a stray round."

Tony took this in then stepped back from the temporary make-shift enclosure. He focused on what feeling he got from each person one by one on every lane to gather in as much data from each of them.

Once done he thought, *Everyone here seems OK today.*

"You all right Tony?" asked Tank.

"Fine. Just thinking," he said. Then he asked "But, given the coverage of gun related deaths, why haven't I heard about this on the news?"

"Great question. Each local police department has a gentlemen's agreement with their news outlets because many officers use these ranges themselves. It is a crazy-ass way to kill yourself, but you have to give it to them that it is very responsible."

Dumbest thing I've heard, but makes perfect sense coming from a man who makes his living training others by protecting themselves at the business end of a gun, Tony thought.

"We're not practicing that today are we?" asked Tony to lighten the mood.

"That would make this the shortest lesson in history," Tank joked. "Let's get down to business."

Chapter 33

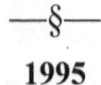

1995

Audrey watched the two police officers pull their squad car out of her driveway and cruse down the street.

Dennis, how stupid can you be!? Why in the world would you only slash her tires and not multiple cars in her neighborhood to make it look like kids? You left a trail, she thought.

Audrey knew exactly what her priorities are.

First, I need to reach Dennis to get this cleaned up. Second, I need to reinforce my computer security with multiple firewall layers because someone is up to something, she thought.

Audrey locked up the house and drove her car in a multitude of directions keeping an eye out for anyone tailing her. She is keenly aware that it's not unusual to have an unmarked officer sitting and waiting until the black and white squad car leaves so they can then follow. Convinced she is alone Audrey finally stopped at a pay phone down by Willamette River at Waterfront Park.

Once through the phone security protocol Audrey asked that Dennis Forman call her back immediately. While she waited, Audrey stood pretending to locate a phone number in the yellow pages from a phonebook hanging from a wire. Her blood pressure should have been going up, but Audrey always seemed to know how to use distress to her advantage on a biological level. Her heart rate always seems to go down in a crisis.

Audrey appears focused on the phone book, but scrutinizes each car that drives by. The maroon Buick coming toward her on her side of the street began to slow down. She took note that the two men in the car are wearing sunglasses on this cloudy day.

What are the chances two men would stop to hassle a woman at a pay phone? she wondered.

Audrey reached her right hand downward attempting to grasp her handgun and realized she may have made a fatal error.

Oh my God! My bag. I left it in the car! Stay calm, she thought.

The car pulled up and the man on the passenger side already had his window down and said, "Excuse me. My knucklehead brother got us lost. Can you tell us how to get back to Interstate 405?"

Audrey stood dead calm realizing she broke a cardinal rule. She let paranoia set in.

With just a slight hesitation she answered, "Keep right on going and you can't miss it."

Before the car began to take off the passenger turned to the driver and scolded, "I told you so."

Audrey listened to the disgruntled diminishing voices as they drove away.

795-UGL, 795 UGL, she thought as she responded to her training to always remember the license plate.

Suddenly the pay phone rang making her almost stumble into the street. Audrey picked up the receiver and said nothing. She waited to hear the exact words.

Hello, this is The American Auto Club calling. We received a message to call this number, said the male voice.

Audrey still remained silent.

"Hello? Adam Hutchins calling for a Mrs. Winslow. At the count of five I will presume you are not Mrs. Winslow and hang up. I don't have all day."

"4, 1, 7, 7, 5, 18"! said Audrey in a stern tone.

"So, where's the fire, Dagger?" he asked.

"Do you have any idea what a mess you've left behind?" Audrey said not expecting an answer.

"What are you talking about?" he asked sincerely.

"Slashing a poor girl's tires?"

"Don't tell me you're going soft on me. We may have to change your code name," he said in a joking tone.

"How could you be so careless?" she asked brushing aside his comment.

"Again, what are you talking about? And calm down for God's sake."

Audrey realized her voice had suddenly become a little too loud.

"I'm talking about a police report that's being looked into regarding a certain day shift employee from the hospital morgue. Her tires were slashed. She called in and couldn't work that day."

"Wasn't that the point?"

"Couldn't you at least have done a few more cars for appearances and make it look like kids did the deed? Now it looks targeted because only one car had slashed tires," she said.

"Oh, that? I didn't have time," he said.

"What...You were late for a poker game?"

"No, I had to catch a plane and haul my ass back here to...well, you know where," he said turning it back on Audrey.

"Are you kidding me!? You flew commercial?"

"Do it all the time. What's the big deal anyway?"

"The big deal is the police were just at my house. They were following up on my recollection of the male employee who screwed up at hospital morgue."

"Relax Dagger. There's no way this can get traced back to me," he said in a slightly condescending tone.

"I should relax? Aren't you missing an important piece of this puzzle?" asked Audrey.

"Like what?"

"Like...you left your prints all over the place at the hospital!"

"No I didn't."

Audrey pulled the phone away from her ear, looked at it with a grimace then said, "Almost everything in the morgue is stainless steel. The easiest material on earth to pull finger prints."

"Why do you think I left prints? Did I become an amateur all of a sudden?"

Confused, Audrey hesitated then asked, "You took precautions?"

"Of course I did! Don't you remember? I wore latex gloves.

Audrey closed her eyes in relief for the briefest of moments. She let out a sigh. She waited for a scolding that she cut off before he had the opportunity.

"Excellent. I remember now. But, there's a bigger piece of the puzzle you may have overlooked."

"I doubt it."

"How many people were with us when I came to pick up those ashes?"

"Do I include the poor soul who took up residence in the box you were given?"

"That's just it. You didn't give me the box. You gave it to Ryan O'Connor."

"So?"

"So guess who these two officers will likely speak to next?" she asked incredulously.

"Oh, I get it. You think Ryan O'Connor is going to sit down with the police and help them with a sketch of me so they can put out an all points bulletin throughout the Metro Portland area. Get the dogs ready for a manhunt and track me down. Is that it?"

"Yes…that's exactly what I think!"

"Take a pill. You really think the police are going to leave the donut shop to track down someone who doesn't exist? Give me a break."

Audrey once again remained silent. This time she wasn't the first to jump back into the conversation.

"And another little item you might recall was the prominent scar I had on my left cheek. It looked pretty real didn't it? I did it myself," he said proudly.

Audrey moved the speaker part of the phone away and took in a deep breath then blew out, her lips forming as if she were going to whistle.

"Your right. I'm being overly cautious."

"You're being paranoid. Is that why you called?" I'm called the Repairman for a reason you know."

"I know. I'm sorry."

"Apology accepted. It's not easy being in the field and feeling all alone," he said with sympathy in his voice.

"I was going to contact you anyway," Repairman said changing the subject.

"Why?"

"I want to know what you thought about your recent visitor."

"Nice guy. I think he has a future. I don't think it will be in tailing anyone very soon, but he's solid."

"You picked him up right away, huh?"

"I think he took an ad out before his plane landed," laughed Audrey.

"You said he's solid. That doesn't sound very solid to me."

"Just a rough start. Was he given any training before coming out here?"

"No. His expertise resides elsewhere."

"I can tell you this. He started out like a lead balloon, but ended up taking off like a missile in the end. Wait until I send you what he came up with. It'll blow your mind!" said Audrey.

"He was there to continue your cyber training. Did something else come up?"

"Just wait until you receive my package. It's on a hard drive buried inside a stuffed animal. He may have revolutionized the way we communicate. I changed quite a lot of it myself, but the guts of what he did is extraordinary."

"Missile. If what you say is true, that name just might stick," he said.

"Huh?" asked Audrey.

"You said in the end he took off like a missile," Repairman said repeating Audrey's words.

"Missile. I guess it's as good as any," said Audrey with a slight shrug of her shoulders.

"You need anything else?" asked Repairman.

Audrey was hesitant to share the information, but decided to bring it up as much for her own safety as for playing for the team.

"Do you know, um...Missile has a very talented brother?"

"We know he has a brother that's a little different, but not so much talented," he replied.

"According to Missile this guy is off the charts when it comes to anything with a computer chip in it."

"I know he's done pretty well for himself in the financial industry...in the tech trading arena. Other than that he's not on our radar."

"We aren't supposed to use names on the phone, but since he's not on the government's payroll I think it would be OK don't you?" asked Audrey.

"Put a military spin on it for me so we aren't breaking the rules," said the Repairman.

"Sam...Echo...Foxtrot...Tango...Echo...Romeo," replied Audrey.

"What's the first name?"

"That's his entire name. He had it legally changed."

"Who in their right mind would choose Sef—"

"Watch yourself Repairman. No names...remember?"

"What's your specific interest in this person?"

"I think he hacked my computer and printer," said Audrey.

"Didn't know you could hack a printer."

"Neither did I and that's the point. He could be a potential asset, but he sounds like an individual who doesn't like to play by the rules," said Audrey.

"You and I would have no idea of what that's like would we?" he chuckled.

"Your right. He's probably a perfect fit. Dagger...out," she said hanging up the phone.

Chapter 34

Present Day

As the training day went on Tony became very comfortable with handling a firearm. His nervousness about firing a gun evaporated with each squeeze of the trigger. After just a couple of hours Tony began to understand the nuances of hand and finger pressure allowing him to enjoy the strategic side of target shooting. He asked many questions and Tank filled him with as much information as he possibly could without making his ears bleed.

Standing behind Tony and watching every one of his adjustments Tank thought, *This kid's a natural.*

"So, you ready for your target test?" asked Tank looking at his watch.

"Do you think I'm ready or do you have somewhere to be?" replied Tony.

"Sorry, I have another client coming in. Just checking the time. You don't have a problem with me working with someone else on another lane do you?"

"I don't care if you double or triple dip as long as I get properly trained," said Tony.

Tank stared, nodded and placed a fresh paper target under the clip then sent it down range to a distance of thirty yards.

"You have two shots to hit the silhouette of the head."

"Now, place your weapon inside the holster in the back of your pants at your waistline just like you practiced earlier today. Take two steps back, turn and face away from the target. When I say go I want you to turn back and take your two shots. Got it?"

"Got it," said Tony as he stepped back and turned away.

Tony calmed himself and waited for Tank to give the go ahead when suddenly something came over him as if ice crystals were forming on his skin from the inside out.

"Go!" said Tank.

Tony didn't move.

"Hey! Geek squad, I said go!"

Tony remained in his frozen state.

Tank walked up behind Tony and with his thumb and index finger popped him on his left plastic ear protection cover.

"What the—" said Tony as he began to reach for his Sig Sauer P226.

"Whoa Tony!" Tank said holding his hands up in surrender. "Keep your weapon holstered!" demanded Tank.

"Sorry Tank."

"What the hell's wrong with you?"

"Um…nothing." *At least nothing I can tell you about,* he then thought.

"Nothing my ass! We agreed to go on my mark. You didn't respond. You stood there like a snowman in January."

"Who's your next client?" asked Tony.

"That's confidential and you wouldn't know him anyway."

You might think that, but I may have already met him, thought Tony.

"Hey, you won't tell me who your employer is so why should I tell you who my clients are?"

Tony nodded, "That's fair."

"OK, let's get back to your test," said Tank calming down.

Tony stepped back into the shelter of his firing lane so as not to see or be seen. With his amplified earmuffs he heard the door open to the range. Tank had turned to get his notebook out of one of his many duffle bags. The feeling, now so strong, Tony stood as still as possible closing his eyes...*Changing Colors.*

The security system conman! Tony thought.

He squeezed two fingers between the makeshift screens to take a peek and saw Stan Davidson the security alarm specialist. Tony's heart rate jumped then settled. He pulled his fingers back and proceeded to dismantle his weapon to buy time to think. Tank, now turning back to Tony, moved in to see what Tony was doing.

"Why'd you do that?" he asked Tony.

"Just making sure before I take my test."

Tank paused then said, "OK, I'll give you points for that. Look, my other client is here. I have to go say hello and get him set up. I'll be back in a few minutes. And put that back together," he said looking at the pieces of the gun Tony had broken down in front of him.

Tony calmly said, "I'll be here ready to go."

Leaning back just far enough Tony watched Charlie Tankerton walking down to the other end of the range.

I wonder what's in that notebook, Tony thought.

Tony quickly put the Sig Sauer P226 back together, picked up a Springfield XDM 9 millimeter and placed it in his waistband holster then double checked on Tank. Tony felt most comfortable with the Springfield and its back pressure safety features. He moved like lightening scrambling to retrieve the notebook. As he opened the bag he couldn't believe his eyes. The duffle bag was filled with notebooks. Quickly rummaging through from left to right he saw each has the year and a letter of the alphabet written on the front of the spiral notebook covers.

How can anyone be so archaic in this day and age of computerization? He could at least use a tablet, thought Tony.

He grabbed as many as he could with one hand from the right side of the bag presuming these would be the latest entries. Tony picked up the one that was already open.

Hastily looking at the page he saw today's date and chicken-scratching of very specific notes. The most alarming feature was staring at him from the top of the page and written boldly; 'TONY JAMES'.

I can't believe he actually uses the real names of someone who was contacted by a government agency that likes to keep their secrets to themselves. Audrey needs to know about this, thought Tony.

Another thought struck Tony as he began to read.

If my real name is in here then the real name for Stan Davidson, the conman, should be here as well, he realized.

Tony turned the page, but found nothing written. He fanned the remaining pages and suddenly found the newest entry for one Mr. Bruno Parrelli of Gresham, Oregon.

That's just west of here. And yet he used the Hertz rental airport location when he visited my house pretending to be a home security systems salesman, thought Tony.

Tony poked his fingers through the paper shroud once again to check on Tank.

I don't have much time. Ah-ha! My phone, he thought excitedly.

Tony took as many pictures as he could, without using a flash, in the little time he had. To his surprise, he had plenty of time to place those back in the bag and grab a few of the first notebooks from the left side of the bag. Changing tactics Tony sped through the first one using his phone's video camera to capture every page. He zipped through the second one getting three quarters of the way done when he felt the pressure to get them back in the bag.

From a distance Tank called out to Tony.

"Hey, geek squad! Come on over here and meet one of the best marksman this side of the Mississippi. You might learn something." said Tank.

From behind the shroud Tony yelled, "Be right there."

Checking to be sure he could get the notebooks back without notice Tony scurried and successfully did so. He began to walk toward the very person he wanted so badly to track down.

One of the best marksman this side of the Mississippi, rang through Tony's mind. *Tread lightly.*

Tony purposely pretended to adjust his weapon at the small of his lower back as he was ten feet from Bruno Parrelli. AKA...Stan Davidson, home security systems salesman.

Bruno and Tony's eyes met. This meeting had shootout at the OK Corral written all over it. Mainly because Tony knew that Bruno Parrelli had bugged his house on the bogus visit about a security system. Tony turned his head and looked directly at the security camera, eyes lingering for a longer time than necessary, sending two messages at once.

You're being recorded on camera so don't do anything stupid, Parrelli. And, yes I remember you from your little visit to my home for these very same types of cameras. Now their working against you, thought Tony.

Charlie Tankerton said, "Guys I appreciate you accommodating me by allowing me to work with both of you on the same day yet separately."

Tony noticed Bruno broke the first rule on the range.

His gun is not on the rest pointing down range. It's in his right hand. What's he expecting? Tony wondered.

Tony raised his right arm and took notice of a slight rapid reflex of Parrelli's hand muscles.

Bruno Parrelli began to raise his arm.

"Whoa! What the hell's wrong with you! Put that gun down! Can't you see he just wants to shake your hand!?" Tank admonished Parrelli.

Tony stood sheep-eyed with his hand extended ready to greet this great marksman.

"Sorry, Charlie. I didn't even realize—"

"Well, I taught you better than that. Time for a refresher course for you!"

He then turned and said, "I'm Sorry about that, Tony."

Bruno Parrelli shifted his gun to his left hand, looked Tony square in the eyes and fired one shot without looking at his target then set the Glock down properly. Bull's-eye…message delivered.

Message received loud and clear. Tank's right. I do need to carry a weapon everywhere I go, thought Tony.

Tony initiated a real handshake this time.

"You look awfully familiar. Are you in the computer industry?" asked Tony testing the man's capacity to think on his feet.

"No, sorry, I'm not," he said calmly giving no further information.

Tony pretended to suddenly remember, "Wait, you're 'The Bug Man'!"

Now let's see what you do with that, thought Tony.

Unfortunately Tank interrupted and said, "Bug man? Have the two of you met before?"

I'm not saying a word. Let's see who blinks first, thought Tony.

"You must have me confused with someone else. I work for a home security alarm firm."

"Right. But, you're 'The Bug Man'." said Tony prodding him along.

Tank said, "OK, knock it off. Obviously the two of you know each other already."

"Now I know who your real employer is…," he said pointing to Tony.

"Oh, and who would that be?"

"You're on the same team as—"

Parrelli cut Tank off before he used his real name.

"I remember now. There was a mix up with an appointment. You're a lucky guy, Parrelli said to Tony."

"Why's he so lucky?" asked Tank.

"Have you seen his wife? She's not only one of the nicest people I've met, but she's also absolutely gorgeous."

"Hmm, the geek's got game. Who knew?" said Tank looking at Tony in a new light.

"Stan Davidson," said Parrelli returning the handshake as an awkward re-introduction.

For the sake of keeping Tank out of it Tony returned the quick handshake keeping his eyes focused on Parrelli's.

"I could have sworn you were known as 'The Bug Man'. Sorry about that," said Tony.

"Did you ever get a security system?" asked Parrelli.

Tony deflected the question and asked, "Why were you driving a rental car the day you came to my house?"

"Um...that must have been when my car was in for repairs," he said just a little too clumsily. "So, what are you doing here?"

Oh, this guy's as quick on his feet as Sam's favorite elephant at the zoo, thought Tony. *Not a good trait for a conman. Obviously not just only a conman if he's here and being touted as a great marksman by Tank.*

"I'm here putting together the last piece of my home security system down there," said Tony nodding in the direction of his target lane.

Parrelli stiffened a little. Just enough to be caught by Tony.

That's all I needed from this guy for now, Tony thought.

"Tank, when you said you were going to split time with another client I didn't know you would be gone this long. How about we wrap it up for the day," said Tony.

"You're right, Tony. Let me go over some basics to remind *Mr. Davidson* on how to behave while on the target range." He gave an angry look at Parrelli.

Within twenty minutes Tony breezed through his test and passed with flying colors. Tank was eager to see Tony in the morning, but Tony had other ideas.

"I think we're done, Tank. It's been a real interesting time. You taught me exactly what I need and your other client proved to me that the best protection is self-protection."

"But, what about your defense training?" pleaded Tank.

"Don't worry about it. I'll make sure you get paid in full. I don't need that kind of training," said Tony.

Tank looked at Tony's height and build and realized he could probably handle himself especially now that he has the training with the great equalizer. They shook hands and Tony was on his way.

Once outside Tony snapped another picture of the only car that could possibly be Bruno Parrelli's. He knew Tank was driving a Chrysler. Tony had the Ford. The only car remaining in the visitor parking lot was a light blue BMW.

I'll call this in to Audrey. She'll fill me in on just who this Bruno Parrelli character really is. There's something wrong with this whole picture. Why would Audrey put so much faith in Charlie Tankerton? He's just a mercenary in my book, Tony thought to himself.

Chapter 35

—§—

1995

Dennis Forman, 'The Repairman', sat at a desk that wasn't his, sipping his morning coffee. He absolutely hated being in the building at Langley. He refused an office, but was assigned one anyway. His office was on another floor and he tried very hard not to use it. Confining him was like incarcerating a Bengal tiger. He'd pace back and forth thinking of things he should be doing elsewhere.

A knock at the door made him stiffen as he automatically began to reach to acquire his weapon at the back of his waistband.

"Sir, this package came in from LA," said a pleasant female voice on the other side of the door.

Dennis relaxed then turned taking purposeful long strides to open the door. The package was presented with a smile.

"Thank you Janine."

Janine Sheppard is an anomaly at the Central Intelligence Agency. Specifically, she's working in the home office as an assistant to a 'newbie' and not out doing fieldwork. She is a stunningly beautiful woman with long brunette hair and an IQ north of 140. She's the entire package. Many of the new male employees visit the third floor just for a glimpse.

"It's been vetted," she said closing the door.

"How'd they know I was in Don Williams' office? And, by the way, how did this pee-on get an office?"

Janine sarcastically asked, "Did you read the Central Intelligence Agency sign out front? We know things. And, I think you know how he got an office."

Dennis responded with a roll of his eyes. He saw the package had originated in Portland and then routed through Los Angeles. He was trained to know packaging codes.

This is what Audrey was talking about, he thought.

Forman lifted his head and watched her walk back to her desk.

Wow! Somebody's a lucky guy. No wonder why people around here call her 'Miss America', he thought.

Instead of trying to find a letter opener in Williams' desk drawers, Dennis reached down without looking and pulled up his left pant leg retrieving a switch-blade from his ankle knife holder. He made quick work of the tape and returned the blade to its home.

I hate this damn Styrofoam stuff. It sticks to everything! he thought.

Finally, the pink and gray fuzz of a toy elephant's trunk appeared. He grabbed it and lifted the stuffed animal out without regard for the mess he was making.

Turning the toy so he was looking at it face to face he said, "So, you're going to revolutionize the way we communicate. I doubt it," he said to the toy.

Dennis didn't open the elephant, but he could feel it weighed way more than it should. He picked up the phone on the desk and called for Janine.

She quickly entered and Dennis asked, "When is Williams due back?"

Janine checked the appointment calendar then said, "He's scheduled to be in tomorrow. Is there something I can do for you?"

"Yes. Give him this package and have him give me a call. Better yet, just give him the toy and get rid of the box."

Don handed the stuffed elephant to her.

"Ooh, heavy little thing. It'll look cute right here on the corner of his desk. I'll make a note on his task list. Is this a priority?"

"It is," said Dennis watching her set the fuzzy toy down just so.

The following day Don Williams got to work before Janine. He entered his office, saw the elephant, but went straight to his calendar. He saw that Janine had made a priority entry regarding the little visitor sitting on his desk.

He picked the elephant up and he could easily tell there was something inside. Protocol dictated he send it down so the contents could be analyzed. Just then, he heard a familiar soothing voice.

"Good morning, Don."

"Hi Janine. What can you tell me about this," he said pointing to the toy.

"It was delivered yesterday. Dennis Forman opened it."

"Forman? Why do I have it then?"

"He used your office yesterday."

"Damn it Janine—"

"It's a well known fact he's used just about everybody's office around here. He even tried your father's once," she said pleasantly letting him know she had no choice in the matter.

With a heavy sigh Don said, "You're right. Sorry."

"That's OK. Do you need anything from me"?

Don, standing holding the gray and pink stuffed animal said, "Yes. Send this down to Nate in the lab and have him call me when he figures out what this thing is…besides a stuffed elephant."

Within the hour the building shook and a low rumbling nose came from underneath the structure.

Wide-eyed, Don grabbed hold of his desk calling out to Janine. The white frosted glass from his door completely shattered. He looked through and saw that almost every door encountered the same fate. He couldn't see Janine.

He waited for a moment just in case there was another rumble.

"Janine! You OK!?"

As he got up Janine slowly rose up from under her desk and said, "Yes! I'm…physically fine!"

"Please get on the line and find out if that was an earthquake!"

"Don, I lived in California for ten years. That was not earthquake!"

"Then what was it?"

Just a few minutes earlier computer lab assistant, Nate Treemont, picked up the stuffed elephant and felt the

315

extraordinary weight and began to squeeze the middle. He felt a hard structure buried within its belly. Nate saw no value in the toy so he ripped it apart at the seams. To his surprise he found a hard drive. As he pulled the hidden contents out, Nate didn't realize he had just disconnected a trip-wire. Flipping it over, he then read the words written in bold black marker...'HI DONNY - BOOM!' Just as the message sunk in, the hard-drive exploded shooting ball bearings and nails throughout the lab. It laid waste to everything and everyone in its path. Nate Treemont was killed instantly. His right arm obliterated and never to be recovered.

Chapter 36

—§—

Present Day

Tony drove home from the shooting range thinking of his day with Charlie Tankerton. In the forefront of his mind was his encounter with Bruno Parrelli, the 'security alarm salesman'. It was then that Tony realized just how unpredictable his new world can be. He turned on sports talk radio to get his mind off the perils of humanity only to find the topic of another sports figure being arrested to be of no interest to him. His mind quickly wandered back to the shooting range. He originally thought there was no way he had any plans to actually carry a firearm on him. But, after his encounter with Bruno Parrelli he was having second thoughts.

I need to give Audrey a call. More importantly I need to give her a call with some evidence of Charlie Tankerton and Bruno Parrelli. And those notebooks. I need to look at the pictures and video. While I'm at it I need to finish up with Audrey's computer files. I've got a lot to do, he thought.

Tony arrived home to find Jacquelyn on the phone in the kitchen. As he walked past her toward his office she motioned for him to stop. She put the phone on speaker and a female voice rang clear as a bell.

"...so we are honored to invite you to speak at the next city-wide school district in-service meeting," the voice said.

Tony gave her a 'what's this about' gesture. He was trying to recognize the voice.

She held up her index finger to him then said into the phone, "I'm honored and looking forward to it, but don't you think it would be best to have Mrs. Conway speak since she was just given the distinction as Teacher Of The Year?"

"You'd think so, but everyone I spoke to recognizes that you know what you're talking about. Between you and me that was more of a political choice anyway. Can you meet me at school tomorrow night for a brief meeting?"

"Tomorrow night? Can't we meet during the day? Maybe right after school?"

"I'm so sorry, but I have a conflict. I guess it's tomorrow night or never," the female voice said in a passive-aggressive tone.

Suddenly, Tony realized who Jacquelyn was speaking with...Agent Elizabeth Wolf. Or was it her sister Danielle?

Only one way to find out, he thought.

He motioned for Jacquelyn to accept the meeting. Jacquelyn was taken by surprise at this knowing full well he didn't like her to be alone on campus at night. But, she trusted her husband with her life. She also knew he would accompany her.

Once off the phone Jacquelyn turned to Tony and asked, "Why do you want me to go back to school at night of all times? There's no reason to schedule a meeting like this in the first place. A simple email would suffice," she said.

"Exactly what I was thinking," he said.

Tony walked over to the refrigerator and removed the phone number from the sticky-note and showed it to Jacquelyn.

"Call this number and then tell her you just checked your schedule and can't make it till later. And please put it back on speaker," said Tony without further explanation.

Jacquelyn questioned him with her eyes, but pressed the digits anyway. On the third ring the same voice answered. She gave a shoulder shrug to Tony.

"Hello?" she answered.

"Hi again. I'm so sorry, but I just checked and that appointment time won't work for me after all. Can we make it an hour later?" said Jacquelyn feeling like she was drowning.

"Who is this?" asked the woman on the other end of the conversation.

Tony had written a question on a piece of paper and quickly handed it to Jacquelyn imploring her to ask.

"This is Danielle isn't it?" asked Jacquelyn with a confident tone along with a look of confusion at Tony.

"I'm sorry. Who's is this?"

Tony had already prepared and handed her another note.

"We just spoke about the in-service meeting tomorrow night," said Jacquelyn.

"I'm sorry; I'm in the middle of—"

Another quick note from Tony.

"Oh, I'm sorry. I thought I was calling the number of one of our new substitute teachers. She gave me her number if I ever needed—".

"Jacquelyn I'm just kidding around with you," she said in a totally different tone.

Tony had already slipped her another note saying "*She has caller ID...she knows it's you.*"

"Oh, good. I thought I misdialed at first," Jacquelyn replied.

"What time did you say the meeting is tomorrow?" the woman asked.

Tony did a victory fist pump. *Two different people, same voice*, he thought.

"We just spoke about it. You were the one with the conflict," said Jacquelyn kindly.

Tony mouthed the word 'perfect' and gave the OK signal to Jacquelyn.

"Oh, right. I turned off my tablet so I don't have my calendar open. Sorry. Hang on just a moment."

"That will be just fine. Meet you in your classroom?"

"Very funny. You know very well we set the meeting for the library conference room," said Jacquelyn.

"Of course. I just turned my tablet back on and see it now. I'll push it back one hour. Thanks for calling me back Jacquelyn. I'm looking forward to seeing you," she said then ended the call.

Jacquelyn checked to be sure the line was cleared before she said anything to Tony.

"That was the same voice, but definitely not the same person! You have some explaining to do Tony," she said.

Tony enlightened her about the two twin sisters. Jacquelyn was not particularly happy about what she heard.

"So, which one was I just talking to?"

"That was agent Elizabeth Wolf."

"So I really was talking to Danielle Green when you came home?" asked Jacquelyn.

"That's exactly right."

"But, why would she want to meet me at school at night?"

"That's the million dollar question. And one more thing, I was told agent Wolf is on vacation. So why is she meeting you tomorrow night?" said Tony.

Tony dropped his briefcase off in his office then heard Sam and Nick coming through the back door. He greeted them with big hugs and kisses.

"Hi Dad," said Samantha.

"Hi Dad," echoed Nick.

"Did you guys have a fun time next door?"

"Yup. They got a new puppy!" exclaimed Sam.

"Can we get one?" implored Nick.

Dodging the question Tony asked, "What's the puppy's name?"

Nick looked at Sam. She stared back then said, "We don't know. We just called him puppy."

The kids were all giggly and ready to bolt so Tony said, "Homework first then wash up for dinner."

"Are you cooking, Dad?" asked Nick.

"You're Mom and I haven't decided yet."

"If you do cook, I want pepperoni on mine," said Nick.

"Just cheese for me," Sam said.

They took off with Sam in the lead.

I really should learn how to cook, thought Tony.

Jacquelyn just gave him a wry smile.

While the kids did their homework at the dining room table, Jacquelyn and Tony sat in the living room talking quietly. The TV provided privacy for them to talk. Tony told her all about the security systems salesman. He left out the part about being threatened with Bruno Parrelli's left-handed bulls-eye shot.

"I'm all done with my homework," Sam announced.

Jacquelyn got up and sat with the kids to check Sam's work then checked to see if Nick needed any guidance. While Jacquelyn did this, Tony decided to go down the hallway to his office.

I need to look at that notebook information before I call Audrey, he thought.

Tony placed his laptop into the docking station so he can use both monitor's and a full sized keyboard. Connecting his phone he then clicked through the photos he had taken at the target range. Once through those he then watched the video he took of the other notebooks.

Jacquelyn walked in asking about what they want to do for dinner then fixated on the left monitor playing the page turning video Tony had taken with his phone. She stood quietly for a moment just watching. Tony had fixed his eyes on Jacquelyn's facial expression.

"I know I shouldn't have taken—"

Jacquelyn cut him off saying, "Go back just a little."

Tony was surprised that Jacquelyn didn't give him the business about snooping around in someone's personal belongings. He paused the recording then began the rewind process with the images flying by.

Jacquelyn said "Stop!"

She pulled up a chair and sat on the edge of the seat next to Tony.

"Go forward a little, but go slow," she said as if talking to one of her students.

What's so interesting, wondered Tony.

Both of them looking at the monitor, Tony felt at ease working side by side with her.

"Right there!"

Tony paused the video.

"Back just a little and go very slow," she said as she took complete control.

OK by me. I have no idea what you saw, he thought.

As the recording played backward Tony finally saw what Jacquelyn had seen. He pressed pause and it was right in front of them big and bold on the twenty-two inch monitor. Tony and Jacquelyn looked at each other in disbelief then back to the still-framed monitor. Tony quickly printed out the image.

"Mom? Dad? We're hungry," shouted Sam from the kitchen.

"Be right there," said Jacquelyn transfixed to the image on the monitor.

She turned to Tony and said, "Is that what I think it is?"

Tony took the paper out of the printer and both of them took in the meaning. They looked at each other again in disbelief.

"How did this training guy—"

His name is 'Tank'," said Tony.

"How did he get this? More importantly, why does he have it taped into a notebook?" asked Jacquelyn.

"Apparently there's way more to Tank than I imagined," said Tony.

Both of them stared back at the image of a birth certificate as big as can be on the monitor in front of them. The certificate was for that of twin girls born minutes apart from one Audrey Shelton. Their names? Danielle and Elizabeth.

Tony looked for the name of the father. The line is blank.

"Does that mean what I think it means?" asked Jacquelyn.

"If you think it means Andrew Shelton is not the father you could be right or you could be wrong. Without a name we don't know," said Tony.

"This guy...Tank. Is it possible he had this made up for some reason?" asked Jacquelyn.

Tony clicked on button and froze the second screen. It showed the front of a green spiral notebook with writing that was not like the other notebooks. This one was entitled 'DAGGER'.

"I wonder what 'DAGGER' means?" questioned Jacquelyn

Tony side-stepped and said, "Jacquelyn, all the other notebooks just had a date and a letter of the alphabet on them."

"Well, is there a better way to hide something than with a title only he knows the meaning in a pile of what looks to be training records?"

It then hit Tony like a ton of bricks. *Audrey's computer and the picture*, he thought.

"Mom? Dad? We're really hungry," shouted Samantha.

"Yeah. Really hungry," Nick's voice chiming in.

"Leave this for now. Our children come first. We can get back to this later tonight," said Jacquelyn.

We?

Chapter 37

—§—

1995

With chaos all around her, Janine spoke into the phone and said, "Thank you. I'll tell him."

She stepped lightly due to the glass and debris as she made her way to Don Williams' office.

Talking through the hole in the door where the frosted glass had been previously she said, "It was an explosion in the lab."

"Please don't tell me…"

"It was the contents of the toy elephant you sent down. Nate's dead…I'm sorry."

Williams sat so still he felt as if his heart was going to jump out of his chest.

I killed Nate, he thought.

Janine sensed what her boss was thinking and said, "You had nothing to do with it, Don."

"The hell I didn't. I'm the one who specifically asked for Nate to look at the package. If it weren't for me he'd still be alive."

"That's not true."

"How could it not be true?"

Janine paused to contemplate how she should break the news then flatly said, "Nobody in the lab survived."

Williams' eyes seemed to fade into the black color of night. His shoulders slumped in defeat. He then placed his hands over his face.

"How could I be so stupid," he quietly said to himself.

Janine, still standing at the door said, "There was no way you could have known. It had been vetted."

Without lifting his head Williams quietly replied, "Give me a few minutes, will you Janine?"

Once she was out of sight Williams opened his lower right-hand drawer with a key. He removed a metal box and unlocked it as well. Williams placed it on his lap, opened the hinged lid then gazed upon all the threatening letters he had received over the past few months.

This can't be a coincidence, he thought.

Within a week after the explosion the CIA building at Langley appeared as if nothing had happened. The lab had been re-built with eight inch reinforced steal and an additional six inches of concrete. The power of government funds at work. The people's money. Not a single news story was to be found anywhere. The Agency made sure of that. Dennis Forman made contact with Audrey to get the details of who she used in LA to send the hard-drive.

"The guy's name is Sefter. I can't tell you how I found him—"

"You don't have to. You told me about him before, remember? I know it's Williams' brother and Jeff Statz' son," said Forman cutting her off.

Audrey was surprised, but didn't let on as she said, "Then why are we talking?"

"I want to know why you would use someone out of our network when sending a package as important as you said this was."

"Are you questioning my loyalty?"

"Why aren't you answering my question?"

"I thought it would be very safe to extend our resources to a family member of two of our own."

"You were gravely mistaken weren't you?"

"Are you saying Sefter was the one who placed the explosives in the stuffed toy?"

"We're not sure if Theodore "Sefter" Williams is on our side. He's a wild card with an agenda all his own. I don't like his track record. Why did you think you could trust him given his background?"

Because I met with him right after he dodged his brother, Don, just after he went out to see him in LA, she thought.

"He's Jeff Statz's son and Don Williams' brother. I didn't think I could go wrong," she said.

"Next time stay within the network. It's there for a reason. No need to go off protocol."

"I'm terribly sorry about Nate and the lab team, but you'll have to convince me Sefter had anything to do with it. He seems to be very sweet and harmless," lied Audrey.

"His name is Theodore Williams and I'll let you know if there's any hard evidence that we uncover. For now, he's a Person of Interest. Why are you defending him? People have died."

Audrey paused to think for a moment then said, "I guess it's because I chose him and didn't consult with you before I used someone out of our approved network."

"All right. I presume you have a copy of the program so send it to me right away using proper channels. I'll catch you later," said Forman hanging up without allowing Audrey to say goodbye.

Good. I'm pretty sure he bought it, thought Audrey.

Audrey went home and unzipped the throw pillow from the love seat and extracted her copy of the CPT program.

I have to get this to Dennis right away. But, before I do I need to make a special copy for myself and add a line of code to track Sefter's communications. If he's as good as I think he is, he's about to become very dangerous. Useful, but dangerous. He's a genius when it comes to moving money around, she thought.

Audrey stayed up most of the night writing the perfect line of code that even someone as skilled as Sefter shouldn't discover. She set the dormancy spectrum so tight it becomes just about invisible. Audrey will send this copy to Forman and hope the CIA lab won't find the hidden line of code.

Two days later Dennis Forman was once again sitting in Don Williams' office. Dennis was sitting in Don's chair. It was at least an hour before Williams was due to arrive. Easily connecting the dots, Forman quietly began unlocking the drawers to the desk.

When he got to the bottom right drawer he said, "Hello. What have we here?"

Twenty minutes later Don Williams unlocked his door to find Dennis Forman sitting at his desk. Hands clasped behind his head and feet up on the desk.

"Damn it Forman! You have your own office. Go use it for a change!"

Forman helped track Williams' eyes to the metal box sitting in front of him on top of the desk. Williams was speechless for a moment then caught his breathe.

"You want to tell me what's going on or should we go see the DCI?"

Williams dropped his briefcase and inadvertently left the door open then sat across from Forman.

"I can explain," he said.

Forman remained silent looking calm stretched out behind the desk.

"About six months ago I started getting these letters," he said with his eyes on the metal box.

"And when were you going to tell someone about them?"

Williams stuttered, "I...I thought I could take care of the matter myself."

"What is it with everyone going off book these days?"

"Huh?"

"Never mind. Are these from your brother?"

"How do you know about Sefter?"

"Because THEODORE is a POI," Forman said forcefully.

"Are you kidding me? Sefter wouldn't hurt a soul."

Forman stared at Williams then said, "Your right. He wouldn't hurt anyone. He'd just kill them quickly."

Williams looked away as he thought of his friend Nate Treemont. The guilt he felt was palpable. Forman seized on William's feelings.

"Tell me where I can find your brother."

Lifting his head and meeting Forman's gaze Williams said, "I have no idea where he is. I just got back from LA. He was supposed to meet me at the airport, but he didn't show. I took a taxi to his apartment. He wasn't there either. I waited, but he never showed."

"Well, we're going to pick him up and question him for causing the deaths of everyone in our lab."

"If he doesn't want to be found, he won't be found. He's got a lot of money and can be anywhere on earth within hours. Besides, there is nothing in those letters that links him to the lab bombing."

"Are you defending him?"

"Just giving you facts, Dennis."

Forman paused just long enough to make it uncomfortable.

He finally asked, "Are these all the letters? Or are you holding back?"

"Of course not. That's all of them. They were all delivered here and vetted for anthrax and other poisons just as protocol requires. If you haven't noticed, some of them don't have postage."

"Which means he delivered them himself?" asked Forman.

"I don't know who delivered them."

Janine had heard enough as she lurked just outside of Williams' office door looking busy. She went back to her desk and picked up her purse and quietly and swiftly exited the building. Walking two blocks east, she stopped at the bank of payphones that lined the street.

Audrey answered, "Hello?"

"My son is in trouble," said Janine.

"Which one? You have three."

"The one you just met with in LA."

"How'd you know about that?" asked Audrey.

"Have you forgotten who you're talking to?"

"Right. Sorry. What kind of trouble?"

"Repairman has picked up a scent that he mailed letters to Don Williams."

"The computer geek that was just out here? What's he got to do with anything?"

"I think you know," said Janine.

"Tell me or we're just playing a guessing game."

Janine paused then said, "Their brothers."

"I know that," chided Audrey.

"Half brothers, but they don't know. We raised them as full-fledged siblings and told no one," said Janine.

"Are you telling me they have separate mothers?"

Once again a long pause from Janine then, "Just the opposite."

It was Audrey's turn to take a long pause.

"This isn't safe. I'll call you back on a secure line—"

"No. All lines are being monitored," said Janine.

"Right. Tell me what you need."

"I need you to run interference or they'll eventually find out I sent, and even delivered, some of the letters on my son's behalf."

"Why in God's name would you do that?"

"It's a long story and I'm short on time."

"Then tell me what you need from me," said Audrey.

Janine explained that she needs an absolute air-tight alibi when it comes to why her fingerprints are on the security box and the letters themselves.

"You didn't wear gloves, Janine?"

"Now is not the time for an 'I told you so'. Remember, I know about—"

Audrey cut her off sternly by saying, "Don't say another word!"

"Then you'll take care of this?"

"Consider it done."

Audrey hung up then Janine did the same. However, Janine made one more call.

Chapter 38

—§—

Present Day

Jacquelyn and Tony spent quality time with the kids over dinner. Tony could tell that his bride was eager to get back to his office and continue to unravel the mystery they had uncovered together.

Once back in Tony's office he and Jacquelyn took the same seats just prior to dinner. The kids were watching a show on TV so he and Jacquelyn didn't have to whisper.

"That's amazing that Audrey has children. I've never heard her mention them before. I also have the feeling she acts as if her husband doesn't even exist. She never speaks of him and he's never at any company functions," said Jacquelyn.

"Your right. She mentioned him once, but she made it sound like he died. Anyway, back to the subject of Audrey not talking about having children. There's a good reason for that."

Jacquelyn didn't need to ask.

"She's said all along she and Andrew never had children," said Tony.

"Why would she lie about something like that?"

"Technically she hasn't been lying."

"Tony, how can you say that with proof staring you in the face?"

"Because, she has said she and *Andrew* have never had children. I've never heard her say she's never had kids. Big difference."

Jacquelyn looked at Tony like he had three eyes then said, "Splitting hairs aren't you?"

"I'm learning how these people think. In their world this isn't a lie," said Tony.

"I don't think I like their world," said Jacquelyn.

"Well, then I don't think you're going to like what I have to tell you next."

"Before you say anything, are you sure we aren't being listened to and are you sure they don't know you told me about what happened in Washington, D.C.?"

"I'm confident they don't know," Tony said calmly.

After a slight hesitation this put Jacquelyn at ease.

Then Tony said, "I made a copy of Audrey's personal computer hard-drive without her permission."

Surprisingly, Jacquelyn didn't bat an eye.

You're not even a little upset...hmm, thought Tony.

"OK, to begin with, we're going to search and cross reference anything that has to do with Elizabeth, Danielle, Charlie Tankerton, Simon Swan, Audrey and Andrew Shelton from her data files."

"Can you do that?"

"Her files are encrypted with multiple firewalls surrounding them. It'll take awhile, but I have the software to put it on auto-pilot. The tricky part is to set certain parameters properly so as not to get locked out."

"If that happens then the information is useless?" asked Jacquelyn.

"There's that. But, more importantly a signal could be triggered and she would be notified exactly what's going on and where."

"I don't think you should play around with something like that Tony."

"First, I know what I'm doing. Second, there's something not right going on," said Tony turning his chair to face Jacquelyn completely.

"But, what if you do trip that trigger thing?"

"Jacquelyn, I need to try."

She paused then said, "I know you've made up your mind already and there's not much I can do here. If you find something let me know."

Jacquelyn got up took Tony's hands and gave him a peck on the top of his head.

"You have my full support."

"Thanks Jacquelyn. You don't know how much that means to me."

Tony ran a successful simulation run and was ready to activate an exploratory extraction program. He sat back, ran everything through his mind, then clicked 'Start'. The program began without locking him out. Tony didn't realize he had been holding his breath. The extraction continued to run well into the night.

The next morning Jacquelyn sauntered into Tony's office to find him sitting upright and fully asleep. She touched him lightly on the shoulder.

Tony jumped out of his chair, turned around and pulled his pistol from the holster in the back of his pant's waistline.

Jacquelyn screamed.

Tony quickly lowered his weapon and let out a sigh and said, "You scared the hell out of me!"

"You're scared!? How do you think I feel? Put that thing away!"

Tony looked at the gun in his hand and lifted his eyes to meet Jacquelyn's and said, "Sorry."

"Just put it away. I'm fine with you having it as long as you protect this family. In a weird way I'm actually relieved you reacted that way."

Tony stared in disbelief.

"What? You think I relish the thought of meeting some imposter tonight without knowing you were well prepared? Now I know you're taking this seriously. I'm guessing it's protocol to carry at all times," she said calming down.

Protocol? Carry? I've never heard her speak like this before. I don't think I talk like that around her, thought Tony.

Tony slid the weapon back into its holder at the base of his back then gave Jacquelyn a big hug.

"I'm really sorry Jacq—"

Suddenly a soft 'bing' sound came through the computer speakers indicating a hit on one of the cross references. Tony sat back down to see the read-out on the screen to the right as the program continued to run on the left.

It read; New Folder>Shopping>Gifts>Friends>Female>Jewelry>Brace lets>Gold>Miss America>CI4551196262

"What does it mean Tony?"

"It means there's a file buried under a folder with eight sub-folders with some kind of information that links at least two of the names we placed into the search. Do you know anyone who names a computer folder 'New Folder''?"

Jacquelyn furred her brow then asked, "What's all that other computer data after it?"

"It tells me the folder has been encrypted and protected with extreme measures," said Tony as he examined the line of code.

"So it's a file we can't get to?"

"Oh, we'll get to it alright. Count on it. Once I know the pattern we'll be able to open it undetected," Tony said confidently.

"You're sure no one has detected anything yet?"

"You'd know it if it was."

"How?"

"Let's just say it wouldn't be my gun to be the only one pointing at you today."

Jacquelyn's eyes opened a bit wider.

"Relax. I know what I'm doing."

"I don't doubt that but, I'm thinking of Sam and Nick. Should we maybe get them some place safe?"

"Jacquelyn, please relax. We are safe. Nobody knows what I'm doing. If you hear a siren sound coming from the computer speakers then it's time to panic. But, I don't see that happening," said Tony.

"I'm going to put together a contingency plan just in case," she said.

'Contingency plan'. Where is she getting this stuff? wondered Tony.

"Good idea. You work on that. I'll work on this," he said.

The search program ended an hour later with only the one hit. Tony examined the protection surrounding the folder and each of the sub-folders. He saw the pattern and devised a work-around.

Here goes nothing, he thought.

As the program time icon rotated on the monitor to his left, the right one showed a slow scroll of computer language that would read like Greek to almost anyone else. Tony kept a close eye on this monitor.

Once the scrolling had stopped, Tony ran it once again and proclaimed it safe to attempt to open the first folder using a specialized spyware program. He inhaled then held his index finger over the enter button. Once depressed there was no turning back. He executed the keystroke then exhaled and waited.

The screen to his left had changed to what looked to be like bars on a music amplifier. All nine of them were green and moving up and down as the program worked on opening the first folder entitled 'New Folder'. Tony's attention was on the first bar in green and the need for it to level out rather quickly. If the color turned yellow he knew he was headed for trouble. Red means he's busted.

Tony held his finger over the escape button just in case. This would execute an immediate stop and hopefully avoid the trigger that was built into the first gradient firewall.

"Come on. Level out," he prompted.

It did. The first bar steadied then turned solid green without further movement.

"Yes! One down…eight to go."

In succession, each bar followed suit. After fifteen minutes Tony was looking at all but one bar that was popping up as if playing whack-a-mole. It was the last sub-folder and the most important one at that.

Tony whispered, "Please."

Suddenly, Tony thought he saw a split second of yellow. He just about pressed the escape button, but he wasn't sure if he really saw yellow or if he imagined it. His heart pounded. It seemed like a lifetime. A bead of sweat formed at his temple.

"Please," he implored once again.

Just as he spoke the solid green bar of success showed its pretty little face.

"Yes!"

He removed his hovering index finger from the keyboard then flexed it a few times cracking his knuckle along the way.

Tony inserted a flash drive that looks like a Mont Blanc pen when closed. He made a few quick keystrokes and downloaded the contents of the files to it. He carefully closed out of everything on his computer fastening the flash drive into his shirt pocket.

Jacquelyn stepped into his office just as he turned off the last monitor.

"Well, I didn't hear any sirens. There aren't any goons with guns in the house. I assume you were successful?" she asked.

"This part…yes."

"What do you mean 'this part'?"

"I'm not going to open the other files on my computer especially here at home."

"Where are you going to open them and how? Did you email them to yourself or something?"

"Yeah. Something like that," Tony said trying to shelter Jacquelyn from knowing too much.

"So, where do we go to extract the data?" she asked.

Extract? Data? We? What's going on with her? Tony wondered.

"I'm going to open the files using someone else's computer."

"Who's computer?"

"Not sure exactly. Maybe when I'm on a call to a client. They leave me alone all the time mainly because they only care about getting their computer system back in proper working order. But, more importantly their just too busy and have other things to do."

"That's smart. So, we're safe," said Jacquelyn prompting him to say yes.

"I think so. At least for now. I still haven't seen the information. It could be nothing."

Jacquelyn stood quietly then finally said, "I'm making a run to the store. Do you want anything?"

You were so concerned only moments ago and now you're just running off to buy groceries? Something's not quite right. Maybe I've scared her, thought Tony.

"Jacquelyn, are you OK?"

"Yes. Why?"

"It's just…you're suddenly taking this all in stride."

"Is there anything I can do about it? I mean, I can't take any real action, can I?"

"No, I suppose not," said Tony.

"Then I'm going to the store. Last chance if you want anything," she said in a soft tone.

"No, but thanks," said Tony scratching his head.

Chapter 39

—§—

1995

After hanging the phone up from her brief conversation with Janine Sheppard, Audrey sat back in her office chair and pondered who the father could be if it wasn't Stan Williams. Numerous candidates came to mind, but none seemed logical.

Audrey had to come up with a plan to protect her investment in Sefter. She left the office and called Dennis Forman.

"To what do I owe the pleasure," said Forman to Audrey.

"I got to thinking about using Sefter as a courier and —"

"You mean Theodore Williams," Forman injected immediately.

"Right. Anyway, I was thinking we should rattle his cage on this explosive device that killed Nate and the others."

"I thought you and he were tight?" Forman said sarcastically.

"I've met him and have gotten to know him a little. I think we would have a head start if I went back to LA and did this myself. Besides, I'm already out here in Portland. I'm only a short distance away."

"Your timing couldn't be better. I've just opened a Level Two investigation on him to see what we can find."

"Why a Level Two?"

"I only want certain people around here to know about it."

"You just told me."

"You have access to Level Two. Why shouldn't I tell you?"

Audrey shook out the cobwebs and said, "Right, I forgot. Tell me what you've got so far and I'll go see him today."

After hanging up with Forman, Audrey drove to another payphone downtown and called Anarchy Venture Capital in LA to let Sefter know she was coming to see him. She then made contact with Janine Sheppard to let her know.

Anarchy Venture Capital began as Sefter's way of putting his financial talents to work while networking with like minded anti-government individuals. He made many people enormously rich while compiling a fortune for himself at a very young age. While most of his clients spent their money raging against 'The machine', Sefter began a life of remaining mostly underground sharpening his passion and thirst for knowledge through computer hacking.

Knowing full well that Forman might give an order to put eyes on her and Sefter, she moved through the city of LA making sure she lost anyone who might possibly try to tail her. She told Sefter exactly where and when to meet and how to get there. He appreciated her professionalism and trusted her skills.

"So, what's the big deal?" Sefter asked Audrey as they sat across from one another drinking coffee in a small empty café.

He reminds me of someone. It's his eyes, she thought.

"The big deal is you killed seven people at the CIA! That's what's the big deal!"

"I didn't try to kill them. I was trying to blow up my half-brother."

"You know Don is a half-brother?"

"Sure. You'd be surprised what can be found out when information flows freely."

"So, you found out hacking into a database somewhere then," said Audrey.

"Your words, not mine."

"Sefter, do you realize how much this places me and Andrew in jeopardy by you putting a target like this on your back?"

"How so?"

"Come on Sefter. Your one of the smartest people I know."

"Maybe when it comes to investing, computers and hiding money for certain people who work for the most secret agency in our government...yes," he said.

"Come on, that's not fair," she said.

"Your right," he said smugly.

"Thank you," said Audrey calming down.

"No, I mean it's not fair. Life's not fair. I learned that at a very early age. It never will be fair as long as agencies like the one you work for have the ability to run over anyone who gets in their way. I particularly hate the IRS," he said coldly.

Audrey took a good look at him and tried to take in the features of his face. She knew Janine is his mother, but

345

she didn't know who his biological father could be. There was something familiar. Especially his eyes. She thought about an elaborate way of trying to find out then quickly realized his defiance is his weakness and went after that.

Quick and simple, she decided.

"You're good, but don't overestimate yourself," she said.

"Why not?"

"You seem to have everything under control, but you don't even know who your real father is," she said irreverently.

Sefter stared at her then said, "Is that why you're here? To prod me into telling you things that I don't want you to know?"

"You can't tell me, Sefter."

"You really think I don't know?"

"I know you don't," she said leaning in to emphasize her point.

"Trust me. I know," he said taking a sip from his coffee.

"Prove it. Who's your real father?"

He hesitated before answering then said, "Don't waste your time trying to look up any records. They've all been changed. Sometime in the future I'll send you proof of who my real father is, but for now let's get to the true reason you're here…your precious private stolen millions.

"Sefter!" scolded Audrey.

"I'm sorry, your private stolen money that currently resides in the Cayman Islands with your husband who just built a Wi-Fi network on the island. Would you like me to tell you the account number?"

Audrey was shocked he knew about this and for the first time in a long time she was speechless.

"Yes, Audrey I know way more than you think I do. But, as long as we work together, your secret is safe with me. By the way, I love that new communication program you developed with my brother Donny. The improvements you made are tremendous. There's no way he could have created such a clean and ingenious program. He's an ideological fool."

Again, Audrey was shaken by Sefter's knowledge.

I need to find a way to either rein him in or I'm going to have to eliminate him, she thought.

"OK, here's why I'm really here. Have you ever considered how much you could gain by being on the inside of the CIA?"

"Why would I surround myself with the very people who are taking American freedoms away?" Sefter scoffed.

"Look at it from another angle. If you're on the inside you have almost unlimited access to as much information as you desire."

"I pretty much already have that."

"No you don't or we wouldn't be sitting here," said Audrey.

Sefter looked at her for an abnormally long period of time.

This is a good sign, she thought.

"I don't see it," he finally said.

"You don't see the benefits of being on the inside of the most cutting edge agency in the world?"

"No, I really don't. I'm my own boss and do as I please. I may not have as much money as the pathetic government monkeys budget for the CIA, but I have enough to keep me amused."

Time to change tactics, thought Audrey.

"Your mother would love to see you safe."

Sefter bristled and said, "Leave my mother out of this. She did her best."

"She's very concerned."

"She'll be fine," he said dismissively.

"Look, a highly regarded agent has just opened an investigation against you. Do you really want your mother to get caught up in all this?"

"I know about agent Forman. He just filed is inquiry. I saw the file."

Audrey was dumbstruck at how quickly Sefter knew about Forman coming after him.

"How could you possibly know?" she asked.

"I'm rich, inquisitive and care about my freedom," he said in an answer that almost seemed rehearsed.

He followed up and said, "Let's get to the point of all this, shall we? Your concerned about your precious money if I get caught up in Forman's investigation. It hits too close to home for you."

"That's only part of it."

"What's the other part?"

"I promised your mother I'd see to it you don't get caught up in this thing."

Sefter stood. Tossed a $100 bill on the table.

"Don't worry about me. Worry about the team your husband wants to put together some day."

He began to turn to leave.

Audrey reached out and grabbed his wrist and sincerely asked, "What are you talking about?"

"You don't know?

"No, I don't," Audrey said with pleading eyes.

"I guess being on the inside isn't all that it's cracked up to be."

"Where did you get your information?"

"Andrew himself. I'm his first recruit."

Sefter turned and walked out leaving Audrey pondering if he was telling the truth or trying to divide and conquer.

Chapter 40

—§—

Present Day

On her way to the grocery store Jacquelyn dropped the kids at her mom's. She then stopped by the school office and checked the district's computer to see if the meeting was in-fact really on the schedule. To her surprise...it was. She called Tony on his CIT Smartphone and told him to check his personal phone. She then left her voice message on that phone. Meanwhile, Tony found the perfect client and opportunity to look at the file he extracted from Audrey's computer. Not once was he disturbed. With total focus, Tony tried to move as quickly and efficiently as possible. To his surprise he discovered not just one file that his cross reference program found, but it had actually located two.

"How could I have possibly missed that one," he said quietly.

He opened the first file that was a simple spreadsheet of CIT's income and expense report from years earlier. The look of it was that of a macro view of the financial health of the company.

Under normal circumstances this would bore me to tears, but this wouldn't have been encrypted if it weren't part of whatever this puzzle is, thought Tony.

As he read the columns on the left-hand side of the spreadsheet he found one entry that seemed to stick out from the rest.

Why only three letters...AVC? he wondered.

He looked at the far right column and saw a total amount of $6.56 million deducted from the ledger. No explanation of any data to be found anywhere within the spreadsheet. He didn't have time to sit and ponder all the possibilities.

Next he opened the bonus file. It was a text document.

Sefter, is that a person's real name, nickname or code name? Maybe it's a company name, he wondered.

To his surprise he found it to be an email attachment letter from Sefter to Audrey. He quickly read the one paragraph letter;

Audrey,

It's been quite awhile since we met at the coffee shop in LA. I told you I knew who my biological father is, but I wouldn't say who. You doubted that I really knew. You challenged me. You should know by now not to doubt me. I don't play fair with people who doubt me. I like you so you might get a second chance. If you challenge me again, I'll crush you. I said I would send you the name in the future. I usually keep all my promises, but I've decided to let you try and learn who it is on your own. Try to realize, we're not exactly on the same team. I'm not really on anyone's team. I'm looking out for myself. The question you should have asked is how did I come to know about the secret funding operation of the Central Intelligence Agency. So, now you know that I know. What will you do? By the way, who's Danielle?

Sincerely,

Sefter

p.s. Don't worry about your cut of the money. It continues to grow leaps and bounds in my company,

Anarchy Venture Capital. How do you like the name? We'll keep moving it every six months or so. I was hired to do a job and I will follow it through.

Tony couldn't believe what he just read. He shook off the shock and once again realized where he was and time is of the essence. He safely removed the Mont Blanc pen look-a-like flash drive and put it back in his shirt pocket.

Anarchy Venture Capital. Is this for real? Who the hell is this Sefter person and what money is he talking about? Secret funding? Tony wondered.

His hands shook as he packed up his work. He had the manager sign the appropriate paperwork and left the building as quickly as possible.

I think I have a ticking time bomb on this flash drive, he thought as he touched it. *I wonder if I should call Audrey and come clean about this. I might be in over my head. This is bigger than I thought.*

Tony pulled out his CIT Smartphone from his briefcase. By second nature he quickly pressed the button to view the screen and saw he missed a call from Jacquelyn. He listened to her short message then deleted it. Prior to listening to Jacquelyn's message on his personal phone he erased the thought of placing a call to Audrey.

As he started the car he thought the obvious.

AVC...Anarchy Venture Capital! That's what AVC means on the spreadsheet!

He began to place a call to Jacquelyn using his CIT Smartphone then quickly dropped it on the passenger seat as it were radio-active. Tony then picked up his personal phone without checking his messages and called Jacquelyn letting her know to keep Sam and Nick at her parent's house and meet him at home.

352

Once there, Tony told Jacquelyn what he found on the flash drive. She encouraged him to go with his initial instinct and call Audrey since he was so new to this kind of work. Jacquelyn was scared and felt honesty should be the best policy.

"Not necessarily in this case Jacquelyn. Remember, I took this information without Audrey's knowledge. I'm not proud of what I did, but I'm now glad I did it. Besides, I'm finding that keeping information then using it at the right time is very important."

"Oh…right. I forgot you *stole* that from her so that makes a difference," she said with an emphasis on the word stole.

"Hey, take it easy on me."

"What's gotten into you, Tony? You don't do things like that."

"Jacquelyn, I did it for us."

She held a lengthy pause then said, "Sorry. You didn't deserve that. I know you wouldn't do anything to hurt me or the kids. So, what should we do?"

"Nothing at the moment. You go to the meeting tonight as planned. I will be with you as always. At this point everyone at school expects me to accompany you on campus at night anyway."

"Are you nuts!? Whoever's meeting us there is not a person to tangle with," Jacquelyn said emphatically.

"It's not until 8pm. We have plenty of time to put a plan in place," said Tony with confidence.

Jacquelyn paused, stared at Tony then said, "You like this stuff don't you?"

Tony didn't answer as he was already deep in thought.

Chapter 41

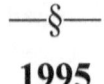

1995

After meeting with Sefter, Audrey remained in the coffee shop for an additional thirty minutes continuing her vigilance to make sure Forman hadn't sent anyone to keep tabs on her. The narrowing list of Sefter's possible biological fathers kept rolling over and over in her mind.

Logic won out as she finally realized, *It could be anyone. Hell, it happened to me. But if he knew, why is he being so secretive? Same reason I didn't tell Andrew I suppose. Now's not the time. I have to get back home.*

Once back at Portland International she made contact with agent Forman to try and ease his mind about Sefter. She has too much at stake to allow a full blown investigation into Sefter to derail her and Andrew now.

She went home and booted up the CPT program to communicate with Andrew. After writing a rather abrupt note about his knowledge of Sefter, she sat back and waited for him to respond. Fifteen minutes went by without an incoming email so Audrey sent another saying, 'WHERE ARE YOU?'.

After another ten minutes she gave up and turned the computer off. Since Sefter's little stunt with her printer she also turned off the power strip.

Her home phone rang.

"Hello?"

"Go to the payphones at the corner of 5th and Couch streets," the mechanically altered voice said then hung up.

"Who is—"

Audrey placed the receiver back into its cradle and did as she was told. Traffic at this corner always seemed steady no matter the time of day. She took in every parked car and person nearby and burned them into her memory. She scanned the buildings across the street.

The third phone on her right began to ring. She glanced at her watch to appear casual. Wearing skin colored latex gloves Audrey answered the call without saying anything.

The same altered voice said, "Maverick...not secure or contained."

"An—I mean Maverick? Is it really you?"

"No time. The person you met with at the coffee shop in LA must be protected at all cost. Our financial future relies on him," said the voice then hung up.

Audrey stood a little straighter slowly placing the receiver back in its cradle.

Why would Andrew contact me this way? It's not like him. How does he know that I know about Sefter? Ah, Unless he read my note and this is his reply. Wait...that can't be right. Something's wrong.

Audrey had a feeling she was being watched. Maybe she was being paranoid, but then again maybe that's how she seems to stay one step ahead. As she stood silently in front of the pay phone a plan began to play out inside her head. She quickly picked the phone back up and pressed '0'.

"Operator"

"Hi, I was just having a conversation and the call was interrupted. Will you please re-connect me?"

"I'm sorry for the inconvenience, but I'm not allowed to do that," said the operator.

"But, I have no idea what phone number to call him back," Audrey sweetly implored.

"That I can provide. Please verify the phone number you are calling from."

Audrey read the number off the pay phone then added, "The number is local."

The operator gave Audrey the number. Audrey thanked her then smiled as she fished for change to put into the coin slot. Once the proper dial tone came to life she placed the call.

"Trinity Corporation, how may I help you?"

Chapter 42

—§—

Present Day

It was time for Tony and Jacquelyn to head off to her school for the 8pm meeting. Jacquelyn became increasingly tense as the time neared. Tony had shut the door to his office. He practiced pulling his firearm from the back of his waist a couple of hundred times. Tony put on a sport coat to conceal his weapon. Thanks to Tank, he knew full well he was breaking the law taking a firearm onto school property.

"I don't care. If I have to, I'll shoot anyone who threatens my bride," he said softly in cold monotone voice.

Just as he straightened his collar Jacquelyn opened the door and said, "It's time to go."

"Are you OK?" asked Tony as he drew her into his arms.

"I'm nervous," she said closing her arms around his waist.

Suddenly she pulled back.

"Is that—?"

"It's just in case," he said as calmly as possible pulling her back in.

There is only one entrance and one exit to and from the school campus for safety reasons. With the various school shootings around the country in recent years, the school district made it more law enforcement friendly by creating a one-way in and one-way out roadway system.

Tony and Jacquelyn road in silence. They took the time earlier in the day to review what may or may not happen. Tony had created multiple contingencies leaning heavily on his instincts. He slowly drove past the entrance of the high school.

"Tony, you missed the entrance."

"Just going to take a quick cruse around before we head in for the meeting."

Hmm, no other cars in the parking lot, thought Tony.

Finally Tony parked in an area that did not provide much light.

"Why are you parking way over here?" Jacquelyn asked in a genuinely sincere tone.

"I have my reasons," Tony said in that same monotone voice.

Jacquelyn looked at him and noticed a very different man next to her. She knew when he meant business and she was grateful to be on his side.

They approached the main entrance doors on foot. They found them locked just as they should be. Jacquelyn used her key to unlock the outside door. Tony entered first with Jacquelyn following right on his heels.

Tony stopped suddenly in the vestibule. He turned his head slightly to his left and cocked it a little, barely narrowing his eyes...*Betrayal*.

"What's wrong?" whispered Jacquelyn.

"It's nothing. How far is it to the conference room?" Tony asked.

"I'm not very good with distance," said Jacquelyn.

"Is it the length of a racquetball court or—?"

"That seems about right. Maybe just a little bit more. It's on our left down the hall."

"So about forty to fifty feet?"

"I guess," she said not really sure.

Jacquelyn used her key card to enter the building and they both walked through the threshold. The hallway was dimly lit. Lockers lining both sides. Tony's right hand at the ready if he needed to draw his firearm.

"Shouldn't there be more lights on?" asked Tony.

"Not necessarily. The school is trying to conserve energy even when meetings are scheduled."

Jacquelyn could see a glimmer of light from the conference room. She pointed it out to Tony. He nodded his head. They continued slowly down the hallway. Tony put his index finger to his lips as they stopped short of the room.

He concentrated deeply almost closing his eyes. The feeling he got and the words received were not what he was expecting.

One familiar and one not. How can this possibly be? he wondered.

Tony whispered, "I don't like this. You have your car key?"

Jacquelyn nodded her head affirmatively.

"Good. You need to leave."

"But—"

"Trust me. You really need to get in the car and leave. I'm going in."

Tony took a deep breath and stepped into the conference room. As he walked in all the remaining lights turned on due to a motion sensor. It almost blinded him for a moment. He then heard the familiar voice.

"Welcome Tony! It's so good to see you again," said agent Elizabeth Wolf.

Tony looked around the room as his eyes adjusted to the light.

"Cat got your tongue?"

"Elizabeth, what are you doing here?" Tony asked.

"Knowing you, I wouldn't doubt you probably have a good idea."

"Not a clue," said Tony with eyes still searching the room.

"Tony. You know I know your about your ability. You can stop looking around the room."

Jacquelyn was listening closely just outside the room. She didn't know what to think. Her instinct was to walk into the conference room to be at Tony's side. However, she stayed disciplined and remained with her back against the wall by the door hanging on every word.

"You're right, I can stop searching the room," he replied.

Tony walked over to the high-backed conference room chair and found a very pretty older woman, legs crossed, sitting perfectly still. She kept her head below the top of the seat backrest out of Tony's view. She swiveled the chair to meet Tony's gaze.

"Hello Mr. James. Very impressive. I've heard so much about you. How did you know someone else was in the room with agent Wolf?"

"Who are you?" asked Tony.

"I'm the one who called this meeting. And, nice job deflecting my question, by the way."

"If you wanted to meet me why would you call a meeting with Jacquelyn?"

"One can't be too careful can they?"

Tony tried to connect the unfamiliar feeling and word that had been delivered to him just before entering the school. He didn't understand...yet.

Betrayal...what's that about?

The woman stood, calmly pressing out the few wrinkles from her slacks. She's taller than most women. Almost as tall as Tony. Her hair and make-up done in a manner that would normally take most men out of their comfort zone. The work she had done made her look at least ten years younger than her real age. She is a beautiful woman. Tony, being married to Jacquelyn, was certainly used to this every day.

Without so much as a flinch, Tony did not avert his eyes from hers. He could tell immediately she used direct eye contact as an intimidation tactic.

She has no idea who she's dealing with when it comes to that, thought Tony.

The woman began to turn yet held her gaze with Tony as long as possible then she slowly walked toward agent Wolf and stood next to her.

"You still haven't answered my question," said Tony.

"Which was...?"

"Who are you? What's your name? he asked bluntly.

"My name is Janine Sheppard."

"And why do you want to meet with me?"

"Let's sit down and discuss exactly that," she said waiting for Tony to take a seat.

Tony walked directly over to the right side of the windows that spanned almost the entire length of the room. He turned the blinds to the closed position.

"Paranoid Mr. James?"

"Cautious. Is it Mrs., Ms. or Miss?" Tony retorted.

"Smart move with the windows. It's Janine."

"Thank you, Janine."

Agent Wolf did not sit down so he stood back up.

"Going somewhere Mr. James?" asked Janine.

"I am unless agent Wolf joins us at the table and you start calling me Tony."

"Come, sit with Tony and me, Elizabeth," said Janine moving a chair for her.

"So why am I here?" asked Tony.

"You have something I want," said Janine.

Tony didn't respond.

"Elizabeth said you have an interesting ability to know the true nature of a person. It that correct?"

Tony shifted his eyes to agent Wolf then back to Janine Sheppard without answering.

"Based on the fact you could not see me when you entered the room and you knew someone else was here tells me she's correct. So, what is my true nature, Tony?"

Run Jacquelyn...run! he thought.

"Are you with the CIA like agent Wolf," he asked.

"What a natural. You really know how to avoid answering questions don't you Tony?"

"You tell me."

Janine looked at agent Wolf and said, "You were right. He is perfect."

Tony kept his hands resting at his sides out of sight for quick access to his gun.

"Perfect for what?" asked Tony.

"Once again, nicely done...trying to take control of the conversation. As much fun as this is, I don't have a lot of time. So, let me get right to why we're here tonight."

I hope you're gone Jacquelyn, he worried.

"I used to be with the CIA. I'm not anymore. I know about the Savant Syndrome Division. It's a stupid name by the way. Anyway, you have an ability and are positioned perfectly and can work for ten times the amount of money the government is paying you. I want you to work for me."

"No thanks. I don't even know you," replied Tony.

"A direct answer. You must really mean it," Janine said in a calm sarcastic tone.

She leaned in across the table and said, "I think you will change your mind. All you need to do is slowly get up and check on your bride who should be just outside the door."

Tony's eyes widened. He thought about grabbing his weapon, but saw agent Wolf was just as prepared and she has more experience. Tony called out to Jacquelyn to come into the room.

"Jacquelyn?" He paused then said, "It's OK. You can come on in."

Please be gone. Please God, I hope she ran, he thought.

No answer. Tony then got up with agent Wolf standing at the same time. He quickly walked to the open doorway. No Jacquelyn.

Thank God! Smart girl, he thought.

Tony turned back to face both of them and said, "Thanks, but no thanks. I'd like to say it was a pleasure, but I wouldn't want to lie."

He walked out of sight then sprinted through the hall, the vestibule doors and finally outside. Tony ran toward the area where he parked the car and stopped cold. The car was still there.

She was supposed to leave, he thought.

He approached their car carefully ducking down just in case. Hoping Jacquelyn was hiding in the car waiting for him before she left the parking lot. Tony remained behind the back bumper closing his eyes to focus. He didn't sense her presence. He checked the car.

Damn it! Where can she be? he desperately wondered.

Tony realized he would have sensed her even if she were unconscious. This made him feel just slightly better.

Where are you, Jacquelyn?

Chapter 43

—§—

1995

Audrey stood frozen still hanging onto the payphone receiver at Fifth and Couch Streets. Quickly she realized her phone conversation with the mechanical voice was generated within the CIA. She placed the phone back into its cradle.

OK, if that wasn't Andrew...who was it?

After subtly scanning her surroundings she headed for home. It took her an extra hour to do so. Audrey used every trick in the book to identify if anyone was tailing her. Once home she booted up her computer and checked for a reply from Andrew. It was there. She checked the time-stamp.

This was sent at the exact same time as when I answered the call at Fifth and Couch. I doubt that could have been Andrew. He would have had to be at a payphone and not in front of his computer, she deduced.

She sent a new email to him asking about the phone call. The reply came back within minutes confirming he had not placed a call to her. His last sentence put an end to her questioning the possibility it was Andrew on the other end of the line at the payphone. It read; WHAT PHONE CALL?

She wrote him back explaining her situation. They corresponded back and forth over the next hour hatching a plan to figure out who's playing the imposter. Audrey got to work right away. She went to the heart of downtown and called Dennis Forman from another payphone.

After protocol was satisfied Foreman asked, "What can I do for you?"

"Are you on a clean line?" she asked.

"Secure and contained."

"Maybe you didn't hear me. Is it CLEAN?" she asked emphatically.

"No. Let me call you right back," he replied knowing Audrey wouldn't react like this unless she had a good reason.

Audrey's payphone rang and she picked up, but did not say anything once again just in case.

After a few moments she heard Forman's voice say, "Secure, contained and *clean*."

"Thank you Repairman. Can you tell me who, within the Agency, has access to information about Operation Monopoly?"

Dennis was surprised to hear Audrey employ the actual name of the operation used to position the CIA to create a revenue stream from the corporate world and bypass the political budgetary process.

"Are you OK, Dagger?" he asked sincerely.

"I don't know. Can you tell me who else knows?"

"The only person I can tell you for sure is the DCI."

"Nobody else?"

"Not that I'm aware. Why?"

Audrey told him about the phone call from within the CIA and the mechanical voice, but left out the part about Sefter. This is part of the plan she and Andrew agreed upon to localize the leak by giving only partial information to a handful of people.

"How the hell could someone know about that particular OP?" he said with his voice level elevating.

"Where are the files stored?" she asked.

"The only files on this one is in the Director's safe," said Forman.

"Then who has access to his safe?"

Forman hesitated for a moment then replied, "I would think only the DCI himself."

"Do you really believe he was the one that called me using a voice scrambler?" she asked.

"No."

"Then who else knows or has access?"

Forman remained silent for a long period of time.

"You still there?" asked Audrey.

"I'm here. I was just thinking about all the slow progress of transferring paper files to the new encrypted digital format that's going on within the Agency," he said as if talking to himself.

"Are you saying the contents of that file has been transferred?"

"It's possible. I don't really know." he said.

"How do we find out?" she asked.

"I'll do some digging on my end. You're the CEO of a computer company that is now tied to the Agency. You may have a window of opportunity."

"How so?" Audrey asked to make sure to understand completely.

"This might be the perfect time for the CIA to hire an agency approved computer company capable of doing a better job of the file transfer. Also, what a perfect time to ultimately pay themselves for a job that needs to be done anyway."

"That's brilliant! I'll get right on it!" said Audrey excitedly.

"Let me know when you have things in place and I'll help you from here," said Forman.

"One more thing. Can you think of anyone on the inside that would have the intelligence and balls to engage Maverick and me?"

"You mean besides me? I'll have to think about it," he said.

"One quick detail that I think is very important," said Audrey.

"What's that?" asked Forman.

"The caller knew An—Maverick's code name. Again, only a few people know this piece of information," said Audrey.

"Hmm…that'll narrow my search considerably," said Forman.

"OK, I'll put the wheels of CIT in motion here and you work on your short list. Let's compare notes no later than tonight or tomorrow morning."

"You know you can count on me, and Dagger, watch your back. Someone has information they shouldn't. I have skin in this game too. If someone knows about the OP then they likely know my involvement as the morgue assistant. I refuse to get caught up in this, you hear me?"

"Then we both want the same thing," said Audrey.

Audrey hung up first, closed her eyes then leaned her forehead on her arm still holding the receiver on its cradle and thought, *Perfect. He's exactly where I want him. He'll save my neck to save his own.*

She walked three blocks south. Ducked into the Sheraton Hotel making sure nobody was following her. Stepping into an enclosed phone booth, complete with a permanent stool to sit upon, she made her next call.

"Janine Sheppard speaking," she answered.

"Hi Janine...its Audrey."

"Audrey, how are you today?" she asked cheerfully.

"Could be better. Can you speak freely?" Audrey asked knowing perfectly well she couldn't.

"Call me at the number I used last time I called you. Do you still have it?"

"Yes."

"Give me ten minutes," Janine said.

Janine approached the payphone then hurried the last few steps because it began to ring. Lifting the receiver she didn't say hello. She listened only.

"Janine?" asked Audrey.

"Sorry Audrey. People were nearby," she said.

She couldn't say hello because people were nearby? That's not right. I'm betting she wasn't sure if it was me calling. Who else could she possibly have taken calls from at this very same phone? Sefter? Easy enough to find out so I'll get right to the point, thought Audrey.

"Janine, I need your help. Agent Forman was involved in a covert OP, code name; Monopoly. Do you have access to the records?"

"Why? Is something wrong?"

"I want to make good on my word and protect Sefter," Audrey explained.

"Why would my son have anything to do with a CIA OP?"

"You're going to have to trust me on this, Janine. Do you or don't you have access?"

Janine hesitated as her mind seemed to go in different directions at once. She didn't want to give up too much information, but her son was somehow involved and she couldn't allow him to become exposed.

Very carefully she said, "I don't currently have access."

"What if CIT became involved in the transfer of our paper files to the new encrypted digital format. Could you find a way to obtain access then?" asked Audrey.

"I think so, but—" Janine began.

"Good. My next call is to involve CIT in helping with the transfer of those files. I don't want any of my people looking at the data because CIT was the first acquisition of many in Operation Monopoly. It would be a huge mistake for me to go poking around as well," said Audrey.

"That's understandable," replied Janine.

"Once CIT has the authorization I will give you a call back and provide you with the proper clearance to access the file and then you can make sure Sefter is protected," said Audrey.

"When will this take place?"

"Today," Audrey said without hesitation.

"OK but, what if I get caught?"

"You won't. I guarantee it," Audrey said convincingly.

"How can you guarantee something like that? You don't know for sure."

"You've known me long enough to know I keep my promises," replied Audrey.

Janine paused then said, "OK, I'll wait for your call. But, remember I'm doing this for my son."

"Understood. I'll talk to you soon," said Audrey hanging up the phone.

OK, two down and one to go, thought Audrey.

She placed more change in the coin slot then punched in the digits. The call was going through. Audrey peered through the phone booth glass making sure nobody seemed out of place.

"Williams," said the voice on the other end.

"Don this is your new friend out in Portland and please don't say my name out loud," she said quickly.

Williams' face turned serious then he asked, "What can I do for you?"

"Well done. I think we taught each other something during our time together. I understand you're involved with the digital transfer program. Is that right?"

"Yes."

"Do you have the authority to bring an outside asset on board to move things along at a much quicker pace?"

"Yes. How do you know we're behind?"

Audrey by-passed his question then proceeded to engage him in conversation about helping him with the data transfer project and the need for more resources to bring the undertaking in on time. He made the decision that Audrey was right. CIT would be a perfect fit and all preliminary background work could be eliminated since she was now CEO.

Once he hung up with Audrey he pressed the button on his phone to summon Janine Sheppard. Janine had just barely made it back in time to answer.

"I'll be right in," she said leaning in toward the speaker phone.

Janine found Don Williams standing and staring out the window.

He turned and said, "Please have a seat."

She sat on one of the two chairs opposite William's desk. Williams walked behind Janine and closed the door then returned to sit behind his desk.

"Janine, what do you know about CIT Corporation located in Portland, Oregon?"

Janine's face remained placid, but she felt as if all blood had drained from her body. She held her breath.

She finally said, "Nothing…why?"

"I want you to add CIT to help facilitate bringing in our digital transfer project in on time."

How in the world did she get this done so fast, thought Janine.

After a few more directions from Williams, Janine left his office, closing his door, and walked back to her desk. She was amazed at how quickly Audrey could turn the switch on to access the digital transfer program.

Her phone rang.

"Janine Sheppard," she answered.

"It's me. Are you all set?" asked Audrey.

"Yes. How did you—?"

"I'll be in touch," said Audrey just before hanging up.

Audrey had her confirmation that Don Williams controlled who could have access with regard to the data transfer program. She also found he had the authority to add CIT to work on it as well.

He has more power than I thought.

Audrey made a serpentine route back home to inform Andrew via the CPT email program. They communicated back and forth as Audrey gave Andrew all pertinent information regarding each player in the scheme they had concocted.

Andrew became adamant that they had to set Foreman and Williams up to force them out of any decision making authority. Audrey didn't understand as she thought it would serve them better to remove Janine and maybe Sefter.

Their wildcards and disposable, she thought.

Andrew's next email came as a surprise when he flat out told Audrey to do as he says. She knew then something was not adding up.

He's never treated me like this before. He never would have gotten to where he is without me, she thought.

Audrey replied telling him he was likely correct and she would take the appropriate measures. However, she had her own plan to execute.

Chapter 44

—§—

Present Day

Tony, now sweating, remained crouched behind his car at the back bumper with only two thoughts running through his mind.

Where are you Jacquelyn? I pray to God you ran!

Then his worst fear began to creep into his thoughts before he corralled it.

What if they—? Stop it! Now is not the time. Think logically. Where would she have gone?

He realized he needed to focus like he's never focused before. Every impulse in his body was telling him to run and search the area looking for Jacquelyn. Instead his logic did in fact return. By instinct he closed his eyes, using his unique ability, and scanned the area like a sweeping radar tower.

Turning slowly from right to left he cocked his head slightly stopping as if boring his mind through all the elements in his universe.

A sudden vibration was so invasive to his process he nearly jumped out of his skin! It's his phone. A text. He quickly pulled the Smartphone out and saw it was on the secret side of his phone. UNKNOWN CALLER.

'GET OUT OF THERE NOW!' it read.

Tony, stashing his phone back in his pocket, closed his eyes once again trying to locate any human personality trait in the darkness. Then finally a hit; *conman.*

His beads of sweat suddenly felt like icicles knowing now who was out there. He reached his right arm behind him and pulled his firearm from his waistband holster. Tony almost racked the slide placing a deadly projectile into the barrel then remembered it was already set for action. His phone vibrated once again.

TEXT FROM UNKNOWN; 'STOP AND THINK WHAT YOU'RE DOING! PUT YOUR WEAPON AWAY!'

He stared at the words on the screen in disbelief.

Who, and how is someone watching me?

He then realized the illumination from his phone screen was a perfect target for Bruno Parrelli, the conman. Tony's memory flashed back to the firing range and Parrelli's left handed bulls eye warning.

One of the best marksman this side of the Mississippi, remembering Tank's words.

Tony hadn't pinpointed Parrelli just yet, but knew if he stayed where he was he was an open target. He quickly began to move to the rear driver's side of the car when a shot slammed into the exact place he had just vacated a second ago.

He fell in behind the wheel of the car hoping this would provide the protection he had only seen on TV and in movies. Tony knew he couldn't stay here very long. He closed his eyes once again and focused. Just like trying to find the source of his concern in Audrey's office mirror he found the exact location of the source.

Parrelli's on the roof next to the air conditioning unit, thought Tony.

With eyes still closed Tony readied himself to take a shot. He fought the urge to open his eyes now knowing the precise location of the shooter. Somehow, his special skill had taken over and it was as if he could see Parrelli's silhouette even in the dark of night. This came as a surprise and was a huge paradigm shift in Tony's view of his ability.

Tony also remembered Tank telling him if he ever needed to use his weapon at night, the flash would blind him for more than a few seconds. That wouldn't be a problem for Tony tonight. At the moment his 'vision' was better with eyes closed. His breathing slowed to that of a marathon runner taking a nap. Then, with eyes still shut, he quickly turned and fired three rounds over the hood of the car at what his internal sensor told him to be the source of Bruno Parrelli.

Tony swiftly dropped down and quickly duck-walked to the front driver's side wheel waiting for a barrage of lead to come his way. His eyes open now. To his surprise not a single shot was fired in return.

Did I actually hit him or did he move? If he did move, is he trying to get to a better location so he has me in his sights? I'm not staying—.

His Smartphone vibrated once again momentarily making him think he was hit. Reality quickly sunk in. Again TEXT FROM UNKNOWN; 'HOW DID YOU KNOW WHERE TO FIRE?'

Who are you and how the hell are you seeing me? thought Tony.

Slowly he moved back behind the front tire then sneaked a peek at the front corner of the school building.

Surveillance cameras! That's got to be it. Whoever it is can see me from the cameras. Is Janine Sheppard and Elizabeth Wolf still in the building monitoring what's going on out here? But, where is Jacquelyn!?

Tony knew he had to make a move or he'd be a sitting duck if Parrelli had indeed moved to get a better vantage point. He could no longer *feel* Parrelli. As hard as he tried…he just couldn't feel his presence anymore.

Maybe he's gone, but I can't just sit here. I have to do something, he thought.

His phone vibrated once again; 'ENOUGH MESSING AROUND. YOU WILL BE PICKED UP IN SIXTY SECONDS'.

Does this person think I'm stupid? These texts are coming in on the secret part of my Smartphone, but no one else except Audrey and Forman have ever contacted me this way before. Am I being played?, he wondered.

Off in the distance Tony heard a police siren and realized it could be on its way to the school. Painstakingly knowing he could be leaving Jacquelyn behind, he quickly got in his vehicle started the engine and sped off at top speed hoping nobody would catch his license plate number.

My God! I'm so sorry Jacquelyn!

Chapter 45

—§—

1995

Audrey sat back in her home office chair staring at her blank computer monitor. She had shut the computer down and unplugged the power cord...thanks to Sefter's hacking talents.

Never in our time together has Andrew ever ordered me to do something so emphatically. Take out Dennis and Don? That just doesn't make sense, she thought.

Audrey chose the people she has confidence in and immediately left her house to make a phone call. She had taken to backing her car into her driveway just in case she ever needed a quick exit. Prior to getting into the car she circled it pretending to look at the level of air in her tires. Peering through sunglasses she scoured the area for cars she knew not to belong.

All clear, she thought.

She pulled out of her driveway making a right turn. About a block ahead she noticed a black sedan with tinted windows pull out from its parking spot in the street after she passed. She made a few extra turns and still the car was behind her.

Are you tailing me?, she wondered.

After verifying her Glock was in her handbag, Audrey continued her maneuvers to expose the possible tail. After several more obscure turns she was now convinced someone was indeed following her. She traveled to the western edge of downtown Portland still watching the black sedan a half block behind her. Audrey drove watching her rearview mirror as much as looking through the windshield at this point. Because of wearing sunglasses, she made sure to only move her eyes and not her head. At times she even turned her head to pretend to look left and right, but kept her eyes trained on the black sedan in the rear view mirror.

It was no longer important for her to lose whoever was tailing her. She now wanted to know who it is. Since Audrey finally had two lanes to work with she gunned her engine to make a yellow light so as to look like she was trying to get away. She watched as the black sedan also gunned it even though the light had changed to red. As soon as the black sedan was at its highest speed Audrey veered into the left lane and slammed on her brakes.

The person driving the black sedan had no choice but to slam on their brakes just a little too late. This gave Audrey an opportunity to try and view the person driving as he went two car lengths past. The tinting wasn't as dense as it appeared from a much farther distance.

Audrey was stunned.

"Jeff Statz!?"

Audrey pulled up next to his car, rolled her passenger window down and gave a 'what's going on' motion.

He pulled his car over into a curbside parking space. Audrey pulled in right behind. She grabbed her handbag, swung it over her right shoulder then placed her hand in position to use her weapon as it was concealed inside the handbag. She took note that the black sedan didn't have any extra lean to one side indicating to her no one else was in the vehicle.

Jeff began to open his door and Audrey shouted as she briskly walked toward his side of the car.

"Close the door and open your window Jeff!" ordered Audrey grasping her pistol inside her handbag.

He complied.

Audrey stopped short of the open window then said, "Hands where I can see them on the stirring wheel Jeff!"

As soon as he did so Audrey approached resting her arm in her handbag on the open window frame. Statz knew what she was holding in her handbag.

"Audrey, I can explain—" he began.

"Zip it Jeff! Tell me who sent you?"

"I came on my own."

Audrey surveyed the look on Statz' face. She couldn't tell if he was lying or not.

"Now why would you do that?" she asked.

"Let's not do this here," he said.

"I can't think of a better place for a quick explanation as to why you were tailing me. Your pretty bad at it. Do you know that Jeff?"

"Look, I don't want to be seen talking with you. Can't we go somewhere private?" he implored.

"Ever hear of this new thing called a telephone? That's a pretty private way to talk to me," Audrey said.

"I couldn't risk it," he said.

"Why?"

"Because, I think someone on the inside at the Agency has gone over the shadow's edge and I believe it has something to do with you."

"Is it your son, Don Williams?" asked Audrey trying to rattle Statz.

"He told you?"

"Yes, but he didn't mean to," she answered.

"Audrey, it's not Donny. He's one of the good guys."

"I don't know what the truth is right now Jeff. Why should I believe you?"

"Because after you called me to help Donny out he and I got together and put our past behind us. I wasn't a very good father to him, but we're working that out because you initiated a call to me about helping him with his career at the Agency. I owe you."

Audrey sized Statz up. Because he is an old friend she decided she was obligated to hear what he came all this way to say.

"I believe you Jeff," she said succinctly.

She lowered her handbag.

"Follow me to CIT, but drive past. Park your car at least a block away, wait about thirty minutes, then come up to my office and we'll talk. And another thing, next time forget the tinted windows. You stuck out like a sore thumb."

"It's good to see you too Audrey," he said with a soft smile.

Jeff Statz is officially the Assistant Director of Cyber Technologies for The CIA. That was in title only. He is something of an enigma. His daily activities were to be the invisible hands of the DCI himself without being on-site. Statz created cutting edge and unique tactics to communicate with the DCI without either of them having to meet face to face. He's very good at his job.

Statz arrived in the building well after Audrey had placed him on her schedule so he would be allowed to enter the elevator up to her office. Audrey decided not to take any chances and had set up an audio recorder.

They sat across from each other on comfortable chairs divided by a glossy oak coffee table.

After a little small talk Statz said, "I don't know how to tell you this, except to be blunt."

Audrey remained silent and looked as calm as could be.

"I know you have CIT set up to assist in the transfer of paper files to our new encrypted digital format so I'll dispense with the background as to why this came about. Someone within the Agency has been passing on confidential information," Statz said.

Audrey remained silent, but wanted to know if Andrew was right or if it was she.

Audrey said, "Why are you telling *me* this Jeff?"

"Because one of them is Andrew."

"Come on Jeff! Are you telling me my husband, who by the way hasn't been near Langley much less in the US, is stealing secrets? I don't believe it."

"I know he hasn't been in country, but I have documented proof of his coordination with an operative within Langley."

"Proof! What kind of proof?" scoffed Audrey.

"A tapped phone line with complete recordings of conversations."

Still skeptical she asked almost as if it were just a throw away question.

"Who'd be stupid enough to have that kind of conversation on an Agency phone?" She followed up by quickly asking, "With who?"

"Code name is Miss America."

"Janine Sheppard? You've got to be kidding me. Are you even sure it's his voice?" she asked.

"I have copies of the pertinent recordings with me. It will be hard, but do you want to hear them?"

"Yes. If you're going to sully my husband's good name then I want to hear the evidence you think you have against him," she said emphatically.

After ten minutes of listening to Andrew and Janine on phone conversations with each other Audrey said, "Enough! Turn it off!"

Statz remained silent. He felt bad that he was the bearer of this news. Audrey Shelton was one of his best students. She stood then walked over to her desk and placed both hands on it. She hesitated then pressed 'Stop' on her hidden recorder.

"You've been recording this meeting?" asked Statz in a soft tone.

"Yes. It's what we're trained to do Jeff. You of all people know that."

He nodded in affirmation with an almost imperceptible grin.

"What's so amusing?" asked Audrey.

"Nothing…just that you've come a long way since training. I like the fact you set up a recording for our meeting. It shows tremendous growth."

Audrey disregarded Statz' compliment and sat back down with him.

"Based on the background noise, that is not an Agency phone," she said emphatically.

"No, it's a payphone within walking distance from the building."

Audrey quickly realized Janine Sheppard was under surveillance within the Agency. She also thought about her recent phone calls to that very same payphone.

Statz, always thinking one step ahead said, "Don't worry. I deleted your phone calls to her."

"Why?"

"Because I believe you are the one person who can get her out of this mess."

Audrey was stunned.

"Are you trying to protect Janine and Andrew?"

"Again, sorry to be blunt, but I don't really care about your husband. I care for the mother of my son."

"You mean sons...plural."

"No I mean Donny."

"What about Sefter?"

"I am not his biological father Audrey."

Really...no time like the present to ask, she thought.

"Then who is his biological father?," she asked pointedly.

Statz hesitated. He knew the next word out of his mouth will change Audrey forever. She stared at him with a quizzical expression on her face.

"Andrew," he said succinctly.

Audrey's eyes opened wide, but said nothing at first.

Finally she asked, "My Andrew?"

Statz looked at her and wanted to ask, '*is there another Andrew we've been discussing'?*, but he knew she was trying to process what he said. He just nodded.

Audrey had thought about it before. Janine and Andrew in the field, working long hours together, but she always managed to push it far enough away. She knew 'Miss America' was transferred out of the country for a little over a year. Now she figured she knew the reason.

"One, I don't want to believe you and two, you said these were the 'pertinent' parts of your recordings. They lack context. For all I know you could be setting me up for a fall. Though, I can't for one second think you would do that to me."

"Audrey, I'm going to leave these tapes with you. Do with them what you want. I'm going to take a stroll downtown and will be back in about an hour. When I get back you can either work with me or against me. I do not mean that to be a threat. I know under normal circumstances I would lose. But, these aren't normal circumstances. I want to protect Janine. The question is...how much do you want to protect Andrew? I'll see you in about an hour."

Chapter 46

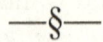

Present Day

The idea of Jacquelyn being held against her will, or worse, almost drove Tony into a blind rage. He could feel the emotional torture building within surrounded only by the shadows in the night. He pulled his car over, killed the engine then listened for the police siren up at the school. It finally stopped, but he then heard more sirens in the distance getting closer.

I have to do something!, he thought.

He knew if he even came near to school he'd run into trouble.

Think! How can I find her?

Then, for some odd reason, he remembered something Audrey said about how she had her technicians at CIT check out her Smartphone and as soon as they began to poke around she was contacted and chastised for it immediately.

I have to call Audrey. There's no other way. I need to find Jacquelyn!

Tony made the call.

"Secure and contained," answered Audrey.

"Dagger, this is —," Tony stopped.

"Radar is that you?"

Tony pulled the phone away from his head and looked at it in disbelief.

OK...that's not Audrey, he thought.

He put the phone on speaker then said, "What do *you* want?"

"Do you seriously think we would just let you walk away from us?" said agent Wolf.

"Where's Audrey!?" Tony demanded.

"Nice try. Remember, I know your verbal deflection tactics. I told you before, nothing really is as it seems."

"What it seems like is your playing on the wrong team. I don't like who you're associating with," said Tony.

A new familiar voice came on the line and said, "That's not very nice Tony. We just met," said Janine Sheppard.

Well, I met the real you when I stepped into the vestibule of the school entrance. I don't have the context of what 'Betrayal' means, but I know it can't be good," thought Tony.

"Your more than just some kind of savant aren't you? I am impressed with how you handled yourself in the school parking lot."

I knew it! She was using the surveillance cameras!

"Tell me Tony, how did you know the location of the person on the roof?"

"You mean Parrelli?"

Janine and agent Wolf looked at each other with expressions of total surprise on their faces.

After a brief pause Janine asked, "Now why do you think that person's name is Parrelli?"

"Why waste your breath asking a dumb question when you seem to have all the answers."

"Now, now Tony. I have something you want and you have something I want. Elizabeth says you're the trustworthy type. Would you like to make a deal?"

Oh my God! She has Jacquelyn!

Tony didn't know what to say. Janine jumped in to fill the void.

"How would you like to work for me and make millions of dollars?"

Tony's mind raced thinking, *She doesn't have Jacquelyn? She left, but didn't take the car. Thank God! But, where is she?*

Tony lifted his gaze as a car's headlights illuminated him briefly as it made a turn. He noticed what appeared to be a smudge on the lower part of his windshield. He leaned in closer. There were letters written in small crayon-like writing on the outside of the glass. He squinted in the darkness, but couldn't make out what it was. He checked all around then got out of his car to read; 'WHERE WE MET-J'.

His heart pounded with excitement in his chest.

Jacquelyn! You're at Floyd's, where we first met! So smart!

Then he heard Janine Sheppard squawk at him once again. He got back in the car.

"So, how's Parrelli?" asked Tony.

"You shot him in the shoulder so he's being attended to. Back to my question. Are you interested in making some real money? It's easy work," she said.

I actually was right and accurate with my shot? he thought.

Then he replied, "I answer to the people who hired me."

"If you're talking about Audrey Shelton then you might as well make some real money working for someone you can trust," she said derisively.

"What do you mean by that?" asked Tony.

"I dealt with Audrey long ago. She has nowhere to go and nowhere to hide with me around."

"I don't understand," said Tony sincerely.

"I thought you said he's bright," Janine said to agent Wolf.

"Listen, Elizabeth will come to you. Just tell us where you are and—"

"I may not be as bright as some, but I'm not as stupid as most," said Tony ending the call.

He started the car, turned off the automatic headlights and floored the gas pedal on his way to Jacquelyn. After a few blocks he turned the headlamps back on. He pulled into Floyd's parking lot and quickly parked the car. Running toward the entrance of the building he heard a voice.

"Tony!"

He stopped dead in his tracks. Tony turned and saw two silhouettes approaching him. One tall and one much shorter. Then he heard what he longed to hear.

"Tony!" shouted Jacquelyn.

She jumped into his waiting arms with tears filling her eyes. He held her off the ground so happy to see her. Then the larger silhouette slowly walked closer. Tony set Jacquelyn down and stepped in front to protect her. Then he recognized agent Dennis Forman.

Confused, Tony asked, "What are you doing here?"

Jacquelyn stepped out from behind Tony and said, "He got me out of the school. I was in danger and didn't even know it. He brought me here."

"And you just trusted him?" asked Tony.

"I was running to the car when I heard a cell phone ring. It was on top of the trunk of our car. I answered and it was Audrey Shelton. She told me this man would keep me safe and take me anywhere I wanted to go," said Jacquelyn.

Tony looked at Dennis and said, "Thank you. But, how did you know?"

"We always keep track of our problem children," said Forman.

"Is that what you think I am...a problem child?" asked Tony.

Forman smiled then said, "Not you...Miss America."

"Miss America?" Tony asked totally confused.

"That's her code name. Her real name is Janine Sheppard."

Tony's face showed surprise then changed back to confusion as he said, "Wait a minute. She really is an agent for the CIA?"

"Was an agent. Long story. Let's get both of you somewhere safe and I'll give you the short version."

"I'm not going anywhere until we know our kids are safe," said Jacquelyn.

"Audrey took care of that. Trust me. Let's go," Forman said.

"Where are they?" demanded Jacquelyn.

"With Audrey and another agent at her house. Trust me, it doesn't look like it, but it's a fortress," said Forman.

"Wait. One more thing before we go anywhere. How did you know Jacquelyn and I would be at the school tonight meeting with Janine Sheppard and agent Wolf?"

Forman was stunned. His eyes narrowed as he cocked his head slightly.

"Agent Elizabeth Wolf was with Miss America?"

"If you still mean Janine Sheppard, then yes."

Forman reached into his jacket and removed his Smartphone. He began to turn then stopped and asked, "Are you sure it was agent Wolf and not someone who looks like her?"

"I know it wasn't Danielle if that's what you're asking," said Tony.

Forman was stunned once again.

"How the hell do you know about Danielle?" he asked boring his gaze into Tony's eyes.

Tony swallowed hard.

Chapter 47

—§—

1995

Audrey sat staring at the microcassette in her CIT office after Jeff Statz had left. Her imagination began to run wild thinking of Andrew and Janine together. Quickly a vision popped into her mind.

Their eyes! Andrew and Sefter have the exact same eyes. Why didn't I put this together before?! she wondered.

She began to question the notion that Andrew leaving the country had anything to do with Operation Monopoly and their private plan to siphon off some of the money for themselves and Forman. She had a difficult decision to make. Confront and forgive or search and destroy.

After what seemed to be an eternity of pondering and connecting the dots Audrey stood tall with a steely determined look on her face. She picked up the microcassette and held it firmly in her hand.

"You picked the wrong person to mess with," she said sternly.

She set the wheels of her plan into motion with a phone call to Dennis Forman. She called his latest burner phone.

"How did you get this number?"

"I have my ways. Are we secure?"

"Yes, of course."

"Dennis, we have a problem," Audrey said flat-toned.

"We or you?" he replied.

"We both have a problem. I just found out Jeff Statz knows that you facilitated the transfer of funds from CIT to the offshore account."

"So? That's what I was supposed to do."

"So, I'm not just talking about the money for Operation Monopoly. He knows about our plan to take some of the money and split it between you me and Andrew."

"How the hell would he know that? And why the hell aren't you using proper operations protocol?" he asked.

"Your right, I'm sorry...Operation Boardwalk. Satisfied?" she asked.

"Yeah...I am. Don't be so casual about our off the books OP," he scolded.

"OK, OK," she said sounding sincere.

"Alright, back to my question. How the hell would Jeff Statz know?" asked Forman.

"Jeff Statz just paid me a visit here in Portland and told me so himself."

Forman remained silent as he ran through the possibilities then asked, "Why would Jeff Statz visit you all the way across the country when he could have spoken to you by phone unless this is something he or the DCI views as a very delicate matter?"

"I asked him and he thinks we have a mole inside the Agency and he said he couldn't trust anyone within the building at Langley."

"Did he say who?" asked Forman.

"He told me, but I don't know if I'm supposed to say anything," Audrey said baiting Forman.

"Come on Audrey! You mean to tell me you're starting to play by the rules now? Give me a break!"

Audrey gave a long pause as if she were thinking it over then said, "How do I know it isn't you?"

Forman chuckled and said, "If it were me we wouldn't be having this conversation."

"Oh, and why's that?"

"Because I wouldn't be dumb enough to get caught! Now tell me and I will make it my personal mission to destroy whoever it is."

I knew I could count on you, thought Audrey.

"It's Janine Sheppard."

"Son of a —", he began then quickly asked, "Are you kidding me? How do you know? Are you sure?"

Forman was absolutely stunned. Audrey filled him in on her version that Janine appears to be ready to divulge or sell the Domestic Covert Operations Tactical list, known within the Agency as 'D-COT'. He was stunned at what he was hearing. If it had come from someone else he'd disregard it out of hand.

"Who's she supposedly going to sell the D-COT to?"

"This is hard for me to say, but it's...Andrew," she lied.

"That makes no sense! Why would he do that, he's on the list?"

"Are you sure about that?" Audrey asked in a leading tone.

"Wait…You're right! He was purposely not placed on the D-COT list because he would be off US soil for most of Operation Monopoly. This new way of providing the CIA with its own funding for domestic covert OPS completely bypasses the budgetary process in Congress."

"But, you and I are on the D-COT list, aren't we?" Audrey asked in a leading tone.

"So, Statz comes all the way out there to tell you Andrew and Janine are coloring outside the lines. Why would he tell anyone? Why not bring both of them in and take care of it quietly? It doesn't add up."

"Because he knew I'd make a big deal out of it and he wants to keep this quiet."

"OK, let's back up a minute. Why do you believe Statz?"

"He played phone conversations between Andrew and Janine. He's caught them with their hands in the cookie jar."

"If he has recordings and you heard them and are convinced of their authentication…then I'm on board. I have my own ideas, but what do you need me to do," asked Forman.

"First, avoid Jeff Statz at all cost and be hyper-vigilant when communicating with anyone in person or over the phone. He could be listening. That's why I called you on your burner. Second, I need you to help me find a way to move the money from the Cayman's to a Swiss bank account without Andrew's knowledge. I need to not only protect our money, but I need to protect him too."

"Are you nuts!? We might just as well walk into the DCI's office and turn ourselves over to him. There's no way we can do that!"

"I didn't say we're actually going to move the money. I'm just asking for you to help me find a way to do it. There's a big difference."

"I can't wrap my mind around the fact Janine and Andrew cooked something like this up."

"Well, believe it or prepare for the consequences. I'd rather you remained steady and take care of Operation Boardwalk with me."

"So, by moving some of the money, you want to show leverage is that it?" asked Forman.

Something like that, thought Audrey.

"Now we're on the same page," Audrey quipped.

"So, what does that really do for us?"

"It ultimately isolates Andrew and prevents him from complete autonomy over the money. He'll be a little more pliable if he's no longer in charge of it."

"And what about Janine?"

I have something special planned for her, thought Audrey.

"Call me when you know who's been given the authority to release the money. And Dennis, make it look like Janine Sheppard's fingerprints are all over it...not yours."

"What am I...stupid all of a sudden?"

No, but Andrew will pay a price and Janine Sheppard will pay a greater price, thought Audrey.

"Talk with you tomorrow," she said then ended the call.

Chapter 48

—§—

Present Day

Tony was between a rock and a hard place. On the one hand he knew he needed to tell Forman how he came upon knowing about Danielle. On the other, he wasn't so sure what the consequences would be admitting to him he copied and hacked Audrey's personal computer.

"This parking lot isn't the best place to be discussing something like this," said Tony.

"Well, this is where it's going to take place," Forman said forcefully.

"So you want Jacquelyn to hear every detail? Shouldn't we be doing something about Janine Sheppard and agent Wolf?" Tony asked, but meant it as a statement.

Forman paused, standing perfectly still, staring at Tony.

"You always seem to find an out don't you?" Forman said in a irritated tone.

Tony remained locked in on Forman's eyes.

"Just tell him Tony," implored Jacquelyn.

Forman took his gaze off Tony and looked wide-eyed at Jacquelyn.

"You know how he came about this information?" he asked sternly.

Thinking quickly she said, "I just want him to tell you whatever he knows so we can get out of this parking lot. I don't feel safe and I want to see my children," she said.

Forman narrowed his eyes as the realization seeped in that she was indeed right. He could feel the slow burn of losing this round.

Later...I'll bust him wide open later, thought Forman.

"I'm taking you both to Audrey's house."

"If you're looking for Sheppard or agent Wolf I can help," said Tony.

"Yeah...help by being in the way."

"Dennis, I can feel them before you can see them. It's dark. Don't you see this as an advantage?" asked Tony.

Forman paused then realized Tony's ability could be an asset to him.

"Alright," he said.

"But, what about Jacquelyn? I need to know she's safe," said Tony.

"Do you remember agent Bobby Stark?"

"Yes."

Forman looked at his watch and said, "He's at Audrey's right now. She'll be safe with him."

On the ride to Audrey's Jacquelyn pleaded with Tony not to go after Janine Sheppard with Forman. She knew this was to no avail, but tried anyway. They entered the house and the kids came running to Jacquelyn as if they were on a sleepover. This lowered Jacquelyn's stress level ten-fold.

Agent Bobby Stark and Forman slipped into the kitchen while Sam and Nick showed Jacquelyn and Tony the fort they built in the living room using blankets and sheets. Tony backed away quietly and entered the kitchen. Both Stark and Forman stopped talking and turned their attention to Tony.

"This is private," said Forman.

"No, this is personal," said Tony.

"How do you figure?" asked Forman.

"They went after Jacquelyn to get to me."

"Don't flatter yourself," Forman derided.

"Oh, I'm sorry. Was it you they tried to recruit to their new version of the SSD team? Oh, that's right. You're talent is being the biggest ass in the room! I completely forgot how rare that is," said Tony walking directly toward Forman.

"What did you just say?" asked Forman.

"You heard me," said Tony ready for a fight.

Bobby Stark jumped in and said, "Tony, he's really asking you what you just said. Is it true that agent Wolf and Janine Sheppard tried to recruit you to a civilian version of SSD?"

Taken off guard Tony responded with a confused, "Yes."

"Tell us exactly what went down and what was said," Forman said as his demeanor changed dramatically.

Tony, Bobby Stark and Forman sat at the kitchen table as Tony left out no detail.

Then Tony asked, "Where's Audrey?"

"She'll be here in awhile," said Stark.

"That didn't answer my question," said Tony.

"She's in her car and on her way. Satisfactory answer?" asked Forman.

Kind of, he thought.

Tony nodded then asked, "How do you know?"

"I just know. Leave it at that," Forman responded losing his patience again.

"Bobby, will you check the perimeter of the house? I don't want any surprises," said Forman.

Stark exited the kitchen through the back door, weapon drawn. Just then Forman's phone rang. The screen showed 'UKNOWN CALLER'. He answered then placed the phone on speaker so Tony could listen as an extra set of ears.

The scrambled voice coming through the phone said, "Hello agent Forman. It's a pleasure to speak with you."

"Who's this?" he asked.

"Are you alone?"

"First answer my question," he replied.

"Let's just say this is a voice from the past." Are you alone?" asked the scrambled voice.

"What does that matter?" asked Forman.

"I'll take that as a no. Who else is with you?"

"Cut the bull!   What do you want?" Forman said forcefully.

"Still have that short fuse I see."

Without so much as a whisper of notice Forman ended the call.

"Why'd you do that?" asked Tony.

"What's there to gain? We would have just gone round in circles. If it's Miss America, she'll call back. In the meantime let's get set up for a trace when she calls back."

Forman used Tony's phone to call Langley and quickly put the trace at the ready. Tony never even knew about this feature on his phone. Forman's phone rang out once again. He answered without saying a word.

The scrambled voice said, "That was very rude of you agent Forman. I see you still haven't any manners."

"The call was dropped," answered Forman.

"Do you really expect me to believe that Dennis? I'm surprised you aren't using someone else's phone."

"Janine, I know it's you. Why the scrambled voice bullshit?"

"Janine. Ok, I'll go by the name Janine if that's what you like. Why have you protected Audrey Shelton all these years?"

"What are you talking about?" asked Forman.

"You have always been to the rescue for her haven't you?"

"What would you have me do?"

"Let me make this point very clear. I have no interest in harming anyone. What I want is to meet with Audrey. I'll be frank. I was thrilled to hear the news when her husband died. Heart attack wasn't it?"

"That's pretty cold," said Forman trying to keep her on the line.

"I'm cold? Compared to Audrey Shelton I'm as cuddly as a litter of puppies. How can you defend her with what you know? Very hypocritical of you."

"I'm not the one using a scrambler. At least I'm up front with everyone I talk with."

Tony, still monitoring his phone waiting for the screen to complete its trace, finally saw its success. He quickly held it up to Forman.

"So why call me?" asked Forman.

"Because I believe in her black heart she actually trusts you."

"So?"

"So, I want you to deliver her to me along with your newest asset, Tony James."

"Why would I do that?" asked Forman.

"Do you remember the nonsense you sent Mr. James to San Diego for? I believe if you check with your local police department the kid has already called in another bomb threat."

"Tony already ruled him out as an imposter. We checked him out as well. No ability whatsoever," said Forman.

"Maybe not, but he sure can create havoc. Can't he?"

Forman took Tony's phone and pressed what appeared to be dozen digits. When he stopped, Forman had a sly grin on his face. He handed the phone back to Tony for him to see for himself.

"He's just a punk who kills innocent people and a cry for help," said Forman.

Tony looked at the screen on his phone and zoomed in on the exact location using his index finger and thumb to expand the map. He couldn't believe his eyes. The red dot pulsated just like his own personal phone with his security system.

CIT, thought Tony. *She's calling from CIT!*

Just then agent Bobby Stark came back in from his appointed rounds. Forman gave him a signal to keep quiet. Stark didn't understand, but gave Forman a hand gesture that all is clear and remained silent. He sidled up next to Tony and looked at the red pulsating dot. He knew exactly what this meant.

"Let's just cut to it. Tell me where you are and I will personally come to you and we can work something out."

"Nice try. Tell agent Stark I say hello."

Forman gave Stark hand gestures telling him he must have missed something outside. She's got eyes on the outside of the house. Stark gestured back telling Forman he saw nothing out of the ordinary.

Forman took a shot and said, "Will you give agent Wolf my regards?"

"What does agent Wolf have to do with anything?"

"Apparently you have her set up in a sniper's nest near Audrey's house," said Forman.

"Oh, that. Just a simple precaution. You know all about planning an OP, don't you."

"So why not fire on agent Stark?"

"Because, he's not a threat at the moment. Trust me, if he made a wrong move he never would have been able to go back in and report to you."

Tony stepped outside the kitchen door while neither Stark or Forman were paying attention to him.

Agent Wolf where are you? he wondered as he closed his eyes and began scanning the area.

Tony felt the lump at the back of his waist to verify he was well prepared just in case. He walked to the back of the house, stopped, continued to scan, but felt nothing.

Just before he rounded the corner at the front of the house he stopped. Focusing as hard as possible he tried to locate where agent Wolf could possibly be hiding. It hit him as quickly as lightening strikes...*actress.* He focused even harder to pinpoint her location.

She's on the move, he thought.

He crouched down behind a bush at the northeast corner of the house. Footsteps quietly maneuvering. Then he heard what seemed to be an unlikely sound.

"Tony?"

He froze. Kept his eyes closed and could visualize agent Wolf as if he were looking through night vision goggles. Once again he heard his name.

Am I actually hearing my name or am I just imagining it, he thought.

"Tony, is that you?"

He tilted his head, found the location, then opened his eyes.

Either take her out or trust her. I'm not sure, he thought.

Tony finally spotted agent Wolf carrying a sniper's rifle, but with the business end facing the ground.

Why would she reveal herself and not have her weapon at the ready? he wondered.

He reached behind his back and grabbed his firearm, then duck walked one foot behind the corner of the house between the bushes. He kept one eye on her.

Elizabeth? he whispered.

She crouched down, froze then said, "Is that you Tony?"

"What are you doing?" he answered.

"I'm here to protect you and everyone in the house. Audrey's orders," she said quietly as she swiftly moved up against the front of the house.

"Everything points to you either playing both sides or worse. How can I trust you?" asked Tony.

"I told you all along, nothing is really as it seems. I'm here because Don Williams has had his doubts about Forman for quite some time. Audrey is picking him up at the airport as we speak. You have to trust me like you did back in D.C.," she answered.

"There I had no choice. This is different," said Tony.

"Tony, we're both on the same side. I'm going to drop my weapon, stand up and place both my hands on the house. I know you have a gun so either you can trust me again or shoot me. Either way all this ends tonight."

Tony quickly moved from the corner of the house to stay partially hidden by the shrubbery pointing his Springfield XDM 9mm out in front of him. As soon as he was convinced he was indeed talking with the real agent Elizabeth Wolf he showed himself completely.

"Keep your hands on the house," he said.

"Tony, my rifle is down there. I'm in no position to harm you or anyone else. I'm here to help."

"I want to believe you," said Tony.

"Do you have your phone?" she asked.

"I do."

"Call Audrey. She'll confirm everything. I've been monitoring Forman for the last two weeks."

"I was told you were on vacation," said Tony.

"Don't be so naive and believe everything you hear."

"I don't," he said repositioning his feet for a more sturdy base.

Suddenly, another bolt of lightning struck him to his core. It was as if something took hold of him and placed him in an automatic mode. He moved to his left like a cat, fired three shots then stood as he watch her fall into a lump on the front lawn.

Chapter 49
—§—
1995

Audrey had a hard time getting back to sleep after waking at 4:35am. She got to her office at CIT before 6am. She had a big day ahead of her. Knowing she would have complete privacy she took the next step in her plan. Audrey took out one of her burner phones and called Andrew.

Looking at caller ID, Andrew was confused and answered the call without saying a word.

"It's me," she said.

"What's wrong? This is a breach of communication protocol. Are you OK?"

"No, *we* have a major problem," said Audrey.

"It's so good to hear your voice. There's no problem we can't handle together," he said.

"You're going to be called back to the States. I needed to give you a heads up as soon as I found out."

"I don't understand."

"Someone tipped off a member of Congress about Operation Monopoly. They're going to subpoena the DCI. You know what that means."

"But, who would do something like that? Only a handful of people know about this OP."

"Jeff Statz is convinced there's someone at Langley somehow playing politics with this. I don't have many details. Do you have any idea outside of the team who would do something like this?" she asked knowing the answer, but interested in his.

"I haven't told a soul," he said without hesitation.

Liar, she thought.

"Good. Get your house in order and transfer our funds to BVVA Bank of Zurich at noon Portland time. We need to secure our future with that money," she said.

"Audrey, I don't understand. If we go through with Operation Boardwalk won't we, scratch that, won't I be putting myself directly in the cross-hairs?"

"I won't let that happen. I have a plan."

"Tell me," he said.

"I can't. Gotta run. Remember to transfer our share at exactly 9am your time. Not a minute sooner or later."

"But, how the hell are they going to resurrect me? I can't just go back to Portland and say 'Sorry, my death was only temporary'."

"I'm sure there's a plan in place. I've got to go," she said emphatically.

Audrey ended her call with Andrew. She then placed the next call to Forman.

"Up and at it early I see," said Forman answering the call.

"Have you had the chance to take care of business?" asked Audrey.

"Everything will be taken care of in about an hour."

"What's holding you up?"

"Williams isn't in yet. He has to approve the transfer."

"You can't involve Williams!" exclaimed Audrey.

"Why not?" asked Forman.

"He's not part of the OP," she said.

"How do you figure? His name is on the ORG chart in charge of authorizing transfers."

"He may pull the trigger, but he's not officially part of the OP. You know that. For all he knows he's authorizing a simple budgetary transfer," she said.

"It seemed strange to me that he'd be the trigger-man, but I really didn't care. He still seems so green," said Forman.

"He's not as green as you think. You're going to have to find a way to go around him."

"And how the hell do you expect me to do that?" Forman asked.

"Have you ever noticed his communications and paperwork?"

"What do you mean?"

"You need to pay closer attention. He uses the same electronic signature on everything. He may be a computer geek, but in this case he's running with the big boys in the real world." Technology can be used against any of us Dennis. She paused then asked, "Is Janine in yet?"

"Haven't seen her. Should be here any minute. Why?"

"Let me know when she's at her desk. You still office hopping?"

"Of course. Oh, I get it. That's perfect! I use his office all the time. No one will suspect a thing. That is unless he walks in while I'm taking care of business."

"I'll provide you cover while you're in his office. Just take care of it and let me know. Oh, and do not, under any circumstances, use an agency phone to call me. A simple call or text from a burner phone will suffice."

"What, all of a sudden I'm new? Remember who the handler is and who the field operative is here," Forman said in an irritated tone.

"Sorry. Just watch for Janine and we'll talk later," she said ending the call.

Almost on cue Janine walked through the front door. Once through security she headed straight for her desk. It was easy for Forman not to be noticed. All eyes were on Janine. This was one task he didn't mind one bit. Janine's phone rang just as she sat down.

"Janine Sheppard," she answered.

"Oh, hi Janine. I thought I was being connected to the archives department. How've you been?"

"Is that you Audrey?"

"Yes. How are you?" Audrey asked, playing along as if they hadn't spoken in a long time.

"I'm doing well. Just got to my desk. Is there something I can do for you?"

At that moment Forman walked by and gave Janine a good morning nod and a motion with his thumb letting her know he was going to use Don Williams' office once again. She shrugged her shoulders dismissively.

Audrey said, "Well, maybe you *can* help me. Do you have a copy of the Scranton file? I need the latest sanitized revision."

Janine had not yet started her computer and said, "I literally just walked in when you called. It will take a few minutes, but I'm sure I have it. You know how these computers take so long to get going. Do you want me to call you back or just send it?"

"Can you talk while you boot up?"

"Sure. What's up?"

Audrey kept Janine on the phone until she received a text notification from Forman. It read; 'DONE'

Audrey finished with Janine then placed her next call.

"Talk," he answered.

"So, you still interested in sticking it to the politicians while helping your mother?" asked Audrey.

"Do you have any idea what time it is here in LA"?

"Yes. The same time as it is here in Portland. Wake up and listen to me. I have a way for you to set your mother up for life, financially, at the expense of your friends on Capitol Hill." she said.

"They're not *my* friends, but I'm listening," said Sefter paying closer attention now.

"At exactly noon, Cayman time, Andrew will be accessing the funds and transferring much of it to a Swiss bank account. The second that money hits I need you to transfer it into an account for your mother," she said confidently.

"So, he's still enjoying the weather down there."

"Focus will you?" Audrey said sternly.

"Why should I do this?"

"Because your mother is about to be taken in for questioning," said Audrey.

"So she gets questioned by the police. Big deal," said Sefter.

"Not the police. The CIA. You have no idea what happens in an interrogation within the confines of a CIA safe house," she said in a ominous tone.

"You and your spook friends are really sick. You know that?"

"Of course I know. We wouldn't be in this line of work if we didn't have a screw loose somewhere."

"OK, so why would my mother be in trouble?"

I'm so glad you asked. Because she will have appeared to steal millions of dollars that's earmarked to fund clandestine OPS bypassing normal budgetary channels, thought Audrey.

"Because Andrew told me he has someone chosen to fall on their sword in order to pull this off," she lied.

"Who?" he asked.

"You don't need to know," said Audrey.

Sefter gave a long pause. Audrey remained silent. The first person to speak would likely lose. He either trusts her or he doesn't.

"You're husband knows how to play hardball when he has to. It's a good trait. I'll set up the new account and monitor the noon transfer," Sefter said breaking the silence.

Yes! thought Audrey.

"Make sure you can't be traced. I made a promise you would not get caught up in this mess," she said.

I didn't say that it was a promise out of loyalty. But, a promise is a promise, she thought.

"So what's this going to do to Andrew?" asked Sefter.

"In the end…nothing."

412

"How can you be so sure?"

"You're going to just have to trust me on that," she answered.

"And what about my mother?"

"She'll be set for life," answered Audrey.

Out of the picture, but set for life, she thought.

"Why don't I just give her the money and save all of us the time and hassle?"

"Because there are forces at work that you just simply know nothing about," Audrey vaguely answered.

Another long pause.

"If you think this will help my mother, only slap Andrew on the wrist, but stick it to some politician, then I'm in," said Sefter.

After a few more instructions Audrey ended her call with Sefter. She switched phones once again, then contacted Forman to let him know what was about to go down.

"…and don't act strange when you hear the news that Janine has been taken for questioning by Statz. But, keep tabs on her and let me know where they take her," said Audrey.

"You really think this is going to work?" asked Forman.

"Only one way to find out. What's the alternative?" asked Audrey.

She ended the call.

Chapter 50

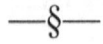

Present Day

Hearing the sound of gunfire out on the front lawn instinctively made Forman and Stark duck down while in Audrey's kitchen. They drew their weapons and moved toward the front of the house while making sure Jacquelyn and the kids are OK. Giving them quick instructions he and Stark went back through the kitchen door then quickly outside.

Agent Wolf stiffened then tried to make herself small at the sound of the three shots fired from Tony's gun. With adrenaline pumping she couldn't locate where she had been hit. She couldn't believe he would actually shoot her.

"Get down!" shouted Tony with authority.

Agent Wolf dropped like a rag doll shuddering in disbelief. Tony moved like a panther in the night toward her.

"Please let me live," agent Wolf cried to Tony.

He stopped, looked down at her, then reached out his hand to help her get up then said, "I just did."

"I don't understand," she said trembling.

With just enough light from the street lamp agent Wolf saw Tony looking behind her. She took Tony's hand and turned her head. Lying in a lump on the grass was a body. A body Tony had just taken the life from.

Stunned, agent Wolf stammered, "Who...Who's that?"

"Her name is Danielle. She was quickly moving toward you with a knife," answered Tony purposefully looking for recognition from Elizabeth.

Agent Wolf immediately ran over and fell to her knees next to the body. She turned the camo painted face toward hers. Recognition quickly set in.

"Danielle was going to kill you Elizabeth. The knife is still in her hand. She threatened Jacquelyn," Tony said in a cold tone.

"But, how did you know who this is?" asked Elizabeth.

Tony didn't acknowledge her question.

Agent Wolf raised her eyes toward Tony, still holding his 9mm. Then instinct and training kicked in.

"We have to get out of here, right now!" she said.

"Why? I didn't do anything wrong. She was about to kill you," said Tony.

"No! The danger is coming from within this house. We need to go right now!"

"I don't understand," said Tony confused.

"I'll fill you in on the way, but right now we need to get the hell out of here. Trust me!"

Tony's mind raced ahead and defaulted to his instincts knowing, for some odd reason, he needed to trust agent Wolf at this moment. It also helped knowing he was armed. They took off running to the west toward a black sedan agent Wolf parked three blocks away.

Once in the car she asked, "Do you have your phone with you?"

"Yeah, it's in my pocket," he said.

"Put your gun away and give me the phone," she said in an all business tone.

"Why?"

"Because you can be tracked with it. Now give it to me," she demanded.

He reluctantly handed her his phone. She quickly got out of the car, violently crashed her heal onto it, then kicked the pieces into the curbside sewer grate. Getting back into the car they promptly drove off just barely exceeding the speed limit.

Forman gave hand signals to agent Stark. They went in opposite directions once outside in the backyard. Each man stopped and dropped when they heard three quick bursts of gunfire. Each remained on the ground just in case they had been spotted and could be fired upon. Forman first realized he was not the target then Stark's deduction skills brought him to the same conclusion. They both arrived at the opposite sides of the front corners of Audrey's house.

Each independently scanned the area. Forman was the first to see the body lying on the grass. Stark concealed himself and covered Forman as he belly crawled to the motionless body. Forman reached out and found the person's neck. He blindly checked for a pulse. Nothing. He moved the head so he could see the face. Shocked he then checked for a birthmark on the neck.

"Damn it!" he whispered.

Stark remained at the corner behind the same shrub Tony had just used to hide himself. Agent Stark called out to Forman.

"Dead or alive?" he asked.

Forman, scanning his surroundings, finally said, "Gone."

"Who is it?" asked Stark.

"You don't want to know," said Forman.

Stark quickly moved to hover over the body.

"Oh my God! That's Elizabeth Wolf!" he proclaimed.

Forman didn't say a word. After just a few seconds he told Stark to call it into the Agency before the police arrived. This would provide both of them precious time rather than being detained by local law enforcement.

"I'm pretty sure they have 'Shot Spotter' here," said Forman referring to the equipment law enforcement uses to pinpoint exactly where shots are fired.

"Where's James!?" agent Stark asked in a violent tone.

"Get on the phone and get a trace on him. We need to find him," said Forman.

Regaining his composure agent Stark asked, "You want me to track him or do you want someone else brought in?"

"For now, you do it. Right now I need to get downtown to CIT. We'll have to split up," said Forman.

"Why CIT?" asked agent Stark.

"Because that's where Janine Sheppard's phone call to me originated."

Chapter 51

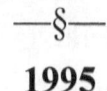

1995

At precisely 9am in the Cayman Islands, Andrew transferred all the funds into the account located in Zurich, Switzerland just as Audrey instructed.

I hope you know what you're doing Audrey, he thought.

Once the confirmation was electronically returned to him he felt the urge to contact Audrey, but decided against it. He thought her phone call to him was too dangerous so he was resolute to show her his superior restraint.

Meanwhile, in LA, Sefter immediately went to work and placed the funds Andrew just transferred into an account in his mother's name. Not even thirty seconds had passed. He used software he created and used many times without incident. His cloning program even provided the needed security to send the confirmation to him acting on behalf of Andrew. The bank has no idea he is pretending to be Andrew Shelton. He then called Audrey.

After looking at caller ID she answered quickly and said, "Right on time."

"All set. Every penny is now in my mother's name and the bank is none the wiser," said Sefter.

"Are you sure?" she asked.

"No. I just made all that up so you would be proud of me. Of course I'm sure."

"Thank you Sefter. Your mother will eventually be proud of what you have done for her."

"What do you mean eventually?"

"You don't want to be implicated so stay in the background and let this play out no matter what you hear. Got that?"

He remained silent.

"Sefter, Do you understand how important it is you remain anonymous in all this? If you get caught interfering with an ongoing clandestine OP you will be—"

"Yeah, yeah I know. I'll be thrown into a black hole, deprived of food and water and maybe never see the light of day ever again. I get it."

"I'd like to say you're way off, but you may be closer to the truth than you think," she said trying to scare him from taking any action.

"Let's not have any contact until I think enough time has passed and the circumstances warrant it," said Audrey.

"Have a nice life Audrey," Sefter said ending the call.

Audrey made a call to Janine at Langley. She didn't trust calling her directly so she went through the switchboard. Part of her plan.

"Janine Sheppard speaking," she answered.

"How do I keep getting you when I call someone else," said Audrey knowing Janine's line is being monitored.

"Oh, hi Audrey. Did the switchboard transfer you to me again by mistake?"

"I'm in a bit of a hurry, but I would love to talk with you. When you get a chance give me a call later. We'll catch up on things. For now, will you please transfer me to Don Williams?" asked Audrey.

Audrey hoped Janine got the hint. She spoke to Williams pretty much about nothing then waited.

Almost an hour went by then her phone finally rang out. She looked at caller ID and saw 'PAY PHONE' on her display. The call she has been waiting for.

Audrey answered in silence.

Janine waited, but just couldn't hold out any longer and said, "Audrey. It's me."

That's one reason you didn't make it in the field; no patience, thought Audrey.

"Oh, hi Janine. I'm glad you called. The Scranton file you sent me wasn't the latest version. Can you check to see if you have the most recent one on your computer?"

"I don't understand Audrey. I thought you wanted to talk about something other than the Scranton file. My mistake," she said.

"What did you think I wanted to talk to you about?" asked Audrey trying to lead her into troubled waters.

"I thought you might have information about what we talked about previously," she said vaguely.

"What do you mean?" asked Audrey.

"Why are you being so shady?"

"You know me Janine. I don't do shady very well. If there's something you need to ask me just ask."

I get it. You want deniability because you're at risk in the field, thought Janine.

"I'll just come right out and ask. Is my son protected?"

"You mean Sefter?"

"Yes. Who else?" Janine asked impatiently.

And there's the dagger! thought Audrey.

"He's safe, sound and doing very well for himself. You've been a good mother," said Audrey.

"Thank you Audrey. You're a good friend," said Janine.

Just then three black SUVs rolled up with fully tinted windows. Men in suits with sunglasses and ear pieces got out and moved on Janine Sheppard so quickly she didn't even have time to hang up the phone. Audrey heard everything.

That's for screwing around with my husband. Thank you Jeff for monitoring this call. I expect you to repay me for turning in a traitor, she thought.

Audrey had tipped off Jeff Statz that Janine set up an off the books OP stealing the money Andrew was scheduled to transfer. Statz monitored the transfer and the phone call then proceeded to detain Janine Sheppard. He wanted her taken outside the building at Langley. Audrey came through.

Statz asked Audrey if Andrew was in on the sting or would he have to pick him up as a traitor as well. Audrey protected her husband and told Statz the sting was completely Andrew's idea. Statz was truly pleased with his power couple in the field.

Audrey's phone rang once again. This time the screen showed it to be Dennis Forman.

"Good afternoon," Audrey said in a sweet tone.

"Not that good," said Forman.

"What's up?"

"You were right. Janine Sheppard was just taken into custody. They've taken her to Langley Air Force Base," he said as if this were big news to Audrey.

"Do you know the reason?"

"Not yet. It just happened," he said.

"How do you know where they took her?"

"The head of detainment at Langley AFB is an old Vietnam buddy of mine. He called me as soon as she was brought there."

"Why would he care?"

"Let's just say there aren't many women who look like her. He knew where she worked and my ties to the Agency."

"And I just spoke to her earlier. Just before she put me through to Don Williams. What a tragedy," said Audrey.

"What did you and she talk about?" asked Forman.

"Nothing really. I called to talk to Don and was put through to her. She is his assistant so I guess that makes sense," lied Audrey.

"Don't give me that crap! I can count on one hand the number of times you went through the switchboard. You always call direct. What gives?" he demanded.

"First, watch your step. Second, go check for yourself that I requested the Scranton file from her then I spoke with Williams."

Forman paused. He always has had a real good BS meter. It was going off in his head right now. He let it go for the moment because he couldn't speak to Janine for confirmation that Audrey did in fact request the Scranton file from her before transferring her to Williams.

"OK. If you say so. But, what about my share?" he asked.

"We're done. If you can think of a way around this please let me know. Now, we need to figure out a way to bring Andrew back," she said.

"You mean back to the US?"

"I mean back to life. How do we bring him home when it is a well known fact he died of a heart attack?"

"That's easy. Just chalk it up to him doing a short stint in the witness protection program," Forman said simply.

Audrey thought for a few seconds then said, "That's a great idea. I didn't think of that. People would buy it. Plus, he wouldn't have to give any details because everyone knows nobody talks about why they went into WP," she said eagerly.

After her phone call with Forman Audrey called Jeff Statz and explained the best way to bring Andrew back to Portland…via a period in Witness Protection. He loved the idea. Andrew could resume his life back home without hardly any downside. A few questions from some people, but nothing he couldn't handle. Jeff would make the arrangements.

Audrey was ecstatic. She nailed Janine Sheppard and now Andrew would be home and held to the agenda she will set. Audrey called Andrew with the plan.

She smiled and thought, *The money is gone. It's back to its original purpose of privately funding CIA covert OPS. Nothing I can do about that. He and I lost a bundle, but Andrew has lost a lot more than money.*

Chapter 52

—§—

Present Day

Agent Wolf held onto the steering wheel tightly as she drove Tony away from Audrey's house. Tony sat quietly in the front passenger seat trying to sort out his feelings about taking another human being's life.

"Are you OK Tony? You're awfully quiet."

Tony remained silent staring through the windshield lost in thought and emotion.

"Hey! You did what you had to do," she said turning to look at him.

Slowly, Tony turned to look at agent Wolf and calmly asked, "Is it wrong that I don't feel bad?"

"You're probably asking the wrong person. You just saved my life so I obviously think you did the right thing. When did you become such a good shot?"

He didn't answer.

"You amaze me Tony. I know agents that have been in the field for years and would never have done what you just did as well as you did it," she said not to cheer him up, but to state a fact.

More silence from Tony.

"Are you sure you're just a computer geek with a special ability or are you a well trained covert operative I know nothing about?"

This got Tony's attention.

"As brief as it was, everything seemed to move in slow motion all of a sudden. It was as if I were playing a game and every tangible nuance afforded me some kind of insight to what was coming next," he said looking out the passenger window.

"Well, I'm glad you were there," she said not really understanding what he just said.

Tony turned and looked at the attractive redhead. For the longest time she kept her eyes on the road. Finally, she couldn't ignore his gaze.

"What?" she asked.

"Why were you working with Janine Sheppard at the school?" he asked.

"Did you forget what I told you back in Langley?"

Tony just stared at her. His emotional equilibrium was off after what he had just done. He didn't answer.

"If you recall I told you 'nothing is really as it seems'. Do you remember that?"

Tony couldn't forget. It's what helped him get through the ordeal. As he sat in the passenger seat he made a conscience effort to feel the lump of firepower pushing against his lower back. It made him feel prepared just in case.

"So, what did you mean by that?" asked Tony.

"This whole business is based on compartmentalization. Every person has been isolated into only holding one or two pieces of the puzzle."

"I don't understand what that has to do with you tipping me off," said Tony.

Elizabeth side-stepped his comment and said, "If, for instance, I don't have the full picture of what's going on then I can be told anything and I will play my role knowing it is part of the whole. Trust is the key."

'Play my role'...just like an actress, he thought.

"What are you telling me? My role was to kill?" he asked.

"No. That you have one piece of the puzzle and shouldn't jump to conclusions," she said.

Still reluctant to completely put his full and complete trust in her he asked, "So do you have any idea of the big picture?"

"Bigger than yours," she said plainly.

"How so?"

"I'm not at liberty to tell you," she answered.

"Stop the car," Tony said in a calm tone.

"I'm not stopping," she said almost irritated at Tony.

"I am telling you to stop the car now."

"No."

Tony's right arm moved so quickly and had the business end of his firearm pointed directly at Elizabeth's head. He didn't say a word.

"So, you're going to shoot me? Is that it?"

Silence from Tony.

"Put that away. We're on the same team Tony!" she scolded.

In a cold calculated tone Tony slowly said, "Are we? Last time…stop the car."

Elizabeth turned and looked into his eyes searching for the usual signs of someone who's bluffing and found none. She pulled the car to the right and slowed to stop on the shoulder of the road.

"Now what Tony? Are you going to take my life just like to did my sister back there?"

"You know you have a twin sister?" he asked suddenly taken by surprise.

"Yes. We were split up at birth. I found myself wanting to be the good cop. She wound up being the bad cop. What do you think I was doing covering Audrey's house?" she asked.

"I have no idea. I only have one piece of the puzzle, remember. All I know is you and Janine Sheppard are working together and placed Jacquelyn in a situation that pisses me off!"

"I was at Audrey's house, at Audrey's request, to protect you and your family," she said knowing the eyes of a serious man.

"Protect us from what?"

"Not what…who," she said flatly.

"You mean Janine Sheppard?"

"No…Forman."

Tony narrowed his eyes just a fraction and tilted his head just slightly letting her words hang in the air.

"What do I have to fear from Senior Special Agent Dennis Forman," he asked as if interrogating her.

"Tony, I know you understand this to be the truth. Your ability to see through someone who's trying to BS you is something you need to rely upon right now. Forman is not your friend. As a matter-of-fact, he's your enemy."

Somewhere in the deep recesses of his mind this seemed to register with Tony. His grip eased on his weapon. His eyes opened just a little and his body seemed as if it relaxed somewhat. Ever the professional, Elizabeth took note of the change in Tony's demeanor.

"Tony, will you please point the gun away from me?" she asked politely.

He held steady. His brain seemed to be still sputtering after killing another human being. Then something tugged at him from what seemed to be a world away.

"Forman said you were on vacation. Is this your idea of a vacation?" he asked.

"Please lower the gun and I'll tell you everything."

"First tell me something I can believe."

"San Diego."

"What about it?"

"I saw you notice the woman who wore the straw hat."

"You were there?"

"How do you think the floppy haired kid with the bright tennis shoes got away," she said.

"So it was you that helped him?" he asked as he lowered the gun.

"Yes. Audrey asked me to make sure you were safe. But, that's not all. Either Janine Sheppard or Dennis, is behind the murders of all those people. Tony, after the explosion, I watched you look for the bench that had been obliterated. Who do you think called out your name so you would come into the building?"

His eyes opened wide with the memory of hearing someone call out 'Tony' as he sat on that very bench. It was enough to make him get up and walk into the NBC building.

"That was you?" he asked totally surprised.

"It was."

"I don't understand."

"You shouldn't. You only have one piece of the puzzle. That's what I've been trying to tell you," she said.

"Then Forman really is the bad guy? How so?"

"Let's just say he has a different agenda these days."

"But, that doesn't explain why you were with Janine Sheppard."

"It's because you are the key to so much Tony. Do you remember Director Williams telling you that?"

"How did you know he said that? You weren't there."

"Another time and place Tony. Right now we—"

Tony was suddenly struck with the reality of his situation. He jolted upward as if he were stuck by a cattle prod.

"Turn the car around! We have to get back to Audrey's house!"

"Are you nuts! You're being tracked down like a dog as we speak. Why would we—"

"Because that's where Jacquelyn, Sam and Nick are!"

"But—"

"Either turn this car around or get the hell out!"

Elizabeth put her hands up in a 'calm down' gesture and said, "Let me finish one sentence. It only takes the police two minutes to respond to a 911 call. They are safe. Forman wouldn't stick around for them. He's long gone," she said.

"I have to make sure!"

"Wait Tony. Does Jacquelyn have her cell phone with her?"

Tony immediately understood where agent Wolf was going with this and quickly answered, "She does. Give me your phone."

Tony called Jacquelyn from yet another burner phone agent Wolf had stashed under the driver's car seat. He then made sure Jacquelyn and the kids were alright. The police had already arrived and Forman, along with agent Stark, were nowhere to be found. This brought relief to Tony. He told her he would explain later where he was and why he had to leave. Jacquelyn was shaken, but holding strong for the kids.

"We heard gunshots Tony," said Jacquelyn.

"I can explain."

"What's to explain. The police said it must have been some kids driving by or something," she said.

Tony paused then cautiously asked, "So, nobody's hurt or anything?"

"No. Should there be?" she asked now suspecting more information was available.

"I can honestly say nobody is hurting. Take the kids to your Mom and Dad's. I'll meet you there later," he said.

"But—"

Elizabeth nabbed the phone from Tony and ended the call.

"What are you doing?"

"Not fun to be cut off mid-sentence is it? This is a burner phone. It doesn't mean it can't be traced," she said as she disassembled it into just a few parts.

Tony understood. He didn't like it, but he understood. Agent Wolf rolled down her window put the car in gear and proceeded along the road tossing each piece of the phone about two miles apart along the roadside.

"So tell me why we need to be concerned about Forman," said Tony.

"First tell me how you knew that was my sister," she quickly answered.

"Forgive me for saying, but you don't seem too broken up about it," said Tony.

Chapter 53

—§—

1995

Holding out his ID badge, Special Agent Forman remained seated behind the steering wheel and waited for the guard to verify he is on the visitor's list to enter Langley Air Force Base. Once confirmed he drove directly to the detention center. He grabbed his satchel, got out of the car and walked through the door marked LAFB D-10.

Gotta love the lack of personality we give our boys in the military...LAFB D-10, thought Forman.

Once inside he was greeted with a slight pang of melancholy. Even though he was Navy and never in the Air Force, the sights, sounds and precision of a military base brought him back to days gone by. Mike Gussek, a big mountain of a man weighing about 280 pounds of complete muscle, interrupted Forman's trip down memory lane.

His deep voice called out, "What's a squid like you doing hanging around us flyboys?"

"Flyboy? You couldn't fit behind the steering wheel of a bus! "Everest...how the hell are you?" asked Forman.

"I'm good. It's good to see even a Navy man such as yourself," chuckled Gussek.

"Is it possible you're an even bigger mountain now?. How do you stay in such great condition?"

"I'm in charge of the steroid test schedule around here," he said with a wink.

Forman and Gussek got caught up quickly then jumped right into the reason for the visit.

"I gotta tell ya, this is the finest looking detainee we've ever had here. She's been a pleasure to host," said Gussek.

"Host. You turning into one of those paper pushing zits that can't say the word prisoner?"

"Technically she's not a prisoner. She's only being detained here until tonight."

"What's so magical about tonight?"

"She's being moved."

"By who?" asked Forman.

"You know who. Her...employer," Gussek said quietly.

"Has anyone been here to talk to her?"

"Yeah, two suits. They asked her questions for over six hours yesterday."

"How'd she hold up?"

"Now I wouldn't have knowledge about something like that," Gussek said with a hint of sarcasm.

"And I'm the King of Sudan. Tell me what they were asking about."

Gussek said, "Follow me."

Though Forman was not a small man by any stretch of the imagination, he was dwarfed by Gussek as they walked to his office. Gussek filled Forman in on his opinion of Janine Sheppard's fragile state of mind. He went into detail about the line of questioning the two men followed.

"Did she admit to anything?" asked Forman.

"I've seen a lot of guilty people come through these doors and if she's one of them, she's got me fooled," said Gussek.

"So, you're still eves dropping then."

"I have a video of her interrogation," said Gussek reaching for the tapes.

"You're the man!" said Forman stashing the recordings into his satchel.

"Well, anytime spooks come in here I know the law could get tossed aside," Gussek said.

"Is she allowed visitors?" asked Forman.

He opened a file and said, "Only from the Central Intelligence Agency."

They both smiled. Gussek led Forman to a lower level to where Janine Sheppard is currently residing. He opened the door and let Forman enter. Once in, Gussek stepped back out and locked the door.

The detention room is a 12x12 foot box with a small table and two chairs that are bolted and welded to the floor. No windows and soundproofed. A permanent cot secured in the same manner in one corner.

Once Everest left and closed the door Forman took out a small transistor radio and turned the volume way up. It was tuned to the Oldies station. Blue Suede Shoes by Elvis was playing. He knew Everest would likely try to listen to their conversation. This would prevent him from doing so. He also knew he wouldn't have to explain the reason for the radio to Janine, a former field agent.

"Dennis! I'm so glad to see you! What are you doing here?" she asked bolting up from the cot.

"I just stopped by to see how you're doing," he said.

Janine quickly backed off. Her mood changed in an instant.

"Who sent you?"

"To be fair, Jeff Statz approved my visit. But, I'm not here to extract information other than to ascertain how you're holding up."

"Right," she said slowly and in disbelief.

Forman knew he would have to gain her trust, but really didn't have that much time on his side. They talked quietly for a few minutes with Forman asking non-threatening questions. He knew she had enough of those already and more to come. Her guard finally came down and Forman could get to the real reason for his visit.

"I don't get it. Why are you here?" he asked bluntly.

Janine hesitated then realized she needs to trust someone and said, "They think I stole money from some secret offshore bank account."

"And you didn't? he asked frankly.

"Come on Dennis. I have no idea what their talking about," she said emphatically.

"Why you?"

In exasperation she said, "I don't know."

"Did they at least divulge the location or the amount of the money that you supposedly had something to do with?" he asked carefully.

"No."

"Janine, I'm going to give you some advice and it's essential that you listen. You need to go back to your days as a field operative and think that way as long as you are being held for questioning," said Forman.

She nodded.

"Their questions had to reveal some details of why they think you have anything to do with stealing money. Is it private money? Physical money? Bank money? Bonds? What kind of money?"

Janine's eyes lit up then said, "It's money in some offshore bank. I don't know the exact amount, but I know it's in the millions of dollars."

"You wouldn't be here if it were only fifty bucks. What bank?" *Please don't let it be the money Andrew, Audrey and I were going to split,* he hoped.

"First they wanted me to talk about some bank in the Cayman's. Then one of them mentioned a bank in Zurich, Switzerland. I don't know. Those are the two I remember."

"And what did you tell them?"

"Nothing! I have no idea what their talking about!" she said raising her voice.

"I understand. You have to lower your voice. Just breathe," said Forman motioning with his hands. "So, if I have this right, they think you took money from a bank account in the Cayman's and a bank in Zurich?"

"Apparently. Wait, that's not quite right. I think they believe I somehow moved money from a Cayman's account to some Zurich account," she said.

"Audrey," he faintly whispered in frustration without realizing it was audible. He lowered his head.

"What?" asked Janine.

"What?" Forman asked right back lifting his head.

"What did you just whisper?"

"I didn't whisper," Forman said forcefully.

"I swear you said 'Audrey'," she said slowly.

"No...I—"

Janine stared at Forman then said, "This whole thing is a set up! Listen to me. Who do you know has the means and skill to make someone look like they did something even though their innocent?"

"Come on Janine. She wouldn't do something like that. I know her as well as anyone and there's no reason in the world that would make her set you up like this," he said.

"There's one reason," said Janine in a much quieter tone.

Forman just stared into Janine's beautiful silver gray colored eyes.

"I'm going to tell you something that has to stay between you and me. I will only tell you if you promise to help me get out of this mess and then ultimately take Audrey down," she said coldly.

"I'm listening," said Forman.

"Good for you, but you didn't promise."

Now she's thinking like a field agent again, he thought.

"I promise," he said.

"When I was in the field. Do you know who I worked with?" she asked in a leading tone.

"Andrew Shelton," answered Forman.

"Do you know why I left the country for almost a year?"

Forman shook his head.

"I swear if you tell anyone else, I'll hunt you down too," she said with rage in her eyes.

"Cross my heart. I won't tell a soul," he said.

"I got pregnant. The Agency didn't want an image problem within the ranks so they sent me away. They gave me the ultimatum of coming back to work in the capacity I'm in now or to never have the chance to work in the field again."

"Why would you getting pregnant cause the CIA to have an image problem?"

"It's the reason I believe I'm being set up by Audrey."

"I'm sorry Janine, but I'm not connecting the dots."

"Andrew Shelton is the father."

Forman's eyes just about shot out of his head.

"That's right. Andrew and I got very close while working on a particular OP. One thing led to another and suddenly I'm pregnant."

Recognition came to Forman. He chased his memory of Andrew's operations and finally landed on one in particular that landed him in Hamburg, Germany. It was called Scranton because of the battle for the black market iron ore money that the United States wanted for the steel industry.

"Are you saying you and Andrew have a child together?"

"Yes. We have a son."

"Do I know him," asked Forman.

"I don't think so. He's extremely smart. He's in finance."

"Finance…huh?"

"No. Don't even think that. My son would never do something like this to me," she said almost crying.

"Maybe not, but you and I know Dagger would."

"What's your son's name?"

"I shouldn't have said anything. Leave him out of this."

"If you want my help I need to know all the players in the game. You know how important that is," said Forman.

Janine remained silent for about twenty seconds then finally spoke.

"Sefter. His name is Sefter."

Chapter 54

—§—

Present Day

Traveling down the road agent Wolf said, "My biological sister and I didn't know each other at all. I've never met her. She became something akin to a ghost once she found out I knew about her."

"If you were split up at birth then how did you even come to know about her?" asked Tony.

"I'm not proud of this, but when I was assigned to pick you up back in D.C. and take you to meet Director Williams, agent Forman told me something about you and I got curious. So, I sneaked a peek at your jacket."

"Why do you people always call a file folder a 'jacket'?" asked Tony in a slightly irritated tone.

"When we go through training it's just part of the vernacular. I think it goes way back," she answered.

"How would a file on me have anything to do with your sister?" he asked.

"I'm getting to that. In your file lists everyone you associate with."

"Are you serious…everyone?"

"As a covert government agency we're nothing if not thorough."

Tony waited for her to continue while bouncing along in the passenger seat of her car.

"I separated your work associates from your personal ones. I noticed something irregular with one of the names."

"Who?" he asked.

"Ryan O'Connor," she said.

"Why him?"

"There's so many good reasons not to tell you Tony, but after what I've seen tonight I think you and I are going to be working together for quite some time."

"You don't have to tell me if you don't want to, but have you been permanently assigned to the Savant Syndrome Division or something?"

"No. It's just that I know a natural field operative when I see one. And, you Tony, are the real deal. Don't be surprised if you're asked to widen your scope of work for the Agency."

"I have no such plans. As a matter of fact I don't know if I'll even continue in my current capacity the way things are going."

"Why's that?" she asked.

"Because I've been given only one real assignment so far and look what it's led to."

"I know you feel bad about taking another person's life, but she's really just another enemy of the state. She would have killed me if you hadn't taken action."

"Still, she's your sister."

"To me...only on paper," said Elizabeth.

Tony abruptly said, "Tell me why Ryan O' Connor's name stuck out."

"He's my father."

Tony turned to look at her in disbelief. Not too much can stifle him, but this news took him totally by surprise. She looked straight ahead at the road in front of her leaving Tony to decide how to process this information.

"So you're telling me when I was detained in D.C. and he entered the room you pretended not to know him?"

"Yes."

"Why?"

"Let's just say a diversion was required at the time," she said.

Ryan O'Connor is her father. He's never spoken specifically about who he stays with when he travels to Washing D.C. I wonder if Audrey knows, he thought.

"By the way, you're the only person who knows so I'm asking you not to tell anyone, OK?"

"OK, but why tell me?" said Tony.

"You just saved my life. Somehow it's a way of thanking you. Maybe just a reaction to thinking how close I came to—," she said trailing off.

"So, who's your mother?" he asked pointedly.

"None of your business," she said.

"You're fine with telling me who you father is, but you won't tell me about your mother?"

Elizabeth remained silent. He didn't push it. Tony stared at her features trying to see if he could recognize any similarities of anyone O' Conner may have introduced him to. When the streetlights hit her just right he thought he saw a resemblance. It was so fleeting he really couldn't tell so he shook off the thought. Before Tony knew it, he found their car crossing the Willamette River heading into downtown Portland.

"Where exactly are we going?" he asked.

"CIT."

"Why?"

"We were monitoring Forman's phone and that's where Janine Sheppard called him from."

"So you think he's meeting her there? Why doesn't someone from the FBI just arrest him and Stark?" Tony asked.

"Bobby Stark is clean by the way. There's no evidence tying him to Forman's activities. So you know, the CIA doesn't just operate covertly on foreign soil as most Americans think. We have so many things going on in the US you wouldn't believe. We work with the FBI, but prefer to work alone. We don't necessarily play well together. But, we're getting better," she answered.

"What's he done wrong?" asked Tony staying on point.

"At the moment I can't tell you," said Elizabeth."

"Can't or won't?"

"Can't," she said.

"Why would you possibly think I would participate in whatever the hell this is without knowing all the facts?"

"Because Audrey Shelton is in grave danger," she said.

This made Tony quickly reconsider. His mind raced to find the logic, but realized he would be wasting his time and energy without all the facts. He knew they didn't have that kind of time.

Audrey comes first, he decided.

"Who's joining us at CIT?" he asked.

"Nobody."

"We're going in by ourselves?" asked Tony in dismay.

"Yup."

"Why would we do something so stupid as that?" he asked.

"Because Forman's good and the bigger the party the better his intel becomes. I have you and that's all I need."

"Are you kidding me? I don't even know what's going on," he said in a frustrated tone.

"Tony, you just have to trust me. I know I can completely trust you. You know the layout of the building, especially Audrey's office."

You still haven't answered me exactly what you were doing with Janine Sheppard at Jacquelyn's school. Tread lightly Tony, he thought.

"So, you think Janine Sheppard is holding Audrey in her office?"

"That's where the call originated from so it makes sense."

"But, won't she know you guys have been onto Forman and get out of there?" Tony said in a hopeful tone.

"No, she has no idea we're after both her and Forman," she said.

"Really? So what's the plan once we're in the building," asked Tony.

"You go in first and use your ability to tell me who's in there. Here's an earpiece transmitter so we can communicate. It's very sensitive so we can hear each other even if we whisper," she said handing him the equipment without taking her eyes off the road.

This makes absolutely no sense. One full-fledged CIA operative and me going it alone. I don't think so. There has to be a better way, he thought.

Agent Wolf parked the car a few blocks away from CIT. She popped the trunk. They both got out and moved to the back of the vehicle. She opened the trunk door completely and reveled a cache of weapons fit for a small army. Tony was stunned at the sight. Agent Wolf began packing and slamming ammo magazines into various firearms.

"You use a Springfield 9mm right," she said.

"Yeah. How'd you know?"

She looked at him like he was stupid then said, "You had it pointed at my face earlier, remember?"

"Right...sorry," he said sheepishly.

"I'll call for backup if the need arises. Does that make you feel any better?" she asked.

Tony nodded.

Once sufficiently packing enough weaponry they took off running toward the back of the CIT building. Tony knew of a side entrance that would not likely be covered. They entered and Tony led the way to the stairwell. Once they reached the 32nd floor it seemed they could go no further.

"Now what?" asked agent Wolf barely breathing heavier than normal.

"Now look around. Are you at all familiar with fire codes?" he asked scanning his surroundings.

"Yes, but what am I supposed to be looking for?" she asked.

"The only way to get to Audrey's office is by reaching this floor then taking another elevator to the 33rd," said Tony.

"Got it. There has to be another way out in case of fire," she said looking for anything out of the ordinary.

Tony then saw it. A slightly darker area in the ceiling right in the corner.

"There," he said pointing.

"How are we supposed to reach that?" she asked.

"I'll give you a boost," he said.

She looked at him like he's nuts then said, "I suppose the only other alternative is that I boost you, right?"

"That right," Tony said looking down at her with a smile.

Tony linked his fingers together and agent Wolf stepped one shoe into the finger web. They rhythmically counted to three and she was lifted up high enough to feel around for an opening. Once found she began to move the piece that covered the disguised ceiling entryway to the 33rd floor. Tony guided her to place both feet on his shoulders. He held her ankles tightly. Quietly she slid the ceiling piece to produce a dark opening. From her pocket she took out a flashlight and saw the fire escape ladder. Placing the flashlight in her mouth she gently unlatched it and Tony held on as they both eased it down until it securely reached the floor.

"You have any idea where this leads?" she asked while looking at the opening in the ceiling.

"Actually, I have a pretty good idea," he said quietly.

"Good. Then you go first," she said as she pulled her snub-nosed Glock from one of her pockets.

Tony held out his hand. Agent Wolf looked confused and handed him her gun.

"Not that. The flashlight," he said.

"Oh…right," she said a little embarrassed.

Tony quietly climbed the ladder into the opening and disappeared. He looked around to get his bearings by imagining Audrey's office layout. He then peeked his head back out and told agent Wolf to climb up and follow him. She did so without hesitation.

Once they were both securely walking on a steel beam Tony stopped and whispered, "If Forman's the bad guy then why would he help Jacquelyn after she left the school?"

He didn't wait for an answer. Tony saw the elevator box and started to go around. Suddenly it began to move downward. He fell back and almost knocked agent Wolf off the beam.

"Sorry about that," he said.

He leaned forward and watched the opening in the elevator shaft get deeper and deeper.

I hate heights, he thought.

They began to find their way around the elevator shaft when both of them heard the elevator stop. Agent Wolf looked down to see how far it had traveled.

She whispered, "It looks like it's at ground floor,"

"But, that elevator doesn't go all the way down. It should only travel one floor," he said.

"I can only tell you what I see. Take a look," she said.

Tony gripped the steel beneath his feet and leaned in to confirm what she said. He then looked around for the

447

elevator that only travels between floors 32 and 33. He spotted it and realized it was sitting on the 32nd floor.

That's why I missed it. Wait, why did this elevator go from the 33rd floor all the way down. I thought it only traveled as far as the 32nd floor, he thought.

He told agent Wolf about how normally the regular elevator can only travel to the 32nd floor then everyone has to get out and take the other to the 33rd.

"Well, obviously there's an override. We're on the 33rd. Well, 32-1/2 to be exact," she said.

Tony thought about that for a moment then continued on to locate his new destination. He began to shine the flashlight up to the ceiling, which is actually the floor of the 33rd, when he saw exactly what he thought he would find.

"This is it," he said.

A short ladder and this time a handle leading upward.

"Where does it lead?"

"Into a space behind a two-way mirror in Audrey's office. This must be the evacuation route in case of fire," he said.

"Yeah, or in case of something else."

"That would be just like you guys wouldn't it?" said Tony.

"It's not stupid. Let's get up there and be quiet," she said.

Tony went first then helped agent Wolf. Both were squeezed for space as they entered. As they stood, both could now see into Audrey's office. The office lights provided barely enough light for them to see inside the small closet-like room.

"Are you sure this is a two-way mirror and they can't see us?"

"Positive," said Tony.

Tony's stomach turned as he saw a small camera pointing into Audrey's office.

Oh my God! Audrey put a camera in here! I wonder if she knows I made a copy of her hard drive! he thought.

Agent Wolf saw the camera and grabbed the flashlight from Tony. She put it under her shirt to dim the light as much as possible just in case it could be seen from inside the office. Bending down she followed a small round cord to a Wi-Fi router and noticed the router was not functioning. Tony had followed the light beam as if he were gliding to his death. When it reached the router he exhaled knowing it was not able to send a feed via Wi-Fi because it was unplugged.

Thank you God! thought Tony.

Agent Wolf turned the flashlight off and whispered, "If that was working, where do you think it sends the video stream?"

"I should be asking you that question," he said.

Both looked into Audrey's office. Tony's head above agent Wolf's.

"Do you see anyone," she asked.

"No, but more importantly I don't feel anyone either," said Tony now comfortable speaking out about his ability.

"I don't get it. I was certain they would be here," she said.

"Maybe they left," he said.

"Maybe their coming back. The lights are still on," she replied.

Just then the sound of the elevator pierced the tranquility of the night. Both Tony and agent Wolf looked at each other figuring somebody was on their way. The elevator continued at full speed then slowed down one floor below and then stopped at its destination…the 33rd floor.

Tony, tilting his head with eyes closed, tried to focus on who's in the elevator.

Three separate feelings accompanied with words were silently delivered to Tony. *Double-edged sword, Mercury and Betrayal.* Then a new feeling and word arrived… *Anarchist.*

OK, we have Audrey, Forman, Janine Sheppard and— ? I don't know that last one, he thought.

"Here they come. First Audrey, Forman with Janine Sheppard! Who's the guy wearing the hat?" he said to agent Wolf.

"Oh my God! This is a rare sighting," she said.

"Why? Do you recognize him?" he asked.

The guy with the hat finally turned and showed his face.

"That's Sefter," she said totally surprised.

The name from Audrey's computer file, thought Tony.

"Who's Sefter?" he asked.

"You wouldn't understand," she said trying to brush him off.

"Clue me in then."

"Now's not the time."

450

"Tell me or I'm out of here," Tony said sternly.

"OK, but just wait. I need to find a way to know what their saying."

Everyone gathered around the table then sat down. Tony and agent Wolf had a front row view. Agent Wolf reexamined the camera setup looking for a way to get sound. Tony remembered seeing a gray box next to the non-functioning router and carefully maneuvered his way past agent Wolf, so as not to make noise, to examine it. He flipped a switch and suddenly they could hear everything being said in Audrey's office. Both squeezed back to their viewing places so they could see each person at the table.

Audrey said something then got up and began to walk directly toward the mirror. The sound kicked in after agent Wolf touched a button on the camera.

"And where do you think you're going?" asked Janine Sheppard pointing a pistol with a noise suppressor directly at Audrey.

"If my body is going to be found I want to at least fix my hair," she said without looking back.

"Only you would think of that at a time like this. However, I can appreciate it. Hurry up. We don't have all night," said Janine.

Audrey stood directly in front of the mirror slowly fussing with her hair. Her hands shaking. Tony and agent Wolf could tell she couldn't see them. They froze anyway.

"That's enough!" shouted Janine to Audrey.

Audrey calmly stopped, turned and discreetly reached behind her placing a small sticky note on the mirror just before walking away in Janine's line of sight to the sticky note.

"Now I'm ready," said Audrey.

"What's does the note say?" asked agent Wolf looking upward at it.

"I have no idea. It's backwards. Do you have something to write with?" he asked.

"Hang on. OK, I'm ready," she said.

Tony began to read each letter, including punctuation, letting agent Wolf know when it was a new word.

"Here we go; !PLEH RUOY—"

"Stop. This is ridiculous. I have a small mirror we can hold up to the note. Since it reads backwards to us we can view it properly using the mirror," said agent Wolf.

She held the mirror up to the note and these words appeared;

'TONY - I NEED YOUR HELP'!

Agent Wolf looked at Tony and said, "How could she possibly know you would be in here?"

"Quick confession. Remember the phone you smashed?" said Tony.

"Yeah?"

"That was my personal phone, not my CIT/Government phone. You owe me two hundred bucks," he said.

Agent Wolf wasn't sure if she should be totally pissed or completely impressed. She decided on the latter.

"Impressive. I told you you're a natural. Tell me, why did you take the chance of being tracked by Forman?"

"Because I'm still not sure if you're working with Janine Sheppard or on behalf of the CIA," he said calmly.

Chapter 55

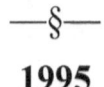

1995

Forman drove away from Langley Air Force Base completely stunned finding out Sefter is Janine Sheppard's son. He then thought about Don Williams and the new connection between the step brothers. Forman knew Don William's father is Jeff Statz. He tried to come up with a solution as to why Sefter sent Williams all those threatening letters.

Could he really be the one who put the explosives in the stuffed animal and blew up the lab? What's Audrey's relationship with this kid? She used him as a courier. Why would Theodore 'Sefter' Williams set up his own mother? There's got to be answers and I'll bet the house Andrew and Audrey know exactly what they are. But, first I have to help Janine. I wonder if Statz has any skeletons in his closet? Forman thought.

"Mr. Statz will see you now," said the personal assistant.

Forman got up, opened the door and sat down on a cushy chair next to a coffee table. He didn't want to give Jeff Statz the perceived upper hand by sitting across from him at his desk. Statz got up, walked over, and sat across from him.

"What's so important you couldn't tell me on the phone?" asked Statz.

"I'm surprised you're even in this office. When was the last time you were here?" asked Forman.

"Get to it Dennis," said Statz.

"I'm here to talk about illegitimate children here at our fine institution," Forman said keeping the subject as broad as possible yet setting the tone to be directly in his face.

Statz, the number two man at the CIA, glared then held up his index finger motioning Forman to stop talking. He got up, reached under his desk, and pressed a button that turned off all recording devices.

"Now, go ahead," said Statz.

"When did you have that installed?" asked Forman.

Statz just waved his hand motioning to Forman it's not important and he should continue.

"OK, then I see this is all business."

Silence from Statz. Forman was used to this.

"A witch hunt is coming. I've spoken to a particular elected official and he's about to launch an investigation into the personal relationships within the CIA," Forman lied.

Dennis Forman can play hardball as well as anyone in Washington. He's not afraid of a single person all the way up to and including the President. He's seen his share of combat and a stint as a POW and feels he really should have died more than once. His survival instincts are becoming legendary. Forman's perspective on life has been altered forever. He lives his life as if he has nothing to lose.

"Who's the elected official," asked Statz trying to hide a slight tone of stress.

"You know I'm not going to tell you so don't even try."

Statz, an exceptionally good listener, decided the man sitting across from him truly is very good at what he does and would never give up one of his sources.

"OK, fair enough. Why is this elected official interested in relationships within the Central Intelligence Agency?"

"Because I told him about Janine Sheppard," Forman lied once again.

"You what!?"

Forman remained silent turning the tables on Statz. He figured he would psychologically spin him around and then get the truth from him.

"Answer me! That's a direct order!" said the usually composed second in command leaning in and pointing a finger in Forman's face.

Hit a nerve I see, thought Forman.

Forman, without moving a muscle, sat calmly and asked, "Would you like to keep that finger or shall I snap it off before I go see the DCI?"

Statz settled back after thinking this was a man who would actually do such a thing, then said, "Sorry Dennis. My mistake."

Now we're on a level playing field. Well, maybe it's tilted my way just a little, thought Forman.

"I didn't tell him about Operation Monopoly. Do you think I'm stupid? That would make me a traitor. I told him about you guys holding Janine Sheppard back because of a pregnancy as a result of getting too close in the field," he lied once again.

"This is a well kept secret. Who told you?"

"Tell me Jeff, if I found out about it this quickly how do you expect to keep anything from the idiots on Capitol Hill?" he asked.

Statz eyed the rough man sitting across from him. He quickly surmised Dennis Forman is much more intelligent than he has given him credit. An uncomfortable feeling came over Statz.

"Is this the only relationship under scrutiny," he asked meekly.

Ah, bones in the closet, thought Forman.

Dennis remained relaxed and said, "You and I know this is not the only relationship worth looking into."

Jeff Statz couldn't believe his ears. He got up and walked to the sun shining through one of the bullet proof windows. As he stared out he became lost in thinking his career could be over. His indiscretions would be used as political fodder. He envisioned having to appear in front of a grand jury. Maybe even televised. He turned and walked back to Forman and sat back down.

"What can we do to turn this around?" he asked.

He must really have something to hide! Take advantage of this opportunity, he thought.

"It's really simple. Move Janine Sheppard to a friendly country. Give her a raise, keep her there working for the CIA in an administrative capacity for awhile then bring her back when appropriate."

"This almost sounds like blackmail. Tell me the truth. Did you have anything to do with her trying to take some of the funds from Operation Monopoly?"

"No. I'll take a lie detector test if you want," said Forman.

Statz eyed Forman and knew he would beat any and all forms of lie detection or even interrogation.

"I believe you Dennis. I also think it would be a good idea to place Ms. Sheppard abroad for a few years until the wolves are at bay. Can you control your Capitol Hill source?"

"You know I can," said Forman.

"OK. This stays between you and me, understand?" he said forcefully.

"Understood sir," said Forman calmly.

Both men stood and shook hands. Forman exited and began whistling as soon as he heard the door shut behind him.

Janine will be grateful and happy. Maybe there's still a way to get my share of the money. Maybe not right now, but sometime in the future, he thought.

Forman's next stop was to the First National Bank of Maryland. He opened up and account under an alias, which included a spouse, and made a rather large deposit. Then he rented a safe deposit box and placed the recordings of Janine Sheppard's interrogation in it Everest gave him. He then realized it could take years before the contents of the safe deposit box may be needed so he set up an automatic withdrawal to fund the rental for decades.

The recordings weren't really worth anything to him, but they would be of value to Janine Sheppard. Forman thought of it as a possible investment in his future. He sent a courier to deliver the safe deposit box key to his buddy, Everest, to give to Janine before they moved her. He didn't want to be seen with her after his meeting with Jeff Statz. He knew if he spoke to her again it could muddy the waters.

458

Next, Forman made a phone call.

"Hello," she answered.

"You sound a little stressed Audrey."

"Well, if you had to deal with the crap I have to immerse myself in everyday you would be a little stressed too," she said.

"Anything I can do to help?"

"It's just that we're bringing Andrew back state-side today. He'll land in D.C tomorrow."

"That's great news isn't it?" asked Forman.

"Of course it's good news. It's just that I'm trying to cut through the red tape so he can come back to Portland and be with me."

"You're talking about his debriefing I presume?"

"Yes. You know how long those can take," she said dejectedly.

"Do you want me to call Jeff Statz and expedite the matter?"

"Actually, I was just about to do that myself. It will mean more coming from me," she said confidently.

Not right now, thought Forman.

"You're probably right. But, if you do need my help, let me know." he said.

"I appreciate everything you do for me Dennis. I will call you if I run into a jam. You didn't call to hear me complain. What's up?"

"I have it on good authority that Janine Sheppard will remain with the Agency in a non-domestic administrative roll," he said without emotion.

"Are you kidding me? She's a traitor! Why on earth would anyone make that asinine decision?"

"Don't get on my case. I'm just delivering the news," said Forman enjoying himself.

"Well, while I'm talking to Jeff I think I'll take care of that as well," said Audrey confidently.

"I wouldn't if I were you."

"Why not? What do you know?" she asked.

"Just leave it alone. Everyone is better off this way," he answered vaguely.

"Did you have something to do with this?" she asked in a harsh tone.

"Let's just say I kept our hopes alive to still benefit from our original goal." he said carefully.

"The money is gone if that's what you're implying."

"Maybe for now. Look, I have to go. Do you need anything?" he asked.

Audrey paused then said, "Yes. I better not call Jeff with the state of mind I'm in right now. But, this can't wait. I want Andrew home. Will you talk to him and try to move his debrief along?"

"I think he'll be open to just about any suggestion I make," said Forman in a cocky tone.

"Dennis, you're good, but don't get too full of yourself," said Audrey almost rolling her eyes.

"I'll handle it," he said realizing he almost tipped his hand.

"Thank you. Talk with you soon," Audrey said before hanging up.

Forman made a call to Jeff Statz and requested an expeditious debriefing regarding Andrew Shelton. Statz asked if Forman took care of the situation on Capitol Hill. He said he did. Statz acquiesced to Forman regarding Andrew.

"He'll be operational back in Portland by tomorrow morning," said Statz.

"Thanks," said Forman.

Statz didn't reply and ended the call.

You're welcome, thought Forman.

Chapter 56

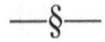

Present Day

"How can you possibly think I would become a traitor to my country," said agent Wolf in disgust.

"You were with Janine Sheppard at Jacquelyn's school. How do you explain that?" he asked.

Tony looked down and saw an ashen faced agent Wolf staring up at him. A look of confusion and wonder enveloped her. She asked him another question. Loudly this time.

"How could Audrey possibly know you would be in here!?"

Tony's earpiece blared so loudly he seemed to wince in pain. He put his right index finger to his lips to quiet her. He pointed to his ear then through the two-way mirror to the people in Audrey's office. Just then, jolted from their conversation, the elevator began to descend. It reached what both Tony and agent Wolf independently determined to be the ground floor. Then, both Tony's and agent Wolf's attention was jerked back to the voice in Audrey's office.

"Everyone sit," Janine Sheppard demanded still pointing her gun at Audrey.

Audrey sat down and crossed her legs trying to continue to show a calm demeanor. Forman, on the other hand, sat forward leaning his arms onto his knees, hands mostly under the table. An overt sign of discomfort or anticipation. Janine waited for Sefter to hold her chair then they both sat down at the oval conference table with Audrey and Forman.

"What a nice young man you've become Sefter. Thank you," Janine said sweetly without taking her eyes off of Audrey.

"Are you in on this Dennis?" asked Audrey.

"Don't answer her. This meeting has yet to be brought to order," Janine said emphatically.

Tony and agent Wolf looked at each other as if Janine Sheppard seems to have lost her marbles.

Banging the butt of her silenced pistol three times on the table she officially opened the meeting.

"Since I should have been married to Andrew and become CEO of this fine money laundering corporation I think it is only fitting that I run this show. Any objections? I didn't think so." announced Janine not waiting for answers.

Audrey appeared to remain calm. She knew there was something not right with Janine Sheppard. Inside, her stomach was turning over and over like a full load of laundry. She got up the nerve and went to work. She had to get Janine talking. Audrey avoided the obvious place to start and ignored her statement about marriage to Andrew.

"What makes you think you should be CEO of this company?" she asked.

"You've been handed everything from the beginning. How hard could it be?" answered Janine in a condescending tone.

Audrey turned her gaze to Forman and asked, "So, you've turned traitor too?"

Forman remained steady and calm. He didn't answer while Janine looked on.

"See Audrey. You have no effect on anything that goes on in this room any longer. Your time is up," Janine said ominously.

Audrey turned her eyes to Janine and asked, "How do you expect to get away with killing me and what will it achieve?"

"I'm not going to kill you and it will achieve everything I thought about over all these years."

"You're not going to kill me?" asked Audrey in a slow methodical tone.

"No. You, my dear, are going to commit suicide," she said adding a faint grin.

"And why would I do that?"

"Because, my dear, your good friend agent Forman caught you after transferring money into your own personal offshore bank account. What justice!" she proclaimed.

"Why would you think anyone would believe I would do such a thing?"

"Because you've done it once before. You set me up! You found out about Andrew and me! You know Sefter is our son!" she said ratcheting up the volume of her voice.

"And how can you believe such nonsense?" asked Audrey boring a hole through Forman.

Janine took note of Audrey's intense stare at Forman and said, "That's right. Dennis came to my rescue. I was transferred out of the country instead of being tried for treason because of this man. I couldn't stand knowing I would never rise to power within the Agency. So, I began a long journey creating a network of people with unique talents to privately fund my organization. Who do you think came up with the idea of Operation Monopoly?"

This struck a nerve with Audrey.

Is it possible it was her idea to covertly fund the CIA by taking over parts of the private sector economy? she wondered.

"Taking credit for a brilliant idea is in bad taste Janine."

"I agree. The DCI never should have initiated it without giving proper credit. However, imitation is the greatest form of flattery. I thought of privately funding certain CIA OPs after a wonderful night with Andrew. You might say he inspired me," she said egging Audrey on.

Audrey decided she was dealing with a nut job and asked Sefter why he was helping Janine.

He said, "The Government of The United States has overstepped its bounds once again. Stealing money from the private sector to torture and kill anyone who gets in its way. I'm just doing my part. Leveling the playing field. If I can do something about it—"

"Is that the real reason?" asked Audrey interrupting.

"I've come to know my mother. I like her and she has finally come around to my way of thinking."

"What...that the government is out to get you?" Audrey asked sarcastically.

"No, not at all. The government can't touch me. I'm helping her because she's my mother," he said succinctly.

"Still can't call her 'Mom' though, can you Theo?" poked Audrey.

She saw she hit her mark. Sefter and Janine both showed looks of anger.

Hmm, nothing from Forman. He's definitely on a different page. Maybe the same book, but definitely not the same page, she thought.

Janine said, "Sefter, get the computer ready. It's time for the great Audrey Shelton to become a traitor to her country."

Audrey couldn't believe her eyes. Sefter put on disposable latex gloves and brought out a white laptop. Then she finally noticed Janine already had skin colored disposables on. She couldn't see if Forman did or not.

My computer! she thought.

After a brief pause Audrey said, "Dennis, you've been awfully quiet. Why are you doing this?"

"I'm just staying the course. Operation Boardwalk died with you taking personal revenge on Janine. So, Operation Park Place was born. I want my money. Simple as that," he said.

"How do any of you think you will possibly get away with this? I have people on their way here right now," said Audrey.

"Audrey, if you think that idiot savant Tony James is on his way here you're sadly mistaken. He's dead. Agent Stark found his body on your front lawn," said Forman.

Audrey covered her mouth in shock.

Tony looked down at agent Wolf and said, "Forman has to know that wasn't me lying on the lawn. Why is he saying that to Audrey?"

Agent Wolf didn't say anything. She turned back to the surreal scene taking place in front of her. Tony then did the same.

"I'm ready," said Sefter with the laptop glowing in front of him.

"Is it ready to transfer?" Janine asked him.

"Just press 'Enter'."

Janine stood and took the computer then glided over and placed it in front of Audrey with one hand. She place the barrel of her gun close to Audrey's temple.

"Now it's time for you to betray your country. Press the button," she demanded.

Audrey looked up at her crazed eyes. She slowly turned her attention to Sefter then to Forman.

"Are you just going to sit there?" she pleaded with Forman.

He didn't move a muscle.

"Press the button," demanded Janine moving the barrel of her weapon closer to Audrey's head.

"If I'm dead I can't press the button," she said knowing it didn't hold water.

Janine snickered, "Either you press it or I take your dead finger and do it for you."

Chapter 57

—§—

1995

Andrew saw them coming before he heard the knock at the door at his dwelling on Cayman Island. Two pasty white men in Hawaiian shirts and wrinkled shorts. Andrew opened the door.

"You two look ridiculous. You lost or something? Hurry up and get in here," said Andrew with authority.

Andrew has known the two men from the Agency for years. They're very good friends. Scott Hanson and Leo Carlin haven't been back in the US for over two years. Both are very average in height and completely non-descript. They are two of the best in the support services group helping multiple field operatives with details like stashing documents or obtaining weapons when needed. They arrived just yesterday. Andrew Shelton, years ago, went through training with both of them. The three of them bonded and became so close during their hyper-boot camp the CIA put them through.

"Do you have it," asked Andrew.

Hanson handed Andrew a sealed envelope with the location and contact information for Janine Sheppard.

"You're not chasing her again are you? I thought you got married?" laughed Hanson.

"No, it's not like that. I need somebody in Germany to facilitate a meeting. Who better than someone who looks like her. Am I right?" said Andrew with a chuckle.

"I wouldn't turn her down," said Carlin to his buddies.

"I need you to do one more thing for me."

"Name it," said Hanson.

"This has to be off the books as well," said Andrew.

Hanson remained stoic while Carlin became noticeably uncomfortable.

"What's up?" asked Hanson.

"Find out what's going on with my status. I'm getting a strange feeling something's not quite right. I'm being brought back to the States way sooner than expected and it just doesn't pass the smell test," said Andrew.

Hanson and Carlin glanced at each other.

"I know that look. Spill it," said Andrew.

"Statz knows," said Hanson.

"Knows what?" asked Andrew.

"Statz thinks the DCI has you in mind to take Statz' job. We don't know the full scope of your current OP, but whatever you're doing here has him spooked out of his mind. Apparently, he's stripping some very good operatives of their power to save his own skin."

"Is that right," said Andrew in a calm thoughtful tone. "What else have you heard?"

"Just bits and pieces really," said Carlin.

"So, tell me."

"They're just rumors, so don't quote me on this. I've heard something about privately funding the CIA without the knowledge of our elected officials. It's just a stupid rumor. I'm not even sure it's worth bringing it up," he said.

I'm sure glad you did! Audrey doesn't know it, but she may have saved me from a jail sentence, he thought.

"Is that it?" asked Andrew as if it were no big deal.

"Can't think of anything else. How about you Scott?" asked Carlin.

"Nope," said Hanson.

"OK, let yourselves out the back. I'll contact you if I need anything else." said Andrew.

The two men left, each going their separate way. They would walk the beach on their own for a little then head to their next assignment. No time to enjoy the warm sunshine.

Andrew opened the envelope and made quick work of contacting Janine Sheppard. She was so excited to hear from him. She would have been excited to hear from anyone she knew at this point.

He took precautions the call couldn't be traced back to him on his end. They conversed so easily it was as if no time had gone by since they last time the spoke. She filled him in on what happened to her. He became her lifeline back. Andrew laid the groundwork. Once this was complete he knew she would be up for just about anything. Andrew knew Audrey went solo on setting her up. He just had to make sure Janine understood this. In order for him to become a man of power he would need leverage and money…and lots of it. It was time he invested in himself and let his career take a back seat.

After hanging up he thought, *I just need to make sure my finger prints can't be connected to any of this.*

That night he was notified to pack his bags and get to the airstrip by 6am. He was going home. The next morning, through high powered binoculars, he watched what looked like a private corporate jet to the untrained eye, land, taxi and refuel at Owen Roberts Airport. He knew this to be his transport home. Military flights are prohibited to fly over Cuba and the air force would have to log its passengers. His two buddies were waiting on the ground standing watch on each side of the jet's, now unfurled, stairway. Andrew wore nice tan casual pants with a blue blazer and a very out of place large straw hat to cover his face just in case. Hanson and Carlin were also called back and accompanied him on the flight home.

The moderately short voyage to Langley Air Force Base was uneventful. The only time Andrew looked out the window was to see Cuba off in the distance. Hanson and Carlin couldn't stop talking about the various restaurants they were going to visit. They couldn't wait to finally go home.

Andrew, on the other hand, remained in thought about his debrief in incredible detail. He didn't want to get snagged in the Agency's fishing net. He hoped he could be released in a day or two. Once on the ground all three men were dashed off in two black SUVs. However, Andrew rode alone in the second one. Sitting in the back by himself, he noticed they were taking a different route than his buddies.

"Aren't we going to Langley?" asked Andrew.

"No sir. Mr. Statz has arranged a lunch at Congressional Country Club in Bethesda," said the driver.

Andrew nodded and said, "Nice place."

Public place? Why on earth would we be going there? Andrew wondered.

"I'll take your word for it. Never been inside," said the driver.

Instead of pulling up to the main entrance the driver drove around the back of the beautiful building, put the

SUV in park and left the engine running. Quickly, a tall thick man with a military look in a dark suit and sunglasses opened Andrew's door and invited him to exit the vehicle.

Just as Andrew got out two more men sidled up next to him. The first man patted him down then told the driver he was now allowed to leave. Off he drove.

"My clothes are in there," said Andrew.

Without so much as a nod the big man motioned with his right arm to walk with him through the back door. His associates walked as far as the door then stood sentry. Meandering through the pro-shop they finally arrived in one of the more casual restaurants next to the club house. It was completely empty except for two men standing and one sitting at a table.

"Andrew, good to see you," said Jeff Statz as he began to stand. "Have a seat. Look how tan and fit you are."

Who the hell are you and what have you done with Jeff Statz? A sheep in wolf's clothing, thought Andrew.

"Good to see you Jeff," answered Andrew as if he hadn't a care in the world.

Without looking, Statz made a sweeping motion with his hand and the two men guarding him left the room.

"So, tell me about living in the Cayman Islands."

You didn't bring me here to talk about my living conditions, thought Andrew.

"One of the best places I've ever stayed. At least while on the job," he answered politely.

Andrew and Statz talked pretty much about nothing through lunch. Both are experts at talking without really saying anything at all. Once the table was cleared Statz sat back. Andrew could see he shifted into business and listening mode.

"I'm going to debrief you," Statz said.

"Fine with me. Are you sure you want to do it here?" asked Andrew looking around.

"Let's just say we have taken extraordinary precautions over the course of time to utilize a normal setting such as this. It's as tight as a safe house," said Statz.

Now why would someone this high up the food chain do something as low level as to debrief a field operative unless he's looking for specific information only he wants to be in the know about, Andrew wondered.

Statz began with open ended questions about activities and locations. He then moved on to specifics about Operation Monopoly. Andrew noticed the casual shift into more yes-no style questions.

Andrew offered up everything he felt was required, but no more. He obviously stayed clear of his own special activities...Operation Boardwalk. To his knowledge this was only known to himself, Audrey and Forman. He shared his ambitions during his phone call with Janine Sheppard, but never mentioned Operation Boardwalk by name.

"I was alerted to the fact there was, let's call it a new communication avenue, used by you and Dagger," said Statz.

Andrew remained silent. Not because this threw him, which it actually did, but it wasn't a direct question. A debriefing is not to become a conversation if one knew what they were doing.

"What do you have to say to that?" asked Statz.

"What exactly are you asking me?"

Statz knew not to tangle too much with Andrew so he asked, "Did Dagger and you communicate during the blackout period?" he asked.

Thank God! I thought you were going to ask me about that program we used.

"Jeff, you know how it is when you're married. It's tough not to communicate with your spouse over a long period of time. Especially when she just attended your funeral!"

"Understood."

Good. Now move on, he thought.

"Now, what about the call you made to Germany last night? Tell me about that."

Andrew's mouth went dry, but tried to hide his discomfort.

"I made many calls to Germany as requested by you to make sure the funds from Operation Monopoly would stay one step ahead of—"

"A very specific call. This one was just last night and not to any bank. Ring a bell?"

Could he have been listening in? Absolutely, but only from Janine's end. I took precautions. I lose everything if I come completely clean, he thought.

"I did make a call to check on Janine Sheppard. It was kind of you to let her stay within the Agency," answered Andrew.

"What did the two of you talk about?"

Ah, the real reason for him to debrief me, Andrew thought.

474

"I was just checking in on her."

Statz reached into his briefcase and placed a microcassette recorder on the table without turning it on.

"Care to elaborate?" Statz asked.

This is it. He's either got me or it's a bluff. No sense falling on my own sword, he decided.

"What's that for?" Andrew asked looking at the cassette recorder.

Statz ignored Andrew's question then said, "If we need to, we will get to it in due time."

First mistake. Never bluff without giving a small snippet of having your target believe you really have something incriminating. Should have let a pro do this debrief, thought Andrew.

"Jeff, I was concerned about her that's all. You know very well why," said Andrew.

"Yes. Your relationship with her has reared its ugly head once again," Statz said forcefully.

"What are you talking about?" asked Andrew.

"A source I trust has told me one of our elected officials on the Hill may be launching an investigation into the relationships among Central Intelligence Agency employees," he said.

"Trust me Jeff, it's over between me and Janine. I really was just checking on her. You can put that cassette away. There's nothing on it that could possibly implicate me in any wrongdoing. Is it against agency policy to make sure another employee is OK? Hell, I'll talk to the damn Congressman myself."

Statz sat back for a full thirty seconds saying nothing. Andrew did the same. Statz made the first move and reached for the cassette. He rolled it around in his hand as if he were deciding to nail Andrew or spare him from a life in prison as a traitor.

"Your right. Nothing wrong with checking in with a co-worker," he said placing the cassette back into his briefcase.

So, what's your story then?, wondered Andrew.

"Who's intel are you using about this so-called elected official? Sounds a little suspect to me," said Andrew.

"It's important to track down any and all possible leaks that could damage the Agency," said Statz.

Bull! I smell blood, thought Andrew.

"Who are you protecting?" asked Andrew.

Statz didn't answer.

"Oh my God! You're protecting yourself aren't you?"

Statz said nothing.

You're digging yourself a great big hole by not saying anything you idiot! I'll take a ridiculous long shot then let's get the hell out of here, thought Andrew.

"I know about you and Janine," he said flat-toned.

Statz tried, but simply couldn't hide his guilt.

"How did you know?"

"Something like that just can't remain a secret forever," Andrew answered.

Bingo! Andrew rejoiced.

"Look, my main concern is for Donny. I really don't care if Janine falls off the face of this earth. As a matter of fact, it would make my life that much easier."

"Come on Jeff! I've known you long enough to know you're looking out for yourself and that's it," said Andrew to provoke a response.

Statz glared at Andrew. His blood pressure began to rise. He clenched his fist. Like a cat he through a left-handed haymaker and connected with Andrew's left side of his face. Statz' chair had fallen behind him. He stood waiting for Andrew to get up and attack. He never did. He was out cold.

The body guards came rushing in. Statz gave them instructions what to do with Andrew Sheppard.

Andrew woke up in an unfamiliar bed, but could only open his right eye. His head pounded like he celebrated too much on a New Year's Eve. He had trouble focusing using just one eye at first. Then he heard the voice.

"You OK Andrew?"

Sitting up he slowly located the voice and saw Jeff Statz sitting about six feet from him with his left leg over his right and fingers clasped together. Statz appeared to not have a care in the world.

"You sucker-punched me you prick!"

"You deserved it," said Statz.

Andrew sat still for a moment then began to chuckle. His chuckle turned into a full blown laugh. Statz, obviously pleased, joined him.

"You're right. I probably did deserve it. Where did you learn to punch like that?" asked Andrew.

"I was a member of a boxing club growing up in Baltimore," answered Statz.

"What possessed you to slug me?"

Because, if I know you, you were going to get too close to the real truth, Statz thought.

"I'm sorry Andrew. The thought of some puke who bought his seat in Congress questioning my integrity just took me to my limit I guess. It was nothing personal."

What I said was meant to be personal, Andrew thought.

Andrew gently touched his swollen eye and asked, "Will you please get me some ice?"

"On the table to your right," answered Statz.

Lying back, Andrew placed the ice bag on half his face. He remembers everything up until he blacked out by Statz' punch. Then a thought entered his mind.

He owes me. I could use him sometime down the road. This is a very fortunate yet unforeseen gift. He may have punched my face, but I just punched my ticket for my future, he thought.

Statz asked, "Will you forgive me."

"Yes, but you owe me," answered Andrew.

"Good. Come up with a story about how you hurt yourself," said Statz.

"I will, but just remember one thing…you owe me big time," said Andrew.

"Yes, yes…I owe you," repeated Statz.

"OK, just remember that when you're DCI someday," said Andrew.

"Yeah, yeah," said Statz dismissively.

"Are we done with the debrief? I want to go home and see Audrey."

"Yes. Just remember, you've been in the witness protection program and cannot reveal a single nugget of information. People will question you. You've been dead you know."

"That should be fun," said Andrew sarcastically.

"Are you reinstating me as CEO at CIT?"

"No. You're too valuable to remain in one company. CIT will be your cover. I need you to travel to other private sector funding opportunities. I've already given the green light to open up various CIT locations throughout the US. This will give you reason to travel," said Statz. As far as the people in your sphere you might as well still be dead to them.

Excellent! I'm as free as can be!, thought Andrew.

"That's a good idea. I presume you've briefed Audrey," Andrew said calmly.

"Not yet, but within the hour. When you're feeling up to it, you can go home. I've arranged for your flight. You can be back with Audrey by tonight."

"Thanks Jeff. But, not for this," he said pointing at his face.

Chapter 58

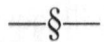

Present Day

The tension in Audrey's office had climbed to an incredible level. Tony and agent Wolf, in the crawl space behind the two-way mirror, both knew they were going to have to save Audrey. Just then the elevator, sitting on the first floor, announced its climb upward.

They both looked at each other in total surprise.

"Maybe that really is Stark," said agent Wolf.

Tony turned and took in the view of Janine Sheppard holding her gun to Audrey's head while listening to the movement of the elevator. He knew they couldn't hear it unless it arrived on their floor.

As if zapped by electricity, Tony nearly jumped out of his skin. His Smartphone buzzed with the arrival of a text.

Agent Wolf, first taken by surprise due to Tony's quick movement, eyed him up and down. Tony began to reach back under his untucked shirt when agent Wolf grabbed one of her guns and quickly stopped Tony from further movement.

"Freeze! You reach any further and I will shoot," said agent Wolf forcefully.

"Woe, hold on! I wasn't reaching for my gun. I stashed my phone next to my gun," he said with urgency.

Agent Wolf stared for a moment then said, "Turn slowly and lift your shirt."

Tony did as instructed.

Agent Wolf took Tony's gun then saw the exact same Smartphone she thought she had crushed on the road near Audrey's house. She didn't understand.

With arms up, Tony said, "You destroyed my personal phone. This is my CIT and government issued phone."

Confused, agent Wolf looked at Tony. Her eyes pleaded with him to explain.

"I didn't trust you. I'm sorry. I wanted to be tracked just in case you really were working with Janine Sheppard," he said.

Agent Wolf lowered her weapon and said, "You are full of surprises. I never suspected you would have your second phone with you. What an idiot I can be!"

"Wait a minute. How do you know I have a second phone?" Tony asked in an accusatory tone lowering his arms.

She handed him both his gun and Smartphone back to him and quickly told him she had been shadowing him ever since he got back to Portland from Langley.

"So it was you opening and closing my garage door?"

"No, that person is lying dead on Audrey's front lawn. She was tailing you and trying to monitor your communication with your wife and also Audrey."

"Back the truck up! You're telling me—"

Agent Wolf interrupted and said, "Quick! Check your phone."

Tony looked at her as if she may be a little off her rocker. He took his phone and his gun. He stored his weapon behind his back then unlocked his phone. The icons appeared.

"I have a new text."

He quickly looked away from the short text to agent Wolf.

"What is it?" she asked urgently.

He showed it to her. Her face was glowing with total surprise.

It read; 'WHEREVER YOU ARE KNOW THAT AGENT STARK IS TRACKING YOU'

Both Tony and agent Wolf turned and looked at Forman. He was still bent down resting his arms on his knees. He kept his eyes down not looking at anyone.

They looked back at each other in almost complete shock then back to the scene in Audrey's office. Janine was losing it.

"I'm going to count to ten. If you haven't pressed 'Enter' by then, I will shoot you in the head," threatened Janine.

The elevator car was coming up. Not close enough for Tony to get a read yet.

"One."

"Can we trust Forman?" Tony asked agent Wolf.

"Two."

"I don't know," she answered.

"Three."

"Why don't you know!?"

"Four."

"Because he's been acting very strange around me for awhile," she said wiping a bead of sweat from her temple.

"Five."

The elevator car was still climbing.

"Six."

"We can't just sit here," said agent Wolf.

"Seven."

"What about Forman?" asked Tony.

"Eight."

Tony closed his eyes, tilted his head and said, "Calculating and —"

"Nine."

The elevator arrived with the ding of destination. Everyone in the office, including Janine looked to the doors as they spread apart. Janine raised her pistol and fired upon the first movement she saw.

Agent Stark fell forward sprawled out. His legs, still in the elevator. He had his weapon at the ready, but it now laid four feet from the blood pooling out of his head. Janine had fired two quick shots with complete accuracy.

Because the elevator is on the same side of Audrey's office as Tony and agent Wolf they didn't know exactly what happened, but could guess by the sound of a body dropping like a sack of potatoes onto the floor after the gunshots.

"Oh my God! Who did she shoot?" asked agent Wolf.

"Stark," Tony said quietly.

"How do you know?"

Tony didn't answer. He barely heard her to begin with. His attention was split between Janine Sheppard, still next to Audrey, Forman and a lightning bolt that had just pierced him. The feeling came with the word...*Covetous*.

What the hell could this person covet so much as to let agent Stark die?, he wondered.

Janine began to remove her left hand from her firing position to turn her attention to Audrey once again. She first looked at Forman and Sefter as they stared at the motionless man lying on the floor.

"See what happens Audrey? Nothing will stop this from happening. I will become so wealthy and you will have become one of the Agency's most notorious traitors," said Janine.

"Sefter, would you be a dear and make sure the man is dead?" her tone turning sweet.

"No. I'm not touching a dead body." said Sefter in disgust.

"OK. I understand honey. Dennis, will you do the honors?"

Forman got up concealing his phone in the sleeve of his long sleeved shirt. He pulled out his weapon and carefully nudged Bobby Stark with his foot. No response. He bent down and checked for a pulse, but didn't expect one.

"Gone," said Forman.

Agent Wolf, in despair, grabbed Tony's phone and quickly wrote and sent a text to Forman.

"What did you just do?" asked Tony alarmingly.

"I texted Forman. We have to know what's going on!" she said.

"Oh my God! What if his phone isn't on silent? He'll be shot and then Janine will know the text came from me! It's my phone! She'll figure out I'm alive and likely nearby. She'll kill Audrey in a heartbeat then come after me!"

Agent Wolf said, "I had to do something! She was about to kill her!"

Tony saw the anguish on agent Wolf's face and knew now was not the time to chastise her for trying to do something to save Audrey's life. He quickly racked his pistol ready to do something. Agent Wolf followed suit. Tony hoped the sounds wouldn't be heard. They both looked intently at Forman.

Forman walked back to his chair without so much as a sound from his phone. He resumed his position of leaning forward and placing his hands on his knees. Hands no longer within sight.

"My God, he just let her kill Bobby!" agent Wolf said in despair.

"Now, back to you Audrey," said Janine with her gun repositioned to Audrey's head.

Janine turned her head looking back toward the elevator door. Stark's legs wouldn't allow them to completely close. It bothered her.

"Sefter, move his legs so the door can close," she said in a demanding tone this time.

"Let him do it," Sefter said nodding to Forman.

"No, you need to grow up. You do it...now!" she ordered.

"Fine," said Sefter.

Sefter crossed the office with long strides and took in the gruesome amount of blood that had poured from Stark's head. He backed into the elevator to move the legs so the door could finally close. As he did so, he was grabbed violently and placed in a headlock and a Sig Sauer suppressed barrel placed to the back of his head.

"Move and you're dead," said the man who was hiding from sight within the elevator.

Sefter, taken completely by surprise, could only move his legs and did as he was told. He couldn't see who was holding him.

"Now, walk forward," said the man using Sefter as a human shield.

The elevator door shut and descended automatically.

Janine, Forman and Audrey all looked at the same time.

"Who's there," asked agent Wolf in a desperate whisper.

"I don't know his name," answered Tony.

"Jeff Statz? Is it really you?" said Janine taken entirely by surprise.

"No way!" said agent Wolf straining to get a good look.

"Who's he?" asked Tony.

"He's the boss," she said.

"Who's boss,"

"Almost everyone's at the CIA."

"Tell me, what could *covet* mean with regard to him?" asked Tony.

"I have no—. Wait! Rumor has it years ago he and Janine Sheppard were personally involved somehow!" she said excitedly.

Tony quickly processed the information.

Audrey tried to will Statz to shoot Janine by glaring at him and slightly motioning with her head. Statz pointed his weapon directly at Forman.

"Hands where I can see them," he said forcefully.

Forman acquiesced by sitting up and placing his palms on the tabletop.

"What the hell are you doing Jeff?" asked Forman.

Statz forced Sefter back into his chair. Sefter looked at his mother trying to get her to shoot the man who just had a gun to his head.

"I'm here for what's mine," said Statz.

"Janine, take a seat," he ordered.

"Not a chance Jeff," she said pushing the barrel of her gun's suppressor against Audrey's skull.

"I'm here to go with you. We can disappear together," he replied.

Janine paused. She couldn't tell if this was somehow a way to let Audrey go or if he was serious. Statz knew his next move.

"Janine, sit down and let me take care of this," he said pointing his weapon at Audrey yet keeping an eye on Forman and Sefter.

He arrived next to Audrey, his back to the two-way mirror, and placed his gun's barrel on Audrey's head. He locked eyes with Janine.

"You're serious, aren't you?" Janine said.

"You don't need another murder on your hands. Not that it matters. We won't be found." He looked down at Audrey and said, "Press the enter key NOW!"

Audrey began to lift her arm as Janine realized her lost love had finally come for her. She took the gun off Audrey and backed up.

"Too slow Audrey!" said Statz.

He pushed the barrel even harder to drive his point home.

Audrey said, "Jeff, may I have one last request before I press this button."

"No, but you may ask once you have pressed it. Do it NOW!"

Audrey had no choice. She pressed the computer button.

Janine was overcome. A smile came over her face. She looked up at Statz with a giddy twinkle in her eyes.

"Janine, please have a seat."

She did.

"Alright Audrey, what was it you wanted to ask?" said Statz still standing over Audrey.

"Jeff, before her last request, we need Sefter to verify the transfer," said Janine.

Janine took Audrey's laptop and set it down in front of Sefter. With a few quick strokes and clicks he verified the transaction.

"It's all there," he said.

"Did you touch the 'Enter' button?" asked Statz.

"No," said Sefter.

"Good. Bring it back here and place it in front of her," he ordered.

Everyone heard Audrey's office phone ring.

Statz said, "If they leave a message it will be the last one you will receive as a living being on this earth."

Agent Wolf said, "I don't see a doorknob so we're going to have to break the—"

Once again the elevator began its ascent.

"Who could that possibly be?" she asked.

"If I've met the person before I'll be able to tell you in just a few seconds," said Tony.

"That's amazing," Elizabeth said almost inaudibly staring up at Tony.

The elevator box was now within Tony's reach. He focused like never before...*Lethal Façade*.

"It's Andrew Shelton," Tony said opening his eyes.

"But, he'll walk right into an ambush just like Bobby!"

The elevator ding made everyone once again look its way. Forman pulled his weapon quickly this time and ducked down just enough so he could see who was about to exit the slaughter box.

The doors opened, Andrew stood in the elevator shocked at the sight of Bobby Stark with a giant pool of blood around his head. He stepped forward then looked up and saw Janine Sheppard, Forman, Sefter and then Jeff Statz pointing a gun at his wife's head.

"What's the hell?" he asked as he walked gingerly across the office.

Now in charge Statz said, "Stop."

Forman stood from his crouched position, but kept his weapon trained on Andrew.

"Nobody shoot...yet," said Statz.

"Dennis, what are you doing!? Audrey, what's happening here!? Jeff, get that gun away from Audrey!"

"We have to help," said Tony.

"The only way I can see getting out of this room is to shoot the glass. I can't find a doorknob anywhere," said agent Wolf.

"Did you hear the elevator go back down?" asked Tony.

"What? No, maybe Andrew locked it thinking he and Audrey would be leaving right away. I bet that was him calling before," she speculated.

"Let's hope your right. And, by the way, there is no doorknob. There's a latch a few inches next to the wood frame of the mirror," Tony said as he grabbed a wooden stick then began exiting the small room.

"Give me the flashlight and take this. Got any gum?" asked Tony.

Elizabeth looked at Tony with confusion, but reached into one of her pockets then handed him the pack.

"Where are you going and why did you give me a pen?" asked agent Wolf.

"To the elevator. Be prepared," he said as he began climbing down the ladder.

"For what?"

"For my signal."

"What's the signal?"

"You'll know it when you hear it," he said as his voice faded away as he walked on the steel beam toward the elevator box.

Tony ditched his earpiece just as he reached the elevator and found a way to quietly climb on top. He found the latch to an opening and silently swung it open toward him and laid it on roof of the elevator car. Lowering himself down through the opening he hung onto the edges trying to feel the floor. The last thing he needed was to make noise and alert everyone of his presence. It would be a fatal mistake. He spread his legs wide and found the two side rails then easily and gently found the floor.

Audrey began to answer Andrew, "It's a set-up. They made me—"

"Quiet!" shouted Statz elbowing Audrey in the head.

Andrew burned with fire and began toward Audrey. Statz froze him in his tracks by placing the barrel of his gun to Audrey's temple once again.

"Jeff, what's this all about!?" asked Andrew in desperation.

"Get over here and sit next to your wife. Nothing better than a little domestic dispute ending in a murder suicide."

"Jeff, Andrew doesn't have to die over this. We can trust him. He's a good man," said Janine.

Statz looked at Janine for what seemed to be an eternity.

"You still have a thing for him or is it because you had his baby?" asked Statz.

Audrey's face showed shock.

"Jeff, you're the only one for me. You know it to be true," she said.

"Do I? Our son at least grew up to be an upstanding citizen following in our footsteps with the Agency. Sefter over there is a spoiled brat that has played on the wrong team since he was in his teens. What did you ever see in this guy anyway?" he asked motioning to Andrew.

Andrew's face had guilt written all over it. If he could figure out a way he would take out both Statz and Janine Sheppard.

"I can explain Audrey," pleaded Andrew.

"No Andrew. No explanation necessary. You see Audrey...Andrew and Janine had a child together. He's sitting right over there. What a guy!" said Statz.

"You're no better," said Audrey.

Statz gave her another elbow to the head this time knocking her unconscious.

"Jeff!" exclaimed Andrew.

Janine sat with a slight grin looking at Audrey. She enjoyed that.

"Here's what's going to happen. I'm going to shoot Audrey first then you. A lover's quarrel. After that we'll mess up the place then disappear like ghosts in the night. Someone will find you and then figure you two had a dispute that got out of hand."

"You're missing one important fact," said Andrew.

"Two field operatives dead. You're nowhere to be found? I don't think you've thought this through all the way. Forget this and Audrey and I will—"

"You're wrong Andrew. Janine will disappear, but I'm sticking around for a little while so I can direct the investigation myself. I'm pretty sure the conclusion I draw will satisfy every law enforcement agency. After that, I resign propping up Forman to take my position."

Andrew looked at Forman.

"So this is why you're in on this? A promotion?"

"No, not just a promotion. I'm really not that interested in his job. As a matter of fact, I don't think I could stand his job for more than a minute. I want my money that you and Audrey took from me."

"First Stark then Audrey and me? You're turning traitor and murdering your friends all for money?" Andrew asked Forman.

"I've served my country in ways you can't even imagine. What do I have to show for it. Not a damn thing! It's my opportunity and I'm not letting it slip away again," Forman said forcefully.

"He has a point," said Statz turning to Andrew.

Tony found a way to easily fixture the stick precariously close to the 'Open Door' button using the wad of gum he chewed along the way. He rested the top of the stick gently on the metal frame of a charity poster along the inside of the elevator car. He then climbed back out making sure the stick was within easy reach.

Perfect, he thought.

Chapter 59

—§—

1995

Andrew's jet landed at Portland International Airport at 10pm. It taxied to the gate where the wealthy people normally arrive. Andrew liked it. Audrey was waiting inside. She was told by Jeff Statz Andrew would be the only passenger on the plane. Her excitement got the better of her. She got up and stood in the doorway looking for the jet door to spring open.

The door finally opened after a few minutes and Andrew appeared. Audrey couldn't control herself. She ran through the tunnel to meet her husband.

"Andrew!" she shrieked with joy.

Andrew dropped his carry-on luggage and caught Audrey jumping into his arms and wrapping her legs around him. They kissed hard.

"Ouch!" said Andrew.

Audrey pulled back to find out what was wrong. She looked at him and couldn't believe his swollen eye. She jumped down and examined his face.

"What happened?" she asked in a concerned tone.

"Not here. Let's go home," he said smiling.

On the ride home Andrew told Audrey exactly what had happened.

"Jeff Statz punched you?" she said in disbelief.

"Sucker punched me," he corrected.

"That doesn't seem like him. You must have really provoked him,"

"Yeah, I'm kind of proud of that," Andrew said in a fun loving tone.

In the back of Andrew's mind was the burning question of why Audrey didn't follow through on his plan to set up Forman and Williams. They talked all the way home.

Once there, they barely got through the front door, clothes began being ripped off and strewn as they groped each other all the way to the bedroom.

The next morning, Audrey got up first and made a pot of coffee. The smell finally penetrated Andrew's senses. He got up and found Audrey at what used to be his desk.

"At work so early?" he asked as he leaned against the framework between rooms.

"This has been pretty normal for me since you had to go away."

"You look good there. It fits you," he said sincerely.

Audrey misread him and said, "I know this is going to be hard for you, but—"

"I meant what I said. You belong exactly where you are. I'm happy to take on new my responsibilities."

"When Jeff told me, I wasn't sure you would even go along with it," she said.

By the way, I have no intention of letting you back into any position at CIT. As far as I'm concerned, I'm in agreement with Jeff Statz. You're still dead to almost everyone. I love you, but I'm not an idiot, she thought.

Andrew took her by the hand. She stood, grabbed her coffee mug, and he led her to sit with him on the couch.

"So, how was it, sleeping in your own bed for a change?" Asked Audrey

Andrew stared at her just a few seconds longer than he realized.

Yes, that could be taken either way, she thought.

He answered, "I can sleep anywhere as long as you're by my side."

"You are quite the charmer Mr. Shelton."

"And you are quite amazing Audrey."

They sat quietly for a few moments enjoying their hot beverages. They had a lot to get caught up on, but all in due time.

Andrew said, "I've put into motion a plan for us to still get our money."

A little perturbed Audrey said, "Forget it. Why take the chance? There's too much attention on this OP."

"That's why it will likely take years to execute," said Andrew.

Audrey took another sip as they touched fingers while their hands rested between them. She looked into Andrew's eyes. She burrowed deep. Like the old days, it seemed as if she were being drawn into another dimension. Something in his gaze reached out to her. But then again, it always had. Then it dawned on her.

It can't be! I don't believe it! I'm imagining this, she thought.

"What's wrong?" asked Andrew.

Audrey withdrew her hand and said, "I still don't get why Jeff Statz would do your debrief."

"You'll have to ask him. Tell me about what went down with the explosion at the lab in Langley," replied Andrew.

"Don't want to talk about it huh?" she said.

"What do you mean?" asked Andrew as he reached her hand once again.

"Your debrief. You changed the subject," she said.

He reached out and placed his hand on hers then said, "I have no idea why Jeff would do the debrief. He really seemed lost. It was to my advantage to let him do it rather than someone who's actually good."

Once again Audrey stared into Andrew's eyes.

"Andrew, do you know who is responsible for the lab explosion?" she asked.

Misreading the meaning behind her question he said, "It wasn't your fault. How could you know?"

She pulled her hand away.

"No. I know it wasn't my fault." she said sharply. "I'm asking you, do you know who's responsible?" she asked now irritated.

"Sorry, I didn't mean to imply—"

"Are you forgetting who you're talking to? Of course you meant to imply it was my fault for using someone who wasn't credentialed."

"Where is this coming from Audrey?"

She got up and walked back to her desk leaving her coffee on the table. Audrey closed her eyes as she placed her hand on the chair of her desk.

It can't be, she thought.

"Audrey, I'm really sorry. We've been apart too long. It was insensitive of me to even bring the subject up," he said pleadingly.

Audrey felt a jolt of rage. She took in a deep breath then let it out. This calmed her just a little.

"Please come back and sit with me," said Andrew.

She turned, walked back and sat at the furthest point away from Andrew on the couch and asked, "Do you know who I used for that package?"

"Of course I know. Dennis told me, but you aren't blamed," he said.

"Who did I use?" she asked.

"Some kid in LA," he answered.

"What's his name?" she asked quickly.

"I don't like this Audrey. I can tell your questions have a destination in mind. I'm glad you didn't do my debrief. Where are you going with this?"

"All right. Tell me about Sefter," she said.

"Who?"

"Sefter. The kid from LA."

"What kind of name is that?" he asked.

"Don't try and slip around this Andrew. Tell me. I can handle it."

Full comprehension came to Andrew's face.

"My God! You know don't you?"

"Tell me and we will never speak of it after today," Audrey said bracing herself.

Andrew knew Audrey so well he could tell she was tracking like a laser guided missile on the truth. He loves her and doesn't want to lose her. But, she views lying to her is worse than the problem.

"I made a mistake. The result of that mistake is that I have a biological son. His given name is Theodore. I had no hand in his upbringing. I've sent money, but that's it," said Andrew facing Audrey straight on.

Audrey slapped Andrew's face. The same swollen side from Jeff Statz' sucker punch.

"How could you!?" she said.

Andrew didn't flinch though the physical pain was dwarfed by the emotion pain and guilt he was feeling right now.

"Audrey—"

"Who is she?"

Andrew hesitated. He didn't like being slapped by his wife no matter the circumstances. His ego rose to the occasion.

"I'm not going to tell you," he said.

"Yes you are!"

"It's enough for me to be punished by you. I don't think it's fair to punish anyone else," he said.

"Trust me, punishment will come some day," she said in a menacing tone.

Andrew shifted gears and said, "What law firm did you hire recently?"

Audrey was taken by surprise, but stayed the course and said, "What does that have to do with your infidelity!?"

"He got what he deserved," said Andrew.

"What are you talking about?" she asked.

"Who do you think pulled the trigger?" Andrew said going for the jugular.

"Oh my God! You shot Simon!?"

"See Audrey, I'm not the only one who made a mistake. You did too," he said.

"You almost killed him!"

"If I wanted him dead he would be," Andrew said stone cold.

"He'll walk with a limp for the rest of his life. How could you?"

"How could you?" Andrew pounced.

Audrey, breathing hard said, "Get out! I want you out of my house."

"You mean our house. No. I'm staying right here until we work this through. We're both flawed people. People who do things for our country that can sometimes be disgusting, but essential. We're two of a kind. I love you and though you don't feel it right now, you know you love me. We're good for each other. Who else could possibly make a better team than us?" said Andrew.

Audrey heard his words, but they hadn't sunk in right away. A single tear rolled down her face. Andrew leaned toward her, hesitated, and she allowed him to wipe it away.

"We're going to get through this Audrey. Both of us have made mistakes," he said.

Andrew stopped talking and waited for Audrey to process the past few minutes. He knew her to have one of the most logical minds and was confident she would see things in the proper perspective.

Audrey let out a long breath then said, "We've both made mistakes. I agree. But, you and I weren't even serious yet when Simon and I got drunk and—"

He took her hands into his.

"You may not have been serious about me, but Audrey, I knew I was going to marry you. I flipped out. I'm sorry."

After a long pause Audrey said, "This is going to take some time to heal. For now, I don't want you doing anything for CIT."

"I started the company and I'll do whatever I please," he said offended.

"No. You won't."

"I'll just get the new board together and—"

"And what? There is no board. I am the board. I have full autonomy."

"Of course there's a board. By law you have to have one," said Andrew in a preaching tone.

"You're right. Technically there is a board, but all votes have been assigned back to me. So, when we get the other CIT locations set up across the country I want you visiting them Monday through Friday every week of the year. I only want you home on weekends to keep up the façade."

Andrew put up a fight, but realized he was just arguing to win a battle. He finally realized this is his opportunity to win the war...Operation Park Place with Janine Sheppard.

She'll soften her stance over time. I give her credit. I never thought of having a board with one hundred percent veto power.   Good for her.   I can wait, he thought.

Chapter 60

Present Day

Tony used the flashlight and surveyed the ceiling as he climbed above Audrey's office. He knew the light from it would not be a factor. In the crawl space...yes. Here...no. Panning left to right he saw exactly what he needed...steel beams with plenty of room to crawl upon.

He plotted his route and calculated approximately how many seconds he would have. Sweat rolled down the sides of his face. His heart was pounding then slowed as he began visualizing his strategy.

Tony then pressed the top of the stick which in turn put pressure on the 'Open Door' button inside the elevator. He prayed the stick wouldn't fall. It didn't. He got up and began quietly crawling like a cat to his destination on the steel beams he had routed in his head.

Ding, the elevator rang out once again.

Oh, please Tony, don't, thought agent Wolf.

Sefter ducked under the table knowing his mother, Forman and Statz would certainly be firing upon whoever walked out of the delivery box of death. Each trained their weapons on the yet to be open door. Andrew, with all his field experience and training, froze and gazed upon who could be visiting his wife's office.

Tony reached his position and removed his weapon.

Andrew moved into a stance to shield a still unconscious Audrey just in case someone came out shooting. Statz and Janine Sheppard both stood in a

Weaver shooting position. They were standing tall with equally balanced weight on both legs. Confidence exuded from them.

The door began to open.

Statz gave the go ahead to begin shooting once the door was completely open. Bullets pounded the inside of the elevator car as if a fully automatic machine gun were being used.

Tony lifted and removed one of the ceiling tiles. He took aim and began firing. First he hit Janine Sheppard in the head. Next he fired upon Jeff Statz and hit him twice. Once in the back and neck. Tony then moved his eyes and firearm left and hit Forman in the shoulder. The shot forcing Forman to fall and drop his gun.

Agent Wolf, seeing a red spray from Janine's head then slump to the floor, unlatched the door and entered the office through the secret passage that is the two-way mirror. The gunfire ceased as quickly as it began.

Sefter peaked out from under the table to see who they had killed this time. To his surprise, he saw an empty elevator. He tentatively stood up.

From behind him he heard, "Don't make a move! On your knees!"

Agent Wolf zip-tied his hands, stood him up and turned him around.

"What the—"

Sefter saw the carnage. Then he saw a person lowering himself from the ceiling. His eyes open wide as can be. Tony moved quickly to Andrew and Audrey.

"Are either of you hit?" Tony asked Andrew as he gave a once over checking the still unconscious Audrey.

He then gave a look to agent Wolf, but didn't say anything. His eyes projecting a focus not seen by Elizabeth before. She looked at him with astonishment written all over her face.

How the hell did you even think of this!? she thought.

Tony closed his eyes and surveyed the room accessing his ability. In this moment he suddenly found he trusts his growing ability more than his eyesight.

Double Edged Sword, Lethal Façade, Anarchist, Actress and Mercury. All alive, he thought.

Wait...Mercury! Forman's still alive, he thought.

Tony startled agent Wolf by his quick movement toward Forman.

"What are you doing?" she asked.

Andrew, gently holding Audrey, took in everything around him like a sponge. He watched Tony as if he were looking on through the glass of a stadium racquetball court. He had seen Tony play so many times. Once again, Tony was a step ahead of his opponents. However, to Andrew, right now Tony just seemed paranoid.

Before Tony could reach him, Forman reached for his Sig Sauer P229 pistol and, left-handed, pointed and squeezed the trigger. One pop from Forman's gun and Tony instinctively fired a deadly shot into his chest.

Tony froze as Forman dropped back onto the floor. His chest filling his shirt crimson red. He watched as Forman breathed no more.

What have I done? Was it necessary? he questioned.

Instinct kicked in once again and he quickly kicked the weapon from Forman's hand, felt for a pulse and realized he had indeed taken his life. Tony closed his eyes as he knelt next to Forman's body.

"James!" he heard as if coming from a time and place far in the distance.

"James! Help me over here!" shouted Andrew.

Tony looked toward Audrey, but couldn't find Andrew. He quickly stood. Andrew was kneeling on the floor over agent Wolf. Tony ran to help while noticing Audrey still remained unconscious.

Appearing lifeless, blood was oozing from agent Wolf's abdomen.

"Come on Elizabeth! Hold on!" shouted Tony.

Suddenly both Tony and Andrew felt a light touch on their shoulders.

"Let me have a look," said a battered Audrey standing and holding a cloth.

Before Tony got up he swiftly grabbed the Mont Blanc pen from Elizabeth's pocket in one quick motion. Audrey knelt down and applied pressure where she was hit. Elizabeth winced in pain giving the first sign she was still alive.

She opened her eyes, but in a rapidly fading state.

Looking directly at Audrey she said, "Mom? Where's Dad?"

"Shh," said Audrey.

Elizabeth's eyes seemed to be coming into focus a little more.

"Where's Dad?" she asked again.

Tony moved closer and said, "Ryan's not here Elizabeth."

She winced in pain once again then slowly and almost in a whisper, "Not Ryan...my Dad...Simon."

Tony moved back. He looked at Andrew and he saw him adjust his collar. He knew this had to be a difficult thing for him to hear.

Audrey said, "I've made a call honey. You're going to be OK."

Chapter 61

Present Day: 6 Months Later

$\mathbf{A}$t Portland International Airport, Tony leaned over and kissed Jacquelyn from the driver's seat of their minivan. He got out and slid open the side passenger door. Tony gave Sam and Nick kisses on the top of their heads then big hugs.

"Take care of Mom," he said looking at them both. "I'll be back tomorrow. Maybe we'll go to Cannon Beach and check out the haystacks."

"Yay!" they said in unison.

Jacquelyn couldn't help it. A single tear rolled down her face as she knew their lives may never be the same after his upcoming meeting at Langley. They had talked about it and agreed destiny surely has knocked upon the James' family front door. She gave Tony her full support with whatever may come their way. Jacquelyn realized she may have to share Tony with the government of the United States for awhile. At this moment, she felt more love for him than ever before.

Tony said goodbye and began walking toward the automatic circular airport doors. He turned and gave one last wave to the kids then touched his finger tips of his right hand to his lips and blew a kiss to Jacquelyn. He turned then disappeared into the airport building.

The house just outside the Washington D.C. area didn't look like much, but it blended in with the others in the middle-class neighborhood. Nobody could tell the windows were blast-proof. Not much could penetrate the Kevlar lined layer underneath the drywall inside. This is one of many CIA safe houses.

Tony was escorted in through an underground passage from the bomb shelter fortress they call a garage. He entered the living room and was greeted with smiles and handshakes.

"There he is," said a well dressed silver-haired man that looked like he should be in the movies.

Relentless, came the word.

"I'm Martin Atwater, newly appointed Director of the Central Intelligence Agency. It's so good to finally meet you," he said with a smile that could blind.

"Thank you. Nice to meet you, Martin," said Tony.

Audrey grimaced at Tony's use of new DCI's first name. *I think he'd do that to the president. But, I love it!* she thought.

"Hello Andrew."

Sorry, I'm not sure why, but I still don't trust you, he thought.

Then he finally got to the redhead looking pretty healthy for someone who had been bleeding from the gut just six months ago.

Tony put his hand out for a handshake. Elizabeth looked at him almost cross-eyed.

"Get that out of here," she said.

Brushing his hand aside, she gave him a big hug. Tony was taken by surprise at this show of affection. It was a short embrace. She shook her head at the look on Tony's face.

"Don't flatter yourself. I hugged you because you saved my life."

Tony gathered himself and said, "You look no worse for the wear. How do you feel?"

"I'm just about one hundred percent," she replied.

"I have to ask. How did you come up with that plan and then execute it all on your own?"

Atwater jumped in and took control.

"Everyone please take your seats. We've got a lot of ground to cover," he announced.

Audrey, Andrew, Elizabeth and Tony each sat down in the living room in a semi-circle with Atwater in control.

"First things first," said Atwater motioning to the security detail.

The serious looking man spoke into his wrist communication device and gave a command for someone to take his place. Within seconds another man entered taking his post, freeing him up so he could walk toward Atwater.

"Thank you Neal," said Atwater.

Neal Sanders, Head of Detail, handed him a small package which appeared to look like a jewelry box of some sort. Everyone stood. Tony was the last to stand. He had no idea what this was all about. Atwater walked over to Tony.

"Anthony Alexander James, on behalf of the United States of America and the Central Intelligence Agency, I bestow upon you the Distinguished Intelligence Medal. Your exceptional work in the line of duty exemplifies the attitude, intelligence and actions of one who has gone above and beyond the call of duty. I am proud to honor you today."

Atwater opened the box and presented Tony with a silver dollar-sized round bronze medal. On its face it had the eagle with shield and arrows. Along the perimeter it had the words 'Central Intelligence Agency For Distinguished Service'.

Tony was surprised at the weight of the medal. Atwater and Tony shook hands. Everyone in the room clapped and either came over to shake his hand or give him a hug. Tony was not privy as to how rare this private ceremony took place and felt a little embarrassed by the fuss.

"Thank you, but I hope agent Wolf has one coming too," said Tony.

"Tony, this isn't just some token pat on the back thank you prize. This is the highest honor the CIA bestows. The rest of the world gets to give their awards in front of TV cameras. But, we're the CIA. We do this in private. You deserve it. I don't. In my debrief I told how you single-handedly took action without hesitation. You saved my life twice in one day. At CIT, it was your unique plan. You executed it to perfection. You deserve this. Congratulations Tony," said Elizabeth.

Perfection? You almost died, thought Tony.

Atwater let a few minutes of congratulations go by then shut it down.

"Alright everyone. Let's sit and move onto other business."

"First, Tony, how'd it go with the shrink?" he asked bluntly.

"What do you mean?" asked Tony not willing to discuss his sessions in front of a group.

"Are you over the emotion of the lives you've taken?"

"I'm sure you get a write-up or I wouldn't be sitting here," answered Tony.

Atwater didn't respond at first. Tony wasn't sure how to take this guy. The only thing he knew about him was the word *Relentless*. Everyone in the room remained silent, including Tony.

When Martin Atwater wanted to make someone very uncomfortable he would simply use his steely blue eyes and wait for them to crack. However, Tony appeared immune.

After a long silence Atwater said, "So it's true. Everything I've read about you says you're smart. Also a smartass. But, you're right. I did receive a report from Dr. Monroe."

"Then you know me better than anyone else on earth. Because, of course, I told Dr. Monroe all my thoughts and feelings and was one hundred percent truthful," said Tony sarcastically.

Atwater sat back, gave pause looking at the others then smiled and said, "I like this guy." He turned to Tony and said, "You and I are going to get along just fine."

"What do you mean?" asked Tony.

"I don't understand your question," said Atwater back to Tony.

"You're assuming I'm still moving forward with my role within your Savant Syndrome Division? I've only had one opportunity in San Diego to serve in the capacity for which I was hired," said Tony.

"No, I never assume. And, based on agent Wolf's recollection of the events that took place in Portland, I think you had plenty of opportunity and did utilized your ability to its full potential on many occasions. Effectively I might add," said Atwater.

Hmm, I guess I didn't think of that, thought Tony.

"So, what are we doing here?" asked Tony.

"I've decided to continue to allocate funds and resources to SSD keeping Don Williams on as its Director."

"OK, so what if I've decided being part of SSD just isn't for me?" asked Tony stirring the pot.

"That's just fine because, as of today, we want you to become a full-fledged field operative without the distinction or restrictions of SSD. You are now fully CIA," said Atwater.

If I want to be, thought Tony.

Audrey could tell Tony was heading down the trail of defiance. She needed to head him off.

"Tony. Without you none of us would be here today. You have something special and you can make a tremendous difference for what faces our country. Both foreign and domestic."

"Audrey, I've heard this speech before," said Tony.

"And it came true," she said.

He glanced around at the faces looking at him then turned to Audrey and said," Looking back, I guess you're right. But, the disloyalty and actions among some of the people within this agency is enough to make me question why anyone would join such a dysfunctional organization."

Martin Atwater jumped in and said, "That's why I'm here Tony. I've been tasked to make sure we have no other instances like we just went through. I've already taken corrective action to assure anyone who works in the Agency stays on the right path. You've undoubtedly looked into my credentials. You will find me to be fair and to run a very tight ship. And, I won't give up."

Yeah, I gathered that from you already, he thought.

Audrey smiled knowing Tony probably had a handle on Atwater even before he sat down.

"Here's the rub. I love my family. I love my life in Portland. I couldn't live with myself if I were to be away from them for lengthy periods of time. I'm going to have to say n—"

"Wait! Before you say no I want you to be fully trained, go on one field OP then make your decision. Is that fair, Tony?" asked Atwater.

This guy sounds like me, he thought.

Tony remained silent for about ten seconds then said, "What about Jacquelyn?"

"What about her?" asked Atwater.

"The last time I had a meeting like this I was basically ordered not to tell Jacquelyn anything. She was used and placed in harm's way by Janine Sheppard. I can't live with myself if the same applies in this situation," said Tony.

"You know now agent Wolf had her back at all times. She was never in danger. She'll need to sign a document, but I see no issues barring you from telling her most things."

"Most things?" asked Tony.

"I can't let you divulge certain intel that would place our country or its citizens at risk. You can understand that, can't you? Besides, based on Dr. Monroe's report, you only trust one other person living on this planet and that's your wife. It would actually be beneficial for you to have that sounding board. We'll soundproof your house for you," Atwater said with a knowing look.

This guy has his act together, thought Tony.

"I'll talk it over with Jacquelyn and let you know."

"You're telling me this didn't cross you mind before you arrived today? I'm willing to bet you and your wife already had a conversation and she told you to use your best judgment. Am I right?" asked Atwater.

I give him credit, he is persistent. No, RELENTLESS, but he's right, thought Tony.

"All right, my answer is yes providing my family is given full protection, I can remain living in Portland and a few questions are answered here and now."

"Such as?" asked Atwater.

"Audrey, Elizabeth called you 'Mom' and she said her father's name is Simon. Was she out of her mind in pain or is this true?" asked Tony.

"Why would that matter to you Tony?" asked Atwater.

Tony kept his gaze on Audrey.

Atwater, not used to his questions being dismissed, asked Tony, "What's it to you?"

"Let's just say it's a matter of personal trust," answered Tony.

"She is my mom," said Elizabeth glancing at Audrey then to Tony.

"And who's Simon?" Tony asked Elizabeth.

"His name is Simon Swan, an attorney living in Portland. He's my real father."

"So, why pretend Ryan O'Connor is your father?"

"I'll answer that," said Audrey. "I gave birth to twins before Andrew and I were married. I had a small emotional breakdown and gave her up to the person Andrew trusted most. It was the right thing to do as you can see," said Audrey proudly looking over at Elizabeth.

Andrew forcefully said, "It was likely the hardest decision Audrey has ever had to make. Let's not beat her up about it, OK?"

Now I know why I don't trust you! My bet is you had something to do with the other twin, Danielle, and Simon Swan and didn't tell Audrey. Why deceive her? I know you two weren't married yet, but that's no way to treat Audrey even if she's no angel, Tony thought.

Tony gave Andrew a knowing look daring him to say another word. Andrew got the message.

How could he possibly know? thought Andrew staring in wonder at Tony.

"So, why does Ryan O'Connor believe Elizabeth to be his child?" asked Tony.

"Because I slept with him then told him the baby was his," said Audrey beginning to become irritated with Tony.

Tony caught Elizabeth's glance and she gave him a facial message pleading him not to pursue this further. Tony obliged, but had one more item for Atwater.

"I'm not looking for an answer to this. I'm just wondering. How could it be that the people who are charged with protecting America's interests seem to spend such a significant amount of their time creating and living within their own conspiracies?"

Atwater said, "If you weren't looking for an answer you wouldn't have brought it up. So, I'll answer you. I'm proud of who we are as an agency. We are all human and have incredible strengths. Unfortunately, with the job of protecting an entire nation under the cover of darkness comes some tremendous pressures. At times the pressure can get to almost anyone. A single decision can send any one of us down a path that is less desirable. Never-the-less, we have a greater responsibility than any one of the pieces of this incredible puzzle we call the United States of America. No one is infallible. Even you Tony. Tell me, did you color outside the lines even just a little, while bringing this to a conclusion?"

Does he know about me copying Audrey's computer hard-drive? I should have kept my mouth shut. He really is relentless, thought Tony.

"This was trial by fire. I tried to start anywhere I possibly could. I then realized I needed to rely on the fundamentals. It was as simple as remembering the first rule of puzzle-solving."

"You didn't answer my question, but I'm curious. What is your first rule of puzzle-solving?"

"Ever since I was little I've always believed there's a game to be played within any game. Sometimes rules have to be bent because your opponent is pushing the boundaries," Tony answered calmly.

"You mean cheating," said Atwater.

"Almost cheating," answered Tony.

"What's the difference," Atwater asked.

"Nuances create a whole new dimension. It almost creates a completely new competition. Rules cast shadows like a tree on a sunny day. But, the earth is always rotating so the landscape is constantly changing. I've always found this dimension to be almost as much fun as the game itself. I guess you can say I love playing where shadows conspire."

"You still didn't answer my question. What's your first rule of puzzle-solving?"

"Edges first."

— The End —

www.ingramcontent.com/pod-product-compliance
Lightning Source LLC
Chambersburg PA
CBHW031050260626
47172CB00001B/4